In August 2007, dear husband Jeff, you said to me:
"If you want to write a book I'll be supportive."

You had no clue what you were saying.

1

Fun and cool.
~ Peyton Graham, age 11

I found *Finding Angel* to be an interesting mix of drama, humor, and fairytale all mixed into one. I would recommend this book to fairytale lovers around the world.
~ Esther Young, age 11

Finding Angel was awesome! I can't wait for the second book.
~ Mackenzie Herrell, age 13

Finding Angel makes you dream that underneath what we see, there may very well be a magical world.
~ Madison Graham, age 13

A truly inspiring tale. With the perfect mixture of mystery and magic, every page leaves you wanting more.
~ Kaylee Williams, age 13

Finding Angel, it's the good kind of weird.
~ Priscilla Graham, age 15

An amazing book, written by a very talented author! From the moment I started it I couldn't put it down—the characters grabbed my attention with their humor, self-sacrifice, and all too human mistakes (the dragons were really cool too!). My only issue with this book was that it ended too soon! I just have one question: When will I get to read more about Angel and her friends?
~ Katie Patchell, age 15

It was fabulous! In my opinion you can hold your own with J.K. Rowling.
~ Barbi Herrell, analyst

It is a story I think about when I'm not reading it, the characters and story stay with me. I find the story believable and interesting with characters I can imagine meeting and getting to know. I can't wait to get to the next one! A tightly woven tale, thoroughly enjoyable!
~ Kecia Strock, homeschooling mom

Intricately plotted and well-written, with characters that leap from the page and into your heart—*Finding Angel* is a rare gem in a sea of "blah." The storyworld is an enchanting blend of magic and science, populated by a menagerie of fantastical creatures. It kept me reading late into the night.
~ Christian Miles, teen author of *The Scarlet Key*

Finding Angel is a wonderful story that swept me into another world. I found myself wishing to visit Toch Island, discover my Talent and adopt a pet dragon, and I'm a middle-aged mom! Kat Heckenbach is a gifted writer, who has created a memorable cast of characters. I grew to love them as their adventure unfolded, and my only disappointment was that the story had to end.
~ Shawna Williams, author of *No Other*, *In All Things*, and *Orphaned Hearts*

This one will captivate you.
~ Amy Deardon, author of *A Lever Long Enough*

A delightful, engaging story full of magic, wonder, and mystery…an imaginative world where surprises are around every turn.
~ C. S. Lakin, author of *The Wolf of Tebron* and *The Map Across Time*

Charming on its surface…also roiling with hidden peril. Opening *Finding Angel* is like opening a living jigsaw puzzle. Reading it becomes the delight of joining the enchanted pieces even as they change shape into dragons and mushrooms, or whisper clues with the rustle of leaves, or merge of their own accord into pictures within pictures sparkling with magic.
~ Sherry Thompson, author of *Seabird* and *Earthbow*

A magical breath of fresh air and discovery. Angel will charm you.
~ Diane M. Graham, author of *I Am Ocilla*

kat heckenbach

FINDING ANGEL

Editors: Diane M. Graham, Amy Deardon, Grace Bridges

ISBN: 978-1-927154-13-7
Published by Splashdown Books, New Zealand
http://www.splashdownbooks.com

~Losing Angel~

Smoke billowed above the forest. A man stood in the center of the burning trees.

He stared down at his hand as the flames licked his fingers. Fire seared his skin, but the feeling of power that surged through him consumed the pain. His anger had caused the fire…fury that the little girl had escaped… fury that the stupid little boy standing outside the ring of fire had helped her.

But it didn't matter now. He would find another way. The power was worth it. The power was worth everything. He merely had to learn to control it.

And to make it permanent.

Fire twisted and danced around him. He held out his burning hand and concentrated. The flames on his skin snuffed out like a candle. Blackened tissue marred his forearm; heat gnarled his fingers. Anger boiled inside him once again.

But this time he funneled the emotion, and focused on the furnace surrounding him. The fire crackled, and swelled, and then a portion drew back. A gap opened up, forming a pathway out of the flames. The man smiled, cracking the crisp skin on his cheek. *Just like parting the Red Sea.*

When he emerged, the boy was gone.

Chapter One
The Beetle

Angel hopped off the school bus and darted toward the back yard, dirt from the driveway kicking up around her ankles. She leaped over the hedges that separated the front yard from the back. Leaves and pine needles slid and crunched beneath her sneakers as her eyes trained on her favorite spot, her reading tree.

The tree grew near the back fence at a thirty-degree angle. Angel had no idea what had knocked the oak over, but it stayed rooted at that odd slant. Someone had also chopped off the top of the tree, leaving one single branch that pointed straight up. Angel walked up the trunk of the tree, turned and sat, leaning against the branch.

A whisper of electricity ran the length of her back where she pressed against the branch, as if energy were traveling into her from the tree. She gasped and looked around, but saw nothing unusual in the back yard. The tree itself looked perfectly normal. Still, it *felt* different. It felt…magical. Or at least what she'd imagined magic to feel like.

She ran her fingers over the rough bark, following a trail down the angled trunk as she leaned forward, stretching her tall frame to its fullest. The tingling surged through her hands, and she yanked them back as if she had been burned.

The thought of burning trees sent a wave of nausea through her. She pulled herself back and leaned against the branch again, inhaling deeply to calm herself. Why was just the thought enough to make her feel this way? The answer had to be buried in her past—but her past was hidden.

And she still had no memory of anything before that day seven years ago.

Except a fear of forest fires.

She looked again at the lichen-speckled bark. Normal. *Just my reading tree. Same as always.*

She willed herself to think of other things. Happy things, like the fact that school was finally out. No more research papers and history projects. No more *teasing* for three more months. And she had the satisfaction of knowing that she'd set the curve for the final exam.

The sound of crunching footsteps bolted her out of her daydreams. Zachary had obviously heard the school bus and come to find her. She peered out the corner of her eye and smiled at her little foster brother.

"Angel, you've got to come see what I've caught!" He tugged on her arm, his blue eyes pleading for her attention.

"It's not another beetle, is it, Zack?" She pulled her arm free and turned to face him. "I've just gotten home. And you've shown me zillions of them already."

"Not like this one. It's huge and it's got silver flecks all down its back. I've been searching online, but I can't find out about it anywhere. *Pleeeease* come in and help me. Mom's gonna want you in soon anyway."

Ugh, more insects.

She hopped down from her tree, and followed Zack to the house, passing Mr. Mason's small vegetable garden and feeling the desire to skip along, now that summer had arrived. She was so caught up in her thoughts she nearly tripped over one of the many stray cats that called her back yard home.

"Vander! Watch where you're going!"

The flame-colored tom scampered away, twitching his torn ear, the result of a fight with the cat next door. Angel watched him as he scrambled across the back yard heading directly for her tree.

He vanished.

Had he just ducked underneath the tree and taken off through the hole in the chain-link fence? She peered past the bent oak, trying to see into the neighbor's yard, searching the vast spread of green for the cat. Nothing.

Her eyes trailed back to the tree, where a strange shadow obscured a portion of the trunk, and then it, too, disappeared. The same sensation that had hit her when she arrived at the tree returned.

"What ya lookin' at, Angel?"

Zack's small voice filtered into her mind, quelling the nausea, and she pulled her attention back to her favorite little guy.

"Nothing, I just thought…never mind. Come on, let's go." She resumed her walk to the house, taking hold of Zack's hand.

The sound of clanging pots issued through the open window. Josh and Jacob bickering over the TV remote competed with the kitchen clamor.

Angel burst through the back door, grabbed the remote out of Jacob's hand and tore down the hallway, shadowed by Zack. She stopped at the doorway to the dining room that offered a view straight through to the living room. Josh and Jacob's matching heads of jet-black hair spun around to glare at her with dual sets of piercing green eyes.

Before the boys could come after her, Mr. Mason stormed into the room, eyes narrowed. "Boys, on your feet!"

Josh flexed a brawny bicep at her and Jacob's angular face distorted into a sneer, then they turned to their father and rose to follow him out the door.

"Why'd you do that?" Zack whispered. "Now he's just going to play another prank on you."

"I couldn't resist. Besides, you know his pranks never work on me."

Jacob had once drawn mustaches on the faces of the mythical creatures depicted on Angel's favorite posters. She'd grabbed a rag, knowing it was a waste of time to try and wipe off the ink, but it had come off effortlessly. Later, she found the marker he'd used lying on the floor, and it was a permanent one. Oh, well, at least her stuff wasn't ruined. And he was always hiding her belongings, but she never failed to find them within minutes.

She entered Zack's room and sat at his computer desk. Zack sat down on his bed, his feet dangling next to a wicker basket of resin animals and bugs. Shelves lined the walls, filled with books about dinosaurs, reptiles, and insects, and boxes of rocks, egg shells, and anything else he found interesting. Posters on his wall illustrated the solar system, the inside of an ant mound, and the life cycle of a butterfly. The only real indicators of his young age were a Mickey Mouse alarm clock on his nightstand and a stuffed duck nestled on his pillow.

A small wire cage sat beside his second-hand computer. Inside, a beetle, easily four inches long, clung to a broken piece of tree branch. The color of midnight, it sparkled with starlight specks of silver. Angel drew in her breath.

She shoved Zack's homeschool books out of the way and sat at his desk. The math workbook on top was fourth grade level. Angel chewed the corner of her lip—what she wouldn't give to homeschool with him and get to move at her own pace. Mrs. Mason said she couldn't handle both of them because "schooling Zack is like schooling seven kids" with all his energy and curiosity. But next year most of Angel's classes would be available online…

The computer was on, and Angel pulled up the list of sites Zack had already visited. She didn't see how she could improve on his search. It was usually her going to *him* for help online. Zack was the one person she never felt geeky around because he was even more of a brain than she was.

"So what do you think Dad was talking to Josh and Jacob about?" Zack asked as Angel stared at the computer screen.

"Hmmm, don't know. Probably work he's got planned for them this summer. Jacob's gotta really behave for a while after his last little trick."

"He's just happy his restriction's over. Mom really laid into him when he got home that day." Zack's expression remained serious as he spoke, but Angel knew deep down he thought the prank was funny. A grown-up brain and grown-up morals didn't mean he was any less a little boy.

"Yeah, I wish I could've seen that. At least I got to see the shiner Josh gave him. Jacob's so smart, but he just doesn't use it. C'mon, how stupid was that? You'd think he'd realize, when you're a skinny sophomore and your brother's a junior and the *quarterback*, you don't steal the mascot's uniform right before the homecoming game."

Zack's serious expression cracked into a wide grin and he walked over and put his arms around Angel's neck.

"Thanks for doing this for me, Angel."

"I'm not really doing much of anything, so far, little man."

This beetle had her baffled. Nothing she pulled up looked remotely like it, and she was getting frustrated when Mrs. Mason's voice echoed down the hall.

"Kids, it's dinner time. Josh and Jacob, quit fighting and get in here!"

After helping Mrs. Mason clean up the kitchen, Angel curled up in the upholstered chair in the corner of her room to read. The feminine furniture wasn't really her taste, but the set had belonged to Mrs. Mason. To make the room her own, Angel covered the walls with posters of unicorns, winged horses, and dragons.

She was immersed in a book when Mrs. Mason poked her head through the door.

"Lights out, sweetie. The rules don't change for summer."

"Yes, ma'am. I was just finishing this chapter." Angel held the book up and Mrs. Mason's forehead crinkled.

"Can't you pick a different kind of book for once? Something realistic. What is that thing on the cover anyway?"

"A griffin. It's a kind of magical creature."

Mrs. Mason stepped farther into the room until she stood next to Angel. "You know magic isn't real, right? Why spend so much time reading about it? Focus some more time on your art. Your drawings are getting so good."

"I will. And I'll turn the light off soon, I promise. Just two more pages."

"Good girl. Sleep well." Mrs. Mason leaned in and kissed Angel on the forehead. "I love you."

"You, too. Goodnight."

Angel watched Mrs. Mason walk out of the room and that strange, unsettled feeling stirred in her gut again. *She sounds like the kids at school. Why do I have to defend what I like to everyone?*

Angel could think of only one person who was more of an oddball than she was—a girl from school who claimed to be a witch. Melinda Watkins dressed in black every day and everyone thought she was a freak. Angel befriended her because she knew what it was like to be *different*, but Melinda's fascination with Ouija boards and Tarot cards gave Angel the creeps. She was always trying to contact the psychic realm and find out if the boy she had a crush on that week liked her back.

Angel thought Melinda was into all of it to get her father's attention. He was a scientist who'd written a few books and always traveled to give lectures and such, gone so often Angel had never met him even though she'd been to Melinda's house several times. Melinda said he insisted there was no psychic world, no spirit world, or human souls, and he laughed at her *toys*. Angel felt sorry for her.

Then one day Melinda quit coming to school, and when Angel tried calling her, the phone number had been disconnected.

Angel heard her door creak, and turned to find Zack carrying the cage that held his beetle.

"It's singing," he said, rubbing his eyes.

"What? What do you mean singing?"

"I don't know. It's making a funky noise. Like chirping, only like music, too. It's keeping me awake."

"Well, just put it on my dresser. It won't bother me. I'm not feeling very sleepy anyway." She closed her book and sat upright in her chair.

"Promise me you'll find out what it is for me tomorrow?" he asked and yawned.

"I promise. Now set it down and get back to bed, little man."

Zack crept over and put the cage on Angel's dresser, and then made his way back across her room.

"Good night, Zack…" she called after him as he scuffled out her bedroom door, his strawberry-blond locks sticking out every which way.

Angel sighed and turned out the light, then slid into bed and pulled up the covers. She'd barely closed her eyes when she heard it…soft, strange…

Singing, indeed.

It wasn't like a voice actually, but it wasn't an ordinary insect chirp either. Angel found herself climbing out of bed and walking toward the cage. The beetle's silver flecks sparkled in the dim moonlight that filtered through the thin curtains. She couldn't see how the beetle made the noise; it wasn't moving its legs or its wings, and it sat perfectly still while Angel watched and listened. There seemed to be meaning in the sounds the beetle made, but each time she came close to grasping it, it slipped away like a wisp of smoke.

She stood in front of the dresser for a few more moments, and then opened the top drawer. She reached under a stack of T-shirts and pulled out the silver charm bracelet that she kept safely in there. It was her most precious possession, the one thing Jacob would never dare to hide from her. He tried it once—only once—because Angel became so angry Jacob swore he saw sparks on her fingertips and crackling in her flaming hair.

The bracelet was her only link to her past. She'd worn it the day she was found.

The Masons called her Angel because most of the charms on the bracelet were letters—A-N-G-E-L. The other charm was a heart-shaped locket with an engraving on the front. A small inscription on the back read "Happy Birthday," and was dated only June 27. The Masons had assumed it meant Angel's birthday, so that was the day they used to celebrate it.

She wrapped the bracelet around her wrist, noticing she now had to clasp it in the next-to-last link. It was beautiful, if a bit scuffed, and she never wore it anymore for fear of losing it. It may not have seemed extraordinary to anyone else, but without that locket her past would be lost forever. The one thing she could never understand was what the locket contained. A tiny chip of wood. She had never removed the wood, assuming that she or someone else must have put it in there for a reason.

But why?

As she slowly spun the bracelet around her wrist, something on the locket caught her eye and she flipped on the light. She looked closely at the engraving on the front. What she had always thought was a flower now seemed to morph into a different shape. There were still vines around the edge, but as she examined it, the center appeared more like wings than petals. Open wings, not a blossom after all. And the wings belonged to a very strange looking beetle.

The singing stopped then, and quiet abruptly filled the room. Angel turned to the beetle in the cage. It stood, perched on the broken branch, with its wings flared out—a living replica of the engraving on her locket.

Chapter Two
The Stranger

The following morning, Angel stretched as she forced herself awake. She had slept fitfully until the wee hours of the morning when her body finally gave in and she sank into slumber. All these years she had thought the engraving was a flower. How could she have not noticed? She unclasped the bracelet and placed it gently back in her dresser drawer, then took another look at the beetle in the cage. It seemed to be staring back at her with its tiny, bulging eyes.

"Where did you come from?" she whispered. The beetle fluttered its wings and crawled to the back corner of its cage. Angel decided to try searching at the library since she was having trouble finding it online. She preferred books to the computer anyway.

Josh agreed to give Angel a ride into town after lunch since he and Jacob were meeting some friends at the movies. At least that's what they told Mrs. Mason. More than likely, they were going to hang outside the theater with their friends.

As she climbed into the back seat of Josh's restored Maverick, a rustling in the bushes grabbed her attention. The bush shook with a force too great to be caused by one of their cats or an armadillo. Before Angel could take a closer look, Josh hit the gas and peeled off down the driveway.

"Why do you have to do that?" Angel shouted. "There's no one out here to see you—you're not impressing anyone. And, Jacob, close the window, it's messing up my hair!"

Few cars traveled the stretch of highway leading out from the Mason's road, and Josh sped along with nothing to deter him. Angel gripped the back of Jacob's seat until her fingers cramped. Josh was forced to slow down as they approached the city, but he cut in and out of traffic, making Angel tense up even more and close her eyes until she felt the car roll to a stop in front of the library.

She climbed out of the car and was tempted to drop down and kiss the sidewalk.

"I'll be back in two hours to pick you up," Josh said through the open window, and pulled out in front of a white SUV so suddenly it had to slam on its brakes. Angel decided that next time she came into the city she would take the bus if Mrs. Mason would allow her.

Thirty minutes later, Angel sat at a large table in the back of the library with books on insects spread out all over. She could find nothing that looked like Zack's beetle. *How completely irritating.* She had never in her life not been able to find what she was looking for. She leaned back in her chair, rubbed her eyes to release some of the tension, and nearly fell out of her seat when she saw the boy sitting in the previously empty chair across from her.

"Sorry," he said. "Didn't mean to startle you. What're you looking for?"

His dark hair was cut short in the back but left long enough in front that his wavy bangs fell across his forehead and into his eyes. He raked his bangs back, revealing nearly black eyes with silver flecks. His loose T-shirt wasn't enough to hide his broad shoulders and arms that were tanned and lean as though used for hard labor. He looked to be no more than seventeen, but his eyes showed a maturity Angel had never seen in any of Josh and Jacob's friends.

She let her heart stop pounding and inhaled. "I'm trying to identify a beetle for my little brother, but I can't find it anywhere. I've searched online, and in all these books, but no luck."

"Hmmm, maybe it's a whole new species and it's not in any of these books." He leaned forward, putting his elbows on the edge of the table. The silver flecks in his eyes picked up the fluorescent light and sparkled.

"Well, then, I suppose I can take him to the museum for them to put on display."

The boy's eyes widened and a flicker of fear ignited in them. But he relaxed again when Angel smiled and shook her head.

"Do you go to Brooker High?" She wondered if he knew Josh or Jacob.

"No, I'm not from around here," he said with renewed calm. "Just… visiting family. I'm Gregor, by the way."

"I'm Angel."

Gregor tilted his head as if in a slight bow, causing his hair to spill into his eyes again.

"Are you staying long?" Her usual shyness was strangely absent.

He intrigued her too, the way he hadn't remarked about her name.

And his accent…

She racked her brain trying to place it. It rang of something distant, yet felt like home.

"I'm not sure. Could be a while. I'm here…sort of…helping out with a project, and it depends on how long it takes." He ran his fingers through his bangs again. "So, you like museums?"

"Well, the art museum across the street has a free exhibit I wanted to see today. A local artist who paints all sorts of fantasy scenes is being featured for the next few weeks. But I promised Zack I'd search for his beetle."

"There's an artist who lives down the road from me back in my home town." Gregor smiled. "She's amazing. Her paintings really come alive."

His last words sent unexplainable shivers down Angel's spine. It was if he'd just shared a secret with her, but for the life of her, she couldn't figure out what it was.

He turned his head and eyed the art museum through the library window. "Why don't we go check it out?"

Angel stared at him in disbelief. If she'd told Josh or Jacob she wanted to see an art exhibit, they'd have said there's no way they'd be caught dead in an artsy-fartsy place like that.

"Well, I really shouldn't. I promised my brother I'd find this beetle."

"If you're sure then." Gregor pushed himself back from the table and stood. " Nice meeting you, though. Good luck with that." He tipped his head to the books spread all over the table. As he walked away, Angel noticed he was wearing leather boots and long black pants. *He must really not be from around here.* It wasn't even the end of May, but in Florida that meant hot.

Angel watched him walk around the long wall of books and disappear, and then she peered out at the street. Moments later, she caught sight of him entering the art museum. She couldn't believe it; he really did want to see the display.

She stood by the window, looking back and forth between the pile of books and the art museum. There was a little over an hour until Josh would be back to pick her up. She straightened the books quickly, and then headed out of the library.

Cassie and her two lapdogs, Heather and Tamara, stood outside the museum entryway. Cassie's voice carried from the other side of the street. "Did you see his clothes? I mean really…boots, in this weather."

She was dressed in the shortest mini-skirt Angel had ever seen and a halter-top that showed off her pointy shoulder blades, and she wobbled in her too-high heels.

Bet her mom doesn't know about that outfit.

Heather, dressed as if she were heading off to a country club for tea, scrunched her nose in distaste. "He looked *foreign* to me. Kinda cute, but *weird.*"

Tamara, in a very expensive but slightly too small shorts and top set, didn't say a word, but laughed at her friends' comments as though they were the cleverest things she'd ever heard. Cassie and Heather only let Tamara into their clique because her father made more money than both of theirs put together.

Angel slipped into the museum entrance and scanned the room for Gregor. Her sandals clicked on the marble floor as she made her way past the signs announcing upcoming displays and events. A security guard sat off to the side of the entrance. The museum seemed nearly deserted. Angel's footsteps quieted when she reached the purple carpet of the main gallery.

The paintings hung on the stark walls, illuminated by fixtures mounted on the ceiling. A huge sculpture of a centaur rearing up on its hind legs loomed over the center of the room. Gregor appeared from behind it, a curious expression on his face, then circled around the statue until his back was to Angel.

She walked silently over to him and whispered, "Whatcha lookin' at?"

He didn't even flinch.

"Not sure. What's this thing supposed to be?" He turned to face her with a smile that said he was very glad to see she'd changed her mind.

"It's a centaur. Half man, half horse. I thought you wanted to see this because you were actually interested in this kind of stuff." Was he going to turn out just like all the other kids at her school, thinking she was strange for being fascinated by mythical creatures?

"Well, I understand those," he said, pointing to a cluster of paintings of unicorns, "and those, over there." He indicated a huge canvas of a griffin with its wings outstretched, and a larger one of a roc perched on the edge of its nest set in the jagged point of a cliff. "But I don't get these human hybrid creatures." There were two paintings of centaurs similar to the sculpture, and a few of mermaids and fauns as well.

"This one looks creepy, I'll agree." Angel stared up at the centaur's snarling face.

"No, I mean, how can a human and a horse…it's just not natural."

He looked so intently at the statue that Angel began to wonder if Heather might be right. Maybe Gregor was from another country and they didn't have art like this, or fantasy stories about centaurs.

"Of course not, they're mythical, like everything else in here," she said, trying not to sound patronizing.

"Right," he muttered, still engrossed in studying the statue. He pulled his eyes from the centaur and flashed an innocent smile.

OK, he's just teasing.

They walked to the wall where the unicorn paintings were hung and Angel said, "They're so beautiful. They look like they'd feel like silk."

He furrowed his brow. "But who would dare to touch one? They're pure magic." He cleared his throat. "I mean…they look like pure magic, don't they?"

She shook her head and moved on to examine the griffin. "I love the way the artist uses the brush strokes to give the fur dimension. It looks like it would blow around if there were a breeze in here. I could never get this to look so realistic."

"Do you paint?" Gregor raised one eyebrow.

"Not really. I like to draw. Mostly with charcoal pencil."

"Are you any good?" he asked as they moved to the next painting.

"I won the school's annual art contest last year." She could feel her cheeks turning pink. "I've still got a lot of room for improvement, though."

21

He smiled, and Angel noticed that the flecks in his eyes picked up the colors in the painting in front of them. "Well," he said, "maybe one day it will be your drawings hanging on these walls."

Angel felt her cheeks heat again, and moved to the next painting.

"Look at this." She pointed to the roc. "Wouldn't want to meet up with her." The roc's beak was splayed open in a threatening cry, and its talons dug into the side of the nest like curved daggers. The perspective of the painting made the giant bird look twenty feet tall.

"Of course you wouldn't," said Gregor, "they're…they look vicious."

Angel turned to the castle paintings and thought she heard Gregor mutter under his breath, "but they're not nearly that big."

They continued around the museum, but Angel was now more interested in Gregor than the paintings. He seemed to be comparing the images in the paintings to his own conceptions and checking them for accuracy. She couldn't shake the feeling that he recognized some of the creatures as if he'd seen them before in real life. He couldn't read fantasy books or he would have known what a centaur was; but he looked nostalgically at the roc and the brownies, the gargoyles and dragons.

A colorful mosaic of a dragon caught Angel's eye. Composed of broken red and purple tiles, the dragon's massive body sprouted wings much too small to lift it in flight. Pieces of steel formed dagger-like fangs. A faceted stone eye of cobalt blue stared blindly as it sparkled under the museum light.

She moved closer to the artwork and Gregor came up next to her.

"They look a lot like dinosaurs, don't you think?" A tenseness pulled his voice.

"I suppose they could." Angel cocked her head. "I never really thought of it before. But I guess I could see how a dinosaur skeleton could fit inside that."

Her comment seemed to give him the confidence to continue, but his eyes remained fixed on the mosaic as he spoke.

"Maybe dinosaurs aren't really extinct. Maybe they're really dragons, and they're just hiding."

"Why would they be hiding? They're huge and they eat people. They don't need to hide from anything."

"What if they're not as horrible as people think? Have you ever looked at a fruit bat? They have exactly the same kind of teeth as a Tyrannosaurus

Rex. Maybe dragons are vegetarians, and they don't eat people at all. Maybe they went into hiding because they got tired of being killed for their scales and claws."

He couldn't possibly be serious, but he didn't sound at all like he was making fun of her.

"Interesting theory," she said, "but I think we'd notice a fifty-foot lizard tromping around, no matter how nice he is." She smiled warmly as he turned to her to let him know she wasn't trying to be mean. He returned her smile, and Angel felt for an odd moment the way she did around Zack.

They continued around the rest of the museum talking and laughing, admiring the skill of the artist, and at times standing quietly side-by-side. When Angel finally looked at her watch, disappointment flooded her as the time registered.

"I've got to go! My brother's gonna be at the library any second to pick me up. I don't want to make him angry, or he'll drive even crazier on the way home." She turned to leave and Gregor followed her through the museum lobby and out the front door.

Cassie and her crew were still outside the museum, but were now sitting on a bench. Cassie's four-inch heels dangled from her fingers as she leaned over her knees. Tamara whacked Cassie in the arm.

"See, I told you," Cassie said loudly, "Just a stupid hick. Look who he's with. Maybe he thinks her *big brain* will leak out on his." All three of them giggled.

"Friends of yours?" asked Gregor sarcastically as they crossed the street to the library.

"Hardly." Cassie always got under her skin. Not that the other kids weren't mean, rolling their eyes when they saw her reading fantasy novels. Even the brains told her they thought she took the books too seriously.

Josh was waiting at the curb and revved his engine as Angel said good-bye to Gregor. Josh started fiddling with the radio when he saw her step up to the car. She waved to Gregor and climbed in, Jacob pinching her leg as she squeezed behind his seat.

"That's for stealing the remote yesterday. I missed half my show." His usual mischievous grin was replaced by a scowl.

Angel settled into the back seat and looked over at the spot where Gregor had been leaning against a tree. He was gone. She pressed her face against the car window, but there was no sign of him in either direction.

"Who was that?" Josh asked sardonically before he pulled the car forward.

"Just someone I met in the library."

"He looks a little strange to me. You need to stay away from guys like that."

"All we did was look at the art exhibit together. What kind of guy *should* I be hanging out with? One of your Neanderthal football buds?"

Jacob snickered and Josh thumped his leg.

"Just be careful. I don't think Mom and Dad would be too happy if they found out you were hanging around the library, or even the *art* museum, with a strange guy." He said the word "art" like it was a complete waste of time.

"I don't think they'd be too happy about your final exam grade in Biology either, if they knew it."

He didn't reply.

The ride home was no calmer than the ride into town, but it wasn't enough to chase away Angel's thoughts about the afternoon with Gregor. She jumped out of the car the second Josh parked in the driveway and ran straight to her room to sketch.

Angel's drawing captured the fiery eyes of the griffin in the painting at the museum, and she'd done a reasonably good job on its fierce teeth and jaws. But the fur...

She pulled a book with a picture of a griffin on the cover from her shelf. She tried the trick her art teacher had shown her and turned both the book and the sketchpad upside down, to take the focus off the subject as a whole and help her hone in on one feature.

Zack burst in and looked hopefully at her. He climbed up on the bed next to where she sat leaning against a pillow adding detail to her drawing.

"Did you find the beetle?"

"Oh, not yet." Guilt niggled at her. "I'm sorry. I searched through a whole stack of books at the library. I'm at a total loss."

Zack's face dropped, but as usual, he didn't stay sad for long. He scooted closer and looked at her drawing.

"That's good. What is it? Looks like an eagle-lion hybrid."

It was hard to believe sometimes that he was only six. "It's a griffin, and you're right. It's a cross between a lion and an eagle. It's not nearly as good as the one in the painting I saw today, though."

"Where'd you see a painting?"

"Oh, I popped into the art museum for a few minutes after scouring every book in the library." She averted her eyes. "Listen, I'm going to go back tomorrow. I'll see what I can find. But I'm going to the museum first, okay?"

"All right, thanks. I gotta go check to see if my computer's booted up yet. I found an awesome dinosaur website yesterday, and I want to look some stuff up about stegosaurus." He slid off the edge of the bed and scampered out her door.

Angel set the griffin picture aside and started working on a dragon. She kept in mind what Gregor had said about dinosaurs, and found that her drawing ended up looking much like a T-Rex with its front legs attached to massive wings. Changing only a few details would make it look like a traditional dragon. All the pictures of dinosaurs she'd ever seen were just artists' renditions anyway, right? And the artists were working off a usually incomplete collection of bones. So, why couldn't they really be dragons?

~Giving Time~

The skin on the back of his hand tugged uncomfortably as he flexed his fingers. He looked up to find the scientist staring at him.

"Is there a problem?" he said, pulling his sleeve out of the way and exposing the scarred tissue on his forearm.

The scientist, a mousy little mongrel of a man, averted his eyes. "No."

"Well, I have a problem. You told me we didn't need the girl. It's been seven years. I want my powers. Permanently. Now."

"I'm very close. The experiments are running well. I just need a little more time."

"Well, until I see real progress, time is all I'm giving you."

Chapter Three
The Discovery

"I don't know, Angel." Mrs. Mason's hazel eyes narrowed as she stood in front of the kitchen counter untying her apron. "You know how I feel about all these new neighborhoods going in out here…the bus will be full of strangers." She wrung her hands as she thought about Angel's request. Angel noticed again how perfect Mrs. Mason's fingernails were despite the fact that she never even polished them.

Josh and Jacob sat at the kitchen table, scarfing down homemade brownies after finishing off two plates of food each. *Teenage boys are pigs.*

"*Pleeeease*," Angel said, "I'm almost fourteen, and it won't be at night. I'll find a mom with kids to sit next to, and if there's anyone creepy on the bus, I'll get right back off and come home. I promise."

Mrs. Mason's face softened. "I'll feel better if you take Jacob's cell phone with you."

Jacob opened his brownie-filled mouth to protest, but Mrs. Mason pointed at him. "Not a word from you. You haven't got a leg to stand on after your last little prank. Besides, you'll be with your brother. You can use his phone if you need it."

"What if I don't want this loser hanging around me all afternoon?" Josh winked at Jacob. "Angel doesn't need to be going into town anyway, she's just going to—"

Angel stood behind Mrs. Mason, holding her hands as if gripping a steering wheel and turning it wildly from side to side. She jabbed her finger in Josh's direction, then ran it across her neck, flopping her head to the side with her tongue hanging out.

"Just what?" Mrs. Mason turned toward Angel.

"Just going to the stupid *art* museum," said Josh. Angel smirked at him from behind Mrs. Mason. *Yeah, you better help me, or no more Mav for the rest of the summer.*

"And what is wrong with that?" said Mrs. Mason, eyeing the two boys. "It's a much better way of spending the summer than watching gangster movies and showing off to your friends. Jacob, give your phone to Angel."

He handed it to her with dramatic slowness, and Angel hugged her foster mom. "Thanks!"

"You call me if you need anything, understand? Actually, call me when you reach town. Zack and I will be here all day, getting started on his summer unit study."

It took Angel a full twenty minutes to make the mile-long walk to the bus stop at the corner where their road met the country highway. She stayed under the canopy of the oaks that reached over the road to avoid the scorching sun. There was a good breeze blowing, otherwise she would have been drenched in sweat even in the shade of the giant trees.

Halfway through the walk she thought she saw something dash behind a tree. When she cautiously walked over to the tree, she found that the leaves on the ground were disturbed, but nothing else. She kicked at a pinecone. *Probably just a stray cat.* She looked up into the tree to see if the cat had climbed into its branches. A tittering squirrel scurried up a branch and out of sight. But as Angel stepped away, the same electricity she'd sensed by her reading tree trailed her spine.

She arrived at the bus stop with only two minutes to spare. The bus pulled up right on time, and Angel stepped through the narrow door, scanning the few passengers. *As if you can tell a criminal by the way he looks on a bus.* There was only a young couple with a baby, and a woman in a suit, her nose buried in a stack of papers in her hand.

Angel found a seat halfway back and looked out the window. The bus pulled forward and soon the trees lining the road sped past. They reached another stop a few miles away, and the bus's brakes squealed. The door opened and a single passenger stepped on. Angel immediately recognized the mop of wavy bangs, which Gregor pushed out of his eyes as he walked down the aisle. He didn't seem surprised to see her, and his face lit up when he reached her seat.

"Going to the library again?" He sat down across the aisle. The bus lurched forward and Angel and Gregor both braced themselves against the seats in front of them.

"Yeah, after I get some brochures from the art museum. I want to use the photos to draw from. What are you doing way out here?"

"Riding the bus." His grin tilted sideways.

Angel laughed, but he didn't say anything else.

"Do you like it out here?" She looked past him through the window behind his seat. All the farmland along the highway was being developed, orange groves torn down and replaced by cookie-cutter houses crammed onto tiny lots. It made Angel sick to see the open country disappear.

"It's okay, I suppose. Did you grow up around here?"

"Sort of. I moved out here when I was six." She was sure some of the kids had heard from their parents how she was found, but she didn't like to talk about it. She let them believe her parents died when she was young and she was placed in foster care with the Masons.

"Where did you move here from?"

"Where did you *come* here from?" She'd answer when he did.

"No place very interesting, I'm afraid. I live on a farm. Quite boring for most people."

"I think it'd be fabulous. Peaceful. I love living out in the country."

He smiled but didn't say anything.

Something stirred inside Angel…the need to tell the truth about her past. *He probably won't believe me anyway. And it's not like I'm ever gonna see him again.*

"I don't know where I lived before, actually." She tried to make it sound ordinary to have no idea where you're from. "I was found walking down the road a little way from my house when I was six. The Masons took me in because they were already foster parents and didn't want me stuck in an orphanage while the authorities tried to find my parents. They thought I'd been traumatized enough."

She held her breath waiting for his comment.

"So your parents were never found then? That must have been hard on you." His eyes searched hers, and she saw genuine compassion in them.

"Well, I was pretty young, and I couldn't remember anything. That was the most frustrating part, not knowing who I was. I'll probably never find out who my real parents are." A lump formed in Angel's throat. It would almost be easier if she *knew* they were dead, and she could just give up the idea of ever being reunited with them.

"So you've been with your family for seven years now?" Gregor asked. "They've adopted you by now, I guess."

Angel's heart sank at his words. And the sparkle in Gregor's eyes dimmed as if reflecting her fallen mood.

"No. Actually, they haven't." She wiggled uncomfortably, his gaze weighing on her. "They've tried, a bunch of times. But something keeps messing it up. Stupid stuff. They didn't have any problems adopting Josh and Jacob, and nothing's going wrong with them adopting Zack now, but…" She breathed deeply. The emotion in her voice sounded strange to her. "No one can explain it. It's almost like someone's trying to stop the adoption. Like someone wants me to be with them, but not…forever."

And not for the first time, Angel wondered if that *someone* was herself.

Gregor didn't push her to tell him more, but something changed about his demeanor. He looked as if he understood exactly what she meant, even more deeply than she did.

When they got off the bus, Gregor stood as if waiting for Angel to direct him where to go.

"So, what do you have planned?" she asked, happy that he seemed reluctant to leave her side. She was afraid the connection she'd felt before had been imagined. But as they stood by the bus stop, everything clicked right back again. Like they knew each other from another place or time.

It wasn't romantic either. Gregor was cute, but…

The feeling was impossible to figure out.

"I just wanted to get out of the house and enjoy some of the stuff you've got here in the city. We don't have museums and movie theaters anywhere close to where I live." It was the first piece of information he'd given her without being asked.

"Don't tell me you've never been to a movie!" She slapped her hand over her mouth. *Like that wasn't rude...*

He raked his fingers through his hair, but didn't seem offended. "Just once. It was a murder mystery. The story was a little obvious, though."

"What do you do for fun, then?" She started down the sidewalk toward the art museum and he moved in step beside her. "I mean when you're not working on the farm."

"I read a lot, and go into town to visit a friend when I have time."

"I *love* to read, mostly fantasy. How about you?"

"I guess you could say...classics."

"Classics? Really? Not *Sports Illustrated*?"

Gregor's eyebrows crinkled, and then he chuckled. "Uh...didn't you say you needed to call home or something?"

Angel pulled the phone from her pocket. Gregor waited patiently while she explained her plans again to Mrs. Mason. Angel rolled her eyes as she said, "Yes...I promise I'll be home in time for dinner."

Gregor followed her into the museum so she could grab a brochure, and they took one more quick walk through the gallery. They stopped in front of the giant dragon mosaic. Angel crossed her arms. "I gave some thought to your dinosaur theory. I can see it happening."

His eyes sparkled, as if he was holding back a comment.

They left the museum, Angel insisting she needed to find Zack's beetle. Gregor tapped her arm with his elbow. "I'm telling you, it's not a species you're going to find. I bet he's brand new." But he helped her look just the same.

After digging through more books, they left the library. Angel scoped the area to see if Josh was skulking about. She saw the Mav in the theater parking lot, but her brothers weren't in their usual spot in front of the building.

Angel looked at Gregor. He wore his same long black pants and boots despite the heat. *That can't be comfortable.*

"Let's go get some ice-cream," she said.

Angel paid for her sundae, and turned as Gregor pulled a handful of coins from his pocket. At least...she'd thought they were coins. He tightened his fist around them, and then opened his hand in front of the cashier. The girl took a crisp five-dollar bill from his palm. Angel scrunched her eyes and shook her head, then went to find a table.

Angel did most of the talking while they scooped their chocolate sundaes. Gregor listened intently, but there were moments when it seemed like he was trying to keep her talking not because he was interested, but to avoid saying something.

Thunder cracked in the distance, and Angel peered out the window at the dark clouds gathering in the pale sky. The wind picked up, scattering leaves and litter across the sidewalk.

Angel should have been making her way back to the bus to get home before dark, but there was no telling what the weather would do and she didn't want to walk home from the bus stop in the pouring rain. She pulled Jacob's cell phone from the clip on her pocket.

"Do you have to be back home soon?" she asked.

Gregor shook his head.

"Hang on then." She called home again. Angel explained to Mrs. Mason what the weather was like in town, knowing it could still be bright and sunny by her house.

"Are you still at the library?" Mrs. Mason asked.

"No, but I ran into a friend and we want to go see a movie."

"You call Josh the second the movie lets out."

"Yes, ma'am. Thank you, thank you, thank you!"

Gregor sat in his chair, staring at Angel, a half-smile on his face.

"Guess we have more time now. And I wasn't kidding about the movie. I think there's something showing in about fifteen minutes."

"Are you really going to ask your brother for a ride after the way he drove yesterday?" Gregor asked as they walked to the theater. The wind was blowing hard, but the rain had barely gotten started.

"I have to. I'd never be allowed to ride home on the bus after dark. Especially since I have to walk our road to get home."

They entered the lobby of the theater and Angel checked the board over the ticket counter. The movie starting next was a gangster flick she wasn't exactly dying to see. It was either that or wait for the following show that didn't start for nearly an hour, so she went to the counter and asked for two tickets. Gregor reached into his pocket, but Angel insisted on paying.

Despite constant action, the movie didn't hold Angel's attention. She turned her gaze to Gregor, hoping he couldn't feel her watching him. He stared at the screen, mesmerized by a movie that was quite ordinary.

Once in a while he'd glance over at her, and she'd snap her head back to the screen. She couldn't get the thought out of her head that he knew something he wasn't telling her—something about her.

The movie was longer than she'd expected, and the sun was sinking in the now-clear sky. It was late enough that Mrs. Mason wouldn't want her walking home from the bus.

She tried calling Josh and got his voice mail. She tried again and again, but kept getting the same message. *He must be in a dead spot.* She walked around to the theater parking lot and saw the Mav wasn't where it had been before. She hadn't thought to call him before the movie, assuming he'd stay in town as late as possible.

The sky was streaked with shades of orange and red, where wispy white clouds replaced the threatening gray ones and caught the spectrum of colors sprayed out by the setting sun.

"Now what?" She didn't want to call home and tell Mrs. Mason what happened, and tried Josh one more time, but with no luck.

"I've got to take the bus anyway," said Gregor. "I don't mind the extra walk. I'll make sure you get home safe."

Angel didn't doubt that he would, but Mrs. Mason would never allow it.

She handled it the only way she knew how, and called home one more time.

"Josh isn't here, and he's not answering his cell," she said. "But my friend can get me home."

"Is it Elizabeth?"

"Um…yeah."

"Her brother's driving?"

"Mm-hm."

"Is he there?"

She covered the mouthpiece with her fingers as she held the phone out to Gregor. "She wants to talk to the driver."

Gregor listened, said a few "yes ma'ams," and handed the cell back to Angel. A dial tone buzzed from the open phone.

"She said you can ride home with me," he said as she snapped the phone shut.

"What did she ask you?"

"Just if I'd been driving for more than a year and if I had a good driving record." His face was remorseful. She'd never seen that particular look on either Josh or Jacob before, and it struck hard.

"I'm sorry I put you on the spot like that, but this was the first time she let me come to town on my own."

They walked silently to the bus stop, Angel berating herself for lying. But Gregor seemed unreal to her, and yet more real than anything she'd ever known. It was like they saw the world through the same glasses, and she felt connected to him in a way she couldn't understand.

"I can't believe you're doing this," Angel said after they stepped off the bus. "You're going to have to walk all the way back in the dark." Gregor only smiled, looking like he wanted to say something but didn't have the words.

They made it about ten yards when a pair of headlights appeared, speeding toward them.

Too fast.

The lights swerved side to side, and bumped as the vehicle ran off the road then jumped back on track. Angel felt Gregor yank her from the edge of the road, the two of them stumbling into a huge oak tree.

She pressed herself against the broad trunk. Her heart nearly stopped. The headlights were incredibly close, aimed directly at them...almost on top of them...

Gregor shoved her...

Into the tree trunk.

But there was no resistance. Silence engulfed her—a momentary nothingness, and then forest appeared all around her.

She skidded across the wet, leaf-strewn ground, losing her balance, and slammed into another tree. A loud *crash* and the sound of crunching metal reverberated through the trees surrounding her. Angel barely registered her location amid a cluster of trees—inside the woods they had just been standing outside of only two seconds before.

A ringing started in her ears, and quickly built to a deafening crescendo. Images rushed through her mind…

Oak and pine trees flew past her as she ran frantically through long shadows cast by the setting sun, her heart pounding and her breath coming hard and fast. She was a little girl of six and terrified, her small feet moving as fast as they could, slipping on leaves and catching on tree roots that threatened to trip her, but she couldn't afford to slow down.

"Mommy! Daddy! Help me!" screamed the sound of her childish voice.

Then a boy with dark hair, no more than ten years old.

He looked scared as she ran toward him, his silver-flecked eyes wide as saucers, but he was brave…he had to be…someone had to save her.

Another voice, that of a man, bellowed from behind her through the dense forest, getting closer by the second.

"Come here! Now! Come here or I'll kill you!"

And Angel was shoved, just as Gregor had shoved her moments ago, through a tree.

Then she was skidding again, this time on her back, her tiny body sliding across the slippery blanket of leaves, the tree roots banging into her, the charm bracelet on her wrist catching the sunlight, which was suddenly much brighter.

And her head cracked into a tree.

The rough bark of the oak tree she leaned on grabbed at her shirt, lifting it, and scraping her bare skin as she sank to the ground. The ringing wouldn't stop and a wave of nausea overcame her. She let her head fall forward and held it between her knees, trying to make her stomach stop churning. The unbearable ringing drove her hands into her hair, her fingernails digging into her skull.

The nausea subsided, and the ringing softened bit by bit so that Angel could loosen her grip, releasing her hair and easing the pain around her ears. Her breath returned in ragged gasps, until she could finally gulp in enough air to exhale. She wrapped her arms around her knees and tried to control the shaking, and then looked up at Gregor, who stood over her, his face hidden in the dark of the woods.

"You…you…" was all she could manage. Gregor squatted down facing her and put his hands on her trembling shoulders. The silver flecks in his eyes danced in the pale moonlight, as tears welled up and poured over his lids.

"Angel, I'm so sorry…I've wanted to tell you all day…but I knew you didn't remember, and how would you believe me?"

She began to sob, not from sorrow, but to release the intense mix of emotions that suddenly overwhelmed her. She knew Gregor. He had saved her from that madman. But where had they been? The trees that she'd been running by were just like the ones in the woods near her house, but there was something distinctly different about the atmosphere. She'd called out for her parents but they didn't come. She tried to picture their faces, but it just made her head hurt again. Had the madman killed them?

And how did Gregor push her *through* a tree?

Sirens sounded, and soon flashing red and blue lights were pulsating between the trees, but Angel couldn't move, and she could see Gregor's eyes suddenly widen in fear.

Angel took a deep breath and swallowed her tears, willing herself to speak. "It's the police," she said quietly, somehow aware that Gregor needed that explained to him, but not sure why. "They're here because of the accident. Just stay still and hopefully they won't notice us." Her voice grew calmer with each word, but her arms and legs still trembled.

"Do you trust me?" Gregor whispered, and Angel nodded. He stood and helped Angel get shakily to her feet, then held his hand up in front of the tree she had just been leaning against. He wrapped his arm around her shoulders and together they stepped through the Gate he made in the tree.

Chapter Four
The Story

They stepped out of the Gate into a well-hidden spot in a cluster of trees near the end of the driveway. Angel still shook, but the nausea was gone, and she found it easier to think without crying now that they were in her own yard. She'd passed through some sort of magic Gateway three times and there was no way she was imagining it. She also realized that, more than anything, she needed an explanation. What had happened to her?

That was going to have to wait, at least until she found a way to get back outside later and talk to Gregor privately. Right then, the most important thing was somehow explaining where she'd been and why she was so shaken.

We really did see a car wreck…

She asked Gregor one question for which she could not wait on an answer. "You're not really staying with relatives or something, are you?"

"No. I'm sorry, I feel like I've been lying to y—"

"Not now. I'm not mad at you. But I need to know if you can meet me at midnight by the back fence."

"Yes, of course, anything. I'll be there and I'll tell you anything you want to know."

She felt him watching her as she walked down the driveway, until she turned the corner behind the house. She entered the kitchen, where Mrs.

Mason was pacing.

Mrs. Mason let go of the apron strings she had been wringing and wrapped her arms around Angel. Then she pulled away and gripped Angel's shoulders, looking deeply into her eyes.

"Where have you been? We've called Jacob's phone over and over. And where are Elizabeth and her brother? I didn't see a car pull into the driveway." Mrs. Mason sounded more scared than angry, and guilt sank deeper into Angel's heart. But she had to see this through. The truth would be impossible for them to believe and Angel needed time to sort things out before she could even think of telling them.

"We saw someone wreck into the trees on the way home." Angel still trembled slightly. "It was pretty bad. Elizabeth's brother had to go back and give a statement to the police, so he just dropped me off at the end of the driveway."

"Are you all right?"

Angel nodded.

Mrs. Mason pulled in a deep breath and placed a fluttering hand over her heart, then breathed out slowly.

Zack appeared in the doorway wearing his pajamas. "Mom, what's wrong?" Then he turned to Angel. "You look awful."

"It's okay, Zack," she said, "I just had a bad day. You go on back to bed and I'll come in to see you in a little bit." He glanced at Mrs. Mason, who nodded to him to obey, and he scuffled back to bed.

"Why didn't you call, or answer our call? We could have come and helped."

Angel hadn't heard the cell phone ring at all, but it could have been blaring in her ear while she fought the horrid flashbacks in the woods and she wouldn't have noticed. She pulled the phone off the clip on her pocket and held it out—the battery had died. Jacob's irresponsibility was finally good for something.

Mr. Mason, entered the kitchen, grim-faced, followed by Josh and Jacob, who looked as though they'd just been reamed. Jacob's face was flushed and both the boys' eyes were bloodshot. Josh swayed slightly as he glared at Angel.

"You okay, Angel?" Mr. Mason's voice was gruff.

Angel nodded.

"Angel and her friend saw a bad accident down the way. Someone ran off the road into the trees. She's just a little upset, but she's fine."

Josh and Jacob's reddened eyes bulged, and Mr. Mason's expression grew even grimmer.

"Was it a truck that hit the trees?"

Angel thought about the headlights…they were too high off the ground to be a car.

"Yes, sir, it was."

Mr. Mason turned to the boys. "Do you see? See what could have happened to you? NOW GET TO YOUR ROOMS!"

He pulled his keys out of his pocket. "They're not to leave their rooms for the rest of the week. I'm goin' to help the police and tell 'em what them boys have been up to." He stormed out and slammed the door behind him.

Josh and Jacob turned sullenly and retreated down the hallway.

"What happened?" asked Angel.

"Your dad found them down at Kevin Johnson's with their friends, drinking. That truck you saw must've been some of them heading home." Mrs. Mason looked devastated.

Angel couldn't believe it. Josh and Jacob had never done more than harmless trouble-making, so she'd thought.

But she had more important things to focus on now.

"I'm going to go lie down."

"Do you want to eat?" Mrs. Mason tilted her head toward the sandwich on the table.

"Can I take it to my room?" Angel asked, and Mrs. Mason nodded. Then she stood up and hugged Angel. Angel hugged back, and felt another twang of guilt. Mrs. Mason had been the only mother she could remember. But after the events of the evening she felt even more determined to go to her parents if they were alive.

Mrs. Mason released Angel, then reached out and tenderly pushed Angel's hair behind her ear.

"Good night, and try to sleep well."

Angel picked up the plate and headed to her room.

She set the plate down on her nightstand, and remembered she'd promised Zack she'd come see him.

He was in bed with the covers pulled all the way up, but his eyes shone over the edge of the blanket. He didn't move when she entered, and she sat down on the edge of his bed, looking into his baby blue eyes.

"What's going on, Angel?" Times like these reminded Angel that he was in fact a little boy.

"Josh and Jacob just got into some trouble. A few of their friends were doing some bad things and got caught. I was coming home with a friend of mine when some of Josh and Jacob's friends wrecked their truck. Everyone's gonna be okay, though. I promise." She smiled reassuringly at Zack, and he closed his eyes.

"You don't look okay to me, Angel. You look like you've seen a ghost."

"There's no such thing as ghosts, and you know it, little man."

Her teasing did nothing to lighten his mood. He opened his eyes again, his serious gaze softened only by his childish features. "You think you don't belong here, don't you?"

Angel's skin prickled. It was as if Zack had read her mind. How could a boy so young sense such a thing?

"Zack, I don't know where I belong. I intend to find out. But you have to understand that no matter where I am, no matter what happens to me, I love you. You believe me, don't you?"

She swallowed. She wanted to assure him that she felt like she belonged anywhere he was, but she couldn't bring herself to lie to him.

His eyes shone more brightly as he blinked back tears. Angel heard him inhale, and his jaw flexed and his hands tightened around the blanket edge as if he was straining to hold back. Angel's chest tightened as his expression scraped her raw. She opened her mouth to speak, but Zack cut in, barely a whisper.

"I love you too, Angel."

He rolled onto his side, closing his eyes.

Angel took a deep breath and rose to her feet, shoving down the emotions that scalded her heart. She returned to her room, a niggling whisper in the back of her mind telling her this would probably be the last night she'd spend in the Masons' house. Her mind reeled as she sat on her bed barely nibbling on her sandwich. What Gregor had done was *magic*. Not the kind of magic performed by illusionists, but *real* magic, the kind she'd read about for years in her novels. And if she knew Gregor from someplace else, then she might be able to do magic, too. And he'd know what happened to her parents, why she was being chased, and who she was before.

She suddenly felt as though every nerve in her body had been triggered, and she didn't know what to do with the energy until midnight when she'd go out to meet Gregor. She sat poised on the edge of her bed, keenly aware of every tiny noise in the house. Josh and Jacob whispered in their room but she couldn't make out the words. The whispering stopped when the door to the garage banged shut, and Mr. Mason's heavy footsteps fell through the hallway to the master bedroom. Angel heard muffled voices for a moment. Mrs. Mason asked something, probably how the boys in the truck were, and Mr. Mason's deep voice murmured an answer. Mrs. Mason's "Oh, thank God!" rang clearly through the door, and was followed by her soft crying.

The house grew completely silent a few minutes later, and Angel crept to her door and peeked out into the hallway. The house and all its occupants were resigned to rest, except Angel and the beetle on her dresser.

The beetle's singing began as it had the night before, and Angel closed her door. She walked over to his cage and carried it to the window where she could take a better look in the moonlight. The beetle's silver flecks danced and sparkled, and Angel remembered the way Gregor's eyes looked earlier that evening in the moonlight in the woods. It wasn't coincidence that he'd appeared in the library the day before. This beetle belonged to him…he'd been in her yard…spying? The rustling in the bushes before Josh pulled out of the driveway the day before…could it have been Gregor?

Angel set the cage down, then grabbed her largest backpack out of the closet and resolutely filled it with jeans, T-shirts, socks and underwear. She snuck into the hall bathroom and took her toothbrush and toothpaste, then came back into her room and searched through her things for items she couldn't live without. There wasn't much besides clothes, what little cash she had, and her charm bracelet.

She examined the engraving once again. She was somehow tied to Gregor and the place he came from. She clasped the bracelet around her wrist, then tucked the backpack under her bed and climbed under the covers fully dressed in jeans and a long-sleeve shirt. If Gregor's clothes were an indication, she was going somewhere not nearly as hot as Florida.

She had another hour to wait, and she didn't want Mrs. Mason finding her pacing around her room, so she lay under the covers with her eyes closed. There was no chance of her accidentally falling asleep, though, with the desire to discover her past forcing the blood through her veins like a raging river.

Just before midnight, she stood in the doorway of her room for one last look at her belongings, her backpack slung across one shoulder and the beetle's cage in her hand. In the middle of her bed lay the note she'd written for the Masons telling them only that she had decided she needed to search for her real parents, and thanking them for all they had done for her the past seven years. *It's not enough. I owe them so much more.*

She crept silently down the hall and into Zack's room, where he lay curled up on his side. She knelt next to the bed, gazing at the curls stuck to his forehead, the long lashes that surrounded those blue jean eyes, the cheeks that pushed out when he smiled at her. And he *always* smiled at her.

Her heart nearly jerked to a stop. Would she ever see his sweet, round face again? Hollowness tore through her, swallowing part of her soul. There was already a hole there that could only be filled by her parents and her past. *It's too much.*

Forcing back the tears that seared her eyes, she leaned forward and kissed his forehead.

Little man… The salty taste of his sweaty bangs clung to her lips as she stood back up. He stirred momentarily, and then snuggled deeper into his pillow, his mouth slightly open, breathing the steady rhythm of peaceful sleep.

"Take care, little man," she whispered, stroking his soft cheek. "I'm going to miss you more than you'll ever know."

She crossed the yard to the back fence, afraid every crunching leaf would betray her and Mr. Mason would come running out to drag her back to the house. But she made it safely through the dark to Gregor, who waited, one leg propped on the base of her reading tree, looking as anxious as Angel felt.

"I believe this is yours." Angel held out the caged beetle.

"Horatio! I've missed you!"

The beetle fluttered its wings wildly inside the cage, its chirping loud and frantic. Gregor unfastened the door to the cage and swung it open.

Horatio flew in circles around Gregor's head several times as though making sure it was truly him, then settled on his shoulder. His chirping melted into a mellow purr.

"I hope he's not been pestering you."

Gregor seemed less anxious now that he and Horatio were reunited. Angel wished she could share in his relief. "He's beautiful, but you know darn well he frustrated the heck out of me. At least now I know where he came from." With more force than intended, she added, "I wish I knew the same thing about me."

Gregor's face dropped, and he leaned against the reading tree. "I'm sorry."

"Stop apologizing. I know you had to lie to me, and I know you would've just told me the truth if you thought I'd believe you. I just want to know what happened. And if my parents are still alive."

"Yes, they are."

Angel's heart nearly burst with joy. She had longed to hear those words for seven years, but she wasn't prepared for the effect they'd have and she nearly dropped her backpack.

Gregor arched his eyebrow and pointed to the backpack as Angel grappled with the strap. "What's that for?"

"I've always known I didn't belong here; I just didn't know why. Now I do, and I want to go back. I want to see my parents." She shifted the weight of the backpack to her other shoulder. "Now."

"It's not that simple." Gregor was letting Horatio crawl around on his hand and watched the beetle's every move. "They're not exactly home right now. Angel, this is going to take a lot of explaining. I didn't expect to find you with no memory of your past." He paused. "This is going to be much more complicated than I thought." His words trailed off to a near whisper.

Angel squinted at him. "I may not remember what happened, but I know I need to go home. Now take me. Do that gateway thing and take me home." She wanted it over with before she lost her nerve.

Gregor set Horatio back on his shoulder, and faced her. He searched her eyes as he tucked his lower lip between his teeth. "You're really sure?"

She nodded.

"Okay…follow me." He held his hand in front of the reading tree.

She stepped quickly behind him and out the other side of the Gate. Gregor stood a few feet away with Horatio perched atop his left shoulder. Tall oak and pine trees surrounded them, and for a moment Angel thought she hadn't left her neighborhood. But the trees were denser, and the air was chilly, unlike the muggy heat of Florida. And the light was different, as if dawn would soon be on the horizon rather than hours away.

"Where are we exactly?" she asked.

"Ireland. Sort of."

She opened her mouth to ask what he meant by that, but he started walking away and motioned her to follow, putting his finger to his lips. They crept between the trees, stepping as lightly as possible, and ended up at the edge of a clearing a few yards away, where a small tent was clearly visible in the early morning moonlight. He stopped, gently grasping Angel's arm and holding her behind a tree. He seemed to be checking over the campsite, which must have met his approval because he continued toward the tent.

"I've been telling everyone I'm camping when I go looking for you. It's the truth, actually. I just don't tell them what I'm *doing* while I camp."

Angel gazed up at the sky through the opening in the canopy. Sparkling stars were spattered everywhere, their brightness undiminished by the ambient light of the moon. More stars were visible in this one small patch than Angel was used to seeing in the entire expanse of sky over the open field behind the Masons' property. The leaves on the surrounding trees glistened in the moonlight, and the faint hoot of an owl echoed through the symphony of chirping crickets.

Gregor walked over to the tent and reached inside, pulled out a blanket and spread it over the ground.

"We could make the walk back to my place right now if you want, but I think we should talk first. You must have tons of questions. Then, you can decide if you want to go on, or you can go back through the Gate. I think if your parents knew about your new life they wouldn't want me just ripping you from it like this." He sat down on the blanket.

Angel dropped her backpack on the ground and sat down across from him.

"I'm not going back. Just tell me what happened. Who am I and why was that madman chasing me?"

Chapter Five
The Answers

"He was someone who killed several people on our island. All we know is he's not from here and he came after you, and we think it was because of your Talent."

Gregor's serious expression did nothing to reassure her, and his words jumped around in her brain as if they couldn't find a place to land. "My what?"

"Your Talent. Your special power that is stronger than the rest. Like my Gate-making. You're a Finder."

"A Finder...What, um..." Angel rubbed her temple and tried to formulate a coherent question.

"You can Find the location of anything, anywhere," Gregor said, "even if it's miles away or buried deep underground. We think Dawric was after you to help him Find something." He sat still, Horatio perched by his ear, no emotion readable by his expression.

Angel studied his eyes. Is he holding back so he won't scare me?

"Let me get this straight. I can do magic like you. And this...Dawric wanted to take my Talent? How do you know? And why are you calling him Dawric if you said you don't know who he is?" The questions poured out of her before she could stop the accusing tone from entering her voice. She expected Gregor to get angry, but he either didn't notice, or chose to ignore it.

"Dawric means 'thief of power' in our ancient language. It's not a name." Gregor leaned forward to let Horatio crawl to the other shoulder. "When an Empowered is killed, their soul becomes vulnerable at the moment of death. It's possible to take their powers temporarily. But when the victim's powers eventually go on to be with them in the Realm Beyond, the murderer loses his powers, too. And he's never the same. His soul is damaged and he becomes...sub-human."

"So how did Dawric kill more than one person if it would do so much damage the first time?" She wrapped her arms around her knees, a sudden chill overtaking her. She was unable to bring herself to ask the question that truly plagued her—*Was he trying to kill me?*

"He must not be Empowered. If he doesn't have powers of his own in the first place, maybe he can't be damaged by losing them. That's what your parents think anyway, and I agree. He never used magic to kill his victims. He always strangled them." Gregor's expression grew more somber, and Angel squeezed her knees tighter.

"So what happened to him? Is he still after me?"

"He's not been back to our island since you disappeared. Your parents are off searching for him while they search for you."

"So my parents know I'm alive!" The words came out of her mouth as almost a gasp. Her stomach tightened. She would be reunited with them; she could feel it with her entire being. But something didn't add up.

"Wait..." She searched the surrounding area as if the answer would pop out in front of her. "Why didn't you just come through the Gate you pushed me through? Then you could have brought me back right then."

"I was planning to. But Dawric showed up the instant I pushed you through. He didn't see where you went, but he saw me and cast me away from the Gate. Then he went into a rage and set the forest on fire. It destroyed the Gate." Gregor took a breath, staring down at the blanket. "I was scared and I didn't think about where I was Gating you..."

"Gregor, you were a *child*, and you saved my life. It's not your fault." She tried to capture his gaze, but he kept his head down. "Besides, you've found me now." The words seemed to comfort him and he returned her look, his face more illuminated now that the sky had lightened with the oncoming dawn.

"Have you been searching this whole time?"

"Yes. I...I found your parents on the edge of the forest. They were unconscious, but I managed to wake your father. He picked up your mother and we ran to safety. I told them what happened. They wanted to start searching for you right away, and find Dawric, and stop him, too."

Gregor became more animated, his silver-flecked eyes reflecting the rise of emotion in his voice. "I insisted on helping, but they tried to talk me out of it. They thought I was too young. They took me home, and we discovered that my parents died in the fire. They must have seen the smoke and gone into the forest to find me. A...neighbor of ours found them in the forest."

Angel didn't know what to say. Guilt shifted inside of her, unsettling her stomach. *If it wasn't for me, they'd be alive.*

The forest was beginning to quiet as the crickets ended their songs, and Gregor continued.

"The neighbor assumed you were killed in the fire, too, and told us it was best that you were gone. He said there are many magical objects out there that could be used for evil, and if Dawric took your Talent he'd be able to find them. Your parents decided not to tell him, or anyone else, that you were still alive. I talked them into letting me at least look for you, that my Gate-making would be useful and I'd be safe because no one would suspect a child."

"Why would they let one person stop them from getting help? Why does his opinion matter so much?" Didn't her parents love her enough to ask the whole town to search no matter what one person said?

"That neighbor is very rich and powerful," Gregor said with a tone Angel couldn't quite identify. "He's got...influence, on the entire island, and could've gotten everyone in a panic. He would have made it impossible for your parents to get *anyone* to help search for you. It was for your safety, and theirs."

His words seemed too carefully chosen.

Angel's head spun with too many details to absorb in one night. But knowing her parents were alive was enough at the moment. It was all she could handle.

They sat silently for a few minutes. The dawn light peeking through the trees reminded Angel that she'd been running on adrenaline for hours. Exhaustion was sinking in. Gregor looked tired too, and he didn't offer any more information.

"I can't go back through the Gate, but I don't know what to do." She dropped her head to her knees.

"Well, I was planning on just having you stay with me until I contacted your parents. I was expecting you to know who you were, though. I guess I didn't think this through well enough. I was concentrating on the search, not on what to do once I'd found you."

"I can still stay with you, though, can't I?" This was going too far, and Angel knew it, but what other choice did she have?

"Are you really sure?"

"Honestly? No. But I can't go back…"

Gregor seemed to be thinking about her words for a moment. "Okay, I'll take you back to my place, but I think we should keep you secret for now. Not let anyone know who you are until your parents come back."

"Because of the neighbor?"

"That, yes. And because it would just require a lot of explaining that I'm not prepared to do without your parents."

Angel nodded and stood up. "Let's go before I fall asleep right here."

Together they folded the blanket and then Angel looked at the tent that needed to be taken down. *I probably should've just laid down on the blanket and slept right here.* But Gregor waved his hand and the tent collapsed into a neat little bundle, which he stuffed along with the blanket into his duffel bag.

He gave her a discriminating look. "I think we should change your hair color. That red will make you stand out. Come here and turn around."

Angel was too tired to question him. His hands slid over her hair, from the top of her head and down her back to where her hair ended at her waist. Then he stepped in front of her and touched each eyebrow.

"That should do it." He dragged his foot across the ground, scraping away a small patch of leaves, then reached down and scooped up a handful of sandy soil. He squeezed his hand around the dirt, then opened his fist. In his palm sat a small, round mirror.

"Here, take a look."

She took the mirror from his hand, turning it over and back to make sure she wasn't imagining it, then looked at her reflection. Her hair was deep brown, almost exactly the shade of her eyes.

"Whoa, way different."

"Speaking of different," he said, "you sound way different, too. That's good. No one would doubt you're not from here."

Angel had wondered about Gregor's accent, but it hadn't occurred to her that she should have one, too. A vague memory surfaced, from a year or so after she'd been found—Mrs. Mason stroking her hair and saying, "You're picking up your father's southern drawl. It's cute, but I miss that funny little accent you used to have."

She handed the mirror back to Gregor. He squeezed and opened his fist again, then let the dirt pour back onto the ground.

"Oh, and you'd better take that off and hide it." He pointed at the charm bracelet on Angel's wrist. " It's your family heirloom and anyone who sees it will know exactly who you are. I'll send Horatio to contact your parents and let them know I've found you, and then I guess we'll figure out what to do next."

Horatio fluttered wildly around Gregor's head.

"Do you know where my parents are?" Angel asked as she picked up her backpack.

"Somewhere in Germany. They think Dawric may be living there. Follow me. I'll Gate us to the edge of my farm and then we can walk to the house. It'll only be a few minutes and you can get some sleep."

Gregor moved toward a tree, held up his hand, and then stepped forward and disappeared. Angel followed. They stepped out on the edge of the forest, where it opened up to several acres of low, rolling hills covered in deep green.

"That's it, right there." Gregor nodded toward a white farmhouse on the other side of the field, dotted with tufts of white and brown. As Angel moved closer, the tufts took shape—sheep and goats dozing in the morning sunshine.

The farmhouse had a comfortable front porch and flowers planted along the sides. A dirt path led to the main road in front, with two horses fenced in on one side. Behind the horses' area was a barn. Off to the other side of the house was a garden, about twice the size of Mr. Mason's and bursting with vegetables.

Charming.

As Angel stood on the step waiting for Gregor to unlock the front door, she felt something soft wind around her ankles. She jumped, then looked down at a skinny gray and white cat with a pointy face and wiry tail.

"Who's this?"

"Angel, meet Shakespeare." Gregor pushed open the front door.

She bent down to scratch under Shakespeare's chin. The gray markings formed a mask around his eyes. The cat followed them into the house, and curled into a ball on the cushioned seat of a wooden chair.

"You can have the spare room in the back." He pointed to a door on the opposite side of the living room.

"Thanks." Angel walked straight through the living room, eyes set on the door. When she reached the bed, she fell on top of the covers without even taking off her shoes, and was asleep in seconds.

Chapter Six
The Farm

Angel's eyes fluttered open. The unfamiliar clock on the nightstand, lit by bright sunlight, read twelve o'clock. Angel sat up and surveyed her surroundings.

What have I done? The Masons are probably waking up right now, reading my note, wondering where I've gone. Angel imagined Mrs. Mason's eyes filling with tears. And Zack…the thought broke her heart.

Everything would be different from now on, even if she decided to go back. How could she take back the hurt she'd caused…or give up finding her real parents?

There was also the magic. She accepted the reality of Gregor's powers as if she'd known all along that they, and he, existed. Well, she had, in a way, hadn't she?

Now she had to find out about her own powers. Gregor had called her a Finder, and made it sound like something special and rare. Excitement filled her, quelled only by the fact that she was putting her life into the hands of a stranger.

But Gregor wasn't a stranger, exactly. He'd already saved her life. Twice. She had to trust him, at least until he proved he couldn't be trusted.

Metallic banging came through the doorway. *Sounds like cooking. Gregor must be up.* Angel calmed herself with a deep breath.

She climbed out of bed and found the door to the adjacent bathroom.

When she was done, she paused to stare in the mirror at her now-brown hair. Her chocolate eyes didn't seem unusual when they weren't contrasted with red hair, and her freckles blended into her skin more, not that they'd ever been that prominent.

She went back into the bedroom. The wall behind the bed held a single painting that depicted a peaceful-looking stream running through a forest dappled with sunlight. A large picture window on the adjacent wall overlooked Gregor's vegetable garden.

Remembering what Gregor had told her before their walk to the house, Angel unclasped her charm bracelet and opened the drawer of the nightstand. The sunlight caught the locket and sent a flash of light into her eyes. Her eyes clouded and her head pounded, and she dropped the bracelet. It landed with a sliding thump inside the drawer.

She slammed the drawer shut and sat down on the bed. The pounding stopped as quickly as it started, but the image of trees zipping by as she slid across the forest floor stayed with her. *Maybe I need to take this more slowly. No questions this morning.*

Angel stood and headed toward the continued clanking of utensils.

Gregor's kitchen was exactly what Angel expected to see in an old farmhouse. Cabinets with a butcher-block counter top held a deep porcelain sink below a square window that overlooked the pasture. A gas stove and an old-fashioned icebox equipped the room, and lanterns glowed on the walls. A mission style table and four chairs sat to the side of the kitchen that opened to the living room. Shakespeare poised on one of the chairs, tail flicking impatiently.

Gregor looked wide-awake despite only a few hours of sleep. Angel still felt slightly groggy, and the muscles in her temples squeezed against her skull. She perked up when he handed her a hot cup of coffee.

"How are you?" he asked, and turned back to the eggs frying in a cast iron skillet. Bacon sizzled in a second pan. The image was incongruous to anything Angel had seen—a teenage boy in front of a stove. Josh and Jacob wouldn't have been caught dead cooking, but Gregor fit the scene perfectly despite his work clothes and heavy boots.

"Much better. What can I do to help?" She sipped her coffee.

"Nothing, really. I'll have this ready in a few minutes. Go ahead and sit down." He cocked his head toward the kitchen table. Angel looked at the chair and her stomach turned jittery.

"Actually, I'll just go look around, if that's okay."

Gregor nodded, and Angel headed toward the living room.

The rest of the house was simple, neat and clean, with a few feminine touches here and there, a remembrance of Gregor's mother. A masculine leather chair sat by the brick fireplace. A hunter green sofa angled to face both the fireplace and the wide front window.

Earth tones decorated everything, punched up by houseplants with bright blossoms. Matching area rugs protected the polished wood floor. Angel ran her hand along the back of the sofa. *So normal.*

A staircase by the front door led up to what Angel assumed were Gregor's and his parents' rooms, but she didn't dare go up there and nose around.

She walked across the living room to the fireplace and gazed at the pictures on the carved wooden mantle. In one, a boy, about eight or nine years old, sat astride a pale Palomino. In another, the same young boy sat next to his mother. His father stood behind them, arms wrapped protectively around his family.

"You look just like your mother," Angel called out. Gregor's mother's long hair draped over each shoulder, framing a round face with a smile that carried all the way into her silver-flecked eyes. His father had blond hair and sky-blue eyes, but shared Gregor's lean build. Angel smiled. *He's the real deal.*

She turned from the fireplace, and her heart leapt at the sight of a bookcase behind the leather chair. It was loaded with everything from novels to cookbooks, with one shelf almost completely dominated by geography books. She ran her fingers over the covers as she read some of the titles—worn copies of *The Physics of Magic*, *Macbeth*, and *Hamlet*. In sharp contrast, tucked on the bottom shelf, sat a dusty but very new-looking history textbook. She stopped scanning the titles when Gregor called her name.

Angel and Gregor lounged on the front steps after breakfast, Shakespeare curled up in Angel's lap. A thousand questions whirled around in Angel's head, but the pain that accompanied her memories stopped her from asking them.

She tried to focus as Gregor told her about his childhood on the farm, swallowing the guilt that burned her throat. The time he'd had with his parents was so finite. It wasn't fair.

"My dad was so patient with me." He stared toward the garden as if he could see his father standing there. "He explained everything about the vegetables and what they needed to grow. He'd let me plant seeds by poking my finger in the ground and plopping them in one by one. It took forever, but he never complained, even though he could have done it in minutes with magic. He made sure I understood that magic was as much a part of the land as it was of us, and taught me that we need to be as respectful of the trees and flowers and grass as we are of people and animals."

Angel wondered what it would be like to be raised by her own parents, growing up with real magic, not just reading and fantasizing about it. She stroked Shakespeare and closed her eyes. *This is not what I expected at all.*

"So…" She opened her eyes. "If I'm Empowered, why haven't I been able to do magic this whole time? I've always been able to find things easily, but that just doesn't seem very…magical."

"It's *very* magical, or it wouldn't have shown up in you at all." Gregor sat up and smiled. "It's your Talent, remember. Your strongest power. Like I said, all you have to do is set your mind on something and you know exactly where it is, even if it's miles away. Most of us can only pinpoint something we've lost in the room we're standing in."

"But I've never done anything else at all magical. How am I going to suddenly start doing it now?" Her stomach tightened. *Maybe it's too late for me.*

"You were born here, and spent six years on this island, far away from the technology that interferes with magic," he said as though that explained it all.

"What do you mean, technology interferes?"

"It's all the waves and particles released by electronic devices. They suppress our magic. I could make Gates when I was around it because I've spent my whole life here and kept coming back to take care of the farm. But my other powers were really hard to use. It should be the same with you."

Angel scrunched her eyes.

"Look, you just need practice. We'll work on it here, where no one will see."

Angel looked at him doubtfully. It wasn't the neighbors seeing that worried her—it was her fear that they'd have nothing to see.

"The neighbors only come around when I'm gone, okay? They used to check on me every day when I was younger, but they figured out pretty quick I could take care of this place on my own."

Angel envied his self-assurance, which seemed to amplify her own insecurity. "They never asked why you were gone so much? I mean, when you were looking for me?"

"I used to camp with my dad all the time, and when I told them I was camping they just figured it was my way of dealing with his death. I guess they were right, in a way." His face clouded.

Angel's heart ached for him. She rubbed her arm to still the chill that crept across her shoulder, and shifted the conversation back to magic. "You'll really be able to teach me?"

"I'll do the best I can." He glanced to the side, where Horatio skittered around the porch floor. "I had to drop out of school not long after my parents died. It was too hard to keep my grades up while working the farm and searching for you. But I'd mastered most of the stuff I really needed for the farm by then anyway. And I've got a friend who owns a bookstore. He gave me most of the books you were looking at in there, so I could study more advanced magic on my own."

"Yeah, but you didn't study everything, did you? I noticed the history book's never been cracked open."

One side of Gregor's mouth curled. He stood, stretched his legs, and then held out his hand to help Angel up. His fingers were strong and callused from labor.

"No time like the present. What ya say we get started with those lessons?"

Angel moved Shakespeare from her lap to the porch floor, and took Gregor's hand. He pulled her to her feet effortlessly.

"I'm all yours. Just show me what to do." Excitement flooded her and pushed aside her fears. This was what she'd dreamed about for so long. Was he going to teach her how to change colors like he did to her hair? She doubted it would be the trick he did with the sand and the mirror. She still didn't feel at all powerful.

"Okay, but let's kill two birds with one stone." Gregor tugged her toward the front door. "We'll go in and clean up the kitchen."

And how is that magical?

Standing in front of the sink, he handed her a dirty dish. "Now, think about *separating* the mess from the plate."

"Wouldn't it be less messy to just make it disappear?" Angel scrunched her nose at the globs of food clinging to the plate. Magic was supposed to be more glamorous than pushing food into the trash.

"Disappear to where?" he asked, then seemed to realize Angel was going to need more explanation. His demeanor changed; class had begun.

"Things don't just disappear. They have to go someplace. First law of conservation of matter. Matter cannot be created or destroyed; it can only change form."

Angel knew that law, but didn't realize it applied to using magic as well. "So what would happen if you *tried* to make it disappear?"

"Well, since that can't happen...like I said...it would have to change form. It would go from matter to energy. You know, it'd explode."

Angel stared at the plate of food as if it was a bomb about to detonate, and Gregor laughed.

"Don't worry, you don't have the power to do that. Now here, get to work."

She took the plate out of his hand, held it over the trash can, and concentrated on pushing the food off, fighting the urge to try to make it vanish. To her amazement, the morning leftovers slid into the trash, leaving the plate gleaming.

"You're good at that," he said with a grin. "I told you your magic is still there."

Angel couldn't believe how easy it had been. "Wish I could have been doing it like this the whole time."

When the dishes were done, Gregor levitated a few of them back into the cabinets.

"You've got to move the air from on top of the plate to underneath it. It creates lift, *sort* of like an airplane wing. It's the same principle, at least. You want more pressure underneath so there's less resistance when you lift the plate up."

Angel tried it with one plate, but after she managed to lift it about six inches, it smashed on the counter top. Gregor brushed the pieces into the trash and set another plate in the middle of the counter.

"Don't just think about the plate. Stay focused on the air as well."

Angel pictured air molecules moving away from the top of the plate and circulating under the rim, increasing the pressure beneath. This time the plate hovered over the counter top.

"Now, slowly ease the pressure to the top and let it lower down."

Angel pictured the molecules again, but this time flowing up over the rim of the plate, little by little. The plate moved downward and hit the counter top with a gentle *thunk*.

After practicing moving the plates straight up and down a few times, Angel sent one through the air to the open cabinet door and it landed on top of the stack Gregor had started.

"That took a lot more concentration than cleaning them."

"It gets easier, once you learn to trust the magic." He set a third plate on the counter.

This time it was a little easier. One by one, dishes floated and landed neatly in the cabinet. Gregor beamed at her.

"Now that you've got that down, how about we try something a little more fun?" His eyes twinkled, and he led her through the door from the kitchen into the back yard.

He gathered some sticks and piled them on top of a flat stone, and then picked two small pieces of flint out of a bucket by the back door. He struck the stones together over the kindling and the sticks were instantly ablaze, with not so much as a spark that Angel could see to get them started.

"Quite the Boy Scout, aren't you?"

He gave her a quizzical look. "A what?"

"Never mind." She may have had a lot to learn about magic, but Gregor knew very little about life beyond his small town.

He stared at the fire and it snuffed out with a puff of smoke. Then he handed her the flint and added a few new sticks.

"Hit those together and concentrate on the energy created by the friction that causes the spark. And remember, oxygen feeds it. Use your mind to bring the air closer to the spark and direct it all toward the sticks."

Angel struck the stones as hard as she could, but her first attempt only created a slight spark, which died within a split second. Her second, third, and fourth tries were no better.

"You've got the spark fine, but you're not bringing the air in to feed it."

She tried again, concentrating this time on feeding the fire. It was harder than levitating the plates because she couldn't visualize *friction*, but the kindling sparked brighter this time and caught flame.

"I did it! I really did it!" She looked at the fire and concentrated on bringing more air to the flame, and it flared up with a loud crackling noise. She relaxed again and the fire died back down. *This is so cool!*

She'd expected to feel a tingling, or energy pouring out of her. Instead, she felt normal but very awake. Like a part of her brain she'd never known existed suddenly started functioning, and she could think more clearly than ever before.

Gregor's voice came softly into her ear. "Now put it out."

"How?"

"Move the air away from it. No oxygen, no fire."

She concentrated, mentally moving the air that surrounded the flame like an inflating balloon—a balloon with the air on the outside and a vacuum inside—and the flame snuffed out like a candle.

"This is awesome! Show me something else."

Chapter Seven
The Foreboding

Angel's comfort on Gregor's farm grew so quickly that her life with her foster family began to feel like a dream. With each improvement in her powers, her connection to her new home strengthened. She became driven to learn all she could about magic. The mental doorway she'd left open to the idea of going back inched closed.

But the future was just as dreamlike, and untouchable. Fear held her tongue when it came to asking about her real parents. Twice she'd pulled the charm bracelet out to see if it elicited any memories other than the night in the forest. Pounding invaded her skull just as it had on her first morning at Gregor's. And on the rare occasion Gregor brought up her parents, her temples throbbed. The night in the forest seemed to have road-blocked her brain.

Gregor used their chores as magic lessons. He told her to imagine her nervous system extending out past her body. If she created a force, like energizing the molecules in the air, she could transfer that energy to the object and make it move. With the same initial directive, she could levitate a cotton ball or a bowling ball. She only had to get the process going, and then the energy within the object took over.

Eggs flew gently from her hand, by the pressure of the air underneath them, toward the basket in the corner of the barn. Huge bales of hay propelled across the field when she and Gregor eliminated the friction between the bales and the ground.

They harvested vegetables by hand because it was just as easy without magic, but replacing the old plants with new ones would have taken ages longer. Gregor touched the old plants, activating the genes that caused the plants to age and die.

"What if that were done to a person?" Angel asked.

"The same thing would happen."

Angel remembered Gregor's comment about Dawric always killing *without* magic. She hadn't given much thought to how it could be done *with* magic.

Gregor had sworn there'd been no sign of Dawric. But what if that was wrong? What if Dawric actually was Empowered? The thought of someone killing her by aging her in seconds, or constricting her veins from the inside of her body…

Gregor opened the bag of seeds and sent them into the air, where they lined up in neat rows and dropped to the ground. He tapped the air with his finger, and the seeds shot straight into the soil. Reassurance washed over Angel as new life replaced what had been destroyed.

Gregor involved Angel in more than the everyday chores, and with summer coming it was time to shear the sheep.

"No matter how many times I do this they're always stunned, like they think they're naked or something. Here, watch."

One by one, he brought the sheep to the barn and severed all the wooly hairs at once. They dropped in unison to the ground in a fluffy pile. Each time the sheep bleated angrily, with eyes wide and accusing.

One particularly skittish ewe broke free of Gregor's grasp and tore out of the barn to the pasture, sending the loose wool into a wild flurry.

"I don't know what's with her, lately." Wool clung to his clothing, piled on his shoulders like snow, but he seemed completely unaware. He gazed out the barn door, staring after the half-shaved sheep as it fled across the field. His brow creased, and he ignored Angel as she called his name.

When he finally snapped out of it, he turned and walked away.

"What's wrong with her?" Angel asked.

"I don't know. It's like she's gone crazy." He paused and raked his bangs out of his face. "C'mon. Time to milk the goats."

Gregor showed Angel how to milk the goats by hand to give her a feel for the movement, and then she was able to do it by magic and milk several simultaneously. As they worked, Shakespeare snuck in to lap milk out of the buckets, until Gregor noticed him. Then the cat found himself floating up to one of the rafters.

"Let him sit up there for a while to teach him a lesson." Gregor stalked out of the barn.

After Shakespeare mewed for over an hour, Angel couldn't take it anymore. She levitated him down and held him to her chest. He rubbed his cheek against her chin and purred, then jumped from her arms and marched straight back to the bucket.

"Yeah, he's learning really well." Gregor stood in the doorway, face flushed and sticky with sweat. "Pretty soon you'll have him trained to eat right off our plates."

Angel gave him an innocent smile and walked over to pull Shakespeare away from the milk.

"You're getting me in trouble, little man," she whispered to the cat.

He gave her a look that said *not my problem*, then jumped out of her arms and sauntered off to the house.

Gregor strained and bottled the milk, then conjured the bottles to various houses around the town. In each bottle's place appeared a small bag of coins and an empty bottle. Gregor gathered the bags and carried them into the house. Angel followed, amazed again by her new life.

Except for one thing.

The one time she'd been horseback riding, the horse was spooked by a gunshot and nearly threw her off. So when Gregor took her out to the barn for the first time to meet the horses, she could barely force her feet into motion. She stopped at the barn door, rubbing her arms to stop the chills.

"This is Romeo." Gregor indicated the palomino stallion that was pictured in the photo above the fireplace. He cleared his throat, but his voice cracked slightly as he continued, "and she's...Juliet." A shadow fell over his eyes as he spoke the name of the small chestnut mare.

Juliet was beautiful, Angel had to admit, with deep, kind eyes. Angel still kept her distance. She was being silly for not just admitting her fear, but each time she saw the strength of those equine muscles, she relived the day at her neighbor's horse farm. Angel didn't see how she could ever control a thousand-pound animal.

At the end of her second week on the farm, Angel had managed to entirely avoid direct contact with Romeo and Juliet. She'd eventually have to tell Gregor the truth, but she allowed herself to be distracted for one more night while she worked on her sketches. She had a good view of Shakespeare sitting in his cushioned chair, rather than curled up sleeping.

The cat stared out the back window of the living room, and Angel sat on the floor examining his profile. When she finished drawing, she looked out the window, searching for whatever had grabbed his attention.

"You see a squirrel or something, little man?"

She strained her eyes but saw nothing in the pasture except sleeping goats and sheep.

A gurgling noise emerged from deep in Shakespeare's throat. Angel spun back to him. The fur down the ridge of his back stood on end, and his teeth were bared beneath curled lips. She peered more closely out the window and finally noticed that one of the sheep lay sleeping away from the rest of the flock, next to the fence.

The sheep's uneven wool bulged in places and was shaved to nothing in others. Angel squinted, and the image cleared enough for her to confirm her suspicion. It was the skittish ewe that had run away during shearing. As Angel watched the ewe, the fence wobbled as if blown by a strong gust of wind, but nothing else indicated a breeze outside.

Shakespeare jumped off the chair and headed into the kitchen as though nothing had happened.

Angel put down her drawing and walked across the room.

"I think Shakespeare saw something out in the pasture," she told Gregor as she stepped into the kitchen.

"He's always seeing things that aren't there." Gregor shrugged and went back to chopping broccoli. "Or it was probably a bug flying outside the window."

No way. Angel had heard that gurgling before from one of the stray cats in her yard—right before she saw a bobcat tear across the field behind the Mason's. And she had always suspected that cats could see things people couldn't.

~Seeing Nothing~

"Why has the boy been back for so long?"

The scientist turned and frowned. "He hasn't found her."

That's not what I asked. "You know this?"

The scientist's jaw twitched. "My last...visit. Everything looked as it always has."

"You saw nothing? No evidence of the girl?"

The scientist shrugged and swirled the test tube in his hand. "Maybe he's given up."

"He hasn't given up."

Chapter Eight
The Town Square

Angel peeked out her bedroom window, searching for signs of whatever had disturbed the fence the night before. She found nothing except hoof prints left by the goats and sheep. Well, there was one set of fresh boot prints, but Gregor had gone into the forest as usual that morning.

She didn't see anything strange over the next few days, but fear clung to her, and bit deep one morning as they gathered eggs.

"What would happen if Dawric came back?"

The egg that had just floated from Gregor's hand dropped to the floor with a *splat*.

"I'm sorry." Angel frowned at the mess on the floor. "I know you said there was no way, but I can't shake the feeling that there was something out there the other night. Shakespeare saw something, I just know it."

"Not possible. Believe me, there's no way Dawric could get past the protection around this island." Gregor cleaned up the broken egg with a wave of his hand and moved on to the next hen.

"But, what if he's Empowered? What if—"

"He's not. There's no way—I promise." Gregor sighed as he reached for another egg. "You're just stressed out because of all these changes."

"Right, changes." *You mean like having my whole world turned inside out?*

Angel stuffed her anger inside, sealing it in with a grunt. Gregor stopped the flight of his egg and let it hang in mid-air.

"You're feeling isolated, I think. Stuck out here with only me and Shakespeare to talk to. And all you've done is work. You need a break. Listen, we're actually gonna be done with everything before lunch today. You want to go into town this afternoon?"

Angel examined the egg in her hand. *A break? That's what he thinks I need?* She ran her fingers over the surface of the sandy-brown shell. *So small and fragile. Just the way I feel.*

"Do you really think I'm ready? *You* say I'm doing well, but I still feel so lost sometimes."

"You'll be fine." His egg resumed its path to the basket. "I know you will. C'mon, let's go clean up and eat, and I'll saddle the horses." He snatched up the basket of eggs and headed toward the house.

Angel still hadn't worked up the nerve to tell him about her fear of horses. Her feet anchored themselves to the ground.

Gregor opened the back door and called to her, "Hey, come on! It's your turn to make lunch."

Angel willed her feet to move, but they refused. *I'm gonna make such a fool of myself! Oh, please let it rain or something. Anything!* She looked up at the crystalline sky. Not a cloud in sight. *I guess I've gotta do this sometime. C'mon feet, let's try this again.* Step by step her feet obeyed, and she made her way into the kitchen.

Despite her nerves, Angel ate everything on her plate. Shakespeare crouched on the floor near her feet.

Something black darted through the open kitchen window, and Angel flew back out of her chair, nearly squashing Shakespeare in the process. Then the black thing landed firmly on Gregor's shoulder.

Horatio!

He began his unusual chirping, and Gregor's brow furrowed.

"What is it?" Angel asked as she straightened her chair and sat down again. She perched on the edge of the chair, her foot tapping anxiously. Shakespeare had stalked off.

"Horatio hasn't been able to find your parents in Germany. He's searched all over." Gregor brushed his bangs away.

Angel's muscles tensed and she fought back tears. *I should never have let myself relax here.*

"Gregor, why don't I use my Finding power to see where they are?"

Her legs tensed even more, lifting her so she nearly hovered over her chair. *Why didn't I think of this before?*

"You can try, but chances are they're too far away. You haven't really practiced. It's not quite the same thing as you Finding my hammer for me the other day. Thanks for that, by the way." Horatio flew off Gregor's hand and landed on the kitchen counter.

"I guess you're right." Angel let out a disappointed sigh, and sank back into her chair. "But if that's the case, I want to start working on it a lot more. They could be in trouble. Dawric could've found them…kidnapped them…" What if she came all this way and found her home, only to have her parents taken away from her before she got to see them again?

"Try not to worry, really." Gregor erased the troubled expression from his own face. "Your parents probably moved on to someplace else, searching another lead. I'll let Horatio rest here a day or two, then send him back out again. We'll find them—*don't worry.*"

The thoughts wouldn't budge from Angel's mind, though. Her heart fluttered and her stomach turned.

I could just go back. But she couldn't forget all she'd experienced. She would wait. But she didn't have to do it patiently.

She stood on the porch, nearly stroking the fur right off a squirming Shakespeare, while Gregor saddled up the horses.

Gregor came out of the barn leading Romeo and Juliet. He tied the horses to the fence and walked over to her, his face twisted like he was trying to stifle a laugh.

"You keep doing that and Shakespeare will be bald." He gently pried the cat from her arms. Shakespeare jumped down and sauntered over to curl up on the seat of the rocker on the porch.

"Why don't we just Gate into town?" Angel tried to sound casual. *So I'm afraid. But really, it would get us to town much more quickly.*

"The horses enjoy the ride, and they need the exercise. Don't you want to see the scenery?" The question remained on his face as he stared at her. "Angel, you look petrified."

"I've, um, never really ridden a horse. Well, not exactly." She crossed her arms in front of her now that she had nothing to occupy her hands. She quickly told him the story of the spooked horse nearly throwing her off.

The signs of laughter melted from his face. "I'd be terrified too if that were my first experience. But Juliet's the gentlest horse I've ever met, and I've trained her well."

He held out his hand and she took it, letting him lead her over to Juliet. The horse's kind eyes looked down as if she understood Angel was afraid, and she nuzzled Angel's shoulder. Angel relaxed and stroked Juliet's silky neck. After a few minutes her courage built and she turned to Gregor.

"Okay, let's do this."

Gregor helped her climb into the saddle, and went over the riding instructions until she felt comfortable with them.

"Remember, I'll be right next to you the whole way."

With no curves to maneuver along the main road, Angel only needed to concentrate on sitting properly in the saddle. Juliet slowed when Angel shifted in the saddle and walked at a steady pace. Angel soon began to genuinely relax and soaked in the scenery as she swayed on Juliet's back.

They passed very few houses at first, spread out along the country lane. Some were little cottages and a few were farms similar to Gregor's, nestled in the rolling hills by the road. The hills became steeper as they stretched closer to the base of the distant mountains, which rose above the forest.

Angel inhaled. Pure air—no pungent exhaust and asphalt. No giant power poles or billboards obstructed her view. No honking horns drowned out the songbirds. The gentle breeze caressed her skin and the sun warmed her. She'd only believed a place like this could exist in dreams.

As they approached the main part of town, the houses came more frequently, and Angel broke the silence between her and Gregor.

"I found Ireland in one of your geography books. And Toch Island. That's where you said we are, right? It doesn't exist according to ordinary maps. I thought I'd never seen it before, not that geography was exactly my best subject. But the book says it's a purely magical island, hidden so it can't be taken over by technological development."

"Yes." He sat straight and tall on Romeo's back. "We've had to resort to islands and enchantments to keep ourselves isolated. The world is becoming so populated that we're running out of places where we can live without interference. Some of us have colonized on the main lands. But it's much harder to keep from being discovered there. There are islands all over the world that only the Empowered are aware of."

"It's beautiful here." Angel surveyed the hills and foliage again. Puffy white clouds accented the bright sky, and the day was crystal-clear. She'd slid into a rhythm on Juliet's back, and felt a surge of connection with the horse. The part of her that called this place home came to the forefront and whispered that she belonged right where she was, chasing away some of the shadows in her mind.

"This place really feels alive, like you're actually *part* of the land."

Gregor's expression said he agreed.

Gregor stopped them in front of a small farmhouse on the edge of the main section of town. They didn't go near the house, but Gregor led the horses through the front gate.

"This is Old Man Brady's house. He was a friend of my parents for years. He lets me leave the horses here when I come to town." After closing the gate, Gregor led Angel into the town square.

Red brick buildings lined the perimeter of a cobbled square directly off the main road. Awnings hung over the painted doors of the shops, which swung open and closed as people bustled in and out. Carved signs swayed on posts in front of most of the stores, but others had their names simply painted on the windows. The shoppers were dressed in an array of styles, from medieval to Victorian to completely modern. Angel was glad she wouldn't stand out in her sneakers and Levi's.

A circular, marble fountain dominated the middle of the square. Water sprayed in arcs around a granite statue of a man in a soldier's uniform seated atop a winged horse. Children chased each other around the fountain, and a few stood throwing coins in the water, their eyes closed as if making wishes.

Benches sat below some of the storefront windows holding all sorts of people, young and old, chatting animatedly, or in the case of one old man, snoring while propped against his walking stick. One young woman scolded her small son for climbing on the fountain wall as she ran her hands up and down his sides, magically drying his dripping clothes.

A skinny teenage boy tugged on the leash of an enormous hound as it snarled at a stray cat. The cat's back arched, fur standing on end, as it hissed. Dogs were not the only pets people had brought. A colorful parrot perched on the shoulder of a man in a bright Hawaiian shirt, and a foot-long lizard clung to the arm of a teenage boy dressed all in black with earrings running up both ears.

They had walked past several stores when the most delicious fragrance wafted out of a bakery. Angel held up her hands to block the glare and peeked through the window. A plump woman in a flour-covered apron waved her hands, directing ingredients into a bowl. Spoons stirred in synchronization in a half dozen bowls along the batter-spattered countertop.

"That's Miss Elsie," said Gregor. "She makes the best muffins you've ever tasted. Maybe we'll grab some on the way out."

Angel pried her face from the window at Gregor's urging, and followed him around the square to the other side of the fountain.

"I want to take you to my favorite place." He lengthened his stride, making it hard for her to keep up. They weaved between people carrying shopping bags, and came upon a path to a little store set off to the side of the square. It looked old but well kept, with stucco walls and round windows on either side of the arched front door. The sign above the door read "The Professor's Roost," and basketball-sized mushrooms poked up through the thick grass in neat rows along either side of the stone path leading to the entrance. Gregor pushed the door open, and the tinkling of a bell announced their arrival.

Chapter Nine
The Professor

Leather-bound books lined every wall from floor to ceiling and were stacked in corners. Several lay open on top of a large, rectangular coffee table in front of an over-stuffed couch. Angel imagined they were filled with things not found in any book she'd seen before.

On the other side of the room, a chubby man sat in one of two straight-back chairs, leaning over the tabletop in between. His neatly trimmed salt-and-pepper goatee matched the salt-and-pepper of his not-so-neatly trimmed hair. The sleeves of his plaid shirt were rolled nearly to his elbow, and the toe of his cowboy boot tapped the floor.

"Hello, Gregor," he said without raising his head from the jigsaw puzzle in front of him. "Brought a friend today, have you?"

"Sir Benjamin, I'd like you to meet my cousin, Angel. Angel, this is Sir Benjamin."

"Nice to meet you." Angel took a step forward.

Sir Benjamin continued staring at his puzzle. After several awkward moments, he finally shouted, "Aha! I've got you!" and grabbed a puzzle piece, snapping it sharply into place. He lifted his head and smiled.

"Pleasure, my dear. Angel—what a beautiful name. What's brought you out here to Gregor's neck of the woods?"

Angel's nerves suddenly overwhelmed her.

"She's staying with me for the summer," Gregor said. "She's from

America."

Angel gave a nod of agreement, and fumbled for something to add.

"This is a wonderful place you've got, Sir Benjamin. I love to read more than anything in the world. I've even thought that one day I'd like to own a book shop." *Yeah, like that didn't sound dorky.*

She scanned the room a second time and moved closer to the table.

"Well, Angel, take a look around—enjoy yourself." His welcoming grin pushed his cheeks out, making him look like a scruffy Santa.

Angel mused over Sir Benjamin's accent. His was a little stronger than Gregor's. Closer to Irish, too—but still not quite.

Gregor sat down across from Sir Benjamin and they chatted while Angel looked around the bookstore. She paused at every shelf to read some of the titles, and picked up a book now and then to leaf through the pages. As she moved toward the back, she came across titles like *Magical Theory* and *Perfecting Your Talent,* as well as other books she'd seen at Gregor's.

She made her way along the wall to the back of the store where there was an over-sized mahogany desk, with great carved lion's feet, papers strewn across the top, and a lantern burning on its corner. Pencil shavings littered the surrounding floor.

Angel rounded the corner to look at some books on the back wall, and let out a squeal that made both Gregor and Sir Benjamin jump out of their seats. On the floor, curled up on a big square pillow with tassels on the corners, lay a metallic green dragon the size of a medium dog. The dragon looked up at Angel, blinked its amber eyes, and tucked its head back under its wing, asleep again in seconds.

"I'm sorry," said Angel breathlessly. "It just…startled me. I-I didn't expect a dragon to be layin' there." She continued staring at the dragon as its side raised and lowered in a steady rhythm, and its breath rustled the tassel in front of its snout.

Sir Benjamin walked over and stood next to Angel. He gazed at the dragon like a parent watching his own child. "Don't worry, Spike's as gentle as can be. Had him since he was a baby. He's getting rather old now. All he ever does anymore is sleep."

"He's full grown?" Angel couldn't hide the surprise in her voice. "I thought dragons were huge."

"Don't they have dragons in America? I could have sworn there were some there when I visited. Of course, that was forty years ago." Sir

Benjamin's brow creased as he scratched his beard.

Angel shifted her weight from one foot to the other. *Uh-oh, how do I get out of this one?*

"Um…I live in Florida, and most of the dragons in America are out west so I've never gotten to see one. Getting too crowded on the east coast for us to keep them hidden." She braced herself for Sir Benjamin's reaction. He raised a suspicious eyebrow, but said nothing.

"Does he breathe fire?"

"Well, the big ones surely can. But you'd be lucky to get a good puff of hot steam out of this old guy."

Angel didn't dare ask another question for fear she'd give herself away. She continued examining the books, stepping carefully around Spike, while Gregor and Sir Benjamin returned to their seats and Sir Benjamin went back to his puzzle. After choosing a book about famous castles, she curled up on the couch to read. She kept her nose buried in a book, but tuned her ears into the guys' conversation, peeking over the pages now and then.

"Diane came in yesterday." Sir Benjamin snapped in another puzzle piece.

"Oh, yeah. How's she doin'?" Gregor leaned back in his chair.

"Good, good. But a bit frazzled. Little Charlie is showing his Talent."

"Really? He's not even a year old, is he?"

"Nope, but he's causing all kinds of trouble already. Oh, I don't envy those parents…" Sir Benjamin shook his head and clicked his tongue.

"What's his Talent?" Gregor crossed his arms. Angel let her book drop a bit farther down.

"Weather-changer. The little imp is starting rain showers in his room when he cries. The only way to stop them is to give him what he wants. Problem is, the rain dries up but the wood floor still gets ruined. They've tried to waterproof the floor, but you know how hard that is. And we've got no one in town with a Talent that can help them right now."

The conversation shifted to Sir Benjamin's study of spider web patterns. He was writing a guide to spiders indigenous to Toch Island. Angel learned from their discussion that Sir Benjamin had been a professor at the university at the base of the mountains outside the town. He'd retired a few years ago and opened the bookstore.

Sir Benjamin waved as they opened the door to leave. "Don't be a stranger, Angel. Any family of Gregor's is welcome here any time."

They walked back down the cobbled path and into the square. Gregor pointed out all the different shops: a pet store with three adorable kittens mewing in the window, a chocolate shop next to Miss Elsie's bakery, a tailor, a small café, and an ice cream parlor all along one side. Across the square, on the other side of the fountain, were a post office, a stationery store, and a few clothing boutiques.

Angel let her gaze run across the storefronts. The brick buildings looked like those she'd seen in small downtown areas before. *So normal, but*…no neon signs in any windows, no tourist shops, no one talking or texting on cell phones. And when she peeked into windows, there weren't any plastic mannequins or blaring fluorescent lights. It was almost like a slice from another era, but not entirely.

The group of children that had been playing by the water fountain were now in the courtyard, levitating toy dragons like remote control airplanes. One dragon smashed into a wall and the little boy flying it burst into tears.

Zack's face flashed into Angel's mind. She could totally see him laughing and playing in the courtyard with the other boys.

Gregor turned Angel's attention to the road that led beyond Sir Benjamin's bookshop. She could just make out a huge feed store, and a pub called *The Dreg*.

Carts full of fresh fruits and vegetables filled an entire side of the courtyard, mingled with tables of jewelry, quilts, and tapestries. Angel tried on a necklace that snaked itself around her neck and clasped together on its own. She found earrings that changed their size to the right proportion for the person wearing them, and others that played music only the wearer could hear. She picked up and examined a silver ring with a huge stone that changed color to match the wearer's hair.

Angel gulped as it shifted to bright red.

A bracelet of thick silver chain reminded Angel of what Gregor had said about her charm bracelet being a family heirloom. She leaned toward him and whispered, "What's the family heirloom thing all about?"

Gregor shook his head slightly, then grabbed her hand. He pulled her away from the crowd and spoke quietly.

"Every family has something of value they pass down, usually to the first born. There are other situations where they get passed to younger siblings, like if there's more than one heirloom in the family. Usually it's a piece of jewelry with some sort of magical property. But sometimes they can be things like tiaras or daggers or even candlesticks."

She tried to picture her mother or father giving her the charm bracelet. Nothing came to her—no visions, no memories at all. No pain either, but that wasn't entirely comforting.

"Hey! Are you gonna pay for that?" the artisan shouted, and Angel realized she was still holding the ring with the now fire-red stone.

"Sorry." She placed the ring back in the velvet-lined tray.

The artisan looked at the ring and then at Angel. "Hey, this is—"

Angel spun and stepped away from the cart. She glanced over her shoulder and saw a man in a gray hooded coat where she'd just been standing. The artisan's face was just visible over the man's shoulder. He nodded toward her.

Angel scurried off to join Gregor. Had the artisan only thought she was trying to steal the ring—or was it the red stone that had him looking so curious? She'd never felt more conspicuous.

They continued on toward a clothing boutique. A dress in the window stopped her in her tracks, and all thoughts of rings and strangers flew from her mind.

"I just want to try it on," she said as she dragged Gregor into the shop.

He shook his head, but didn't stop her.

The skirt billowed around her ankles when she spun. The sleeves flowed down from her shoulders, flaring out at the wrist, and the bodice laced up with satin ribbons. Every inch of the luxurious fabric was a deep purple that set off her pale skin.

"Isn't it gorgeous? It's so medieval princess! What does this mean?" She held the sleeve out so Gregor could see the tag marked with a strange symbol followed by numbers.

"It means you'd have to really be a princess to afford this dress."

After Angel reluctantly returned the dress to the rack, they went to the feed store to pick up the things on Gregor's list. The owner, Roger, was tall and thick, with a military haircut. A bundle of keys fastened to his belt jangled when he walked around apologizing about the mess and searching for the seeds Gregor needed.

"We're changing some of the seasonal stock. Ah, there they are." He handed Gregor a bag of seeds and turned toward a young kid who was levitating sacks of grain across the room. "Hey, Shawn, those need to go in the back aisle."

"Right, boss."

"Looks like you're doing more than changing stock," Gregor said.

Roger huffed a sigh as he stepped behind the register. "This was supposed to be a quick, easy change-over, but we've had to do some serious reorganizing. I swear it feels like we've moved everything fifteen times in the past week. I'm surprised even I can find anything around here, much less my customers." He rang them up, then Angel and Gregor navigated their way through the chaos to the exit.

Angel rode in silence most of the way home.

"You, know, that dress is completely impractical," Gregor said out of nowhere. "Princesses are way over-rated."

Angel nodded, but it wasn't the dress making her melancholy. She was thinking about the town that was so unfamiliar to her and wished she could remember days she must have spent there as a child. Surely she'd shopped with her parents there, maybe even buying a dress from the boutique she and Gregor had gone in. *I might've walked right by people who knew my parents, kids I went to school with…*

Of course, they've probably forgotten me by now.

She dreamed of the day she would walk through the town and it would feel like home, and everyone would know her for who she really was. A day when her memories brought no pain. Or, at least she'd have her parents to help her through it all. She'd be safe from everything, and she'd feel like a whole person again.

-Lying Truly-

The scientist stood there, saying nothing, eyes averted as always.

"I asked if you've been following the boy." Relying on the inept scientist was becoming increasingly annoying. "If you can't find out whether or not the girl is with him, I'll do it myself."

The scientist's head snapped up. "I've followed him. She's here, but—"

"Good. I want her now."

"It's not that simple. Her powers...they're gone. She can't help us anymore."

"You're lying."

The lab was semi-dark, and the scientist shuffled to the side, slipping half into a shadow. "Why would I lie?"

"Because with her, I don't need you."

The corner of the scientist's mouth curled. "True. But without me, you can't get near her."

Chapter Ten
The Finding Lessons

Angel's muscles rebelled the next morning as she climbed out of bed. Her legs nearly gave way when she stood up. She flexed and stretched her hamstrings until she felt able to conquer the walk to the bathroom. *I knew horseback riding was dangerous…*

She entered the kitchen and found breakfast laid out on the table, but only one place setting. Crumbs on the other side of the table showed her Gregor had already eaten.

He must have gone into the forest again. She peeked out the window over the sink and watched the edge of the trees. A figure appeared and Angel recognized Gregor's gait as he walked toward the house. *Why does he go out there so early?*

She left the window and sat at the table. Several minutes passed as she nibbled on cold toast. Then the back door opened and Gregor tromped in, letting the door slam behind him. He walked right past Angel and disappeared into the living room. Shuffling and banging noises, and then Gregor appeared in the kitchen doorway with a wooden candlestick in his hand.

"You said you want to work on your Finding. I think that's a good idea. I've been thinking of the best way to do it. If we go into the forest, I can Gate myself anywhere so we can really test your Talent."

"Really?" Angel let her toast fall to the plate. "What do we—I mean how—what's the candlestick for?"

"This is what you'll be Finding," he said. "The animals will just think it's a stick and leave it alone, and if one did happen to pick it up, it's not valuable."

She wolfed down the rest of her breakfast. Finally, she'd really be doing something. Maybe now she could speed this whole thing up and get her parents home. She felt like she'd been sitting on a fence—part of her looking at the life ahead of her and part looking at the life she left behind. She couldn't bear to give up one for the other, so she waited.

After helping Gregor feed the animals, and a quick visit with Juliet, she changed clothes and stood fidgeting at the door. Her thoughts swayed back to the image of Gregor coming out of the forest that morning. Not once had he asked her to join him, or waited to go later in the day.

Was it because they were too busy? Or because he thought the forest might bring back bad memories? She hoped it was the former, because the latter meant that he was worried enough about her parents to risk it.

Angel stood on the edge of the forest while Gregor made a Gate to a tree she couldn't see. He reappeared moments later.

"Your turn," he said.

Angel concentrated. She'd touched the candlestick before they started to make a connection with it. An image popped into her head—the candlestick lying next to a flamingo-pink flower. She gave Gregor its distance and direction. He guided her through the forest until they reached it. Sure enough, there was the flower.

"That was way farther than anything I've done," she said.

"Yep." Gregor scooped up the candlestick and turned to her. "But we're just getting started. He Gated them back to their starting point. They repeated the process, placing the candlestick farther out each time.

With each venture into the forest, Gregor pointed out plants and insects. Angel gaped at everything as she followed. *He's memorized the whole stinkin' forest.*

"Amazing!" She stared at a vine with bright orange blossoms that opened and closed one after the other like chasing Christmas lights. "And those mushrooms over there—they're huge!" The side of the thick stem swung open like a door, and a bulbous nose flanked by beady eyes poked out. She heard a grunt, and the door slammed shut again.

She stepped off the path and reached up to touch a purple blossom hanging from a tree that looked like a magnolia. The sweet scent tingled her nostrils.

"Don't touch those!" Gregor lunged and grabbed her forearm. "Sorry, but they bite, and I don't have the antivenin." He smiled wickedly and turned back to the path.

Angel glanced at the beautiful blossom. *Was he teasing?* She didn't touch anything else.

As she grew more proficient at Finding the candlestick, they pushed deeper and deeper into the forest. Gregor never put the candlestick in the same place twice, sending them off in different directions each time to better test her Talent. Soon, he was putting the candlestick too far away for them to walk and began Gating them most of the way. Then Angel made sure he'd taken them in the right direction.

As they trekked along, Gregor explained the powers of the magical trees that filled the forest. Their leaves were gold, coppery red, or bronze even in summer time, or deep shades of blue that made the trees look as though they grew right into the sky.

The bark of the Pewter Pine was streaked with what looked like burnished steel, but was so pliable Angel left an imprint of her fingertip when she pressed on one. Most of the trees were named after the metals or metal alloys they contained in high concentrations. The metals acted as a protection for the tree and served as a conduit for the trees' magical powers as well.

"I once found a Platinum Oak," Gregor told Angel after showing her a Silver Spruce, whose spiny silver-green needles sparkled like tinsel in the sunlight. "They're very rare, and incredibly powerful. A tincture made from its leaves can cure nearly any chronic illness. I knew just by touching it I'd be able to Gate my way nearly anywhere in the world. And, well, I've always wanted to see Japan…"

"You've been to Japan?"

"Well, not exactly. I was afraid if I didn't connect with a tree just as powerful there, the Gate could close behind me and I'd be stuck once I walked through." Gregor's eyes brightened and a sly smile turned the corners of his mouth. "So I just stuck my head through. It was so cool. I was looking out over the most beautiful lake, with a red bridge stretched across it. A girl was walking toward me on the bridge and saw my head sticking out of a cherry tree. She nearly fell into the lake."

Angel tried to guess what kinds of animals belonged to the caws, chirps and clicks that filled the air. She caught glimpses of bright feathers and patches of fur now and then, but they were few and far between. She did spot the metallic glint of dragon scales in several branches.

"They nest much lower than the birds." Gregor pointed out a pale yellow dragon perched on a low branch. "They don't need to fear predators the way birds do, but the small ones prefer to live in trees. The larger dragons nest in caves or in the hollows of big trees, but they're rare. The only large breeds on this island live in the mountains." The yellow dragon peered at them curiously and jumped up to a higher branch as they passed below him.

"Angel, check this out!" Gregor led her over to a colossal Bronze Oak. When they reached it, he motioned for her to peek into the hollow. A single, softball-sized egg lay nestled in a bed of moss and twigs. The iridescent oval swirled with wispy streaks of blue and gray.

"That's a dragon egg?" she asked.

He nodded.

She giggled at the thought of Spike making a home in a tree hollow. She couldn't see him giving up his purple pillow with the golden tassels.

"Dragons are just cool." Gregor leaned in as they admired the egg. "They have some of the most amazing traits. Like, they range from eight inches to eighty feet. And the variety of colors and breeds—winged and wingless, some that walk on all fours and some that walk on their hind legs. Some lay eggs and some have live birth. Next to unicorns, they're the most magical creatures out there. They—"

Angel backed away from the nest and looked at Gregor. He'd stopped talking so suddenly and now stood still as a statue. Finally, he blinked and then bit his lip.

"It's weird." He stepped back onto the path and she followed. "That momma dragon must have been gone for some time. I didn't see any tracks around the nest. I can't believe she'd leave her egg for that long." He shook his head as if dismissing a thought. "I'm sure she's fine. I mean, it's not like there's much out there that can hurt a dragon, but..."

"What?" Angel tried to read his expression.

"The forest is noisy, which is normal. But the animals aren't coming out, showing themselves. It's been like that lately, but I haven't been able to figure out why. I've seen nothing else out of the ordinary."

Angel thought of the wobbling fence, but she didn't mention it because Gregor had already blown her off about it.

But then something snapped loudly, a crack that echoed in the trees. Gregor's head jerked toward the noise, his brow furrowed. He walked over and picked up a large branch, then scanned the area.

"This is way too thick to have been broken by something small, but there's nothing around here."

Told you so.

After walking a few more yards, Gregor whipped his head around again. Angel followed on his heels as he ran back to the dragon's nest. It looked exactly as it had before.

"Something's hiding out here, but I don't see any sign of an animal that could break a branch like that. It doesn't look like it was cut by magic, or gnawed. I don't know what would do this. It must be something that camouflages well." He searched the area once more.

"I don't know. Nothing's here. No footprints, no signs of animals at all, except the dragon egg. No blood or anything to indicate a predator. I can't figure it out. I don't think we need to stick around. That momma dragon may come back and if something's been out here she's gonna be mad."

He started down the path, and Angel followed. She couldn't help feeling like whatever had broken that branch was still there and was watching them walk away.

Each afternoon of Finding lessons strengthened Angel's Talent, but she hit a wall after the first week. She thought her Talent should come easier than her other powers.

"You've got to trust your Talent, Angel," Gregor said over and over, but Angel didn't understand what he meant.

"I'm trying!" She struggled to fight back tears. After a deep breath, the tears broke loose, and she wiped them from her cheeks. "I'm never going to be able to Find my mom and dad at this rate. Why was I given this Talent if I can't use it far enough to reach them?"

Gregor moved over to her and touched her cheek, removing a tear she had missed.

"You're not letting the magic happen. You're trying to aim it at the candlestick. Focus on letting your Talent flow through you and *it* will Find the candlestick."

She turned her head away and stared into the forest. *He makes it sound so easy, but I just don't get it. Why is it taking so much work?*

"Why can't you just tell me how to do this?" She expected Gregor to glare at her, but he smiled.

"It's personal. I can't tell you specifically any more than you could explain to me how to Gate. You just have to reach out in your own way."

"Reach out? But I was trying to pull it from inside me…" Angel's brow tightened and she flopped down on a giant toadstool.

"You're trying to do this on your own…okay, I see…" Gregor sat down beside her. "Look, it's like your artistic talent. You're naturally better than most when it comes to drawing, right? But you'd never improve without someone guiding you through the process, another artist who knows what it's like."

"But you just said you can't teach me because you don't have this Talent. So how is this going to help? It's not like I can go around the corner and ask another Finder." She couldn't hide the sarcasm in her voice.

"Of course not, but that's not what I'm saying."

"Okay, so then what do I do?" Angel wiped away another tear that had slipped out. She shifted impatiently in her seat.

"All right, it's like this," he finally said. "We can all use our abilities somewhat without understanding them. Look at the animals around you. Bats, for instance. They use echolocation, but they don't know the first thing about physics. They don't have a clue what sound waves are intellectually, yet they rely on sound waves for their survival. They're not designed to understand physics, only to use certain principles innately.

"That's kind of how we are with our magic powers. They are innate, too—part of our design. They require practice of course, and some learning, just like walking and talking. But our Talents require more than that. They are not meant for us to use on autopilot, like a bat uses echolocation."

"But you keep telling me to trust my Talent, like it's going to do the work for me. This isn't helping." Angel huffed and stifled back another sob.

"That's the point." He lowered his voice. "It's harder to trust something that doesn't come automatically, no matter how innate it is. But that's where you have to start. And then you can work with it to develop it. You keep trying to make your Talent behave the way you want it to, but you have to learn how it operates."

Gregor's words sank in, and excitement flittered inside Angel.

"Like my drawing. If I try to change my style, it won't work because I'm trying to force myself to be a different kind of artist. And just because I'm naturally good at working with charcoals, that doesn't mean I don't have to learn how that medium works and practice those specific techniques. I think I'm getting it." She sat forward and pushed her hands into her knees, smiling at Gregor, and then immediately slumped back.

"What's wrong now?" His eyebrow arched.

She felt more than ever like his little sister. "We're back to square one. No teacher."

"It's not a teacher you need." Gregor's mouth tilted into a crooked half-smile as he stood.

Angel didn't move, and narrowed her eyes. *What on earth is he talking about? How else am I going to learn this if I can't find someone to teach me?*

Gregor seemed to read the question on her face. "Haven't you ever taken something apart to see how it worked?"

"A few times." Dried tears tugged on Angel's face as she smiled at the memory of being happy that one of her toys broke so she could disassemble it.

"Well, think about this…who would be better at helping you understand something—someone who has experience using it, or the one who designed and built it?"

Chapter Eleven
The Cursed Region

Gregor's words awoke a stirring inside Angel, familiar and comforting. How could she not have put it together before? It suddenly seemed only natural that this was the way. Once she realized the truth, it brought the life back into her. She jumped to her feet.

"Put the candlestick out again. A couple of yards farther than last time."

Gregor nodded and then disappeared into the nearest tree. Angel closed her eyes. Now she knew where to direct her focus. The connection to the candlestick came immediately, and Angel felt in herself what she had seen in Gregor all along.

She heard the shuffling of leaves, and her skin tingled as if someone was looking at her, but she didn't want to open her eyes and lose her focus on the connection.

"Gregor, I've got it—I know I'll be able to Find the candlestick anywhere now."

Silence.

Her eyes popped open. A split second later Gregor emerged from the tree.

"Wait, if you just got here…" Angel surveyed the area, but saw only foliage and a lizard clinging to a tree trunk. "Did you see anything? I thought you were standing right here."

"No." Gregor looked at her curiously. "Nothing."

"I swear, someone was just standing right here," she said. "I felt eyes on me."

Gregor's eyebrow rose. "There are probably a thousand eyes on you right now."

"You know what I mean! *Human* eyes. Someone was—oh, never mind."

Gregor shrugged. "Come on, let's make this the last attempt for the day." He headed back to the tree. "I'm getting hungry."

Angel told Gregor the location of the candlestick and followed him to the tree, but before she stepped through she glanced over her shoulder. A Silver Spruce glinted in the sunlight as its branches rustled in the breeze. Angel spotted a patch of gray that lacked the luster of the silvery needles. She squinted to see if it was a dragon perched in a rear branch. *No, it can't be. That would be shiny, too. It looks like...fabric.*

The breeze shifted the branches slightly, obscuring the gray and washing away the feeling of being watched. Angel stepped through the Gate.

When she emerged, something wasn't right.

"This is the wrong direction," she said. She concentrated again. The candlestick was close by and she turned to face the right direction.

Gregor moved up beside her and tapped her with his elbow. "Great job, I was trying to throw you off."

Angel elbowed him back, and started walking toward the candlestick. "I really get it now. It's amazing how much easier my magic is when I'm not trying to force it."

They'd walked only a few yards when Gregor stopped suddenly and swore. "Sorry, I didn't think about exactly where we were...I didn't mean to lead you here."

"What are you talking about?" Where they stood looked just like an ordinary forest. Maybe that was what he meant; maybe there was nothing particularly magical in the area. But then she looked a little farther ahead.

Beyond the trees in front of them loomed a shadowy area. When she stepped forward Gregor grabbed her arm.

"You do not want to go near there." His voice and posture were tense and his eyes lit with warning.

"What is it?"

A dank smell infiltrated the normally fresh forest air, and a chill ran down Angel's spine. That's when the silence became apparent to her. No birds chirped at scampering squirrels, and the towering trees remained stiff and silent like living statues. Something churned inside Angel, telling her to run. Garbled voices echoed inside her head, but her feet froze to the ground. A vein in her temple thumped, then throbbed, and soon she felt like a vice was squeezing her head, but she couldn't bring herself to move.

Gregor stood stock-still as well, until the rustling of leaves broke the eerie silence. A green tendril stretched itself out into the space in front of them, groping along the ground. Angel thought it was a tentacle from some sort of strange animal, but when it stopped only a few yards from her feet she saw that it was a vine, and what looked like suckers were short, thick leaves. The vine continued searching the forest floor, seemingly unaware of Angel and Gregor.

Gregor broke free from his invisible bonds and pulled Angel several paces back, but his eyes remained fixed on the gray-green tendril slithering across the ground. The vine pushed leaves and twigs aside until it revealed something lying in the dirt, dead and half decayed. The tendril wrapped around the animal carcass, completely encasing it, and retracted back into the shadows.

Angel and Gregor stared at the spot where ants swarmed over the loss of their feast.

"That's where it happened. The fire, I mean. The day that…" But Gregor didn't finish his sentence. He pulled Angel toward another tree, Gating them away.

When they stepped through, Angel sucked in the fresh air in a great gasp, and let herself sink to the ground. She wrapped her arms around her knees and looked up at Gregor. He knelt down in front of her, and she could tell by his expression he was berating himself.

"What happened to the forest there? Why is it still dark like that?"

"It was cursed by the fire," he whispered.

"Cursed?"

His voice cracked and his words seemed to sneak out of his mouth against his will. "Yes. Remember, Dawric didn't really know how to control the powers he'd stolen. His rage was sent into the fire and left a curse on the whole area. It's been taken over by plants and animals on the fringe of the fire. At first they were normal, but the curse caused them to mutate, and degrade more and more with each generation. Now everything has changed so much in only a few years because the life, if you can call it that, inside that area of the forest has become like a cancer. And it's spreading."

Despite Gregor's chilling words, Angel felt the color returning to her face as her heartbeat and breathing returned to normal. She reached out, letting Gregor know she was ready to stand, and he released a deep sigh.

He picked up the candlestick and started walking, instead of Gating them back to the farm, as if he needed to burn off some energy.

Comforted by how quickly she recovered, Angel dared one more question. It had been nagging her for a while, every time Gregor reassured her that there was no way Dawric could return.

"Gregor, I hate to even ask this, but how do you know for sure Dawric didn't die in the fire? You said you took off before the fire started, right? So maybe he's dead and that's why he never came back."

"I saw him leave," he said briskly, then inhaled through his nose, nostrils flaring. "Or, at least I don't know how it could have been anyone else. When your parents and I went searching for my mom and dad, we saw a helicopter take off from deep in the forest. We put word out, and for a long time no one could step outside without looking to the sky. But no one has seen a helicopter since then, and thank God, no one has been killed either." Gregor kept his eyes locked in front of him as he spoke, and his hand gripped the candlestick so tightly his knuckles turned white.

For both of their sakes, Angel didn't press for anything more.

"Where did you get Horatio?" she asked after a while.

A smile crept onto Gregor's face. "I found him in the forest, bound up in a giant spider web. Poor thing was chirping like crazy. The spider was sleeping on the other side of the web, but woke up when it felt me cut Horatio loose. I could see the venom dripping from its fangs." He shuddered. "Ugliest thing I've ever seen."

His face brightened again and he loosened his grip on the candlestick. "Anyway, I ducked into a Gate when I grabbed him, and he's been my best friend ever since. I found out I could understand his chirping if I concentrated hard enough. Now I don't even have to try."

"I'm sorry Zack and I kept him from you. He just thought Horatio was really cool and unusual. He would've released him as soon as he found out what species he was."

"Well, you would've never found him in any of your books. Maybe not even in one of ours. As far as I know, he's the last of his kind."

"Can you teach me to understand him? I thought I almost could the night he was singing in his cage. But it kept slipping away."

Gregor tagged her with his elbow. "The way you are with animals? You bet. When he comes back, just listen closely and block out everything but his singing. It'll come to you. I don't doubt it."

Angel snuggled into her bed that night, emotionally and physically exhausted. Something or someone was out there and watching her. She'd hoped she could cling to the idea that Dawric had died in the fire, but Gregor had dispelled that notion.

Gregor seemed reluctant to talk about the source of protection, but at the same time he had complete confidence in that protection. Why? It made no sense to her at all. If the island was protected from unempowereds, then how did Dawric find it? Surely Gregor had thought about that—why didn't it concern him?

Despite her worries, one thing did settle in Angel's heart and make her smile that night. Experiencing her Talent made her feel special, not just different, for the first time in her life.

She also now knew without a doubt that she was made for this place; and no matter how badly she missed the Masons and Zack, or how many fears she would have to face, there was no turning back.

~Practicing Patience~

He lunged forward and pinned the scientist against the wall. "I'm tired of waiting!"

"She's practicing, but it will take time for her Talent to come back. You have to be patient."

He tightened his grip on the scientist's shoulders. "Loan it to me again. I want to see for myself."

The man shook his head, and furrowed his brow. "Not like this. Not while you're angry. You can't control it."

"I'm angry because I am never allowed to practice outside these walls! I'm tired of waiting!"

"Yes…you said that…"

He let go of the scientist's shoulders but did not move away. "I will not wait forever." He inhaled, forcing back the pounding of his heart. Why did the little mongrel have to be right about self-control?

Chapter Twelve
The Puzzle

The following Monday, Angel and Gregor rode into town. The wind sent Angel's hair flying in every direction. For the first time, she relished the freedom it made her feel. And she was finally used to seeing her hair brown instead of red.

She once asked Gregor how he'd changed her hair color. He went straight into annoying professor mode.

"An object absorbs all the light waves *except* those that make up the color you see. White reflects every wave and black absorbs them all. Magically adjusting the surface's absorption and reflection of wavelengths changes the color."

"But in art white is the absence of color. And black is created from pigment. That just makes more sense. Seems like absorbing all the light would make something invisible."

"If you bend the light rays just right, you *can* make something invisible."

"Can you do it?"

"No…it's incredibly difficult. I've never been able to make even a paperclip invisible. Now back to work."

She leaned forward in the saddle, legs gripping Juliet's sides. Her thoughts moved to the present, the forest and its mysteries, and then to the day she'd finally reunite with her real parents.

Even her worries about Dawric nearly disappeared as she allowed herself the freedom to enjoy the ride and absorb the energy from her surroundings. Wobbling fences and broken branches really could be just that and nothing more. Dark thoughts would not steal the joy of seeing Sir Benjamin and Spike again, and experiencing a day in town as someone who felt like she belonged.

As Gregor marched her past the bakery, where Miss Elsie put the finishing touches on a tiered cake, Angel spied the adorable kittens in the pet shop window next door.

"Can we please, please go in and see them? Please…" Angel gave Gregor the most pitiful look she could muster, and watched as his face softened.

"Only for a minute."

She plunged through the door and raced straight to the kittens. The sounds of squawking birds filled her ears, and she detected the distinct scent of cedar shavings. Gregor followed her inside looking as though he regretted his decision.

"We can't take one home, you know. Shakespeare would never forgive me. He enjoys being king of the castle."

"I know," she said, as she picked up a fluffy white kitten. "But they're just so cute." The tiny kitten felt like a squirming tuft of cotton. His miniature claws poked at her fingers, but they only tickled. She held him to her chest and let his downy fur brush her chin.

She picked up the other two in turn, snuggling them both as she had the first, and inhaled their sweet scent. Then she reluctantly turned away from them.

Another pen caught her eye.

Inside laid a sleeping Boxer puppy, its square jaw propped on its front paws. She stared at the puppy but didn't move any closer. It was only a couple of months old, with its head and paws far too large for the rest of its body. Its ribs expanded with each breath, and it snorted and snuffed while its back paw moved as if it were dreaming about running.

The oddest feeling crept into Angel's stomach. It wasn't nausea exactly, but it threatened to become so. The floor tilted under her feet, and she felt the blood rush from her face. She didn't say a word when Gregor asked her if she was ready to go, and followed him. She stopped right outside the door and let the fresh air fill her lungs.

She moved forward into the crowd and found she couldn't concentrate on where she was going. She smacked right into a woman with a frilly shawl wrapped around her shoulders.

"Excuse me, dear, are you all right?" The woman placed a gloved hand on Angel's shoulder.

Angel nodded, mumbled, "I'm sorry," and headed off after Gregor.

When she stepped up to him, his eyes widened. "Maybe the riding was too much for you? I know it was really only your second time…"

She tried to speak, but her jaw clenched as she fought the sudden fatigue. *That must be it, I just over-exerted myself.*

"Why don't you go hang out at Sir B's while I go get what we need." He wrapped his arm around her shoulder as he led her over to the bookshop.

"I'll meet you here after I've loaded up the horses. And we'll take it easier on the ride back home."

She nodded and went inside. At first the place appeared empty, but then Sir Benjamin popped up from behind the desk.

"I was making sure the old boy was still breathing. He didn't even move when I poured the food in his bowl. Worthless lump of scales, but I love him." He flashed a Santa smile. "What brings you by, Miss Angel? And where's Gregor?"

"Gone to get supplies." Angel felt the blood returning to her head and managed a smile.

"Then have a seat. Would you like some tea?"

"That'd be great. Thank you." She made herself comfortable on the couch, and started nosing through a book about magical plants, trying to find some of the specimens she had seen in the forest.

"Interested in Botany?"

She nearly dropped the book onto her lap, and spun her head to find Sir Benjamin standing right behind her.

"Sorry, Angel, didn't mean to shake you."

"It's okay." She reached for the tea in his hand. "I was just looking up some of the plants Gregor showed me. Very different from where I grew up."

"Seems there's a lot of differences between here and there," he said with a wink. He walked over to the table that held his jigsaw puzzle and sat down. Angel sipped her tea, watching him consider the puzzle pieces in front of him.

"Mind if I help you?" She'd spent many Sunday afternoons working on puzzles with Mr. Mason, the only time she ever had him to herself.

"Please! I'd love some help." He jumped up to pull the other chair out for her.

As Angel sat, a stout woman burst into the shop, dragging a yappy little dog on a leash. Sir Benjamin gave Angel a sly wink and walked over to help her.

Angel tucked one leg underneath her and looked at the picture on the puzzle box, a magnificent stone castle with mountains in the background, and a sky of gray clouds marbled with lightning. The castle looked bright and beautiful despite the stormy sky.

Sir Benjamin sat back down as the woman left, and set straight to work.

"I'm surprised Gregor never told me about you." His eyes remained trained on the puzzle.

Angel picked a flowered tree that covered one side of the castle wall and began looking for pieces with flecks of bright purple.

"Well, he wasn't expecting me really, until I came." She didn't realize until she heard herself say the words that it might sound odd.

"Oh. An unplanned vacation, how wonderful. Nothing like being spontaneous, eh?"

"It's not really been a vacation. We've been working pretty hard. I'm not complaining, though. Gregor's great."

The contrast between Gregor and the other guys she knew was even more vivid to her now. He'd been running his father's farm since he was ten. All Josh and Jacob cared about was looking cool and impressing girls. Mrs. Mason always complained about how they needed to get more focused, set some goals, and stop bending to the influence of their school friends. The thought prompted an idea.

"My parents decided to send me to Gregor's place for the summer," she said. "They thought he'd be a good influence on me since he's been so responsible on his own."

"Smart parents you have. Gregor's the best kind of influence, I'd say."

"Yeah, he's taught me a lot already. Things I could never have learned from school."

Angel placed a piece she'd been hunting for a full fifteen minutes. Her Talent gave her an edge in finding the pieces, but it was still a challenge because she couldn't connect with the piece she needed until she actually saw it.

"Would you like more, my dear?" Sir Benjamin waved his hand and the teapot floated toward them.

"No thanks," she said with a sigh. "I think I'd like to look around again. That last piece about killed me."

"Make yourself at home."

He caught the teapot and poured himself a cup, then went back to the puzzle and worked in silence while Angel pulled books off the shelves one at a time. She was careful not to step on the snoozing Spike as she walked behind Sir Benjamin's desk, but did bend down for a moment to stroke his shiny scales. They were cooler to the touch than she expected, and smooth like polished metal. He snuffed and adjusted his wing but didn't wake. Angel gently touched his spiked tail. *A pet dragon. Too cool.*

She made her way to the other side of the room, and glanced on top of the small counter. A book lay next to the cash register. It didn't look at all like the leather-bound books covering the shelves. Angel picked up the paperback and turned it over to read the back cover, bumping the bell on the counter.

"That's for one of the University professors," Sir Benjamin said, before Angel had a chance to read anything.

She looked up.

He smiled tentatively at first, as though he wasn't going to continue, and then his face brightened again. "Interesting guy. He started teaching there the year before I retired."

Angel flipped the book open to the middle. Strange charts and drawings mingled with long, dry passages of text. If Angel was reading correctly, it seemed to imply there should eventually be humans with superpowers. She scanned a few more pages. No mention of the word magic, but what the author described certainly sounded like it.

She looked up from the book. "Have you read any of this?"

"A bit. As much as I could take."

Sir Benjamin glanced at his watch. "Actually, he ought to be here any minute to pick up the book."

The words were barely out of his mouth when the door burst open, sending the bell clanging. In rushed a man dressed in black pants and leather boots, his shirt half tucked in, his gray cloak nearly getting caught in the door as it slammed shut behind him.

No...*cloak* wasn't quite the right word for what he was wearing. It looked like a lab coat, but not the stark, fitted ones Angel was used to seeing on doctors and scientists.

His strawberry blond hair was nearly the same shade as Zack's, and its hue blended into the redness of his flushed cheeks, interrupted only by the most intense ice-blue eyes Angel had ever seen.

Chapter Thirteen
The Good Doctor

"Dr. Damian." Sir Benjamin rose from his chair and strode across the room to shake Dr. Damian's hand. "We were just talking about you. Angel here was interested in the book you ordered."

"Oh, really? See, Dr. Punnett, I told you someone would eventually get interested if you'd put one someplace besides the bottom shelf. You just didn't give it enough time."

"I think five years was plenty enough time. And how often do I have to tell you, I stopped being Dr. Punnett when I retired. Anyway, come meet Angel."

Dr. Damian kept smiling brightly and turned to Angel. She swallowed to stop herself from gasping when his mesmerizing blue eyes fell upon her, and the book slipped from her fingers onto the counter.

"Are you interested in science? I teach Genetics at the University. You're welcome any time to come up and visit. Classes aren't in session for the summer, of course. But most of us in the science department are there every day working on our research." The words sped like a swarm of bees, as if they were all trying to get out of Dr. Damian's mouth at once.

It took a moment for Angel's brain to catch up before she could answer. "I'd love to, but I'll have to talk to Gregor about it."

"She's staying with Gregor Halvard for the summer. His cousin from America."

"Bring him along." Dr. Damian's grin broadened even more. "The more the merrier!"

He paid Sir Benjamin for the book, and set off, shouting over his shoulder, "Nice to meet you, Angel!" The door slammed with a *whoosh* behind him.

Angel and Sir Benjamin were left in silence, except for the tinkling of the doorbell. They had just sat down to resume work on the puzzle when Gregor arrived.

"Ready to go, Angel? Sorry it took me so long. Roger had to search the back to find the grass seed I needed. Took him a while. We could have used your T—" Gregor clamped his mouth shut and scrunched his brow.

Angel nearly popped out of her seat. *Nice save, Gregor.*

"It was great talking to you again, Sir Benjamin," she said. "I feel much better now—ready for the ride home, I think."

"Thanks for taking care of her for me," Gregor added. "Wish we could stay, but this has already taken too long, and we need to get back and unload the horses."

He walked toward the door and Angel followed, but she stopped when Sir Benjamin gently touched her arm. He was holding the plant book she'd been looking at.

"Here, take this. Maybe it will come in handy on your and Gregor's treks through the forest."

"Oh, no, I—"

"Please. I want you to have it." He gave her an imploring look and pushed the book closer to her.

She took it, then leaned forward and thanked him with a kiss on the cheek. She followed Gregor out the door and to the horses, where they climbed on and rode home.

Angel and Gregor spent the rest of the week doing their usual chores in the morning, and either riding the horses in the afternoons or working on Angel's Finding. She'd finally gotten to the point that they would have to leave the island for her to improve. Her lessons had taken them to the depths of the forest, to tree-covered mountainsides, to vast plains so dense with white flowers it looked like a snow blanket. Still, Gregor refused to take her farther than the edge of the island, afraid he would end up losing her again.

He was so insistent about keeping her close to home that she'd refrained from asking him to take her to see Zack. She wouldn't speak to Zack, or even show herself to him, but she couldn't live with the idea of never laying eyes on him again. *Just wait, Gregor. When my parents are back I'll show you how insistent I can be.*

It seemed, however, that day would never come. As Angel sat one evening trying to read Gregor's worn copy of *Macbeth*, thoughts of her parents floated around inside her head making the play even more difficult for her to understand. *The waiting is too much.* She felt like she was on that fence again, gazing back at her old life and forward at her new life. Only this time, everything but Zack felt miles away. She finally gave up on the book.

"It's been weeks, Gregor. I came here at the end of May, and now it's nearly the end of June, and there's been no word from my parents. What could be taking Horatio so long?"

"He's fast, Angel, but they may have moved." Gregor turned a glass figurine in his hand, magically reshaping it into the likenesses of different animals, one after another. "We only know where they were last. And remember, they're looking in areas that aren't exclusively magic, which is why we haven't been able to stay in contact as much as we could if they had their powers available at all times."

Angel understood that, but it irritated her that Gregor wasn't worried. It was more than that. He seemed to be getting too used to having her around. She was sure he wanted her parents to come back, but it would put an end to her living at his farm. Was he lonely? She wished he would be honest with her.

He spent a lot of time in the forest alone during his morning walks, but she had assumed that he used it for solitude, and, well, she didn't know what else. Now she didn't just wonder what he did out there; she was actually becoming suspicious. Other than those times in the forest, he never, ever showed signs of wanting to get away from her. She closed the book in her hands.

"I'll just feel much better when Horatio finds them." She tried to hide the irritation in her voice. "Or at least comes back to tell you where they are."

Gregor settled on forming the glass figurine into a beetle and set it down on the table. He looked at the clock. "It's late. Tomorrow's Saturday, but we still have work to be done." He rose to his feet.

"Tomorrow's Saturday? All day I've been thinking today was Thursday. That means tomorrow's the 27th."

"And…"

"It's my birthday. I'll be fourteen."

Gregor's stoic face broke into a wide smile. ""Your birthday? I guess I can't make you work then, huh? What do you want to do?"

"How about a real walk through the forest—no Finding practice. And a picnic."

"Ooooh…you're a wild woman!"

He ducked as she threw a pillow at him.

~Looking Away~

"Do you have to leave those freaks of nature uncovered like that? They give me the creeps." He would never get used to the strangeness of the animals here. Much less the scientist's fascination with making them even more unnatural. What ever happened to old-fashioned lab rats?

If only the girl hadn't gotten away. He could have taken care of things a long time ago—on his own, without having to help the little mongrel with these ridiculous creatures.

"Just don't look at them," the scientist said. "It's not like they can bother you."

Chapter Fourteen
The Musician

Angel awoke to the aroma of bacon and eggs. Her stomach responded with a grumble. She hurried to the kitchen, where she found Gregor pouring syrup onto a huge stack of pancakes.

"Chores are done, so we can get going after breakfast," he said.

"But…"

Guilt slammed her heart—she'd had such resentful thoughts. Gregor took care of her like a sister, and had spent all that time searching for her. If all he wanted was some company after spending years alone, who was she to complain? She slid silently into a chair. *I owe him my life.*

After breakfast, Gregor packed their lunch, shooing her away when she tried to help. "Not the birthday girl. You go relax."

She settled into the big leather chair in the living room, and picked up one of Gregor's geography books. He had dozens of them, and maps galore of the British Isles, Western Europe, and the East coast of America. It amazed Angel that he had found her at all. But he really understood how his Talent worked, and studied geography to isolate the most likely spots. At first Angel couldn't see how he shot her all the way to America, but he'd explained how water isn't really a barrier. And it had something to do with the way the continents were connected not long ago. It was just as likely to be America as Germany.

He stepped into the living room, picnic basket in hand. She yanked on her sneakers, and followed him to the forest, plant guide in hand.

"I thought you didn't want this to be a lesson?" Gregor's mouth tilted in a half-smile.

Sunlight streamed the forest with glimmering, golden light. They stayed on the main path, where the trees loomed dizzyingly high overhead. Angel felt like she was walking through a huge living tunnel. She stopped at every opportunity to look up the plants she found interesting.

Many had medicinal qualities, such as the palmetto-like plant that controlled temperature and was used to treat fever. Now it made sense why Gregor had cringed when she told him about pharmacies and man-made medicines. Angel picked a small, yellow bud from a plant that acted as a pain reliever and stuffed it into her pocket.

They continued walking along the well-traveled path. A few lizards poked their heads out from behind thick leaves, and a furry snout sniffed at them from the dense underbrush every now and then. But for the most part, the trail was merely filled with the echoes of animal noises emanating from deeper in the trees.

The path extended far ahead and seemed to merge with the giant walls of trees that lined either side. Angel imagined walking for hours and eventually just disappearing into another realm.

They had walked a good couple of miles when Angel finally spotted a clearing through a break in the trees on her right.

"What is that?" She pointed through the trees at what looked like the ruins of an old temple. Great, wide stone steps ascended to pillars and crumbled walls that no longer supported a roof.

"A band of Elves."

Angel had been looking at the building, but now noticed that on the far side of the steps several someones sat around on broken pillars and large pieces of stone. *Elves? Really?*

"I never could keep track of all those terms for groups in biology," she said. "A school of fish, a herd of elephants, a flock of seagulls. They all mean the same, so why couldn—"

"They're not *animals*, you know. They're absolutely no different from you and me." He turned his back to her and set off toward the stone building.

"Wait! Gregor, wait!" She caught up to him and grabbed his shoulder.

He turned to her with fury in his eyes. *Or is that hurt?*

"I'm sorry. Honestly. I didn't mean that at all. It just reminded me when you said *band*...it was just a joke."

His shoulder relaxed under her hand, and she dropped her arm back to her side.

"It's okay."

His eyes still reflected the anger of his reaction to her words, and Angel wondered why he'd taken them personally.

"But, really, when I said *band*, I meant they're *musicians*. Come on, I'll introduce you."

As they approached the stone building, Angel's eyes moved up the height of the immense stone walls until she had to crane her neck upwards to see the windows. Chunks of jagged, colored glass remained seated in the sills, their sharp edges catching the sunlight like prisms and splashing kaleidoscope images on the white walls. The openings were squared at the bottom, but the sides curved in slightly, giving the impression that the missing tops had been arched like the stained glass windows of a church. Sunlight blared over the glass and Angel squinted.

A large stone gargoyle guarded the building from above the dungeonesque door. A thick chain connected the door handle to the wall, the ends meeting within the confines of an iron lock. The building was impenetrable as far as Angel could see, even with the roof missing. Anyone who successfully scaled the walls would still surely meet their death, impaled by the pointed spires of broken glass.

When they reached the base of the steps, Gregor called out, "Kalek! D'ya mind if we watch you rehearse today? This is my cousin, Angel, and she's never seen an Elven band play before."

One of the Elves appeared from behind a column and leaned his shoulder against it, ankles crossed, peering out through the mass of stringy curls that hung down either side of his long face. His lean arms threaded through studded armbands and ended with long graceful hands. Musician's hands.

Like the others, he wore an oversized tunic, belted at the waist, and suede boots. A dagger was tucked in a sheath strapped around the leather pants that stretched over his thigh. It wasn't until he turned his head that Angel noticed the point of an ear poking out of his tangled curls. She bit her lip, heart skipping. *Elves—really!*

"Sure, why not?" he said coolly. "Maybe we'll autograph a picture for you when we're done."

The other Elves laughed, and then three of them scrambled to take their places with Kalek on the platform at the top of the stairs.

Angel hadn't seen any of them carrying anything when they climbed onstage, but in the blink of an eye, they each were in place with a different instrument. One Elven guy stood behind a tall, narrow harp, another held some sort of large flute, and the third sat astride a stool behind what Angel assumed was a percussion set. The drums were all the same height, but of varying widths and looked like solid posts of polished wood with silver grain. Kalek held what appeared to be an ordinary electric guitar. He positioned his hand in front of the strings and spoke.

"One, two, three…"

The music took Angel's breath away. It didn't come directly from the instruments, and there were no microphones or speakers to direct it elsewhere. It emanated from the surrounding forest, the very trees themselves, and drifted down from the sky. Angel could feel vibration in her feet—it even rang from the grass and rocks on which she stood.

The leaves on the trees and bushes changed color before her eyes, from green to red to gold and back, sparkling in the brilliant sunshine. Butterflies swarmed out from the forest, fluttering in yellow clouds around the flowers in the clearing. The music seeped all the way into Angel's bones, stirring her soul.

The Elven band played slow and soulful at first, and Angel involuntarily closed her eyes. The darkness behind her eyelids brightened to a soft glow, which dispersed and swirled, and then coalesced into images of a savannah that was as real to her as the forest in which she stood.

A strange, disconnected feeling overtook her, as though her spirit had been pulled out of her body and transplanted someplace else. It wasn't frightening, only disconcerting at first, and then something surged inside her like an instinct she'd never experienced, an animal hunger that urged her to lower herself to the ground. The positioning of her limbs didn't feel human—more like the way she imagined a cat would feel stalking a mouse.

The deep grass swayed before her, and her strong lioness muscles tensed and twitched, her belly scraping along the ground. The scent of her prey wafted into her feline nostrils as her lungs filled with the dry, pungent air.

She pounced, and her massive paws slid across the grassy plain, her legs spreading out to her sides, becoming raven-black wings that caught the wind and lifted her from the ground. She pumped her wings until she reached her nest and was greeted by the hungry cries of her young. She gazed into their pleading eyes, and her surroundings slowly rose around her until she touched lightly on the ground.

Her raven wings reached below her as they transformed into graceful legs supported by sturdy hooves. The small avian eyes that held her gaze became the big brown eyes of her fawn, full of dependence and innocence that would be nurtured into strength and the will to survive.

The music intensified and increased its tempo, and Angel's heartbeat pounded in time with the rhythm.

Instantly, she ran free on larger hooves, braying into the wind, ranging the hill for pasture in search of green sustenance. No noise or commotion distracted her from her play; no driver shouted at her as at the other pack mules.

Then a harness clamped down on her and subjugated her free spirit. Strength filled her as the earth shrank beneath her feet. She commanded her immense ox muscles to pull the plow to which she was harnessed, tilling the earth for her one and only master.

Her harness unfastened and her massive legs withdrew into skinny stalks and fluffy feathered wings that were too small to lift her large ostrich body into the air. She flapped her wings joyfully, although she could not take flight. But soon her pinions stretched into those of a stork and she left her nest of eggs to tramp around, and then ascend into the air with speed and agility. She laughed as she easily surpassed the horse restrained by his rider.

Kalek moved into ripping tunes, creating chords that reverberated through the treetops and swayed their trunks. Angel became intensely aware of the blood flowing through her veins.

She transposed from free bird to swift horse, galloping and leaping, her mane flowing behind her. She struck terror with her loud snorting and fierce pawing, and rejoiced in her own strength. A trumpet blast resounded in her ear and she quivered. Unable to stand still, she charged into battle, unafraid, speeding past sword and javelin toward the commanding voice of her captain.

As she ran, sleek wings sprouted and fanned out at her sides, while her equine body shrank into the form of a hawk. She took flight, soaring into the sky as the trees disappeared into miniature green clumps far below. A river snaked its way along, curving left and right around the rolling hills. Her keen eyes spotted a rabbit scuttling along in the grass of a field and she dove, the streak of green below pressing toward her at a dizzying speed.

Then she soared once again, back to her nest on the rocky crag of a cliff, her eagle stronghold from which her piercing eyes would detect the next meal for her young.

The music deepened and slowed, and Angel found herself on the ground once more, her powerful behemoth muscles mounted on bones of bronze and iron. She swayed her cedar-like tail as she lumbered across the land, confident in her place as first among the works of her Maker, and she made her way to the raging river that was no match for her strength.

As she lowered herself into the river, her massive body morphed into a more streamlined form, shielded by scales joined one to the next as an impenetrable fortress, protecting the mighty leviathan from being pierced by wind or weapon. She snorted, and firebrands streamed from between the fearsome teeth ringing her open mouth. Smoke poured from her nostrils as she churned the sea like a boiling caldron. Only One stood stronger than she at that moment, and she felt immense joy at being made part of His divine creation.

She opened her eyes and she was Angel again, but the music continued to fill her and she still felt a connection, a sense of her place in creation. When the Elves stopped playing, the music eased out of her body, but not completely, and Angel hung on to it for several moments before she could speak.

"That was amazing!" Her voice sounded harsh compared to the beautiful music.

Kalek leaped down from the top step in one bound, landing directly in front of her.

"Thank you, but it is the stars in the heavens you should speak to," he said. "They are the song-makers. We merely carry their proclamations to your ears, so you can see the evidence of the handiwork around you."

He turned abruptly when Gregor spoke.

"How is Siophra?"

"Fine, as you well know. Do you think I haven't seen you spying on her through your tree-Gates? She knows her place, Gregor. When will you learn yours?" Kalek's cool voice sounded like hardened steel.

He turned back and bowed deeply to Angel, and when he stood he held out a single, thick-stemmed, deep-red rosebud.

Angel took the rosebud in trembling hands. The touch of his fingers sent chills up her arm.

"Just stroke the petals when you want to hear our music. It's not nearly as strong as when we play here, but I hope you enjoy it. It was wonderful to meet you, Angel." His voice was kind again as his onyx eyes looked deeply into hers.

"You too, Kalek. Thank you so much."

Kalek turned and rejoined his friends. As he did, a beautiful Elven girl emerged from the forest on the side closest to the Elves. She walked directly to Kalek's group, her eyes fixed straight at them. She seemed not to notice Angel and Gregor at all. She stood talking to Kalek, and Angel was taken by how different she appeared from the other Elves. Her elegant velvet gown of midnight blue clung to her torso, highlighting her small frame, and draped around her legs, nearly touching the ground. Her sleeves narrowed into points that covered the backs of her delicate hands, and her high neckline set off a magnificent teardrop emerald that hung on a sparkling gold chain.

The girl's black hair was pulled back in a waist-length braid, entwined with golden ribbon. As she spoke to Kalek, she finally glanced in Angel and Gregor's direction, but instead of greeting them, she stiffened and immediately returned her gaze to Kalek.

Angel turned to ask Gregor who the girl was, but he was no longer standing next to her. She looked toward the forest path just in time to see Gregor's boot disappearing into a tree on the edge of the clearing. She darted to the entrance of the path, and started running back toward the house. She'd only run for a minute or two when she spotted Gregor sitting on a tree stump on the edge of the path. She was ready to lay into him for leaving her, but his dejected expression stopped her.

He said softly, "I'm sorry. I shouldn't have taken off like that, but I was afraid I'd lose my temper back there and I didn't want to ruin your birthday by getting into a fight. My fault, though…I never should have mentioned…" He clenched and unclenched his fists, and continued, loosening his voice, "Never mind. Let's go over to the stream. You'll love all the creatures and plants that live along the bank."

Angel wanted to ask who Siophra was, knowing that the Elven girl was whom *he shouldn't have mentioned*, but she took his quick change of subject as a signal that he didn't want to talk about it. If there was one thing she'd learned by living in a houseful of males, it was never push them to talk. Better to just forget about it and move on.

They walked to the edge of the stream and found a flat area to set up their picnic. Angel looked up everything she could in her plant guide—tiger-striped daisies, lily pads that had tails swishing behind them directing their course like little rudders, and mosses and toadstools of every variety.

The trees lining either side of the stream reached up and over until their branches blended together, creating a roof that protected the water from the sun's warmth. A lizard slunk into the chilly water and turned from green to orange. Frogs jumped and plopped into the stream, splashing a rabbit that had come to drink. The rabbit's fur rippled when the cold water hit, and it stood on its hind legs with its nose twitching.

At one point, as Angel read aloud from her book about a tree that emitted a sap used to heal burns, Gregor grabbed her arm and put his finger to his mouth.

She stopped talking at once. He pointed downstream to a spot about fifty feet away, where a doe lapped water from the stream. She was the color of caramel with white markings around her nose, and brown eyes that Angel could see shining from where they sat.

"Beautiful." Angel noticed a bulge on the doe's side and whispered to Gregor, "It looks like she's pregnant."

Suddenly, the water splashed downstream from the doe, and she darted into the thick trees. Angel and Gregor jumped to their feet and dashed to the spot where they'd seen the splash. Gregor reached into the water and groped around under the surface, but pulled up only a clump of decaying plant material. The water rippled unnaturally in a spot on the opposite shore, but there were no other signs of movement.

Gregor stared at the rippling water as if waiting for something to surface. Long minutes passed as he stood motionless, eyes fixed on the unnatural pattern. Finally, he let out a barely audible breath.

"Step back into those trees," he whispered, motioning behind them. "I'm going to Gate over to the other side and check out that spot."

By the time Angel reached the trees and turned around, Gregor was already on the other side, and the strange rippling was gone.

No, wait! There, in the middle of the stream. It just moved.

Gregor saw it too, but he seemed to understand it no better than Angel. He tried throwing several stones at it, but nothing came out of the water, and he never hit the mark because the ripple would shift before the stone hit the water's surface. He finally gave up and Gated back to Angel.

"Oddest thing I've ever seen out here," he said as if to himself.

His tone made Angel's chest tighten.

"Could it be magic? A creature, maybe, that affects the water above it like that?"

"Possibly. Whatever it was didn't get frightened by the stones I threw, so it's not threatened by predators. Glad I didn't try going in after it, if that's the case."

Chapter Fifteen
The Birthday Present

After they finished lunch, Gregor told Angel he wanted to go into town.

"I need to buy you a birthday present."

"You've done more than enough, Gregor. You don't need to buy me anything."

"I want to. You've got no choice." His expression was playful defiance.

She returned his tease with a pretend pout, which quickly gave way to a smile. *He must be feeling guilty about losing his temper, but I won't let him buy me much.* She thought longingly about the dress she'd tried on, but that was out of the question. *Maybe a book from Sir Benjamin's. Yeah, the castle book. That's perfect.*

"Ok, let's go to Sir Benjamin's. I want to tell him how much I like this." She held out the plant guide.

They packed up and went back to the farm, then saddled Romeo and Juliet.

"Don't you ever Gate into town?" she asked on the way.

"Only if I have something quick to do. I usually use it as an excuse to ride."

Sir Benjamin gave Angel a bear hug when Gregor told him it was her birthday. He blurted out, "Wait here a moment. I'll be right back!" and then disappeared out the front door. Angel raised her brow at Gregor.

He shrugged. "That's Sir B for ya."

Sir Benjamin returned with a cake from Miss Elsie's. Pink roses ringed the white icing. Gold icing in the shape of angel wings flanked a single candle. *Happy Birthday Angel* was arced in silver above the wings. Below, a harp made from silver and gold icing played the tune to "Happy Birthday."

Angel stared at the cake, touched. Her birthdays had all been just her and the Masons, with the exception of one sleepover. Which Jacob, of course, had ruined by putting a huge wolf spider in the shower, terrifying all her friends.

Sir Benjamin beamed at Angel. "Can't have a birthday without cake, my dear lady. Now blow out the candle and make a wish."

She closed her eyes. *I wish I could remember my childhood here.*

Sir Benjamin cut them each a piece of cake. Spike gobbled his up in one bite, then tucked his icing-covered nose under his wing and went back to sleep.

Angel and Sir Benjamin spent a while chatting over the puzzle—half the castle was put together, as well as all of Angel's tree. Sir Benjamin asked Angel about her life in America. She talked about the Masons, Josh and Jacob, and little Zack, just changing a few of the details.

"I went to visit a cousin of my own out there once, about forty years ago," Sir Benjamin said. "Hadn't seen each other since we were kids. They'd moved to Chicago—I think that's the name of the city—to get away from 'boring country life.' There was plenty of open space outside the town where they could live and not have their powers discovered, but they kept dragging me into the city. I hated it, and only stayed a few days. I guess I'm just a big ole country boy at heart."

Angel had been to Chicago once, to visit Mrs. Mason's aunt. She agreed with Sir Benjamin. It was way too crowded and noisy. "You definitely wouldn't want to go back these days then," she said.

Sir Benjamin looked off to the side, and a smile pushed out his rosy cheeks. "I met some people that thought they had discovered magic. They wore flowing dresses and tunics, and what they believed were magical symbols on leather strings around their necks. They wandered around telling everyone they could attain magic if we all worked together—not that peace and brotherhood aren't a wonderful thing—but they had their facts all wrong."

He chuckled. "They talked all the time about 'Flower Power' and hung around in the woods trying to 'capture the magic' of nature." He rolled his eyes. "Like you can get magic from sitting around under a tree. And from what I heard, they were always messing with what they thought were magical plants and gave themselves brain damage. Never bathed either." He crinkled his nose. "Good for a laugh, though."

Angel laughed so hard she snorted. "Hippies!" she spit out between giggles. Gregor stared at them both like they were crazy. Angel quit laughing when the bell announced another customer.

Two men entered, both maybe twenty years old. One wore jeans and a T-shirt and the other a tunic and pants that looked a lot like the outfits Kalek and his friends wore.

"We're looking for something with information about trapping," the one in the tunic said. A pointed ear poked out of his long dark hair.

"What do you need it for?" Sir Benjamin asked.

"We want to help with that Lunicor that's on the loose," said the man in the T-shirt. "I've lost two mares already, and Marin here has lost a dragon and his best hound."

"What's a Lunicor?" Angel whispered to Gregor. He didn't seem to recognize Marin, so she assumed he wasn't one of the Elves that had been at the temple that morning.

"It's basically a huge cat, sort of like a panther. They're usually black and are really good at hiding. Very few people have ever seen one. They can slice a horse wide open with their claws." He held his hands up, a good eight inches apart.

Angel cringed. *That's one ginormous panther.* "Is there really one out there?"

"Not that I know of. It might explain why the forest has been so quiet, but there'd be signs other than a few animals disappearing if a Lunicor was on the loose."

"Don't you want to leave that to the expert?" Sir Benjamin asked the men.

"Not at the rate we're losing animals. We know he's the best, but we can't just sit by and do nothing."

Sir Benjamin didn't have a book in stock that would help them, so he pulled out a catalog from behind the counter. He searched through until he found what he was looking for.

"I'm going to have to order this from another shop."

The man in the T-shirt counted out several pieces of paper money and coins. Sir Benjamin tapped the pile of money and it disappeared. Seconds later, a book appeared where the money had been.

"Cool!" Angel flushed with embarrassment when all heads turned toward her.

"She's from America," said Gregor.

Angel shot him a wicked look and went back to the puzzle.

Before they left, Gregor tried to buy Angel the castle book, but Sir Benjamin insisted on not charging him. Sir Benjamin handed Angel the book himself.

"But you gave me a book already."

"Doesn't count. I didn't know you were about to have a birthday." He smiled his Santa smile.

"Well, I guess I'm off the hook," Gregor said, but his face showed his disappointment.

On the walk back through the square, Angel caught sight of the kittens in the pet shop window.

"Please, can we go in and see them again…it *is* still my birthday, you know." She grabbed his hand and pulled him into the shop, but she didn't go to the kittens.

She found herself drawn toward the Boxer puppy in the corner. This time the puppy was awake, chewing on a bone while rolling around from stomach to back. The clamorous cawing of birds was distant and tinny, along with the metallic rattling of cages that drifted through her consciousness as she walked, eyes set on the Boxer puppy.

The puppy dropped her bone and ran to the wall of the pen, putting her big front paws on the rim of the gate. A white diamond marked her forehead above bright, chocolate brown eyes. Her tail wagged furiously, and she whimpered until Angel knelt down in front of the pen. Angel scratched the puppy behind the ears and down her neck and shoulders. The puppy turned her head and licked Angel's hand.

That same strange sensation washed over Angel again, making her stomach squeeze, and the floor shift under her feet. Only, a flash of a vision came, too—a big Boxer running after a ball in a fenced back yard. He wasn't a puppy, though. He was much larger, with a touch of gray marking his otherwise brown and black face.

"You okay, Angel?" Gregor's voice sounded as distant as the birds.

"Yes. I think I knew someone with a Boxer once. An old one with gray on his face. He was so sweet and playful, but I can't remember whose it was…"

She strained to place the memory. Was it a neighbor's dog she'd known when she lived with the Masons? Her perspective in the vision seemed rather low to the ground, as though she wasn't much taller than the dog himself. The familiarity was so strong, but she couldn't get a grip on it.

"Angel," Gregor said, bending close, his voice hushed. "*Your* family had a Boxer. He was full-grown when you were born, and already pretty old when you were lost. Your parents gave him to Old Man Brady to take care of when they left to search for you, but he died two years later. His name was—"

"Rusty!" The name burst from her mouth, and she let her knees drop forward to steady herself. *How did I know that?*

She sat there letting the puppy lick her hands, reveling in the realization that she had remembered something about her past—without the horrible ringing in her ears and nausea that came with her other visions.

Gregor stepped away, but Angel stayed with the puppy. The distant sounds of the birds and other animals scuffling in their cages returned to normal, and she heard Gregor at the register buying cat food for Shakespeare. The puppy rolled onto her back, and Angel scratched her belly, sending the puppy's back leg into a frenzy. She withdrew her hand and stood up when Gregor came back carrying a bag heavy with food. A leather strap dangled from his hand.

"Happy birthday." He held the leather strap out for Angel to take.

"What's this?"

She took the strap, then let go of all but one end, and the other end clunked loudly as a metal hook hit the floor. *A leash?*

"She's all yours." Gregor leaned over to pick up the puppy that wiggled to lick his face.

He handed the squirming puppy to Angel, and she nearly burst into tears. She couldn't find the words to thank him, so she shifted the puppy to one arm and threw the other around Gregor's neck.

"You're welcome already," he said, and backed away when Angel released him. A tear shone in the corner of his eye, but he squared his shoulders and walked out of the pet shop.

Angel smiled. *He thinks I didn't see that.* She carried the puppy out to the horses, holding the puppy's head down to avoid dog slobber up her nose.

When they reached the horses, Gregor fashioned a pouch from a blanket and slipped it over his shoulder like a sling.

Angel handed the puppy to him and he tucked her into the sling. "I think I'll name her Zoe," Angel said. If the puppy had been a boy, Angel would have named him Zack.

As she looked at Zoe that evening, curled up in front of the fireplace, Angel felt compelled to push for more memories. The fact that she'd made it through the vision of her old dog, Rusty, encouraged her in a way she'd not experienced since her return to the island.

"Gregor," she said, apprehension in her voice despite her newfound courage.

He looked up from his plate, still chewing, and waited for her to continue.

"What can you tell me about my parents?" She cleared her throat. "What they're like, I mean."

Gregor swallowed his food and contemplated her. "Are you sure you're ready? I mean, this has been really hard for you. You shouldn't push yourself."

Angel forced down a lump in her throat and nodded. "I think if I want to get past this, to make all the pain go away, I've got to start now. I can't keep being afraid."

"Okay, then. Let's go get comfortable, though. Then you tell me what you want to know." He rose and walked into the living room, taking a seat on the couch closest to the fireplace. Angel chose the big leather chair.

She curled her legs underneath her and leaned her head against the chair's back. The questions came tumbling out. "What are their names? What do they do? Did you know them well?" She steeled herself for the answers.

"Actually, not really well. I knew who they were because y'all didn't live very far from here. But your mom is pretty well known. Her name is Caryn and she's an Artist. Her Talent is painting things that become real. She's the one I mentioned that day in the library."

She snuggled deeper into the chair. *That's right*—he'd said, *"Her paintings really come alive."*

"You mean, she can paint someone and the painting would be able to talk?" It was strange talking about her mother in this way, but it felt like these details would fill the hole inside her, just a little.

"No, not exactly. When she paints something, like a vase or a flower, she can reach in and take it out of the painting. It would be as real as any other vase or flower. But she can't paint people and make them real, or anything else alive. Nothing with a soul."

"So she could paint gold, and it'd be real—or diamonds? She could make anything she wanted and pull it out of the painting?"

"I suppose, but I doubt she'd do something like that."

"But what if someone else got a hold of her painting? Could they pull it out?" It seemed like the greatest Talent—and it was *her* mother that possessed it.

"No, it has to be done by her. She's the one with the Talent. Just like you could never go through a Gate once I've closed it. As long as she leaves the painting alone, it's just a painting."

Angel realized she was sitting up stiffly, and tried to relax her posture again. She let Gregor's words sink in. No real memories came back, but she felt like she held a part of her mother inside her now, something they shared besides bloodline.

"And my father? What's he like?"

"A great guy. His name's William and he's an inventor. His Talent is Transforming. He can Transform any natural substance into any other. Like wood to stone, or vice versa."

"Like you did with that glass figurine?"

"No—that was just the shape. Your dad could have changed the figurine to metal, or wood."

"What kind of things does he invent?"

"Mostly tools. He can take scraps of wood and make all sorts of things, like that hammer of mine. Your dad carved that out of magical wood that has properties which make it never miss the nail it's aimed at. He made a saw for Old Man Brady that could cut through anything, and an axe that never needs sharpening. Sir Benjamin's got a lot of his pencils because they never run out of lead."

Gregor's hammer...

Now she wanted to run out to the barn and feel it in her hands again, smooth wood that had been shaped by her father.

She tried to picture her parents' faces, but the images were still locked away in a part of her brain that she couldn't reach.

"What do they look like?"

"Your mom looks most like you, I think. She's got your same hair and eyes. And your dad is really tall, with blond hair. You look a little like him, but definitely more like your mom."

She searched her memories for something that matched the descriptions of her parents, but nothing correlated. She longed to feel connected to them, to feel like they were already a family. The hole inside of her still gaped, but hearing about her parents made it believable that someday it would be filled.

"Gregor..." She was more nervous about hearing his next answer than anything so far. She closed her eyes and plunged forward. "I think I need to know one more thing."

She could hear Gregor shift in his seat, and she opened her eyes. He was sitting slightly forward, exuding a calmness that seemed to amplify her anxiety. The answer to her question made no difference to him, of course, but it would alter the very fabric of her existence.

"Go ahead," he said.

"Okay." Her heart pounded, but she tried to ignore it and looked down at Zoe, still fast asleep. The puppy's steady breathing calmed her enough to continue. "I need to know my name. I know it can't be Angel or you would have made me change it like you did my hair. I was afraid to ask before, but I think I'm ready now.

"I've fantasized for as long as I can remember about finding my real home. I love the Masons. And I miss Zack." She choked on her little brother's name and her eyes filled with tears. "But this place calls to me. I feel so at home here. I know this is where I belong, even if my parents never make it back." She felt Shakespeare's fur tickle her toes as he rubbed against the chair, and she leaned down and picked him up. She squeezed him to her chest, wishing she could hug Zack one more time.

Gregor still leaned forward, and searched Angel's eyes. He must have seen what he needed to. "Your name is Anna. Anna Kleidon."

Angel tried the name on for size. "Anna Kleidon." No fireworks or trumpets blared, but she felt the name slide into place somewhere in the storehouse of her brain. The fog still obscured the rest of her memories, but the name was there, and she knew it belonged. The name for the person she had been, and still was deep inside somewhere. The person she would become again.

That night, as the crickets sang through the open window, she thought of Zack, wondering what kind of insect he'd found that day. *If only I could bring him here. He'd go crazy wanting to collect everything.* It was impossible…but she could dream.

And dream she did. Of running into her parents' arms…and hearing them say… *"Anna."*

Chapter Sixteen
The Verses

Angel pumped her legs forward and back, willing herself to go higher. She leaned back, legs extended, until gravity took hold and pulled her toward the ground, then up, up, up, tucking her legs under the swing. She swung forward again in a long arc, hair blown into her face, as the earth beneath her feet swept past in a blur. This must be what it feels like to fly…

A woman's voice called from inside the house, "Anna…Time for dinner!…"

Angel let her feet hit the ground, dragging them across the dirt and grass to slow herself down. She didn't want to stop, but Mama was making her favorite…

The swing had barely stopped moving when she felt something grab her wrist…

Angel's eyes popped open, and she bolted upright, something still tugging at her wrist—

Zoe.

"You scared me half to death!" Angel's heart pounded against her ribs, but she couldn't be angry at that sweet face. She got out of bed, and began her walk to the bathroom, when her foot landed in something very *wet*.

"Oh, Zoe!"

Zoe shrank to the floor, head drooping, eyes sagging and pleading for Angel's forgiveness. Angel glanced at the clock. "Not your fault, little girl. I overslept." She knelt down and welcomed Zoe into her arms. She kissed the puppy's forehead and tucked her under one arm. Then she waved her hand over the puddle, gathering it into a shiny liquid ball, and sent it through the window. It landed with a *splat* in the yard.

After a quick shower, Angel went into the kitchen and found scones and honey on the table, but the house was quiet and still. Zoe found her food bowl and munched away. Angel grabbed a scone, drizzled honey on top of it, and walked to the kitchen window to look for Gregor in the pasture. He appeared at the edge of the forest path. She watched him draw nearer—his face was set in a scowl.

She jumped away from the window when his gaze turned toward the kitchen window. He entered through the back door, the scowl replaced by his usual cheerful expression except for a slight shadow around his eyes.

"Finally up, I see."

"Yeah, Zoe dragged me out of sleep."

She reached down to feed the puppy a bite of scone. Shakespeare rounded the corner, shot an annoyed look at Zoe, and walked straight to his food bowl. He turned up his nose at the contents and wound himself around Angel's ankles. She filled a saucer of milk for him, despite Gregor's condemning gaze.

"You spoil him. He may be king of the castle, but that food costs money."

"I'm sorry," she said with feigned innocence. "But I've got to let him know Zoe hasn't replaced him." Shakespeare looked at them with satisfaction and lapped his milk.

Angel sat down at the table and reached for another scone. "Have a nice walk?" She winced as the words left her mouth. *Oops, why did I just say that?*

Gregor's brow furrowed, and he skulked over to the icebox.

"Fine." He wrenched opened a jar of milk, poured himself a glass, and plopped down at the kitchen table.

"Sorry." What could have possibly upset him in the forest? It was his favorite place on the island. "Did something happen?"

"I had business to attend to." His expression told her that she'd better not ask what it was.

There was a sudden crack of thunder in the distance, and then another only moments later and much closer. Gregor got up from the table and looked out the window. Angel glanced out too and saw dark clouds gathering in the sky over the forest.

"Well, let's get outside and get the animals fed at least." Gregor still peered out the kitchen window. "Storm's coming. Can't complain, though. We really need this rain."

It hadn't rained all month, and Gregor had resorted to condensing the moisture in the air into little rain clouds that hovered over the garden, watering the vegetables. Too much longer with no rain, and the grass would suffer too.

The moment they stepped into the house after tending the animals, it began to pour.

They closed all the windows to keep out the lashing rain, and settled into the living room. The blackness of the sky extended in every direction. Angel slumped into the big leather chair. *We're going to be stuck inside for hours.*

Zoe's energy soon had her bounding around the living room, so Gregor tied some old socks into knots for her to play with. They kept her occupied for all of ten minutes, and then she whimpered at the door to be let out. That desire snuffed out as another thunderbolt cracked and she dashed under the leather chair, shivering. Angel pulled her out and wrapped her in a blanket, then curled into the chair again, cradling the puppy protectively. Shakespeare lay in a ball on his cushioned chair, sleeping.

The thundering eventually became an indistinct rumble, but the rain continued hard and heavy. Angel stroked Zoe's belly, and soon the puppy fell asleep in her arms.

"Well, what are we going to do?"

Without answering, Gregor pulled out a checker set and began setting it up on the floor. Angel carefully got up and set the bundled Zoe in the seat of the leather chair.

They played six games before Angel thought she'd die of boredom.

"This never has been my favorite game," she said and got up to scratch the still-sleeping Zoe's ears. The puppy woke and licked Angel's nose, then jumped from the chair. Angel found one of the rolled-up socks and tossed it across the room. The storm still raged outside, but the thunder had diminished and sounded farther away.

Gregor brushed his hair out of his eyes several times as he put away the checker set, and Angel realized that nervous habit had disappeared shortly after she arrived. She watched him push his bangs aside again. *He hates being stuck in here more than I do.*

Angel scanned the room looking for inspiration—*anything to pass the time*—and spied the pictures on the mantle. "Do you have any photo albums?"

Gregor looked at her as if he didn't understand, then a smile showed in his eyes, if not on his lips. "I think there are some in my parents' room." His voice lifted. "I haven't looked at them in ages. You want to see 'em?"

"Yeah!"

Gregor headed up the stairs, and Zoe scrambled after him.

"Zoe, get back here!" called Angel, but Zoe just stopped on the step without returning to her.

"She can come up with us." Gregor continued up the stairs and Angel followed.

Gregor's parents' bedroom was exactly what she expected. Traditional and elegant, with a king size canopy bed covered by a hand-made quilt, a cedar chest centered in front of the footboard. Matching nightstands flanked the bed, and an armoire and bookshelf completed the set.

Gregor opened the cedar chest and pulled out several photo albums. He sat on the bed and opened one.

Angel hesitated in the doorway.

"What's wrong?" Gregor asked. "You're the one who wanted to look at these."

"I feel strange in here. Like I'm imposing."

Gregor waved her over. "For all practical purposes, this is your house too right now. You're welcome anywhere. If my parents were alive, they'd be saying the same thing."

"Okay, okay, you're right. I'm being silly."

She walked over to the bed and sat on the edge, forgetting her insecurity when her eyes caught sight of the pictures in the album. Zoe tugged on her pants leg, and Angel lifted the puppy into her lap.

The album held pictures of Gregor as a baby, standing in his crib, his silver-flecked eyes full of laughter. His cherub cheeks reminded her of Zack when he first came to live with the Masons. Zack had grown so fast back then. How long would it be until she saw him again? *How much will he have changed?* She pushed the ache aside and focused on the pictures in front of her.

As the pages turned, the infant-Gregor grew into toddler-Gregor, and the crib was replaced by a mattress set on the floor.

"My parents had to get rid of the crib when my Talent manifested. It was made from the wood of a magical birch tree and I could Gate right through the sides. I only landed outside the crib, but my parents were afraid I'd end up out in the forest someday."

Angel found herself jealous of his ability to recall his early childhood—even those he knew only from his parents' stories. *All I have are foggy memories I can't even reach.*

"You can Gate through cut wood, not just trees?" she asked. Zoe was wiggling in her lap, so she leaned over and set the puppy on the floor.

"Only if it's from a magical tree. And I can Gate through just about any part of a tree, even ordinary ones, as long as it's still connected to the trunk. The main branches, even the roots. That's why there's no trees on the property. I could've ended up anywhere just playing in my own yard." Gregor conjured the knotted sock from downstairs and tossed it onto the floor for the puppy to play with.

The pictures moved on to family picnics, picking vegetables in the garden, and vacationing at a lake. They looked happy...truly happy. A tear formed in the corner of Angel's eye. *It's not fair. He didn't deserve to lose them.*

She couldn't envy Gregor. Unlike hers, the part of *his* life that was stolen away would never be returned.

Gregor slid off the edge of the bed and began searching through the other contents of the cedar chest. He came across his first shoes, a hand-crocheted afghan made by his grandmother, and several mementos from his parents' wedding.

He stopped rifling around, then shifted as if trying to get a better grip on something and pulled out an intricately carved wooden box. He brought it over to the bed and set it on the mattress.

"I forgot all about this. It belonged to my father."

The box was made of magical wood, judging by the metallic grain. Strange markings circled the sides of the lid, and a clasp fixed it to the bottom.

A forest scene was carved into the lid, so detailed it appeared nearly three-dimensional. The leaves of the trees and the feathers covering the birds popped out like tiny holograms. A multitude of animals peeked from behind the foliage with miniscule wooden eyes. But the focal point was an exquisite unicorn inlaid with a silvery substance that shimmered like metallic light.

"What is it?"

"Inside this is an ancient sacred book. My father was very into history.

I always wanted to have his passion for it, but it was like my brain just shut off when I tried to read about it. Even when I *wanted* to listen to him, the words went in one ear and out the other." A half smile formed on his face and he shook his head slightly. "It was the one thing about me that always frustrated him."

"I know what you mean," said Angel. "History was my worst subject in school. It was the only class I ever got into real trouble in. Once I was doodling on my sneakers and the teacher stopped the whole lecture and walked over to see what I was doing. It was the most embarrassing thing…"

"Well, I just wish I'd paid more attention to him, then I'd at least be able to tell you more about this. All I know is it's very old, and it was really important to my dad. He rarely took it out. I don't even know where he got it. He told me some of the stories from the book, but they didn't make much sense to me when I was a kid. Most of them were about wars and people that seemed to have nothing to do with each other."

Gregor ran his hand over the engraving, letting his fingers glide across as though clearing the way for his eyes to get a better view. Then his fingers slid over the side of the lid, and he cautiously lifted the clasp. The leather-bound book inside was plain and tattered.

Gregor gingerly lifted the book out of the box, and began leafing through the pages. They were thin, but not frail, and the writing matched the odd markings on the lid of the box.

"What language is that?"

"I don't know."

Angel pointed to a passage underlined in faded ink. "Do you think your dad did that?"

"I have no idea. He wasn't the type to write in books, so I doubt it." He kept flipping the pages, and they found several more underlined passages.

Gregor looked up from the book and tapped his finger on the open page. "Hold on…I think I know something that will help." He set the book down on the bed. After checking both nightstands, he sat back down and showed Angel what looked like a three-inch wide magnifying glass with no handle.

"It's an interpreter lens. If you hold it over the page it will show you the words in any language. I forgot my dad even had this. He used it all the time to read through old books. Here, try it."

Angel took the lens from him and held it over the open book. As she moved the lens across the page, the symbols morphed into written English, with just a slightly different grammatical structure. The sections were titled like chapters and divided into numbered passages.

Gregor was right about the tales of war and family lineages. But the underlined passages were statements of comfort and encouragement. Angel flipped page after page, until she found a section that looked like a poem.

The poem was underlined as well, with a perfectly drawn box surrounding it.

Angel guided the interpreter lens over the poem while Gregor occupied Zoe with the knotted sock. The poem didn't rhyme, but of course that aspect may have been lost in the translation. Even in English, the words didn't make much sense, but a whisper of foreboding washed over Angel as she followed the verses. Her hand froze when she reached the last line, and her eyes remained locked on the words.

"Gregor, you have to see this!" She heard Zoe's toenails skidding across the polished wood floor, and the thump of Gregor's footsteps.

"Here," Angel said when she felt the mattress sink. "What does this mean? Can it mean…me?"

Gregor looked over her shoulder and read the words of the poem aloud.

"Powers given in birth
Taken on eternal in death,
As the bearer stands on the threshold.

The place of beginning
The place of ending
Completing the circle.

The spot is marked
By the flame
That burns with no fuel.

The key to the key being found,
The lock can be opened

126

By the key handed over
To the rightful heir.

Inside lies treasure
Beyond all measure
Happily gained when all else is lost.

The guardian shall leave his post
When the hidden path is unmasked
And the truth has been exposed by the substance of man.
The Finder's work will then be complete.

"Wow. The Finder…I don't know. It *is* a very rare Talent, but this could be talking about something that's already happened, maybe even hundreds of years ago." He moved from behind her and sat on the bed where they could face each other.

Gregor's words made perfect sense, logically. But Angel had a sinking feeling in the pit of her stomach. There was something about the other words in the verses, not just the reference to "The Finder." She couldn't write it off so easily.

"What about the first verse," she said. "Powers taken in death. Isn't that what Dawric was doing when he killed? That's what you said, isn't it?"

"Well, yeah, but he wasn't taking the powers on eternally. They were temporary, remember?"

He had a point, but there had to be more to it. She read the verses again. *This can't be coincidence. I'm found by the guy who just happens to have a rare copy of an ancient book with a poem about a Finder and powers being stolen, which according to Gregor hasn't happened in ages on this island. This has to mean something…*

"Gregor, I know you think I'm off-base, but look at the rest of this. It's talking about something that is locked away. What if there's something out there that could give Dawric the ability to keep powers permanently? You told me yourself, that there are magical objects that would be dangerous if Dawric got his hands on them. Your neighbor even believed it enough to scare my parents into telling everyone I was dead. That's got to be something really powerful, don't you think?" Angel looked pointedly at him.

"But what are the chances of me having the very book that tells about it, and you being here to read it right at the time all this is happening?"

"*That's my point*. What are the chances? This is not coincidence. I bet if we searched, we'd find something about this. I bet you anything there's an object, or a potion, or something that would make Dawric able to steal someone's powers and keep them. It would explain why he was after me—you can't deny that."

Gregor's eyes focused as though he were deep in thought. He ran his hand through his hair after a few moments, and Angel knew her words had hit their mark.

"Okay, it might explain that. But regardless of Dawric's motivations, it's all over now. He's gone and thinks you're dead. All that happened years ago. If this were really a prophecy about you, it would've happened back then."

Gregor and his logic!

"Maybe everything that happened was just to keep me out of danger so I could do the work I've been called to do. I was being protected, but now it's time for me to finish, or Dawric really could find a way to get powers and the danger would return. Right now, he could've just gone back to his old life, but if he found me once, he might be able to find me again. If we stop it all before he does, then no one'll be in danger."

Angel's heart began to race with the prospect. Not from fear. She felt like she had a real purpose. She'd been given her Talent for a reason, and it wasn't circumstance that had brought her back home.

"I'm not saying you *are*…" said Gregor, "but *if* you're right, then what are you expecting? I mean, do you think you're here to Find whatever he's looking for before he does?"

"Well, that would be the most logical—"

"Come on, you don't even know what he's after. Which means you can't Find it. What if it's not even a thing? It could be a place, or a person. And it could be well out of the range of your Talent."

Angel breathed in through her teeth, and exhaled slowly. She couldn't let him discourage her.

He reached out and touched her arm. "Okay, I shouldn't give you such a hard time. But you've got to admit it sounds like a stretch. I just don't want you getting worked up over nothing."

"It's not nothing. I know it's not. I can't explain to you *how*, but I know."

He leaned back against the headboard and crossed his arms. "So, what do you want from me then?"

"Just help me look for the answer to this. The verses practically fell into our laps. The rest of the information could be anywhere, but if this is real, then we'll find it. If not, I'll feed all the animals for a month."

Gregor cracked a smile, then opened his mouth and laughed in earnest. Angel felt her cheeks pulling back, and she giggled. The giggle grew into a laugh, and soon she and Gregor were both holding their sides.

When they had both stopped laughing, Gregor looked out the window at the ominous gray clouds and sheets of rain beating against the glass. "Well, we've got plenty of time to work on it. It doesn't look like this is going to let up any time soon. But let's eat lunch first."

Angel looked at the clock on the nightstand. *Two o'clock? We've been up here that long?* She saw that Zoe had found a spot in the corner of the room and gone to sleep.

Gregor put the ancient book back into its box, and he and Angel stood, the mattress springs creaking. Zoe's head popped up off of her oversized paws, and she started whimpering.

Angel hurriedly carried Zoe to the front door, but a bolt of lightning struck as the puppy stepped out. Zoe peed all over the porch. Angel washed it off by directing rain toward the puddle, and laughed. *I finally get the magic I've always fantasized about, and I'm using it to clean up puppy pee. Again.*

After lunch, they started with the only resource they had—the supply of books throughout the house. They eliminated the novels and cookbooks and such, but books like *Infusion of Magical Properties* and *The Physical Constraints of Magic* were definite possibilities.

Hours passed as they pored over pages, even opening the dreaded history text.

Angel went to bed that night listening to the pouring rain and distant thunder. Her fatigue weakened her resolve, and she began to wonder if Gregor had been right. Maybe she was reading too much into a meaningless passage. Disappointment washed over her as she fell asleep.

~Seeking Solitude~

The storm had forced him to leave. He couldn't stand being trapped in that windowless room for another second, with those…things. He took the scientist's notes and pored over them, searching for something that would free him from his dependence on the little mongrel. Without the girl and her power, he needed the scientist's help. Pure science he could handle on his own; but this required magic.

There had to be more that the scientist was not telling him, but he would not force cooperation. It was too risky. He'd already given the scientist enough help to continue the research without him. If he pushed too hard, the scientist might expose him. The townsfolk might believe he'd died seven years ago, but they'd be easy enough to convince otherwise.

And he couldn't take them all on at once. Not until he'd gotten what he'd come for.

Chapter Seventeen
The History Lesson

The rain confined Angel and Gregor to another day indoors. But a good night's sleep had renewed Angel's determination, and soon she sat in the floor surrounded by open books.

Gregor showed more enthusiasm toward the search, but Angel knew his motivations were conflicting. *He's bored, and he just wants to prove I'm wrong.*

"Maybe we should be focusing on the place where the object is found," Angel said. "There seems to be more clues about that." She flipped through Gregor's history book, while Zoe hopped around, nipping at the pages.

"I don't know how we're supposed to figure out the place by these verses," said Gregor. "The place of beginning and ending, the spot marked by the flame that burns with no fuel. Nothing burns without fuel. It's ludicrous. How are you going to get a picture of that in your head to focus on?"

"But what about the key? I know I can picture a key."

"How do you know *which* key? Out of all the ones in the world, c'mon. And according to the verse we have to find the 'key to the key,' whatever that means." Gregor snapped a book shut, and threw it aside.

"Well, then the lock. It's a treasure box or something."

"What, are we pirates now?" Gregor scrunched half his face, squinting one eye. "Arrrgh, ye land-lubbin' fool."

"You're a pain!" Angel turned another page and Zoe nipped at the corner. "Stop it, Zoe!" She shouted a little louder than she'd intended. The puppy ran to Gregor and jumped into his lap.

Angel flipped another page, ignoring Zoe. This was worse than when she tried to identify Horatio. And they were running out of books.

"Why can't we ask Sir Benjamin? He might know something that could help us," she said with a slightly better rein on her temper.

"You know if we ask him for help, he's going to want to know what we're up to. And you're supposed to be dead, *remember?*" A snarl was woven into Gregor's voice.

"But we trust him, don't we? He wouldn't tell anyone, I'm sure."

"Of course we can trust him. That's not the issue. He's like a father to me. Do you think he'd have said nothing about all my 'camping' trips if he'd known what I was really up to? He'd just talk us out of this, Angel."

"But maybe we're supposed to. Maybe…"

"No. Out of the question." He paused and ran his hands through his hair for the fiftieth time that morning. "I shouldn't be telling you this…but he had a son of his own who was killed years ago."

Angel opened her mouth to ask how, but Gregor answered her before the words had a chance to form.

"I can see what you're thinking, but it wasn't Dawric. It was years before that."

Angel sat, dumbfounded, holding a page in half-turn.

"Okay…so we don't ask Sir Benjamin."

She turned to the next chapter of the history book and found herself staring at a map of Toch Island. She read the page that told about the establishment of the island and the University where Sir Benjamin had taught.

An Elven scholar had founded the University in the year 1410. He'd traveled the world studying architecture and modeled the main building after an Arabian palace. He included a museum in the design, with a permanent display of Elven artifacts and areas for rotating displays such as art, weapons, and recovered treasures. An enormous library housed books dating back hundreds of years.

"I completely forgot to tell you," Angel blurted out. "I met Dr. Damian, from the University. He came into Sir Benjamin's last time. He invited us to go see his research."

Gregor squinted at her. "Is he the one with the *freaky* blue eyes?"

Angel nodded, but sneered at him. *You don't have to be snotty.*

"You've met him, then?" she asked.

"Yeah, the year before Sir Benjamin retired. He seemed *nervous* to me."

"It was his first year teaching, for crying out loud. You'd be nervous, too. And his eyes have nothing to do with what he's like. He seemed very friendly to me. Some might call you nervous, y'know. You never sit still for more than a minute."

"I'm not all fluttery like he is, thank you very much." Gregor imitated Dr. Damian's rapid speech with the effect of looking like a rabbit.

Angel ignored him. "Well, I'd like to go see his research. And the University, especially the museum. Have you ever been? You told me there weren't any museums near you, remember?" She eyed him teasingly.

"Sorry, forgot about that one. It's not very big, and it's all pretty much stuff I've seen before. But if you'd *really* like to go…I *suppose* we can plan a visit for when the rain clears up…" He huffed. "If it ever does. In the meantime, let's get these books put away and make dinner. I'm starving. And all this sitting still is making me *nervous.*"

Thunder rumbled in the distance as Angel rested her head against the pillow. Drowsiness forced her eyes shut, and a hazy picture drifted into her mind.

She stood in an area of the forest she didn't recognize, although she knew without a doubt she'd been there before. She was looking for something, and pointed excitedly when she spied a perfectly formed blossom. "There! That one! Paint that one, Mama. I want it for my nightstand." She gripped the comforting warmth of a soft finger with her other small hand.

As with her other flashbacks, she couldn't see her mother's face. It was something, at least, and she let the continuing rainfall lull her to sleep.

On the third day, Angel didn't even attempt to persuade Gregor to do more searching. With the books lined up on their shelves, and the rain finally abating, she looked forward to the outdoors and sunshine.

She spent the morning sketching. She'd created a good rendering of Zoe tugging on the knotted sock and captured the crinkle above the puppy's nose that she thought was so cute. She'd even talked Gregor into sitting for her one time, but he squirmed more than Zoe, and made every excuse to get up and move around.

Angel let Zoe out after lunch, and the puppy burst through the kitchen, tracking little muddy paw prints all over the floor. Angel evaporated the water from the mud, swept up the dry sand with a wave of her hand, and walked into the living room. Zoe was already asleep in front of the fireplace, still sodden and muddy. Shakespeare slunk over and sniffed the puppy, and gave Angel a look that said he was quite glad he had a nice dry litter box to use in weather like this.

"Zoe needs a real walk," Angel said. "She's getting as anxious as you. Maybe after dinner, if the rain has stopped, we can all go together."

"Good idea. Being cooped up like this is starting to make me tense." Gregor said as he paced in front of the window.

"Starting to?" She laughed. "One more day of this and you'd turn to stone."

Gregor's nerves were an advantage for Angel as they played checkers in the afternoon.

"Had enough?" she asked as Gregor kinged another one of her men.

"Enough of the inside of this house, for sure." He raised his head and peered out the window.

The treetops were just visible through the rain-streaked glass. The window framed them like a picture, but Angel was reminded of how vast the forest was. She missed it too. *Who else is feeling the same way as us? Kalek must be going stir crazy too. Of course, he can just play the outdoors for himself...*

"Hang on." Angel jumped up and ran to her room. She grabbed the rosebud Kalek had given her, then dashed back to the living room. "I shoulda thought of this before. We can listen to this and at least it'll *feel* like we're outside."

Gregor's expression instantly turned grim. "That *thing* will not make *me* feel anything but contempt. That group of vagabonds needs to stay out of my forest."

Angel couldn't believe what she was hearing. Kalek had spoken harshly that day at the Temple, but Gregor had admitted he'd over-reacted. He hadn't said a negative thing about Kalek since. Of course, that may have been because Gregor hadn't mentioned him at all—she couldn't remember. Still, he was being ridiculous.

"*You* are the one who introduced us, remember? *You* asked them to play for me! What is your *issue*?" She held the rose as if she needed to protect it from Gregor's words.

"It was a mistake. I should never have taken you there. I—"

"It's because of Siophra, isn't it?" She didn't know why she felt so defensive; she'd only met Kalek once. But Gregor wasn't being honest. They were supposed to trust each other, and if he had feelings for Siophra, why couldn't he just tell her about it?

"You went to see her the other day, didn't you? I saw you coming out of the forest with a foul look on your face. You're in love with her, aren't you? And she doesn't feel the same?" She glared confidently at him.

That must be it. He's in love with Siophra and he was just taking it out on Kalek because Kalek defended her. She didn't know what Kalek's words to Gregor meant, but she was sure that someone with that close of a connection to nature, someone who could bring out the beauty of the forest like that, couldn't have meant whatever Gregor thought he did.

Gregor rose, his face red, hands balled into fists. "Siophra is the most loving person I've ever met!"

"Then it's Kalek…He's in love with her, too, or someth—"

"KALEK NEEDS TO LEARN TO MIND HIS OWN BUSINESS, AND SO DO YOU!" Gregor stormed off to his room, slamming the door behind him.

Gregor didn't come out of his room for dinner. Angel made herself a sandwich, but she couldn't eat it and she dropped it into Zoe's bowl. Shakespeare rubbed against her calves until she picked him up.

"Maybe you should go talk to him." She scratched under his long chin.

After cleaning up the dinner dishes, she decided to take Zoe for a walk herself. She left a note for Gregor on the table, assuring him that they'd be back before dark.

As they entered the main path, Angel knew what she needed to do. She followed the path straight to the clearing with the old ruins, Zoe running playfully along the way. Angel tugged on Zoe's leash to keep the over-excited puppy headed in the right direction.

The temple was deserted when she arrived. Disappointed, she let Zoe off her leash to run.

"You stay right here in this clearing, young lady."

Zoe pounced on a cluster of flowers, scattering an array of colorful butterflies.

Angel climbed the steps of the ancient building and looked closely at the ruins. The enormous height of the walls amazed her. She ran her hand over the door. *This place must have been magnificent at one time.* The wood was rough but beautiful, with an intricate grain that didn't match any kind of wood Angel was familiar with. She noticed markings above the doorway on either side of the gargoyle, but they seemed to be in a different language, and were so worn they would have been unreadable anyway.

"Hello, Angel."

She turned from the door with a start. Kalek stood at the base of the steps, his mass of tangled curls aglow with the golden light of the setting sun. He was dressed just as he had been when she'd met him before, and his lean legs were set shoulder-width apart in the damp grass, his arms crossed over his chest. Tattoos she hadn't noticed before peeked out from under the leather bands on his forearm.

"Zoe! You are supposed to *warn* me if someone comes."

The puppy ran to Kalek and put her paws on his leg, begging to be petted. He scratched the top of her head, then held out his hand. A ball materialized in his palm and he threw it for her to fetch.

"What brings you here, my lady?" His voice was cool and regal—incongruent with his rock musician appearance.

"This place is beautiful. Is it a Temple?"

Why had she thought this was a good idea? She didn't know Kalek at all. Why would he be honest with her about Siophra if Gregor wouldn't?

"Yes it is. Or I should say, it *was*. But you didn't come here to find out that."

He eyed her and stepped closer to the stone steps, but didn't join her where she stood by the door.

136

Angel swallowed and crossed her arms. "Who is Siophra?"

"My sister."

"Why did you talk to Gregor that way when he asked about her? Until this morning I thought you liked each other."

Kalek narrowed his eyes. "It's much more complicated than that."

"But aren't you friends? You obviously know each other well."

"Gregor hasn't told you anything about us?" He moved forward another smidge.

"Nothing."

Kalek scowled, but didn't comment.

"Please, can't you tell me? I hate to see Gregor brooding like this. He won't talk to me about it at all. I just want to understand. Please."

Kalek stood, considering for a moment. "All right," he said finally. "Have a seat. Apparently, there's much you don't know about Gregor, and the Elven of this island."

He joined her on the Temple platform, and they sat facing each other, cross-legged, their faces barely touched by the filtered light of the sun now hanging low in the sky.

His words flowed out smooth and even, as though he was reciting a story he'd memorized.

"Generations ago, Elves and humans freely married, although it wasn't very common. There was one particular Elven male who married a human female. They were very much in love. She gave birth to twin boys, and named them Rastus and Rurik. The boys were the couple's pride and joy. Rastus was technically the first born, having arrived three minutes before his brother, so he was given the family heirloom. He was born with blond hair and blue eyes, and human ears, while Rurik had dark hair, and Elven ears and eyes."

His own Elven eyes shone like polished obsidian in the dusk.

"The boys remained best of friends throughout their entire childhood, but Rurik couldn't escape thoughts of a better life. Rastus was content with farm life, and decided at a young age to continue in his father's footsteps. He loved working the land and spending his time in the serenity of nature. Elves have a gift when it comes to nature."

A teasing smirk appeared on his face, and Angel remembered how the trees and wildlife had responded to his music.

"When Rastus and Rurik were still young men, their parents passed away. They were both heartbroken, of course. As different as they were, they shared a deep love for family. But Rurik became restless with his desire for a different life—a life of power and riches that farming would never provide.

"He approached Rastus with his plan to sell his half of the farm and move away. Rastus became furious. He refused to allow anyone outside of the family to own even part of the farm. He considered it a disgrace to his parents, and knew if he allowed it that it would only be a matter of time before the farm would have to be sold off altogether.

"The young men fought. In the end, Rastus gave Rurik the family heirloom, which was very valuable, as payment for Rurik's half of the farm. He never regretted giving up his status as first-born, but was angry that he'd had to sell the heirloom to Rurik in order to keep the farm. Each man felt the other had betrayed his parents. They parted ways, never speaking to each other again."

Something resembling anger traveled across Kalek's face.

"Rastus continued working his family's farm, and eventually married, having a family of his own. Rurik returned to the Elves in the mountains, gaining power and wealth in their community. He married an Elven princess, and they started a family as well. From that point on, each brother's family proudly held that theirs was the better life. And pride can be a characteristic that is very hard to give up." He spoke with an edge that told Angel pride was something he'd dealt with himself.

"So, did they decide that Elves and humans shouldn't marry or something?" she asked. "That's why Gregor is so upset—he wants to marry Siophra, doesn't he? But he knows it's against Elven law." She lifted her knees and wrapped her arms around them. *No wonder he's so angry.*

"Not exactly." He shook his head slightly. "There was never a law made about such marriages, although they did become much less common. It's more of a personal issue between Gregor and my father."

What? Why did Kalek just tell her that big, long story, just to say that it was between Gregor and Kalek's father?

Kalek's eyes glinted mysteriously. "The last descendant of Rastus still works his farm to this day." He sat quietly, seemingly watching Angel for a hint of realization. Then, he said the words she knew were coming.

"Your cousin. Gregor."

"And what about Rurik's descendants?"

She thought she knew the answer to this, too, but it still made her heart skip a beat when Kalek bowed his head to her, his mass of curls spilling forward and obscuring his face.

"Kalek Halvard, at your service, my lady."

So, Kalek's father would never let Siophra marry Gregor because he's Rastus' descendant. And Gregor must know. The family heirloom lost, huh? No wonder he changed the subject so fast when she asked about it.

"And this family feud has been going on all this time. For generations? Do you agree with this?" Her voice came out sharp and accusing, and her heartbeat quickened.

"No, but I must…respect my father's wishes. Everyone must…" Anger flared behind his eyes and then extinguished. "Besides, their marriage would be inappropriate in other ways as well."

"You mean because they're, like…cousins?"

"No," he said with a sigh. He stretched his legs out over the edge of the steps and leaned against a broken pillar. "The ancestors we share lived so many generations ago that it's not an issue anymore."

"Then why can't they marry?"

"It's Elven custom that when a female reaches eighteen she has one year to choose a husband. Her suitor must be *of age* himself—at least eighteen. Siophra will be turning nineteen in three months. Gregor, however, doesn't turn eighteen until November. Marrying Gregor would be two disgraces at once as far as my father is concerned."

"One month's difference! And an ancient family feud…that's why they can't marry? That's absurd!"

Kalek didn't seem angered by her comment, but he said firmly, "It's Elven custom, and I don't question it. I *can't* question it. Gregor is a good man, and he loves Siophra. I'd be happy if the feud ended, and if Gregor was of age in time to marry Siophra. But as I said, I must respect my father's wishes and the customs of our people."

"Have you told Gregor how you feel about him marrying your sister, that it's not him personally?" She understood that Kalek had to respect his father's wishes, but he didn't have to destroy his own friendship with Gregor.

"Yes, and he believed me at first. I even spoke to my father on his behalf. But my father wouldn't hear of it, and told me in no uncertain terms I'd better keep the two separated. For a while, I looked the other way when they spent time together, and hid it from my father, but…recent events have forced me to step in."

Now she could see why Gregor had gotten upset at the mention of Kalek's name.

"What events?"

Kalek sighed again, as if what he was about to say burdened him.

"Siophra's heart belongs to Gregor, and she's found it difficult to choose a suitor. So my father has chosen for her. The wedding will be on her nineteenth birthday. There is nothing I can do to stop it. Gregor needs to end it now, while their hearts are still able to mend."

"Can't you do something? I mean, Siophra's an adult. What if she chooses to marry Gregor and leave the Elven society? Your father would be angry, but he can't control her life!" Angel was beginning to really see Gregor's side on this. This girl should be willing to stand up for him if she loved him. And Kalek was a grown man. If their father was being unreasonable, it was his problem—it shouldn't affect them at all.

Kalek sat up straight and faced her, his eyes shadowed with fear that he tried to hide by intensifying his gaze.

"You have no idea how powerful my father is," he said simply, and broke his gaze with a finality that told her he'd tell her no more.

In one fluid motion he stood and leaned against a pillar, facing away from her. His grace and agility were such an odd contrast to his tangled hair, leather and tattoos.

Angel felt a tugging on her shirt and puppy paws digging into her leg. She picked Zoe up and rose to her feet. Kalek remained leaning against the pillar, still looking off toward the darkened forest. She stepped over to the Temple door and looked up at the worn engraving.

"What does this inscription say?"

Kalek didn't answer immediately, but Angel waited.

He finally turned to face her again. "Bound on Earth as bound in Heaven. Loosed on Earth as loosed in Heaven."

"What does it mean?"

Kalek stepped over to her, looked closely at the inscription as if he hadn't just told her the words, then put his hand on her shoulder and gently led her to the edge of the steps.

"Like I said, this was a Temple at one time. A very special Temple. *Mori Zede*—Temple of Justice. Criminals were brought here for sentencing, led blindfolded down a trail through the forest. That's where we got the name for our band. They used to call it 'The Masked Road.'

"Anyway, the criminals were given one week in the Temple to cleanse their soul. It was believed that if they succeeded, they would be taken straight to the Realm Beyond. No one could escape, so if the Temple was empty at the end of the week, it meant the criminal was cleansed. Otherwise, he was removed and placed in prison. Unless he was found dead, of course."

They descended the steps and walked out into the clearing.

"Was the Temple found empty often?"

"Many were found dead, a few still kneeling in prayer when they died. I believe those men may have found forgiveness. But the Elders realized that it was impossible to cleanse your *own* soul and locked the Temple up for good."

"What happened to it?" Angel's eyes trailed over the ruins. "And what made the Elders see they were wrong?"

"That's a story for another day. It's getting late." He pointed to the half moon in the darkening sky. "You should go home before Gregor gets worried."

Kalek held his hands out and gathered moonlight into a bright ball that floated slightly above and in front of Angel.

"Here, this will light your way along the path." The moonlight bounced off his onyx eyes, obscuring any emotion they might have shown.

"Thank you." She hooked a squirming Zoe to the leash and leaned over to set the puppy on the ground. When she stood up Kalek was gone.

She made her way safely back to the farm along the main path of the forest, and waved her hand at the ball of moonlight. It rose into the night sky, where it disbursed like a swarm of fireflies zipping off in every direction. When she walked into the house, she was surprised to see Gregor in his father's leather chair. He was sound asleep, head angled to the side, *Romeo and Juliet* lying open on his chest. She closed the book and set it on the side table, unfolded a blanket and covered him, then went to bed.

Chapter Eighteen
The University

"Thanks for the blanket." Gregor's voice was husky with fatigue as he sat in the leather chair, the blanket still covering his legs.

Dark circles under his eyes told Angel he hadn't slept well, and she wondered why he hadn't just gone into his own bed. He looked more hopeless than angry, and Angel wanted desperately to tell him that she understood now, and that she was sorry, but the words refused to come.

"Would you like some breakfast?" she asked in lieu of an apology.

Gregor shifted in the chair, but didn't answer. "You went to the Temple last night." It wasn't a question, and his intense stare dared her to deny it.

"Yes, and Kalek told me everything."

"Did he now?" He didn't sound angry exactly, but she could tell he wasn't happy to hear she'd been listening to anything Kalek had to say. "So you know why I can't be with Siophra, and that Kalek is too much of a coward to stand up to his father and bring happiness to his only sister."

"He told me he *has* gone to his father, and that there's nothing he can do. You don't believe him?"

"I *did...*" He let out a deep breath. "But he's proven whose side he's on."

"How? What has he done?"

"He gave the necklace—*my* family heirloom—to Siophra as an

engagement present. Now it will be passed to her new *husband's* descendants. The other day, when you saw me coming out of the forest, I went to confront him about it. He said he had to give it to her to prevent a huge mistake from being made." He pulled his shoulders back and tapped his chest. "I know the mistake he meant." He slumped back in the chair.

The image of the magnificent emerald necklace popped into Angel's head. *So that's the Halvard family heirloom.* And Gregor hadn't run away just because of Kalek's words that day. He'd seen the necklace around Siophra's neck and knew who must have given it to her.

Angel couldn't bear to see him like this, and did everything in her power to cheer him up. She made them both a huge breakfast of pancakes and sausage, with loads of maple syrup. Gregor hardly spoke a word, but he ate heartily. Angel kept talking to drown out the quiet, telling Gregor funny stories about some of Jacob's pranks, and got a few half-smiles out of him before they had the breakfast dishes cleaned up.

"I'm gonna go get dressed," Gregor said as he put away the last dish.

"Go take a shower first."

"I'm just going to get filthy again. It's sopping wet out there."

"Do it anyway." She crossed her arms and tapped her finger on her elbow, feeling like Mrs. Mason dealing with Josh and Jacob.

"But—"

"Just do it. It will make you feel better."

He grunted and walked away.

They spent the morning doing their chores double-time, hoping to be finished before lunch. Their feet sank into mud puddles all over the pasture, and the lingering humidity made the heat stifling. Gregor was right—they both ended up sweaty and filthy.

"I told you a shower this morning was a waste of time," he said, a hint of a tease back in his voice.

Neither of them spoke about Kalek or their argument, and Angel was glad things were somewhat back to normal. She couldn't bring herself to believe Kalek had lied to her, but she knew Gregor was telling her the truth, at least as he saw it. Like Mr. Mason always said: *"There's three sides to every story. Person A's, Person B's, and the truth."* One day she'd find out the truth, she hoped, but she doubted it would come from *Mr. Stubborn A or B.*

As they sat down for lunch, she said, "We've got time this afternoon to go to the University, don't we? You said we could go check out the museum, and see Dr. Damian's research, remember?"

"If we must." He took a bite of salad and chewed mechanically.

"You don't think it'd be interesting? Didn't you ever wonder about Sir Benjamin's research when he worked there?"

"Sir Benjamin studied animal behavior. He wasn't stuck in a lab all day. I have no desire to sit around watching test tubes boil."

"Fine. You just have to go, but I won't make you enjoy it. Satisfied?"

Mud had seeped into Angel's sneakers all morning, so Gregor found a pair of his mother's boots for her to wear to the University. As she tied up the laces, she caught Gregor staring at her.

"My mom loved those boots."

"I wish I could have met your parents." She finished the last loop.

"You would've loved them. Nothing like the *family* I've been left with, if you can call it that." Gregor's voice caught an edge and he scowled. "A vagrant and his tyrant father who hates me for something that happened ages ago. Ole Aldrik needs to wake up and see what he's done to his family. Ragged old man…should be grateful I'd be willing to put up with such a father-in-law. Not like all the others, who want his daughter as a trophy."

Angel ignored Gregor's comment, but began to wonder how a man like Aldrik Halvard could have fathered a man like Kalek. And if Siophra was anything like Gregor described her, it was even more of a mystery.

When they arrived at the University—Gregor Gating them to edge of the property—Angel gaped at the architecture of the main building. A beautifully mutated Arabian palace with golden spires topping the roof's peaks, their points mimicked by the mountains behind the grounds. But the walls, unlike any picture of an Arabian palace Angel had ever seen, were set with octagonal slate tiles that strangely complemented the golden spires. A marble staircase spanned the length of the main building, with three sets of massive wooden doors open at the top of the steps. Angel craned her neck, unable to see the end of the wing that stretched out to the right toward the mountains.

She and Gregor climbed the marble steps and entered the lobby through the center set of doors. Groupings of chairs and small round tables with clawed feet sat empty, and on one side an old-fashioned elevator's metal grate was closed and locked. A wooden staircase curved up to the second floor of the wing on the building's left. The ceiling of the lobby itself rose to the top of the second floor, and a balcony ran around the perimeter rimmed in a magnificently carved balustrade. An enormous column, easily ten feet in diameter, soared to the peak of the cathedral ceiling. The column was circled at its base by a high-backed bench covered in red leather.

Gregor cleared his throat, drawing Angel's attention away from the room.

"We should visit Dr. Damian first," she said when she saw his impatient expression. "You know, so we can get it over with and have plenty of time to see the museum."

Gregor pointed to the hallway on their right and grumbled, "The science wing is that way."

She followed him down the hall, disconcerted by the eerie quiet. Their feet fell silently on the carpet that ran the full length of the hallway. Doors lined both sides of the hall, polished wood set against textured wall, some marked with signs, and some merely with numbers. Angel peeked into a classroom with desks lined up in perfect rows. A series of painted portraits hung between the doors.

When they reached the end of the hallway, Gregor led her through a narrow doorway that opened directly onto an even narrower spiral staircase. At one point, a woman, whom Angel guessed must be a teacher, passed them coming down, forcing them to press themselves as flat as possible against the wall.

The science wing's smooth, white walls were dressed up only by carved wood baseboards, crown molding, and trim around the doors. Display cases housed rocks, various plants and insects, charts listing chemical compounds, and an illustration of the life cycle of a salamander-like creature.

Gregor looked around the wing as if he wasn't sure which way to go, then walked into an open room where a woman sat behind a desk, scribbling in a notebook. She glanced up from her work and shot them a look of annoyance.

"Can I help you?"

Angel looked at her apologetically, and fidgeted, taking a step backwards toward the door.

The woman's face relaxed. "I'm sorry. I didn't mean to speak that way. I'm just having a hard time figuring out this calculation. If these numbers are correct, I've wasted three years of research."

She removed her glasses, and smiled at them, revealing a single dimple on her left cheek. Her dark hair, deep hazel eyes and olive skin contrasted sharply with her white lab coat. It was just like the gray one Dr. Damian wore and had a nametag pinned on it that read, "Dr. Rena Watson."

Angel and Gregor stepped farther into the room, and Gregor said, "That's okay, ma'am. We're here looking for Dr. Damian."

"His office is two doors down, but he's probably in his lab, which is the next one over. And, please, don't call me ma'am. I don't even let my students call me that—makes me feel old."

Angel guessed Dr. Watson couldn't have been more than twenty-seven. She glanced down at the papers Dr. Watson had been scribbling on.

"What are you researching?"

"The effects of increased levels of different nutrients in the soil on the growth rate of *lilium regenerosa*. It's a plant indigenous to Toch Island that is used in regeneration potions."

"You teach Botany, then?"

Dr. Watson nodded. Angel looked down at her papers again and noticed something...

"You've written that three as a five right there." She pointed to one of Dr. Watson's calculations.

"Thank you!" Dr. Watson went back to scribbling.

The door to Dr. Damian's lab was opened only slightly, so Gregor knocked.

"Come in!" they heard from inside.

Gregor pushed the door all the way open, letting Angel pass in before him. Dr. Damian was watering a tray of seedlings on the counter in the back of the lab.

"Come *all* the way in," he said and motioned them back. His back was to them, revealing hair pulled into a ponytail that reached nearly to his waist.

"Angel! And Gregor—it's been a long time. Just watering my research," he said with a bright smile when they reached him. "Golem Flower. I've inserted a gene segment from the German Bronze Dragon. Now, we can make a tincture from the plant and give it as a vaccine for Dragon Pox."

Dr. Damian rattled on about the Golem Flower, each word nearly indistinguishable from the next. When he finally paused for a breath, Angel quickly said, "You mentioned something about a tour that day at Sir Benjamin's."

"Oh, right…enough about boring research then." He slapped the watering can down on the counter, splashing water in every direction, and ignored the puddle it formed on the floor. "Come, let me show you around."

As they walked through the room following Dr. Damian, Gregor mouthed to Angel, "See, *nervous.*"

Dr. Damian's chatter soon became white noise in the background as Angel examined the room. It looked very much like an ordinary laboratory, but without all the high-tech equipment. Glass Petri dishes were stacked everywhere. Several apparatuses with lenses of varying thickness stood on tables with black stone tops. Angel turned a dial on one of them and watched the lenses change position. *Microscopes. Cool.* She peered into one of the eyepieces.

A scuffling noise came from the other side of a door in the back of the lab. Angel lifted her head from the microscope. Scratching and rattling joined the scuffling.

Angel took a step toward the door. "Um, what's in there?"

"Well, come see." Dr. Damian walked over to the door and waved his hand in front of the knob. The lock clicked and the door popped open. Dr. Damian pulled the door wide so Angel and Gregor could pass through.

The small room was lit only by a single torch, which brightened as the door closed behind them. The scuffling and other noises ceased instantly.

There were several cages along the perimeter of the small room, some empty, some covered in dark cloth. A few contained animals that made Angel drop to her knees for a closer look.

She stared in amazement at a pair of animals that reminded her of skunks, but were anything but black and white. Their fur, despite its silky-soft appearance, was a metallic silver-blue. Their little bluish noses sniffed the air and their marbled eyes stared back at her from sockets set close together below small, perked ears.

"These are for your research?"

"Oh, no. They were found wounded in the forest. No one could get near them to help, so I was called, of course."

Gregor's voice came from behind her. "You're the Tamer, right? That's what Sir Benjamin meant by 'the expert.' You're supposed to be looking for that Lunicor everybody thinks is out there."

"You don't think there is one?" asked Dr. Damian.

"In all my time in the forest I haven't seen any signs of one. No blood, no carcasses. Nothing they normally leave behind."

"How do you explain all the animals that have disappeared? You think everyone else is wrong?"

"All I can say is, if there's really one out there, it's a smart one. To have been able to hide this long, I mean. I can see it escaping us, but not the Elves."

"The Elves are concerned though, aren't they?"

"None that I know. Some Elven guy came into Sir Benjamin's and said he believed one was out there...or at least his friend did. But, according to Siophra, most of the animals that've been killed were sick or pregnant, and they all have been females. And I've always been told that Lunicors favor males."

"Well...thank you, Gregor. That bit of information is surely helpful." Dr. Damian fiddled with his collar and furrowed his brow. His ice-blue eyes looked distant, and his expression pained. The silvery creatures began skittering around in their cage.

Angel turned to Dr. Damian. "What's a Tamer?"

Dr. Damian shook his head as if to clear his thoughts, and spoke in a slow and controlled voice that was nothing like the hurried chatter she'd heard coming from him before. The silvery creatures quieted down again.

"My Talent is to calm animals, any animal, even the most vicious. Not something I'm in need of much as a geneticist, but since I'm in my lab all the time, I can take care of animals like these, that are frightened and won't let anyone else near them. I've been called out to rescue dragons and all sorts of other magical creatures, and I can Tame dangerous animals so they can be caught and then released where they won't hurt anyone. Or, um, disposed of if necessary. I Tamed a winged horse once, and he's been with me ever since. Not too many people have ever even gotten to ride one, so I consider it an honor that he kept me."

"So you'd be able to go near any kind of animal, like that Lunicor, and it wouldn't hurt you?"

"Oh, yes, but it's not always a matter of not getting hurt. I'm probably the only human on this Island that could go near a unicorn. Well, the Elves can, of course, but you know what I mean."

No, Angel didn't know what he meant.

Dr. Damian stepped over to the cage where Angel knelt. "Those creatures that you're looking at now are Gildens. They have the ability to encase things in gold. It's actually a way of storing their food for the winter. When it's time to eat, they just peel off the gold layer and eat what's inside."

One of the Gildens turned around, exposing its other side, which had a shaved patch surrounding a cut that was almost completely healed.

"And over here," Dr. Damian pointed at a cage a few feet away from the Gildens, "is a Fractal Chameleon."

It was nearly eighteen inches long, with scales covered in a kaleidoscope pattern of golds and browns—the colors of the branch it clung to. As Angel looked closer, though, she saw that the pattern repeated, only each time it appeared smaller and smaller as it radiated and swirled out from the center on the chameleon's side. The chameleon was missing one leg, but it appeared to be growing back. Angel wondered if Dr. Damian had used the regeneration potion Dr. Watson had mentioned.

"Watch this." Dr. Damian slipped his finger between the bars of the cage. The branch turned from bark-brown to brilliant red-orange. The chameleon remained still, but it began to change color as well, until its fractal pattern became a swirl of sunburst.

Zack would kill to see this room.

A strange mewing drew Angel's attention away from the chameleon, and she turned her head to find its source. It was followed by what sounded like a lion cub attempting a roar, and then a snort. The sound came from a cage covered in black cloth, tucked into the corner of the room between two cupboards.

Angel moved closer to the cage, and the series of sounds repeated.

"What's in here?"

Dr. Damian looked nervously at the cage. He held up his finger and hesitated for a moment. "Can you keep a secret?"

Chapter Nineteen
The Secret

Gregor shot a suspicious look at Angel, but her curiosity was too much for her.

"Yes, what is it?"

Dr. Damian pulled the cloth from the cage. Sitting upright on its haunches, a creature about a foot long from nose to tail stared through the opening between the cage bars. It looked like a dragon, but was covered with downy fur instead of scales, and was striped like a tabby cat. Its wings were small and its head large in proportion to the rest of its body.

It must be a baby...

The baby dragon-creature repeated its mew/roar/snort and rubbed against the cage bars, its eyes directed at Dr. Damian as if Angel and Gregor weren't even in the room.

Dr. Damian reached into a cupboard and pulled out a jar, mixed a sweet-smelling concoction, and covered the jar with a lid that had a spout like a baby bottle. He opened the door to the cage and the baby leaped deftly into his arms. Dr. Damian put the spout in the baby creature's mouth and it began to drink.

"I found this poor little fellow in the forest. Looked like he'd just been born, still wet, like his mother hadn't even begun to clean him off. He had rolled into the brush, and I heard him crying. The ground was covered in blood, and there was a trail leading off between the trees. His mother must have been taken by predators or something. I couldn't find her body anywhere." His voice was even calmer and smoother than before.

"What is he?" asked Angel.

Gregor seemed curious too, but held back, behind Angel. She could sense his tension. She turned and saw him staring hard in the direction of Dr. Damian and the baby. This was obviously no species he'd ever encountered.

"Have no idea. Never seen anything like him before. I did some genetic testing, and he seems to be part cat and part dragon. I'm calling him a Cagon.

"I'm keeping him in here until I find out what his temperament develops into. Obviously, he's fine around me, but I have no idea what he'll be like in the wild. I'd prefer if you didn't tell anyone about him though, not until I've learned more."

He looked pointedly at Angel when he spoke his request, and she agreed to keep his secret. Gregor remained silent.

The baby Cagon finished his meal, and he climbed from Dr. Damian's arms to the cage where he curled up exactly the way Spike liked to lie when he slept.

Dr. Damian closed the cage, then invited them to his office for tea. Gregor tugged Angel's arm.

She glared at him, then turned to Dr. Damian. "Sure, we've got time."

As they walked out of the lab and into Dr. Damian's office, Angel asked, "Are you enjoying the book?"

"The book? Oh yes, that. It's fascinating, of course." He stepped over to his bookshelf. After scanning the titles, he pulled a book off the shelf and handed it to Angel. It wasn't the same one that he'd gotten from Sir Benjamin's. "This is one of his earlier works."

She read the title, *The Extension of Man*, and this time took a good look at the author's name.

Dr. Blane Watkins. That sounded familiar...

Could this be Melinda Watkins' father? She flipped open the back cover and looked at his photo on the inner sleeve. He had the same black hair as Melinda, and eyes just like hers, but his were filled with arrogance instead of sadness.

Angel flipped through the pages. Diagrams and terminology similar to the other book filled the chapters. No mention of magic, of course, not that she expected it. Magic to Dr. Watkins, she was sure, meant his daughter's Ouija boards and Tarot cards.

"He's quite brilliant," Dr. Damian said. "I'd love to discuss his theories with him, face to face. Nothing like a healthy debate, eh?"

"I'm sure he'd set you straight," said a voice from the door.

Angel, Gregor, and Dr. Damian all looked over at once.

"Hello, Dr. Randall. Nice to be dry today for a change, isn't it?" Dr. Damian laughed nervously.

In the doorway stood a man with a sallow complexion and dull, dirty-blond hair, just beginning to gray at the temples. He wore a gray lab coat like Dr. Damian's. His pants stopped just above his ankles.

"Yes…of course it is."

Angel shot a quizzical look at Gregor. He shrugged, then mouthed, "The rain." Angel glanced down at her mud-crusted boots. *Oh, yeah.*

"This is my friend, Angel, and her cousin, Gregor." Dr. Damian motioned toward them.

Dr. Randall ignored them, but eyed the book in Angel's hand. "That's rubbish, you know. Don't let Dr. Damian convince you otherwise. That author has no idea what he's talking about."

"You don't agree with what he says in this, then?" Angel asked.

"He doesn't even agree with himself." He dismissed her by turning to Dr. Damian. "Can I speak with you *privately*?"

"We can talk on the way to the staff room. I promised these kids some tea. Excuse me, you two." Dr. Damian followed Dr. Randall out the door, eyes narrowed.

Angel opened the book again. Those eyes. Exactly like Melinda's… exactly.

"Gregor, I know this guy. He's the father of a girl I went to school with. She made him out to be a real jerk."

Gregor peered out the door as if he was on guard. He said out of the corner of his mouth, "Sounds like Dr. Randall disagrees with him."

"But Dr. Randall said, 'I'm sure he'd set you straight.' What do you think that meant? He's creepy if you ask me." She walked over to put the book back on the shelf, and a piece of paper slipped from between the pages. The paper flipped open when it hit the floor. It was an American newspaper clipping. And the name Blane Watkins was underlined in the text.

Angel returned the book to the shelf and picked up the newspaper clipping. It was an article announcing a lecture featuring several renowned scientists, dated nearly eight years ago, about the same time the book was published. *Promotion for his book, no doubt.*

Angel reached for the book again, intending to put the paper back.

But Gregor, who had stepped up behind her, grabbed the paper out of her hand and stuffed it into his pocket, whispering in her ear, "He's back."

Sure enough, the second Angel turned around Dr. Damian appeared in the doorway, three mugs floating in front of him. Angel took a mug and sat in a chair across the desk from Dr. Damian. Gregor ignored the tea and plopped down in the chair next to her.

Dr. Damian rattled on about his research. Angel tried to focus on him, but Gregor kept tapping her foot with his.

The moment Angel set her mug on the desk, Gregor popped out of his chair like a jack-in-the-box. He held her chair to pull it out, barely giving her a chance to stand.

"Thanks, Dr. Damian." She gave Gregor a side look. "We've got to go."

"Yeah…I promised Angel I'd show her the museum." Gregor held out his hand to Dr. Damian.

Dr. Damian didn't shake it. "Didn't you hear? The museum's closed right now."

"Why?" asked Angel.

"One of the displays was vandalized. And it's a part of Aldrik Halvard's personal collection."

Gregor's face hardened at the mention of the name. Angel shared his anger. Why couldn't they get away from this guy?

"Come on, Angel," Gregor said. "We've got to go." He turned and left the room.

"I'm sorry, Dr. Damian. Thanks for showing us your lab and everything." Angel ran to catch up with Gregor, who was already at the doorway leading to the spiral staircase.

They descended the staircase and walked back to the lobby in silence. Instead of turning to the front doors to leave, Gregor crossed the lobby to the opposite hallway. Angel hurried to keep up.

The museum entrance was roped off. A woman stood on the other side of the rope, looking through a small notebook and muttering to herself.

"Excuse me," said Gregor.

The woman looked up. Or down, rather. She was taller than Gregor, but had the slim, graceful look of a ballerina. Her face was stern, however, with glasses perched near the end of her nose. She peered over them at Gregor without answering.

"We were wondering what happened to the museum," he said. "I'm Gregor Halvard, by the way."

The woman nodded at him.

"I'm Mrs. Crick." She snapped her notebook shut. "Gregor, I'm afraid something was stolen from the display several months ago and your, um, uncle…or…whatever, has insisted we close the museum until the culprit is caught. He believes there are artifacts in the rest of his collection that may be in danger as well."

"He closed the museum? Huh! He must have known we were coming. He probably did it just to ruin my day." Gregor grumbled something else under his breath.

Mrs. Crick's stern expression nearly cracked. A twinkle settled in her eyes. "I'm sorry, Gregor, but you know probably better than I do that what Aldrik Halvard wants, Aldrik Halvard gets."

"Can you tell me what was stolen? Was it—" But before he could finish, Mrs. Crick was shaking her head.

"Sorry, no. Another one of Mr. Halvard's requests was that we keep that information confidential. I suppose you'd have to take it up with him."

Gregor only grunted in response, and thanked Mrs. Crick before turning to leave. Angel didn't follow.

"Mrs. Crick, I'm Angel, and I was wondering if you have anything I could take with me about the museum. A brochure or something. I was really looking forward to seeing everything."

"You know what, Angel, I do have something you can have. Wait right here."

She disappeared into a room down the hall. Gregor stood in the lobby with his arms crossed.

Mrs. Crick emerged from the doorway carrying a book.

"Here, we were going to have to throw this away. It's about the artifacts in our permanent display, and it includes some other Elven objects of interest. I think there may even be a few things in here that are in Mr.

Halvard's collection. Anyway, the back cover's torn off and we can't sell it like that, so you can have it if you'd like."

"Thank you."

Mrs. Crick smiled warmly.

Angel and Gregor Gated back to the forest edge, and trudged through the still-damp pasture to the house. When they entered the kitchen, Gregor went straight to the table and sat. He pulled the newspaper clipping out of his pocket and read over it several times.

"You said you know this guy?" He looked at her with dismay as she stood by the open door waiting for Zoe.

"I knew his daughter. I never actually met *him*," she said. "But, from what Melinda told me he was really awful." Zoe ran back inside through the open door. Angel filled a bowl with food for the puppy and joined Gregor at the table.

He was looking at the clipping again, deep in thought.

"Melinda was really into witchcraft. She was always trying to predict the future and stuff, like using Ouija boards to contact the psychic world. Her dad was downright mean to her because of it, always telling her she was wasting her time reaching for the spirit world because people don't have souls."

"Witchcraft like that is *not* magic," Gregor said as his head rose and he leveled his gaze, "and you know it."

"Yes, I know it." She crossed her arms. "But *he* doesn't. And neither does she. I wish I could bring her here and show her all this."

"Be careful what you wish for."

"What do you mean by that?"

"Nothing." He directed his gaze back to the clipping and raked his hand through his hair. "Never mind. I just don't get this. Why's Dr. Damian so interested in this guy's research?"

"What's the big deal?" Angel scratched Zoe behind the ears. Shakespeare remained curled in his cushioned chair, ignoring the thump-thump of her tail.

"You're the one who told me about that other book he got from Sir

Benjamin," Gregor said. "The one that was full of all that stuff about humans and super-powers. If he doesn't believe in souls, how can he believe in something that sounds like magic?" His scrunched eyes scanned the clipping as he spoke.

"He thinks it's a genetic trait. I mean, if he's never seen real magic, that would be his logical conclusion. Anyway, he's just a guy Dr. Damian has never even met, right? Quit over-reacting. You just don't like Dr. Damian and you're being picky now."

"You say picky, I say cautious." He lifted his head again. "This Damian guy's treading a thin line, Angel. How do you know for sure he hasn't stepped across already?"

~Keeping Secrets~

"It's none of your business what I do when I am away." He turned from the scientist, inhaling slowly before he reached for another test tube. He would not give into his frustration and allow the man to see him rattled.

The door creaked behind him.

"Started without me, I see," a voice said.

The scientist's colleague, another little rat of a man, who had no idea what kind of research was really going on.

"I'll go grab my notes and join you." Retreating footsteps followed.

The scientist moved to his side and whispered, "He's getting suspicious. You're spending too much time out in the open here. How are we to keep from him that you are really here to help me if you aren't more discreet?"

"Maybe I should reveal to him who I am? He has ways, does he not, of getting what I need?"

The scientist glanced over his shoulder. "He would never do it."

"Maybe I should have a talk with him myself…alone…and convince him." He smiled, the skin on his cheek stretching reluctantly.

The scientist gazed at him with burning eyes. "It's not as easy as you think. Trust me. The girl isn't the best answer. You'll see that for yourself soon."

Chapter Twenty
The Break-in

"Ow! That was my toe!" Gregor cried as the corner of a plank of wood landed on his work boot.

Angel snapped out of her fog and stared at the plank. She'd been distracted for days now. The trip to the University diverted her thoughts for one afternoon, but the verses of the prophecy soon returned to her mind and settled in, begging her attention. Unfortunately, they forced themselves to the forefront at the most inopportune times—like when she was supposed to be supporting a board for Gregor to nail in place

"Sorry, but I was just thinking we need to be searching for the key. I mean, it's not going to just show up on our doorstep one day. And we never looked through any of your maps, you know? Maybe we should be concentrating on the location. And isn't that little box with the symbols in the corner of a map called a key? Maybe one of those has a—"

"It's called a *legend*, too—ooh, spooky, huh?" He reached out and wiggled his fingers menacingly. Then his expression turned to stone. "Really, Angel. This was fine to fantasize about when we were trapped in the house and had nothing else to do. But now it's back to the real world."

Gregor picked up the board that had fallen on his foot, and handed it back to Angel. "Now, come on, let's get this finished before lunch."

But Angel couldn't get the prophecy out of her head. It invaded her every thought and action for the rest of the day. She lay in bed that night, her head whirling as she pondered the first verse for the hundredth time. *Powers given in birth, taken on eternal in death.* Each time she came to the same conclusion. It had to be Dawric. But what did *as the bearer stands on the threshold* mean? A threshold meant a door, but to what?

The place of beginning, the place of ending, completing the circle. That had to mean the island. That's where Angel came from and where she came back to. But could it mean something else as well? Didn't poems often have dual meanings? She tossed and turned on her pillow, but no matter what position she chose, she couldn't stop the verses from flowing through her mind.

The next verse had to be symbolic. Gregor had already pointed out that a *flame* could never *burn with no fuel.* But Angel could think of nothing that it might stand for. *Something flame-like, maybe?* She looked at the clock. Two a.m. This was unbearable. She was exhausted, but she couldn't shut her brain off and go to sleep.

The fourth verse pushed its way through again. *The key to the key being found, the lock can be opened by the key handed over to the rightful heir.* She was back to the lines Gregor had teased her about. The key seemed to be the significant object here, but that wasn't what Dawric was after. What he wanted had to be hidden because the next line talked about a treasure lying inside of something. A *treasure beyond all measure.* That meant something valuable. Or, something…powerful.

And of course it would be *happily gained* by Dawric, if it was what he'd been coveting for seven years. But Angel didn't understand what was meant by *when all else is lost.*

My mind is going to be lost if I don't get this figured out. Or at least get some sleep tonight. She buried her face in the pillow, stifling a scream. She didn't want to think about it anymore, but she had no choice. She finally gave in and let the words of the last verse form in her mind. *The guardian shall leave his post when the hidden path is unmasked.* Something about that struck a chord with her, but try as she might, she couldn't come up with a reason.

Whatever it meant, it would happen when *the truth has been exposed by the substance of man.* That sounded to Angel like a test of some kind. Something to show a man's true nature? The only line that she knew the meaning of for sure was the last. *The Finder's work will then be complete.* And that couldn't be soon enough. Riddles were fun, but not when they tormented you in the middle of the night.

The verses began their rotation through her mind again. *This is maddening!* She sat up and decided the only way to make it stop was to do something about it. The key stuck in her mind the most, and she thought about Gregor's maps again. His teasing words haunted her. *It's called a legend, too.* So maybe she was on the right track. There was only one way to find out.

She tiptoed out of her bedroom, careful not to wake Zoe, and crept into the living room where Gregor's maps were kept. One by one she unrolled them, cringing each time the paper crinkled. She examined every line and symbol for anything that resembled a key. When she reached the last map, she had to admit that Gregor was right. There was nothing on the maps that would help them locate something as small as a key.

Oh, come on! Her fatigue and frustration threatened to send her into a fit. She was totally over being patient. She didn't ask for this to happen to her; so why wasn't she at least being led in the right direction?

She reluctantly began to roll up the last map when she noticed a seal on the corner. Words were imprinted around an unfamiliar symbol, and they looked as if they were written in the same language as the verses in Gregor's book.

She heard the muffled tread of footsteps descending the stairs, but didn't have time to finish rolling the map and get it back on the shelf before Gregor reached her.

"What are you doing?" he asked. "It's the middle of the night."

"I just couldn't get the maps out of my head. But you were right, there's nothing in them that would help us. I did find this though." She unrolled the map enough to expose the seal in the corner.

Gregor didn't look at it. He pushed the map aside. "You've got to stop this, Angel. Look what it's doing to you. You need to get back to sleep."

She put the map back in front of him. *Yeah, don't I wish?*

"Fine," she said, "I'll go to bed as soon you take a look. This seal has the same kind of lettering as the book with the verses."

He hesitated, looking as if he wanted to argue, but then took the map from her and angled it so he could examine the seal.

"This is an old map of my dad's. It's completely out of date. He only kept it because it's one of the first maps of Toch Island. And what difference does it make if it's the same language?"

"Maybe it says something about the key. Let's get the interpreter lens and see."

"It's just a seal. Probably the name of the guy who drew the map, or the person who commissioned him. It looks Elven, but there are so many old languages that make up their culture it would be hard to tell.

"See?" He pointed to other words on the face of the map. "Those are in a completely different language and those over there are in another one. Lots of languages back then were interchanged and mixed together. It doesn't mean the map has anything to do with the book."

"But if we knew for sure it's Elven, even an ancient form, it might narrow down our search. You made us leave the University before we got to see the library. I bet one of the old tomes there could help us. Some of them might've been written around the same time. If it's Elven, I bet Kalek would know."

Gregor snarled and mumbled something that sounded like "traitor" as he stomped back toward the stairs. Each step up the staircase was punctuated by a "humph," the last of which was drowned out by the slamming of his bedroom door.

Shakespeare, curled up on his favorite cushioned chair, lifted his head and looked at Angel as if to say, *I don't know any better than you do*, and then went back to sleep.

But Angel had gotten what she needed. It wasn't much, but seeing the seal in the same language as the book made Angel certain that the prophecy was at least tied to Toch Island. It was enough to let her brain relax, and she drifted off moments after returning to bed.

Neither of them mentioned maps or keys for the rest of the week. Angel felt like she had to walk on eggshells around Gregor, and he acted as if nothing had happened. She hated it. His irritation with her was tied to his anger with Kalek, and he buried them together. Despite his attempt at self-control, it leaked out in little things he said and did. He had to be angry with Siophra too, for not running away and disowning her father.

Saturday arrived. Angel couldn't wait to see Sir Benjamin, and for the first time in days talk to someone who wasn't mad at her.

When she woke, she found Gregor working on a section of fence that had been torn down. One of the sheep was missing as well. The rest of the sheep, and all the goats, remained in the pasture, most of them curled up in the shade of the big wooden shelter.

"It's the ewe that's gone." He was pounding a post into the ground. "She's been acting strange lately. Skittish and temperamental." He slammed the hammer so hard Angel thought he'd splinter the post. "Typical hormonal female."

Angel ignored his comment, not wanting to prove him right. What she really wanted to say was that if anyone had been temperamental lately, it was *him*.

"Why don't you go on into town?" he said, sullenness returning to his voice. "We really need that alfalfa, and I can fix this myself."

His anger seemed to be deteriorating into self-pity. Angel felt her own anger begin to melt, and it was as if she were seeing Gregor with new eyes. He was hurting. All of his other emotions were a result of that one fact. She bit her lip and tried not to look like she was feeling sorry for him.

"You okay riding into town alone?" he asked when he saw her expression.

"Fine. But are you sure I can't help you? Then we can go into town together later." *A visit with Sir Benjamin would do you good*, she wanted to add.

"No, really. I'd rather do it alone. I'll take Zoe for a walk when I'm done. You hang out at Sir B's and help him finish that puzzle of his."

Angel remembered Mr. Mason retreating to the garage to sort things out on his own, and Mrs. Mason always kept her distance when he did that. Gregor must've needed the same thing. So Angel saddled up Juliet and headed into town. It wasn't until she was almost to Old Man Brady's that she realized Gregor was making excuses and would probably slip off into the forest and try to see Siophra.

Angel walked in the door of the feed store. Roger's footsteps echoed as he paced back and forth behind the counter, his face red and his voice booming through the entire store.

"I can't believe this! There's no way my stock can be low like this. No one buys this stuff on a regular basis. Someone had to have broken in here. Shawn, are you *absolutely sure* you haven't seen anything suspicious?"

The store clerk stood blank-faced and pale.

"N-no, sir. Nothing. It must've happened when the store was closed. When you're not here I always keep that door locked."

Angel looked in the direction he indicated. A cabinet hung open in the room behind the counter. It contained an assortment of vials, and the cabinet door had Roger's keys dangling from the lock.

"It *can't* have happened at night. I've been suspicious of something for a while now, and for the last week I've been sleeping here and bringing Rex with me. He'd've barked like mad if he'd seen anyone 'round here at night. And he hasn't made a peep. Yet, three more vials are missing!" Roger slammed his fist on the counter.

At that moment, another store clerk, nervously glancing toward Roger, came up to Angel. "Can I help you find anything?"

Angel wanted to get out as quickly as possible. "Just here to get some alfalfa. I know where it is."

She stepped away as the clerk said, "But—" and walked straight to the far corner of the store. The place was still in chaos, but Angel concentrated, imagining a bag of alfalfa like she'd seen at Gregor's. Her Talent led her to the only one in the store, buried in a messy pile of bagged grass seed.

She shoved aside the seed bags—each was no larger then a lunch sack and only weighed a few pounds even though they were marked with many times that weight. She found the 50-pound bag of alfalfa, also magically shrunk and lightened, and snatched it up with one hand.

The clerk commented as she came back, "How did you know where that was? I thought we were out. It's normally right up here." He pointed to an empty rack at the other end of the counter.

Angel didn't know what to say, and looked around nervously. Roger had retreated through the doorway behind the counter and was locking up the cabinet. Shawn was nowhere to be seen. Angel hadn't thought twice about using her Finding to locate the alfalfa.

"Um…I was just in the other day and saw it there. I didn't realize it was in the wrong spot." She handed the clerk the money Gregor had given her and scuttled out the door before the clerk could ask her any more questions.

Angel practically ran to Sir Benjamin's. Stuff being stolen from Roger, artifacts stolen from the museum. Not to mention the Lunicor, and the broken fence and missing sheep. It was all just too creepy. And it all seemed to have started when she arrived. She needed no more proof that the prophecy was real, but the excitement over being involved was morphing into fear. She thought about what Gregor had said the other day—that it was fine to fantasize in the safety of the farmhouse, but that it was time for real life. His words were true, but not in the way he'd meant them.

Sir Benjamin's place was as bright and welcoming as usual, and Angel relaxed as soon as she walked in the door. She set her bag down by the couch and scanned the room for Sir Benjamin. The door in the back opened, and he walked in, followed by a tall woman with cropped gray hair. She wore a white lab coat similar to the ones worn by the professors at the University.

Sir Benjamin's face lit up and his Santa smile appeared, sending its warmth straight to Angel's soul. "Angel! Come meet Dr. Solberg, our local dragon expert."

"Please, Ben," the gray-haired woman said to Sir Benjamin, then turned to Angel. "It's Kate. Nice to meet you, Angel." The reflection of the lantern on Sir Benjamin's desk danced in the corner of the doctor's thick glasses.

"You too, Dr—Dr. Kate."

"Kate was kind enough to come out and see us on a Saturday. Spike's not been looking too good these past couple of days." There was a crackle in his voice.

"He's going to be okay, isn't he?"

Dr. Kate smiled reassuringly. "Of course he is. Nothing to worry about. The only problem Ben's going to have is getting Spike to take the tonic I've given him."

"You're not kidding about that," said Sir Benjamin. "Spike's the most finicky creature in existence."

"Well, try those tricks I showed you to get it down him. If he's not better in a few days, bring him in and I'll run some more tests at the office."

"Will do, Kate, will do."

"And the biggest thing you need to do is stop worrying. He'll be fine." Dr. Kate peered at him through the thick lenses of her glasses and patted his shoulder.

"Yes, I know," he said, and then turned to Angel. "Kate here has more knowledge about dragons in her little finger than I do in my whole body. We went to school together, and she's the only one who aced every test in Dragon Studies."

"They've always fascinated me," said Dr. Kate with a humble smile. "And now I've got my own practice and a lab where I can study them all day."

"Oh, yes, Angel," said Sir Benjamin, "with your aptitude for science, I bet you'd love to see her lab." He moved around from behind the desk and sat down on the corner. "That reminds me—did you ever make it over to visit Dr. Damian?"

"The other day. It was great. He showed us his lab and some of the animals he's taking care of." Angel had to bite her tongue to keep from bringing up the baby Cagon. Here she stood with a dragon expert right in front of her, and she couldn't say anything.

"How'd Gregor do?" Sir Benjamin looked as if he were enjoying a private memory. "Did you get him past the lobby?"

"He was pretty reluctant to go, but I thought that was just because he's mad at Kalek."

"They've had a falling-out again? Not surprised. Sticky situation. But he's never been too fond of the University. He's...let's just say he likes structure, but it's got to be structure that he creates himself."

"That's Gregor, all right," Angel said, and smiled.

"Be glad he came with you. That means something, for sure." He stood up and turned back to Dr. Kate, who'd begun packing her black medical bag. "Kate, I just remembered something I need to give you. I'll be right back." He nodded toward Angel. "Excuse me a moment." He disappeared through the door behind his desk.

Angel fidgeted while she thought about the situation. Should she chance asking Dr. Kate about the Cagon?

She cleared her throat. "Maybe you can answer a question for me, Dr. Kate."

"Sure." Dr. Kate pulled her glasses off and wiped them on her lab coat.

"Um, do you know of any species of dragons that have fur instead of scales?"

Dr. Kate put her glasses back on. "No, dragons *all* have scales. Fur would be impossible. Why do you ask?"

"Oh, just something I read in a book. I must be remembering the details wrong." It bothered Angel that Dr. Damian had asked her to keep the Cagon secret. Because of the animal's temperament? It'd seemed so gentle. Of course, it was probably being Tamed. Still, she kept wondering...*Why was I so quick to agree?*

"Are you interested in dragons?" Dr. Kate went back to gathering her belongings.

"I've always thought they were the coolest creatures. Spike was the first one I got to meet in real life, though." Angel glanced at the curled-up dragon, his metallic green scales not quite as lustrous as the last time she'd seen him. "Is he really going to be okay?"

"Absolutely. He's old, but Ben has taken great care of him. He'll come out of this just fine. But it's true that he doesn't have too many years left. Ben was lucky to find Spike at such a young age. Maybe he'll be lucky again when Spike is gone." When she finished packing she walked over and stroked Spike's side.

"Take your tonic like a good boy and I'll see you soon." The dragon replied with a snort and touched Dr. Kate's hand with his wing.

"I'd better skedaddle," Dr. Kate said as Sir Benjamin walked back into the room. "Ben, you call me in no more than three days and let me know how Spike is."

"Don't forget this." He handed Dr. Kate a small book. "That should help on your trip."

Angel glimpsed the cover—a French phrase book.

Dr. Kate flipped the pages and smiled. "This is perfect. Thank you, Ben." She tucked the book into her bag and turned to Angel. "Any time you'd like to visit me, please feel free. Ben can give you directions. I love showing off my patients."

She gave Sir Benjamin a quick hug and headed to the door. "Good-bye, Angel, Ben." The bell tinkled as the door closed behind her.

Sir Benjamin motioned to the puzzle and Angel followed him over to the table. They both sat down and started working on the last section.

"Thanks for keeping your promise and not finishing without me."

"Of course. I wouldn't even think of it. Coffee?"

Angel nodded and he waved the pot over to the table.

"So, you enjoyed seeing Dr. Damian's research?"

"It was interesting. But he talks so fast, I couldn't keep up with half of what he was saying."

"That's Dr. Damian." Sir Benjamin let out a small laugh and handed Angel her coffee. "He brought a lot of energy into our department. We needed it, too. It can get pretty stodgy when everyone is so caught up in their work."

"Was Dr. Randall there when you taught?" She took a sip of coffee and set the mug down, then picked up a puzzle piece and began looking for its place.

"Oh, yeah, he's been there for years. Brilliant mind for details. Never needs to use notes during his lectures—he just remembers it all. The students hated him because he expected the same of them. Quite a few of them dropped out because of it."

"Is that his Talent or something? Oh, I guess not, if he expected his students to be as good at it as he is."

"Actually, I never found out what his Talent is."

Angel's head popped up and she widened her eyes. "Even after working with him for years?" She didn't think Talents were something people kept secret. But then again, here Sir Benjamin sat in front of her and she had no idea what his Talent was. Neither he nor Gregor had ever mentioned it, and she hadn't given it any thought.

"No, we didn't see eye-to-eye on a lot of things, so we kept away from each other for the most part. I shouldn't be telling you this." He tilted his head forward, peering between his bushy brows and the top of his glasses.

Angel was too curious to let it drop. She wanted Sir Benjamin to confirm that Gregor was wrong about Dr. Damian.

"He was kind of harsh with Dr. Damian about those books he got from you."

"Not surprised…" Sir Benjamin placed another puzzle piece, flashed a satisfied grin, and continued. "Don't worry, Angel. It's just Dr. Randall's style. He's a bit superior in his thinking, likes to slice people up with words. And Dr. Damian can handle himself. Believe me, he doesn't listen to anyone he doesn't want to hear."

"He seems pretty interested in that author. You know, I think I've seen Dr. Watkins in the newspapers back home. He's a scientist who gave some lectures at a local university." Angel kept her eyes on the puzzle pieces when she spoke, afraid her expression would give away that she knew more about Dr. Watkins than she admitted.

"I remember Dr. Damian saying something once about the man's lectures. I think he may have even gone to see one. But that was before he started teaching here. He was still in grad school, I guess, back in Germany."

Angel dropped her puzzle piece. *Dr. Damian said he wanted to meet Dr. Watkins.* Had he already done so? This conversation was not going where she wanted it to go. She had hoped to clear Dr. Damian's name in her mind, to gain some proof that Gregor's assumptions were wrong. But Sir Benjamin's words seemed to confirm what Gregor believed—that Dr. Damian was being less than truthful and was tinkering in ideas that went against the beliefs of the Empowered.

She realized Sir Benjamin was staring at her, eyes twinkling, looking more like Santa than he ever had before. A lone puzzle piece lay on the table.

"Would you do the honors?" He nodded at the last puzzle piece.

She snapped it into place, and studied the completed image.

The castle's luminescence contrasted against the churning black of the stormy background sky. A fortress of light the storm could never overpower. The castle's magic, its strength, came not from the bricks that composed its walls, but from the craftsmanship of its architect and the solidity of its foundation.

"Just promise me you won't take it apart until after I leave," she said. "I hate seeing all that work disappear in seconds."

"You have my word," he replied with his hand over his heart.

She needed to get going if she wanted to make it home in time for lunch. She walked over to Spike to say good-bye, gently stroking his smooth scales. He really did look like he wasn't doing well, and felt like he'd lost a little weight.

"Don't worry about him," said Sir Benjamin over her shoulder. "He's in good hands. Dr. Kate has never been wrong about him before."

Chapter Twenty-One
The Portrait

On the ride home, Angel mulled over her conversation with Sir Benjamin. Was Dr. Damian lying about meeting Dr. Watkins? What could he possibly have to gain by that? She bent her head forward, focusing on a spot on the back of Juliet's neck.

After several minutes deep in thought, she realized Juliet's gait had changed, and she looked more closely at her surroundings. The area seemed oddly familiar…but she'd never been here with Gregor. It was a neighborhood in a hilly area dense with trees. She looked behind her—she was still on the road that led into the town square. *I missed the turn to Gregor's.*

She couldn't bring herself to turn around. *I've been here before. I know this place. That house right there—it has a green shed on the other side.* As she passed the house, a shed popped into view, green but faded.

She scanned the other houses and recognized features in nearly all of them. Then the road became increasingly steep. She wasn't sure how to handle Juliet on that kind of terrain. She thought about turning back, but the ground leveled off again just ahead. *I'll only go a little farther.* When she reached the level ground, she noticed a small cottage tucked in the trees to her right.

It looked abandoned, but quaint, with a wreath still hanging on the front door. She pulled on Juliet's reins and the horse stopped in front of the cottage. The white paint was dirty-gray in areas, and the blue shutters blocked the view inside. Angel climbed down and tied Juliet to a nearby tree, pausing to build her courage.

She walked slowly up the walkway to the front door. A spot in the back of her head began to throb as she stared at the wreath—hand-made, she knew, by the neighbor two doors down. The porch was covered in dirt and leaves, and the railing had two broken slats. The boards creaked slightly under her feet as she climbed the steps. Her palm slid up the banister, and she felt a familiar bump, a knot in the wood that snagged the smooth motion of her hand.

She reached the front door and put her hand on the knob. It was probably locked, but she had to try anyway. Her heart pounded in anticipation and her hand shook as she twisted her wrist. The knob turned easily, but she didn't open the door. The mailbox on the wall drew her eye, and she read the name engraved on the front.

Kleidon.

The throbbing in her head intensified.

Her hand slipped from the doorknob, slick from the sweat of her clammy palms. It swung open a couple of inches, and the hinges creaked. She froze a moment, unsure of what to do. This was her parents' house… *her* house…and it was full of memories. Would it be too much at once? Maybe she wasn't ready. And she was alone. But could she just turn and leave?

A *crash* resounded from inside the house. She yanked the door shut, and bounded off the steps. Her fingers fumbled as she tried to untie Juliet, but finally the knot gave way. She jumped on Juliet's back and kicked the steed's sides, sending the horse off in a full run.

As they tore down the road, the sound of her own blood rushing filled her ears, and her legs ached with the effort of keeping Juliet under control. The horse turned onto Gregor's road without Angel so much as tightening her grip on the left rein, and didn't slow down until the farm was in view.

When Angel burst into the kitchen, Gregor scowled at her over his half-eaten lunch.

"Where have you been? I was starting to worry." His eyes narrowed and he leaned forward against the tabletop. "I saw your professor, Dr. Damian, in the forest today. He was standing over a dead animal, and he had a knife in his hands, dripping with blood. There is no Lunicor, Angel. I knew it." He slammed his fist on the table, rattling the silverware.

Angel finally caught her breath, but stood speechless. She couldn't process what he was saying at that moment. The information flew through her consciousness, lodging in a corner of her mind to be dealt with later.

"There's something or someone in my parents' house, Gregor. I accidentally found it on my way home—I missed the turn, and it...it all felt so familiar, so I decided to go see if I was right. I heard something crash inside and I jumped on Juliet and we ran home."

Gregor bolted to his feet. His scowl dropped and his face instantly registered concern. "Stay here," he said, rounding the table. "I'll go check it out."

As he headed to the door, Angel grabbed his arm.

"I'm going with you. It's *my* house."

He shot her a look of irritation, but didn't protest and headed straight out to the barn.

"Why don't we just Gate there? It'll be much faster," Angel said, following him.

"If I get in trouble there I want you to have a way to get help." He grabbed the saddle and strapped it on Romeo's back. In moments, they were galloping side by side down the road.

Gregor pushed past Angel when they reached the porch. He made her stop in the doorway as he listened for the intruder. Scuffling noises came from a room in the back. Angel stepped up behind Gregor, then ducked into a doorway on her right. Gregor walked slowly around the staircase and down the hallway. Angel could see just enough to make out a counter and sink at the other end.

She waited as Gregor entered the kitchen, trying to slow her heartbeat and breathing. If he needed help, she couldn't panic. She found herself running her hand through her hair.

Voices soon echoed down the hallway, but Angel couldn't make out the words. She edged closer to the kitchen and saw Gregor crouched and leaning over a lump on the kitchen floor. The lump was covered in ragged cloth, and Angel jumped when it moved.

Gregor turned his head and motioned for her to come closer. "It's just Lucky. He's harmless, but he knows better than to come in here."

"Lucky?"

"His real name is Davis, but everyone calls him Lucky. He used to be fine until people got wind that he believed in leprechauns. It wasn't like he believed in the pot of gold or anything, but he thought they were terrorizing him or something. It's really just sad, now. He's spends most of his time at *The Dreg*. Looks like his wife has gotten fed up and finally kicked him out." Gregor pointed over to a rolled-out sleeping bag and worn duffel.

Lucky began to stir. His eyes popped open and then widened even more when he saw Angel and Gregor, but he lay as if glued to the floor.

"What ya think you're doing here, Lucky?" Gregor asked. "You know better. This house is off-limits. Show a little respect."

"C'mon, Gregor. Gimme a break. I got no place else to go. I was campin' out in the woods, but I needed someplace to hide. Bad things in them woods…" He squinted, and clutched a whiskey bottle to his chest.

"Lucky, you know there's nothing in the forest over here except what that whiskey makes you see. Now get up, I'm taking you home." He held his hand out, but Lucky shook his head.

"There is too!" Lucky sat up, pushing himself against the kitchen cabinet. "I seen 'im, a man in a funny gray coat, leadin' a unicorn. You know they ain't supposed to be touched by humans. He's gonna curse us all!"

He tried to take a swig of whiskey, but Gregor pried it from his hand.

"What man? What did he look like?" asked Angel. What had Dr. Damian said about being the only human on the island who could touch a unicorn? "Was it in trouble? Maybe he was just trying to help it."

Gregor gave her a scathing look.

"Weren't someone trying to help that beast, no way. It weren't fighting him or nothin', but it looked skerred, starin' straight ahead like it weren't sher where ta go. Then 'e jabbed it with his fist and it just went all quiet and followed him along."

Gregor gave Angel another suspicious glance then reached down and hauled Lucky to his feet. Lucky wobbled and leaned against Gregor.

"C'mon. I'll talk to Marie. I'm sure she's cooled off and will let you come back."

"Yer a good boy, Gregor, a good boy…" Lucky let Gregor drag him outside and load him onto Romeo. Angel rolled up Lucky's sleeping bag and stuffed it into his duffel, then joined them outside.

"There's a key in the kitchen drawer by the sink," Gregor said. "Lock up the house and ride straight back home. We need to talk about this." His face was ice.

Angel walked into the house and found the key, but when she got back to the front door she hesitated. *Wait, this is* my *house.* She closed the door and tucked the key into her pocket.

She lifted one of the sheets draped over the living room furniture. Dust floated into the air like miniature spirits released from a grave. The fabric of the couch underneath was vibrant red. *Mom's favorite color. Dad hated it.* She pulled off all the sheets. Red chairs, natural wood tables. Mom, the artist, and Dad, the nature lover.

The throbbing in her head had disappeared and didn't seem to be coming back. She stared at the hallway on the other side of the living room. *Two bedrooms down there.* She stepped across the room and into the hallway. Still no pain.

The first bedroom was decorated in yellow, with butterflies painted above the chair rail. A frilly lace curtain adorned the window. The sunlight streamed into the room, illuminating the dust particles that danced in the air. Even before she peeked under the sheets, she knew the bed was cherry wood. She opened the closet and dresser drawers, but found nothing except a few pink dresses and patent leather shoes.

It was like standing in the middle of a room she had dreamed about over and over but never entered before that moment. Or like walking into a scene from a movie she'd seen many times. Exciting, but surreal.

She ran her hand over the scrolled wood footboard of the bed, and a voice began to drift around inside her head, distant but distinctly female, speaking with the intonation of someone reading a children's story. Angel closed her eyes, trying to let the memory take hold. The tone coalesced into words until she could clearly hear her mother's voice reading *Alice in Wonderland.* She still couldn't see her mother's face, but she relished the memory, and filed it away with the other remembrances of her foggy past.

She continued on to the next bedroom. Once again, she found the furniture covered in sheets, and the bed and dressers bare. A thick layer of dust covered the gorgeous canopy bed, dulling the glossy finish. The matching dresser was as empty inside as it was on top.

Dreadful thoughts pushed past any memories the room might provide. *The house looks abandoned.* Were her parents expecting it to take such a long time to find her? Had they given up hope and moved on to a new life, and Gregor was just afraid to tell her?

The need to learn more drove her back into the kitchen. She threw open every drawer and cabinet and found everything tarnished and dusty. The thick layer of dust on the floor showed only footprints left by Gregor, Lucky, and herself. She slammed the last cabinet door. *Why haven't they been back here?*

She returned to the foyer, and slowly climbed the steps to the loft, her chest tight as she struggled with her conflicting emotions. The memories she'd found meant nothing if her parents had abandoned hope.

The loft was strewn with canvases and drop cloths, with an easel planted squarely in the middle. Paint bottles and large cans filled with paintbrushes covered a table pushed against the wall to her left. Stacks of paintings leaned against the other two walls. She wandered around the room, fingering paintbrushes stiff with dried paint, and her foot bumped into a painting.

My mother's studio. She abandoned this too…to find me. The realization brought stinging tears to her eyes. They hadn't given up on her—they'd given up their life *for* her.

She picked up the painting at her foot. The butter-yellow rose looked amazingly realistic, and Angel felt a tinge of jealousy. She had inherited some of her mother's skill, but she could never have painted something with such depth of color and texture. She stroked the satiny petals, gently at first, and then more firmly, willing her fingers to pass into the painting the way her mother's could. But the stiff canvas pushed back and would not allow it.

Angel carefully replaced the painting and moved on. She felt a draft coming from an open window. She walked over to close it, but stopped short when she spotted bright red hair and a forehead peeking over a blank canvas.

She slid the painting out of its hiding place, and met a pair of very familiar chocolate eyes. A little girl, maybe four years old, wore the same pink dress Angel had seen downstairs, and a silver charm bracelet on her left wrist. Angel moved to the light from the open window to take a better look. The little girl sat in a child-sized chair. *Dad built that chair…for my birthday.*

The breeze cut through, cooling her skin and brushing past the surface of the painting. A slight movement caught her eye. She tilted the painting so the breeze from the window hit it more squarely. *Yes, right there.* A piece of paper was tucked under the painted chair…a rolled-up piece of paper that fluttered silently.

This time when Angel reached toward the painting, she felt a tingling in her fingertips. She inched them forward, but they didn't meet the canvas as they had before. She pushed farther, the tingling traveling up to her wrist, until she was able to wrap her fingers around the rolled-up paper. It felt solid, real. She pulled her hand back out, still gripping the paper.

She set the portrait down and unrolled the piece of paper. Three very familiar symbols were drawn on it. She'd seen them every time she looked at her charm bracelet. They were drawn first separately, and then put together to form a single shape. The shape of a key. And in the corner was a sketch of the same beetle engraved on her charm.

She stuffed the paper into her pocket; and nearly forgot to lock the front door as she dashed out.

She arrived at the farm before Gregor, and paced the living room until he came home. She had no idea how she'd made it back before him, but she was grateful for it.

Until he burst through the front door.

"How can you be so naïve about that Damian guy?" he said as the door slammed behind him. "Even Zoe senses there's something wrong with him. She growled the moment she saw him. I pulled us back behind a tree where he couldn't see us, and then he looked all around behind him like he was making sure no one else was there." Gregor's eyes were wild, and his face flushed. A vein protruded under the skin of his forehead. "Then your dear professor grabbed something out of the animal's stomach and carried it off with him. He's sick, Angel. Really sick."

Speechless, Angel sat as Gregor continued. She perched uncomfortably on the edge of the chair, but didn't dare move.

"When he walked away, I went over and took a look at the animal. It was the missing sheep, the ewe. He killed her, and cut open her womb. I think the thing he pulled out of her was an unborn lamb. I was beginning to suspect she was pregnant, the way she'd been acting. Well, she's not anymore!"

"Oh, Gregor!" Tears seeped over Angel's lids.

"Angel…" His voice came softer. "I'm sorry. But, I'm telling you he's not what he seems. Think about the way he talked about that Lunicor like I was an idiot not to believe in it. He's planting ideas in people's heads. He's a *Tamer*. How do you know he can't Tame people? How do you know the reason he seems so nice to you is that he isn't *making* you think that?"

"Why aren't you affected then?" She scooted back and sank into the leather chair.

"I've got Elven blood, remember? It does have some benefit, even if it doesn't earn me the right to my heritage."

Heritage?

Angel jumped up and shoved her hand into her pocket.

"Gregor, you're not the only one with a heritage…Look at this." She pulled the paper out for him to see.

"Don't change the subject. Didn't you hear a word I said?"

"Yes, every word. But you have to look at this. Please." She pushed the paper into his hand.

He examined the drawings, and his eyes lit with realization. "Angel, this looks like Horatio…"

"I know…wait here." She ran to her room, and pulled the bracelet out of her nightstand. She returned to the living room, clutching it tightly. She drew light from the lantern on the table into a ball to illuminate the charms. "Here, look closely."

Gregor peered at the bracelet. "Why is Horatio on your locket?"

"I don't know, but look at the symbols. Those aren't letters spelling out Angel. That first one is an A, but look at that next one. It's not an N—it looks more like an upside-down horseshoe. I always thought it had been bent. But it's an Omega. Alpha and Omega. The first and last letters of the Greek alphabet. The second verse, Gregor. *The place of beginning, the place of ending.*"

"*Completing the circle*," he said, finishing the verse. "The bracelet is a circle. And the other three are the sections of the key. They're just not in the right order. Look, they must have been switched."

The loops holding the last two charms were not perfectly round, as if they'd been pulled off and then put back on. What Angel had thought was a G was actually the bow of the key, missing a small section. The missing section of the bow, and the shank, looked like an L, and the bit was shaped like an ornate letter E.

Angel said, "It's a good thing someone did switch them, or I'd have been called *Angle* this whole time."

Gregor smiled for the first time all day, but went right back to examining the bracelet. "I need to take these off to see if we're right about this." He waited for her approval before continuing.

She nodded, not happy that her family heirloom was about to be disassembled, but it was the only way to know for sure.

Gregor carefully pried the loops open and dropped the charms into Angel's hand. They seemed too small to make a key that would open anything significant. She fitted the G and the L together, filling in the open part of the G with the short leg of the L. A tiny light emitted from the junctures, and the two pieces sealed together. She added the third piece, the letter E held horizontally to the long end of the L, and the same thing happened.

She now held a small, silver key.

Chapter Twenty-Two
The Protector

"Will you stop moping," Angel said the next day as she walked out of the kitchen after dinner. Gregor had been grumpy all day. She'd expected him to be at least a little cheered up now that they'd found the key. Sure, they had no idea what it would open, but wasn't it proof that the verses were true?

Gregor stared out the window.

Angel's heart sank. Siophra was completely out of reach, and he had every right to be angry and sad. She turned on her heel and headed back to the table. "I'm sorry. That was out of line," she said as she sat down.

Gregor didn't reply, or even look at her. He continued to gaze out the window as if entranced.

She reached over and shook his shoulder. "Gregor, come on. I said I'm sorry. I mean it. I shouldn't have said that. I know how hard this is on you."

He held stone-still, except for the twitch of muscle in his jaw as it clenched. So she told him goodnight, then headed to her room.

She pulled the key from her nightstand, and leaned against the pillow. The palm of her hand tingled where the metal touched her skin. She wrapped her fingers around it and willed it to tell her what it was meant to open. Of course nothing happened. There were no revelations or visions, and her excitement began to diminish. It looked like any other ordinary key.

For all she knew, it opened nothing special. A music box, or a diary, probably.

Doubt set in. Lying there alone, she saw how Gregor could easily forget about the verses. They were all Angel had thought about for days, but she didn't have the distraction of being in love with someone who was betrothed to another.

Her future was in those verses, and she knew they spoke the truth. She needed to have faith that when the time came for action she would be ready. She dug in the nightstand again and pulled out a piece of ribbon, which she ran through the bow of the key and tied around her neck. The tingling began again, this time in the center of her chest where the key rested.

She nestled her head into the pillow, and sleep overtook her.

Gregor's mood was still sour the next day. Angel tried not to be discouraged, and reached for the key every time the tension got too great. She watched him push his food around on his plate after lunch, his eyes glossed over. She had tried to talk to him about dozens of things, and had gotten no response whatsoever, until she mentioned the key.

"Get it out of your head, Angel," he said without looking up. "It's probably just a key to an old family diary or something. Do you really think something that tiny could open anything significant? The lock would be so easy to break if that were all it took to turn it."

It was like he'd read her thoughts from the night before. It only spurred her to be more belligerent. "But what about the beetle that looks like Horatio? That ties it all together, doesn't it?"

"He's just a beetle. Maybe he's the last of his kind, but he could have been as common as a housefly back when that bracelet was made. The game is over. Dawric only wanted your Finding Talent so he could get his hands on something. That's all. There's no real reason to believe you're part of some great prophecy. That book has to be centuries old, and it looks like the information in it is thousands of years old. It's just coincidence."

"Couldn't we at least go back to my parents' house and look for more clues? If it really is just the key to a diary or something, it may still be there.

I promise if we find anything like that I'll drop the whole thing." She put her right hand in the air as if swearing an oath, and Gregor looked up.

"I'm glad you're finally being reasonable, but I'm not in the mood for going out today. And you'd better stay close to home. If someone really is lurking around the forest near your parents' house, you need to stay away from there. Maybe tomorrow." With that he headed to his room.

Yeah, right. And tomorrow it will be, "Maybe the next day." There was no way Angel was going to wait for Gregor to change his mood. She left a note saying she was taking Zoe for a walk and crept out the back door.

Zoe pranced along, tugging on the leash and zig-zagging until Angel unhooked the leash and let her run ahead. The puppy chased something Angel couldn't see, and then gave up and ran back, walking along next to her for a few minutes before running ahead again. The ritual repeated over and over the entire way. Angel picked up her pace.

She arrived at the house, hot and tired. She pulled the house key out of her pocket and unlocked the front door while listening carefully for any strange noises. Hearing nothing but the tapping of Zoe's toenails on the porch, Angel entered. The door shut quietly behind her. She found lukewarm water in the kitchen tap and cooled it with magic. After a drink she was ready to explore.

She ascended the stairs to the loft with Zoe at her heels. Maybe if the *key to the key* was up there, whatever it opened would be as well. But she soon found the paintings calling out to her. Something of her mother was in each piece of art in that room.

She went straight to a stack of paintings leaning against the wall and began to look through them while Zoe sniffed around. Her mother had an affinity for flowers and landscapes. A love of nature that must have drawn her to Angel's father.

Angel came across a portrait of a young girl with red hair but not Angel's chocolate eyes. *Can't be me—I was already gone at this age.* Nothing about the painting was familiar. It didn't have the intensity of emotion Angel had seen in her mother's other works either.

She put the painting down and looked closely at an unfinished portrait of a man with blond hair and blue eyes. She searched for any similarity to her own features, and found touches of herself around his mouth and nose. His eyes were sad despite the slight smile on his face. Angel visualized her mother's hands holding the brush, her skillful strokes capturing the subtlety of his emotions. So much care had been taken with the tiniest detail. Why had she not finished it?

Angel pulled her eyes from the picture after memorizing every inch of the man's face. If it was her father, she wanted to carry the image of his face with her.

She noticed a paint-spattered smock hanging on the wall. The moment she touched the fabric she envisioned her mother standing in front of an easel, wiping her paintbrush on the smock between strokes. But, as usual, Angel couldn't see her mother's face, no matter how she turned the scene in her mind. Angel sighed while she hung the smock back on its hook. *I can see her hands, her back, her hair…why not her face?*

As she stood sulking, a tickling sensation on the back of her neck gave her shivers. She realized she'd never closed the window the day of her first visit.

The window offered a view of the back yard, a patch of grass and scattered flowerbeds in front of the forest edge. Angel leaned through for a better look. A girl with dark hair appeared between the trees and looked directly at Angel, her onyx eyes reflecting the mid-day sun.

Angel bounded down the stairs, nearly tripping over Zoe, and ran out the—thankfully—still unlocked front door. Zoe raced Angel around the corner of the house to the low picket fence that surrounded the back yard. Angel cleared it easily in one bound. Zoe dashed between the slats and beat Angel to the edge of the forest, barking an excited greeting.

Siophra stood waiting in the exact spot where Angel had seen her, as if she knew Angel would come down. She was breathtaking in her flowing gown of deep burgundy. Angel felt awkward and plain by comparison.

The same emerald pendant hung on its sparkling gold chain around her graceful neck—the Halvard family heirloom that rightfully belonged to Gregor. Angel wondered if Siophra knew Gregor would have given a thousand emeralds like that magnificent teardrop in exchange for her hand in marriage.

The Elven girl's penetrating stare revealed nothing of her emotions. Angel wanted to shout at her. *Don't you know how much he loves you? Don't you care?* But she held back her anger and spoke as calmly as she could.

"Siophra, I'm Angel, Gregor's cousin. I saw you—"

"I know who you are. But what are you doing here? You're trespassing." Her manner wasn't harsh, only self-assured.

"There was a disturbance here the other night, and since Gregor agreed to keep an eye on this place for the Kleidons we came to check it out. I was taking a walk with Zoe today and decided to check again, just to be sure."

Siophra's eyes softened, but her face remained tense. "And why…why did Gregor not accompany you this time? He is all right, isn't he?"

"Well, actually…"

Siophra's hand reached nervously for the emerald.

"He's okay. He's fine, but…" Angel steeled herself to ask Siophra the big question. "Do you truly care about that? Do you have any idea how Gregor feels about you getting married?"

Siophra's hand clamped down on the emerald and a single tear crept down her cheek. "Of course I do. I care more than you could know. I love Gregor. But I cannot disobey my father. Kalek told me he told you so. You just don't understand—I *cannot* disobey him."

Siophra was wrong about that, though. Angel understood all too well. She knew from her talk with Kalek, and the comments made by Mrs. Crick, just how controlling Aldrik Halvard was.

"Siophra, I'm so sorry…but I had to ask. Gregor is miserable. He thinks Kalek betrayed the two of you. He hasn't smiled in days."

"Nor have I." Siophra wiped the tear from her cheek, her other hand still wrapped around the emerald. "But please tell Gregor Kalek has not betrayed anyone. He's only been forced into obeying my father's wishes. There is nothing Kalek can do."

"I'll tell him. I knew Kalek wouldn't betray him."

Siophra smiled and her eyes shone through her tears. "Kalek is a lot of things, but he's not a betrayer."

"So, um, what are you doing over here?" Angel remembered Kalek saying something about the Elves living in the mountains. "Do you live nearby?"

"Our family lives east of the Elven mountains. Across the forest, behind Gregor." Her hand tightened ever so slightly around the emerald. "I'm here checking on a unicorn. She's pregnant and she's not doing very well with it. I've been trying to visit her every day to make sure she's all right during the birth. But I've not been able to find her for two days now." Her brow tightened.

The pieces of a puzzle clicked together in Angel's mind, forming an image of a bundle of rags with eyes wide and scared, lying on her parents' kitchen floor.

"Did you say a unicorn?"

"Yes. And she may die without me."

"She's in more danger than you know. The disturbance the other night—it was someone from town, a man Gregor called Lucky. He said he saw someone with a unicorn in the forest. He said the man was trying to hurt it, and that it followed him like it was in a trance or something." Angel's throat tightened. *What if Gregor's wrong about Lucky just hallucinating? Then it had to have been Dr. Damian. And if he killed the sheep, the unicorn might be next.*

"But only the Elven can get near a unicorn," Siophra said. "Close enough to touch it, that is. Except for Dr. Damian. But he wouldn't…" She finally released the emerald and lowered her hand.

"Lucky said the man was wearing a funny gray coat. It sounded to me like the lab coats the University professors wear." Angel watched closely for Siophra's reaction.

The Elven girl's brow furrowed more deeply. "Dr. Damian has always been kind to the animals. He's the one we call when we need help with them. Everyone is relying on him to stop the Lunicor."

"That's what I thought too," said Angel, "but Gregor told me he saw Dr. Damian doing something really awful to one of our sheep in the forest the other day. And he told me the sheep had been pregnant."

Siophra's shoulders pulled back and her nostrils flared. Apparently that was all she'd needed to hear—that Gregor had said it was so.

"Then Dr. Damian cannot be trusted! Kalek was going to talk to him tonight about Taming the mare so I can examine her, but it sounds like he's already gotten to her. And I need to know where she is, or I can't use my Talent. What do we do? She needs my Protection."

"That's your Talent? Protection?"

Siophra nodded. "I can Protect others from specific dangers. I could Protect the unicorn from Dr. Damian if I knew I where she was, the way I was going to help her through her labor." Siophra's eyes, so much like Kalek's, clouded over more deeply, and then widened. "What if he turns on Kalek? We need to stop Kalek from reaching him."

"Siophra, I think I can help. But I need you to trust me, and not ask questions."

"If Gregor trusts you, so do I."

Angel concentrated on the Elven musician. She saw him standing on the Temple steps, putting his guitar in its case.

"Okay, I can tell you that Kalek is at the Temple right now. Go to him and warn him. I'll go to Gregor and get him to Gate us to the unicorn."

"But what if you can't find her?" Siophra looked nervously around, as if she thought she'd spy the unicorn in the surrounding trees.

"That's where I need you to trust me. We *can* find her. Now go to Kalek." Angel was surprised by the confidence in her own voice.

Siophra stopped looking into the trees and focused on Angel's face. "Thank you, Angel." She reached out to touch Angel's hand, her grip like that of someone comforting an old friend. "Hey, since you're cousins with Gregor, it's almost like we're family as well."

She let go of Angel's hand and placed her fingers on the emerald again. Then she turned and headed farther into the forest, disappearing between the trees. Angel stared at the empty patch where she'd stood. *Just like Kalek.*

Angel wanted so much for Gregor and Siophra to be together now that she'd met the Elven girl. She seemed perfect for Gregor in every way.

If only Aldrik Halvard was not so stubborn! And so powerful. And so protective of his possessions. *He even treats his own daughter like a possession, like one of his precious artifacts that has to be locked away so it can't be stolen.*

And then it hit her. Siophra had said her family lived on the other side of the forest from Gregor. *Her father* was the one who told Angel's parents that she was better off dead.

And what Aldrik Halvard wants, Aldrik Halvard gets.

Angel stood there, at the edge of the forest behind her childhood home, with anger bubbling up inside her. This Aldrik Halvard was the one who'd kept her from that home for seven years by sabotaging the search effort her parents could have made. *He's a monster.*

She stomped back over to the house to lock the front door, Zoe nipping at her pant legs. "Come on, girl. We've got to get going. It's time to show me how fast you can run."

Chapter Twenty-Three
The Unicorn

Gregor was finally eating something when Angel returned to the house and entered the kitchen.

"Where've you been?" he said. "I thought you were just going out for a walk. You've been gone for nearly two hours."

"I went to my parents' house," Angel said tentatively as she poured a bowl of milk for Zoe and then joined Gregor at the table.

He started to stand but she put her hand on his arm to stop him.

"Lucky was right. *You* were right, too. Dr. Damian *is* up to something—he's the only one who can get near the unicorn and Siophra said she can't find her. She's gone to warn Kalek because he was going to ask Dr. Damian to help them—"

"You talked to Siophra? How did you—? Is she okay?" He pushed up against Angel's hand, but she held firm.

"She's fine, physically anyway. But she's just as depressed as you are. She told me that you've got to believe Kalek didn't betray you."

"Of course she'd say that. She's so trusting. I won't deny he takes care of her, but he's got no problem saving his own—"

"Gregor, stop it. Why do you have to twist everything to blame Kalek?" She grabbed his arm and locked her eyes on his. "I said we have to find that unicorn. She's pregnant and Siophra is afraid she's not going to make it through delivery. Siophra said she needs to use her Talent to

Protect her."

He pushed against her hand again, and this time she let him stand.

"Find the unicorn," he said.

"That's what I told Siophra I would do, but I need you to tell me how. I've never seen it. I thought it had to be something I'm familiar with."

"You told Siophra about your Finding?"

"Not exactly, but she trusts us. Now, what do I do?"

"Okay…let me think. You're familiar with what a unicorn is. And you're familiar with what being pregnant is."

"Are you sure that's all I need?" So much was riding on this.

"It's not like I said to Find a ladybug!" Gregor nearly shouted. "There are only a few unicorns out there and I doubt there's more than one pregnant one right now. Just try!"

Angel forced her emotions aside and concentrated, envisioning a majestic, pure-white unicorn with a silvery horn spiraling toward the sky, a glittery, glossy mane and tail, and a stomach wide and round.

But the image almost instantly began to change. The pure white fur became smeared with grime and the stomach sank in until it was concave. The shine of the glossy mane dulled and mingled with a muddy brown, and the brightness of the silvery horn faded into pitch.

Angel held her arm in the air, pointing out the direction they needed to travel. When she told Gregor the distance, his eyes narrowed and his jaw clenched.

"That's the University!"

They dashed outside, leaving Zoe whimpering and scratching at the door. Angel's legs were already tired from running all the way home, but she sprinted toward the forest. She ducked through the Gate and stepped out behind Gregor at the back of the University's science wing.

The presence of the unicorn hit Angel the second they arrived, but she couldn't pinpoint it. It didn't make sense. *We're closer—this should be easier.*

"She's here somewhere, but I can't reach her. Something's wrong. Why isn't my Talent working?" She tried again as Gregor paced.

"Focus, Angel. We've got to hurry!"

Focus. That was the problem. She was trying to focus her Talent, the way she had during the beginning of her Finding lessons. She let herself see the unicorn in the state in which her Talent had shown her before, and her hands began to tremble.

187

"She's underground." Angel's voice cracked as the words scraped through her throat. "She's dead. I can see her so clearly now. She's buried right below us."

Gregor seemed unable to speak; rage twisted his face.

"How am I going to break this to Siophra?" he said at last.

"What do we do?" Angel asked. "We can't just dig her up, can we? We need to tell someone about it. But who's going to believe we just happened upon a buried unicorn? We'll be giving away my Talent if we do. And we still can't prove it's Dr. Damian."

"Hmph!" Gregor's eyes were a fiery storm as he stared at the building behind Angel. Suddenly, his expression changed and he grabbed Angel's arm and pulled her through the nearest tree, hiding them behind it.

"What are you—?"

"Shhhh." He put his finger to her lips, and then pointed toward the building

Dr. Damian stepped out the back of the building through a door Angel hadn't noticed. He was accompanied by Dr. Randall and a man in a deep burgundy cloak. The cloak's hood covered much of the other man's face, and when he turned to speak with the two professors Angel saw he wore an eye patch. The hood obscured his other eye, so all Angel could make out was a prominent nose and a thick gray beard.

The man's cloak barely cleared the ground and his hands were covered in black gloves. Why would someone be wearing gloves in this July heat?

"Thank you so much, doktohrs." The cloaked man held his gloved hand out for Dr. Randall to shake.

Dr. Damian stepped back to avoid receiving the same gesture, and the cloaked man held his hand to his head in a mock salute instead.

"I appreciate your help vith zis so very much. I vill contact you to let you know if zis vorked."

"You're very welcome, Dr. Stieber," said Dr. Randall. "I've enjoyed working with you, and I'm sure Dr. Damian feels the same." He tilted his head in Dr. Damian's direction and smiled.

This was not the same Dr. Randall Angel had met in the doorway of Dr. Damian's office. The stern, no-nonsense look was gone, replaced by a warm smile that put crinkles around his eyes.

"Yes, yes," said Dr. Damian. "Anything I can do to help. I still can't believe you're having such a problem. Dragon pox usually doesn't cause such extreme symptoms."

"Vell, your help was exactly vhat ve needed, vasn't it, Doktohr Randall?" Angel caught a hint of sarcasm in Dr. Stieber's voice.

"Truly it was," said Dr. Randall.

His words dripped sugary sweet, giving Angel a creepy feeling, like when Cassie smiled in her direction at school.

"Good-bye for now, gentlemen." Dr. Stieber turned and walked around the corner of the building as Dr. Randall waved.

"Interesting man." Dr. Damian stared straight at the spot where Dr. Stieber had last been visible.

"I'm sure if you got to know him better you'd find him utterly fascinating," said Dr. Randall. "Besides, he may have come to me because of the birth defects but it was you he really needed all along."

It was odd hearing such words of praise coming from Dr. Randall after he had been so brusque the last time Angel had seen him. Had he been in a bad mood that day? Maybe…but it seemed more to her at the moment, as she crouched behind the tree with Gregor, that Dr. Randall was somehow changed. He seemed filled with respect for Dr. Damian, and with gratitude toward him. His expression reminded her of the way the Cagon had looked at Dr. Damian.

The two men stood for a moment without talking, and then Dr. Randall walked about twenty feet, stopping directly over the spot where the unicorn was buried.

"It feels good to work on something that will make a difference in the world. That's what research is all about, isn't it? Progress and discovery. Knowing that your work is paying off after tremendous sacrifice." Dr. Randall smiled broadly. "You never know what will come from teamwork."

Dr. Damian stared at the ground under Dr. Randall's feet.

"Honestly…I think I prefer to work alone." He turned abruptly, but stopped when Dr. Randall spoke again.

"I guess that means you don't want my help with that unicorn Kalek Halvard told you about. He said she was pregnant. That *is* my area of expertise…"

"No," Dr. Damian replied, his back still toward Dr. Randall, "I think I can handle it. I'll have Siophra with me." He walked back into the building.

Dr. Randall looked down at the ground as if to see what had previously grabbed Dr. Damian's attention. He stretched his thin mouth into another grin, tapped the ground with the toe of his shoe, and then headed back into the building.

"We need to get to Siophra and stop her." Fear creased Gregor's forehead and hollowed his eyes.

Angel concentrated on Siophra. "She's at the other end of the forest, sitting on the edge of a bed. She must be home."

"I'll never be able to get near enough to warn her."

"But isn't she safest there? She probably doesn't even know Kalek has spoken to Dr. Damian. He wasn't supposed to come here until later. Besides, she already suspects Dr. Damian. She's not going to go near him."

"I want to warn her anyway. What if he goes after her?"

"What we need to do is find Kalek and tell him in case Siophra hasn't talked to him yet." Angel focused on Finding Kalek; but she couldn't get an image of him or a sense of his location.

"I'm not Finding him."

"He's probably at the cliffs then. It's, um, farther than I've let you practice."

Angel clenched her jaw. *He lied to me about the strength of my Talent. Figures.*

Gregor held his hand up to the tree they were hiding behind. "Come on. I can Gate us most of the way, but we'll have some climbing to do when we get there."

~Protecting Plans~

"He believes I'm gone. Loan it to me, so there is no chance of him seeing me."

The scientist shook his head. "No, you must stay hidden."

"Hide? Why should I? Loan it to me...I am ready."

"You've gotten better. But you're not the only one." The scientist grinned. "I believe the girl has improved her Talent enough. It is time for one last thing before we need her, though."

"You're sure you can get the other one? Even with her Talent?"

"Of course. You know all too well what I am capable of."

He knew, but he did not trust the scientist. "Just be careful. Do not draw attention."

"Don't worry...our plan is...ahem...*well protected.*"

Chapter Twenty-Four
The Scream

They arrived near the top of a rocky incline. The sound of crashing waves rolled over the peak and the familiar scent of salty air tingled Angel's nostrils.

She began the climb behind Gregor, following a path worn into the rocky ground, toward a peak that cut into the sky ahead of them. Her legs strained as she pushed up the incline, and her shoes slipped on the fine pebbles and dust. Gregor had to stop more than once to wait for her. He was impatient, she knew, but he didn't express it. His silhouette rose above her with the sun glaring behind him and he looked stronger than she'd ever seen him.

They finally reached the peak, and Angel gazed down at the shore below. She'd never seen the ocean from this vantage point, and its vastness awed her. The crystalline blue water formed foamy crests that looked like strings of pearls being swept onto the sand. The crashing of the water echoed off the rocks, a more formidable sound than the gentle lapping of the waves that slipped over the sandy, gulf coast beaches of Florida. A flock of small dragons flew overhead, the bright sunlight glinting off their scales.

She saw no sign of Kalek.

Gregor began to descend the crumbled staircase of boulders that led to the beach far below. He carefully chose the precise spots on which to place each step and pointed them out for her, never moving too far ahead. The rocks felt solid enough under her feet, but images bombarded her mind—bumping and crashing and bones crunching as her limp body tumbled down the steep slope.

Lizards disappeared into the cracks between the rocks as they passed, and at one point a hissing sound issued from a deep crevice. Angel prayed that whatever it was would stay hidden inside.

Step by step, Angel made her way down without falling. Gregor led her between two huge boulders where Kalek sat on a large plateau, staring toward the sea as if trying to unravel its mysteries.

"Have you come to fight with me again, Gregor? Because I'm really not in the mood. Actually, I'd appreciate you leaving. Angel, you can stay." Kalek's voice was smooth as polished stone, like the onyx of his eyes that continued searching the ocean in front of him.

"I came to warn you to stay away from Dr. Damian," Gregor said in a strained voice, "and to ask you to make sure Siophra does *not* meet him today. She's in danger."

Kalek ignored him.

Angel stepped up next to Gregor and poured every ounce of her fear into her voice. "Kalek, Gregor's right. He saw Dr. Damian with one of our sheep and she was slashed wide open. I've already told Siophra, but she may still be in danger if she returns to the forest to look for the unicorn on her own. You need to tell her the unicorn is dead. It was, um, laying behind the University and we found it when we went to, um…" Angel couldn't think of an explanation.

Kalek didn't seem to need any. He stood and looked past Gregor, directing his gaze at Angel alone. His eyes blazed.

"You're sure about this?"

Angel nodded.

"Lead the way, then."

He waited for Gregor to head back up the rocks and let Angel go next. Gregor chose a steep return route, forcing Angel to lean in toward the slope to keep her grip. She kept her gaze planted firmly on the rocks in front of her face and concentrated on the destination above her head.

With the peak securely in sight, Angel reached to grab the next rock. It pulled loose in her hand and knocked her off-balance. She tried to catch herself with her foot, but that foot slipped past the side of the rock below her and her shoe wedged into a crevice. Kalek grabbed her and held her steady, but she was afraid to move her other leg and she didn't have the leverage to get her foot out of the crevice.

She clung to the rocks and refused to loosen her grip so she could move into a position of better footing. She'd been thinking only of the other side of the incline. Now images of jagged boulders overtook her mind, and she swallowed a scream. *I'm never going to make it back...*

Kalek's and Gregor's voices echoed in her ears, drowned out by the roaring of the surf below. The waves threatened to climb the rocks and wash her away, smothering the life out of her with their icy wet hands. The rocks wanted to jump out from below her and let her slide freely into the depths with only their jagged edges slowing her fall. She closed her eyes and dug her fingers into the rock, which cut her hands and cramped her muscles.

Finally Gregor's voice broke through the din that filled Angel's ears.

"Angel, just move your left foot inch by inch to the right. You've got to get your legs closer together so Kalek can pull your other foot out. There's a rock you can brace yourself on. I promise you'll be fine—we're right here, you won't fall. Please! Kalek's got to get to Siophra before Damian does!"

His words hit her brain like a bullet. Siophra was the one in true danger. She braced herself and focused. *Okay, foot, move.*

Her foot obeyed. Her shoe ground against the rock but it moved. Little by little it traced the curve of the rock until she had to let go and grope for the rock to its right. Oh, how she hated that feeling. One foot wedged, the muscles in her calf pulled awkwardly, and her weight borne only by her hands. But then her left foot hit solid rock again and she was able to shift her weight and release the strain on her right leg. Kalek worked her foot loose, and Angel released the breath that fear had frozen in her lungs.

At the top of the peak she sat on the ground to collect herself. Her hands were covered with tiny cuts and her ankle was bruised, but otherwise she was fine. She cast her gaze down momentarily and gave both men a subdued thank-you.

Gregor urged her with a meaningful look. She concentrated on Siophra, and nodded to him, indicating that Siophra was still in her room. As they headed down the slope leading away from the cliff's edge, Angel took great care to kick her feet into the ground solidly each time she took a step and soon they reached the trees.

Gregor Gated them to a spot just outside the Halvards' property line and Kalek dashed toward the house.

Gregor and Angel waited in the trees just off the Halvards' land, which was surrounded by a ten-foot brick wall. Gregor fidgeted and muttered under his breath, pacing back and forth between two trees.

"I could Gate right to her window if it weren't for those dogs. I know the old man got them just to keep me away. I swear he trained them to recognize my scent."

The dogs paced in time with Gregor, the thumping of their feet so loud Angel imagined they must be the size of horses.

"What is taking him so long?" Gregor stopped pacing and slammed the side of his fist against the wall. The dogs' steps increased in volume and rhythm until it sounded like the earth was being pummeled with rocks. Barks, deep and fierce, rumbled from behind the wall, and claws like iron nails scraped against the bricks. Then the elephantine paws hit the ground with huge *thuds*, and the dogs returned to their pacing.

"It's only been fifteen minutes," Angel said. "Kalek must be talking with her."

Gregor glared at her. "Only fifteen minutes? Only?" His nostrils flared. "This is killing me. We need to do something. Can you at least Find Dr. Damian? Make sure he's not in there with them?"

Angel nodded and concentrated. A faint image formed, hazy, blurred. It flickered in and out of her mind, but never gained focus. And she had no sense of direction or distance.

"It's not...I can't..."

"What?" He stared at her, fingers tucked into his bangs.

"The image won't form. It's like I can't really get a signal...it's so weird."

Without warning a figure appeared at the top of the wall and Angel screamed, causing the dogs to barrel toward the wall and dig into the bricks once again.

"Shut up, you mutts!" Kalek jumped down to the ground like a cat, graceful and lithe, and slunk toward Gregor.

"She's not there. I searched the entire house. She must have already gone out into the forest. We had to have missed her by seconds."

"Why did you have to tell that nut she'd meet him in the forest?" Gregor poked Kalek in the chest with his finger. "Instead of playing on the rocks you should be going out there with her! If she were my wife she'd never spend a moment alone, and she'd never be in danger."

"Gregor!" Angel pushed herself between the two men. "It's not Kalek's fault you can't marry Siophra. You've got to stop taking it out on him."

"Stay out of it! You don't understand." He continued snarling but put his hand down to his side. "He's supposed to be a man. And he was supposed to be my friend."

"I'd never do anything to harm my sister," said Kalek, "no matter how misguided her affections may be. And if you'd rather stand here and fight you'll have to do it alone because I'm going to find her."

Gregor froze. He looked at Angel and implored with his eyes. She'd caught the words too—*find her.*

But Kalek had already walked into the forest. Angel ran after him, trailed closely by Gregor. She reached to grab Kalek's arm, but before she could, he stopped in his tracks. He cocked his head to the side, eyes closed, focusing his attention as though he were trying to sense something unseen.

"Did you hear—?" His eyes popped open and he cocked his head again. "That's Siophra!"

Angel concentrated on the Elven girl, and spun to face Gregor. She mouthed Siophra's location. Gregor Gated through the nearest tree, and Angel and Kalek darted through after him.

They found Siophra crumpled on the ground of a small clearing, her hair covering her face, leaves scattered around her still form. Gregor dropped to his knees and tentatively touched her shoulder, then gently rolled her onto her back. A dart protruded from the center of her chest, circled by a small crimson stain.

Angel's throat went dry and her legs threatened to give out.

Gregor trembled as he reached for the dart, poised on his knees, eyes blazing. He tenderly pulled the dart from Siophra's chest, and then plunged it into the ground next to him.

Angel stood breathless as she watched Gregor's hand press against Siophra's neck, and then slide down and grip her wrist. His shoulders dropped as a sob escaped him.

"No…no…no…"

His hands became more frantic as he checked her pulse again and again. Then he leaned over her and placed his palm against her breastbone and pressed…

Angel swung her gaze to Kalek, who hadn't moved toward Siophra. He stood as he had before, perfectly still, ears keened for a sound only he had heard, but this time his hand poised over the dagger strapped to his thigh. Then Angel heard it too—the faintest shuffling of leaves, and an almost inaudible snap of a tiny twig. Her heart skittered through its next beat.

Kalek's dagger was in the air, thrown with perfect precision, and found its mark in a tree on the other side of the clearing. He and Angel dashed to the tree, only to find a small torn piece of gray cloth embedded into the bark with the dagger. Quick crunching footsteps retreated into the forest.

When they peered around the tree they caught only a glimpse of gray clothing before it disappeared amid the dense foliage.

Kalek dashed between the trees, gone before Angel could take the first step after him. She stood helpless, gazing into the empty trees. She heard Gregor behind her as he tried to breathe life back into Siophra—she kept her back to them, unable to bear the image without Kalek by her side. The moments stretched far too long as she waited, heart fluttering and tears burning her eyes. She bit her trembling lip. *Hurry, Kalek, hurry. Be careful…*

Kalek finally appeared, anger etched on his face, and shook his head at Angel. He passed by her and walked solemnly toward Gregor and Siophra. As he knelt down beside them, tears welled in his eyes.

Gregor's hand cupped Siophra's head and he pressed his mouth to hers. Angel could hear the breath he tried to force into Siophra's lungs. Then, he released her and began pressing her breastbone again. His hands and the front of her dress were smeared with blood, and a crimson line trailed from her mouth.

Siophra's eyes still shone like polished stone, but they were empty now. Strands of hair clung to her face, which was far too pale. Her lips stood out against the ghostly white skin, purple-blue. Kalek let out a gut-wrenching howl that tore through Angel, shattering something inside her.

"Gregor, stop," Kalek said, and grabbed Gregor's wrists.

Gregor wrenched away. "No…no…she's not dead…she'll breathe…I just have to..."

Kalek grabbed him again, fingers digging into Gregor's arms. "Gregor, now! No more!"

Gregor lifted his face to Kalek and shook his head. His mouth opened, and his lip trembled, but no words came out. He sank back until he was sitting, legs bent beneath him. He pushed both hands into his bangs, over and over, smearing blood across his forehead. His breath came ragged and gurgling. Angel found herself straining to take in air.

Finally, Gregor leaned forward, wrapped his arms around Siophra, and pulled her to his chest. His fingers brushed her hair from her face as tears streamed down his cheeks.

"Siophra..." His face lowered slowly toward hers, until his lips touched her forehead. He took another ragged breath, and kissed her lips one final time.

Angel began to sob, her lungs tightening, pulling away from her ribs. Her arms burned with the need to embrace him, both of them. She stepped forward, and then stopped. The air tingled with the grief of the two men in front of her and she had no place disrupting them. She forced herself to stand still, watching, aching.

Gregor continued cradling Siophra, tears streaming down his cheeks, the silver flecks in his eyes like tiny flames. He didn't protest when Kalek reached over to smooth Siophra's hair and slide his graceful fingers over her eyes, closing her lids. Now she looked more peaceful, and Gregor drew back to drink in the beautiful face.

Kalek looked at Gregor, silently pleading Gregor to allow him something—Angel didn't know what—as his hand reached to the back of Siophra's neck. The magnificent emerald on her chest slid as the chain unclasped, and slipped off into Kalek's other hand.

Sorrow roughened Kalek's voice. "I did *not* give this to her as a wedding present. I gave it to her as a reminder that she, no matter who she calls husband, will always truly belong to you. Just as this belongs to you." He opened his hand to show Gregor the emerald gleaming in his palm.

Gregor didn't speak. He sat, Siophra secure in his arms, tears dripping from his chin, staring at Kalek as though he wasn't sure what to believe.

Kalek continued, "I had to give it to her, Gregor. It was the only way to save you both. If I had returned it to you before my father's death he would have only come to stake his claim over half your farm. He would've forced you into selling your family's land, or brought you into bankruptcy by charging you a fortune to rent his half. He told me that when I begged him to give you back the necklace."

"I didn't need this back, Kalek," Gregor said hoarsely. "She was all I wanted from your father." He gazed down at Siophra.

"And she would have come at a higher price." Kalek pounded his fist on his knee. "My father told me he'd frame you and have you arrested for stealing the necklace, claiming you were using it to force Siophra to marry you. He'd be able to take everything from you, Gregor. The necklace, your land, Siophra. And you'd spend the rest of your life in prison. I couldn't let that happen. I had to get the necklace someplace where my father wouldn't dare touch it, so I gave it to Siophra. That pleased him, and I knew he'd leave you alone. And Siophra could have at least a piece of you."

Gregor opened his mouth to speak, but Kalek cut him off.

"The suitor my father chose is *old*, Gregor. He'd have only had Siophra for a while, and then when he and my father both died, you'd be free to marry her. I didn't tell you what I planned, knowing how much you loved her and that you'd try to stop anything that put Siophra in another man's arms. But the loss of our friendship would have been worth it if my plan had worked. I knew your love was strong enough to survive until Siophra was free."

Gregor gazed back down at his beloved, and when he raised his head, Angel could see by his expression that he believed Kalek.

"I don't care what your father does with my land now. Nothing else matters to me, not even my family's farm, without her…" He choked back his sobs, then softly kissed Siophra's forehead.

Angel tasted the salt of her own tears running over her lips.

"I have to bring her back home for burial," said Kalek, "and I'll tell my father to end the feud, or I will leave him myself. He no longer has Siophra to use as a bargaining chip. And he cannot stand the thought of leaving this world with no heir, but if he does not leave you alone, I'll disown myself from the family." Kalek's voice was back to its cool timbre, but his eyes were tear-filled and his face was hard and angry.

"I'm going with you." Strength had returned to Gregor's voice also.

"Yes, my brother." Kalek pushed the emerald necklace into Gregor's hand, and then helped him stand. Gregor still held Siophra tightly against his chest, her delicate frame weightless in his strong arms.

Angel stood silently, watching the two men, tears of joy now mingling with her tears of sadness. They were reunited in Siophra's death, but Kalek's friendship would be a pale replacement for Siophra's love.

Without a word, Kalek and Gregor looked at Angel, and she nodded.

"Don't worry about me," she said. "Whoever was here is long gone by now, and I'll take Kalek's dagger."

"Of course. Be careful," Kalek said.

The men turned, and Gregor Gated them both through the nearest tree, leaving Angel alone in the clearing.

Angel wiped away the tears that wet her cheeks, and inhaled. Anger swelled, displacing her sorrow. Her trembling fingers tightened into fists as she stalked toward the tree that held Kalek's dagger.

She braced her feet against the ground to give her the leverage she needed to withdraw the dagger. When it pulled free from the tree, she stumbled back, and tripped over a root. The dagger flew out of her hand when she landed. She spotted it several feet away, lying next to the dart Gregor had removed from Siophra's chest. But when she got closer, she saw it wasn't a dart after all. It was a hypodermic needle—a *plastic* one—something never used by the Empowered, who only used natural materials. The needle itself was far thicker than any Angel had seen.

There was still a small amount of liquid inside the syringe, and as Angel stared at it the plastic began to dissolve as though the liquid were eating it away. She quickly conjured a small glass vial from the cupboard at the farmhouse and poured the liquid into the vial. The glass proved impermeable to the liquid and Angel dropped the syringe to the ground while she capped the vial. When she looked back down, the plastic was completely gone and all that remained was the silver needle. She melted the needle and molded it into a small bead so that it couldn't pierce her and dropped it into her bag along with the vial. She grabbed Kalek's dagger, Found her way back to the main forest path, and walked the distance to the farm.

Angel took the vial out of her bag and hid it in her nightstand. She sat on the bed, examining the intricate engravings in the blade of Kalek's dagger, and began to wonder about Siophra's murderer. Obviously, the prime suspect was Dr. Damian. He had the motivation. If he was really the one killing the mother animals, then naturally he'd want their Protector out of the way.

But how did he get the needle?

Angel thought back to the day in his lab. The room was completely lacking in modern technology. And he even went to Sir Benjamin for books. He seemed to not have any real connection to the ordinary world.

Except for the newspaper clipping that was inside his book. But attending Dr. Watkin's lecture had nothing to do with hypodermic needles. And it didn't make him a murderer.

Angel concentrated on Dr. Damian. This time the image came through. *Why didn't it before?* He was brushing down his winged horse outside the University. He looked flushed and disheveled...but did he look like someone who had just committed murder?

There had to be something else going on. Maybe Dr. Damian was killing the animals on the island, but there could be someone else, totally unconnected, with a plan of their own. Someone who had no qualms about killing humans.

There was only one possibility...Dawric. The verses were coming into play again, and Angel was still convinced that Dawric had a part in fulfilling their predictions. *The place of beginning, the place of ending, completing the circle.* It had all started with Dawric searching for her...it could have to end with him finding her.

But why kill Siophra? How did that tie in? Unless he wanted her Talent. Angel rolled the dagger's handle in her palm. *But, Siophra's Talent hadn't even Protected her.*

Wait! Protection. What did that verse say? The guardian shall leave his post. Could Siophra be the guardian? Angel felt like she was assembling two different puzzles whose pieces had all been put in the same box, and there were pieces that looked like they could belong to either puzzle. One puzzle scene showed two men with two different motives, and the other showed one man with multiple motives; and she had no way of sorting them out.

At the moment she held one puzzle piece that needed placing, and it might give her a start on the others. The poison that killed Siophra. But what could she do to test it? Who could she go to that could analyze the poison in the vial? The most obvious choice would be Dr. Damian, but he was also the most obvious one she could *not* go to. Sir Benjamin no longer spent time in labs, but…

Dr. Kate, the dragon doctor! She said she had her own lab, and maybe she had the equipment necessary to test toxins. And she'd told Angel to come by any time.

She set the dagger on her nightstand and leaned against the headboard, sighing with resignation. *Oh, Angel, you can't just walk in off the street and ask Dr. Kate for this kind of help. You only met her once!*

But what other choice did she have? The liquid needed to be tested somehow. The type of poisons used on the island would be very different from poisons found in the ordinary world, which were mostly man-made. Maybe, just maybe, if the poison turned out to be something that originated on the island it would turn the pointer toward Dr. Damian. It would still be incredibly difficult to convince everyone that their trusted Tamer was a killer, but at least Angel and Gregor would know.

But if the vial had something else in it, a man-made substance, it could mean something else altogether. An idea was burgeoning in Angel's mind, and if she was right about that liquid…

She would take the contents of the syringe to Dr. Kate, and that was that. She'd just have to figure out a way to convince the dragon doctor to help her without drawing suspicion. And if her guess was on target, she'd have even more proof for Gregor that the verses were coming true.

Chapter Twenty-Five
The Dragon Lady

Angel waited hours for Gregor's return, sketching to pass the slowly creeping time. Eyes covered pages in her sketchbook; they were all she could draw. Deep, penetrating eyes, full of pride and devoid of love. Dr. Watkins' eyes...and Melinda's sad eyes.

What had happened to her? Had Melinda found anyone else who'd look beyond the black clothes and Ouija boards?

Angel wished Melinda could be here, and see real magic for herself.

Gregor finally walked in the door just when Angel had decided to go to bed. Dark shadows circled his eyes, and he dragged himself through the doorway like a sleepwalker. Angel waved the door closed behind him and then sat beside him on the couch. She wanted to put her arms around him or take his hand, but she only cried silently at the sight of him.

"She's really gone." His voice was hoarse from crying, but his tears seemed to have run out. "I thought Ole Aldrik was going to kill me, Angel. I really did. But Kalek grabbed him and dragged him into the next room. I could have exploded just sitting there. Siophra was still so beautiful, and she just looked...peaceful. I kept thinking she had to be sleeping, and her eyes would open and it would all have been a big mistake..."

His voice broke and the tears Angel thought had run out sprang up and spilled out of his hollowed eyes before he buried his face in his hands.

This time Angel did reach out, and held him until his shoulders pulled back and squared. He directed his gaze toward the window, but it didn't hide the tears sliding down the side of his cheek.

"He'll never admit he's wrong. Even after all Kalek told him, he still blames me. He thinks she must have snuck off to see me. He took the necklace, then had his brutes 'escort' me out. Kalek's going to stay home until the funeral, but he told his father that unless the feud ends he'll disown the entire family. It won't end though. He'll stake his claim on half the farm now and torment me until..." Gregor sniffed and his jaw tightened. "None of it matters now. The old maggot can have the *whole place* for all I care. If I can't share it with Siophra I don't want it at all."

"Would he really take the farm like that? Is he that cruel?" asked Angel.

The misery she saw in Gregor's eyes said, *yes, crueler than you know.*

Gregor rose from the couch and headed toward the stairs.

"We'll find a way to stop him, Gregor," Angel called to him as he took the first step up.

"I just don't care anymore. He can have the farm. All I wanted was for him to let me love his daughter. I would have appreciated her the way he never did."

"I know you would have, Gregor. I know you *did*. And so did she."

A faint hint of a smile played on his lips before he turned and climbed the rest of the stairs.

Angel pulled Zoe onto the bed with her that night. Zoe gave her a confused look, but licked Angel's cheek before snuggling up against her chest. Angel pulled the covers over both of them, and let her head fall to the pillow. In moments the fabric was soaked with tears.

The image of Gregor's tortured face burned behind her eyelids. He had lost everything, just as she had so many years ago. She cried for him, and for herself. They had only each other right now.

The house felt hollow around her, empty because the two people inside it were empty. She tightened her arms around Zoe. The puppy's warmth and soft breathing soothed her, and she closed her eyes. Her thoughts quieted as soulful music slid through the bedroom window.

Angel awoke with Shakespeare crouching on her chest and breathing up her nose. "Me-aw," he said when her eyes popped open, and then continued kneading his paws into her skin. She pulled herself out of bed, tucked him under her arm and carried him to the kitchen.

The room was empty and quiet. No coffee aroma filled the air, and the dim sunlight shining through the kitchen window seemed reluctant to enter the room. Angel filled a bowl of food for Shakespeare and walked outside with Zoe. She found herself peering into the forest, looking for the rustling of branches at the edge of the trees. But there was no sign of Gregor. She fought the desire to Find him.

She did only the bare minimum of work that day, partly because Gregor wasn't there to help her, and partly because she was anxious to get to Dr. Kate's. The note she left on the kitchen table said only that she'd gone into town. Gregor would be concerned, and angry, if she told him the truth.

The idea of going to the authorities popped into her head one more time while she rode toward town. But since she didn't actually have the syringe, or even the needle, she didn't think she'd be taken seriously. What kind of help would that be? The whole town already knew animals were being killed, and they would soon all know that Siophra was poisoned as well. Angel couldn't very well report that she'd seen a plastic syringe that didn't exist anymore. And Mr. Halvard had most certainly already initiated the search for Siophra's killer. He probably had an entire Elven militia scouring the island.

Until Angel found out the liquid's composition, she didn't want to let on that she and Gregor suspected Dr. Damian, just in case they were wrong. No one would believe them with Aldrik Halvard disparaging Gregor's name.

Actually, there was one person who would believe them. Angel smiled as she thought of Lucky and his hallucinations. What a great witness he would make...*Yes, Your Honor, I saw a man in a gray jacket leading a unicorn through the forest. He was followed by a group of little green men holding pots of gold.*

Angel could have led the authorities to the unicorn, but how would she explain how she knew it was there without giving away her identity and sending the town into a panic? Mr. Halvard was angrier than ever over the loss of his daughter and if he got wind that the *Finder* was back, well, Angel couldn't even imagine what he'd do. And when he found out Gregor was harboring her in his home…

No. This is my only choice.

Angel urged Juliet to move faster.

She'd used her Finding to locate Dr. Kate, and turned Juliet in that direction after they passed Old Man Brady's and the town square. The winding road led into a neighborhood, and Angel followed it to the building that housed Dr. Kate's lab. She scrunched her eyes. *Her office is in her house?*

Angel approached the huge, concrete house with shells embedded in the outer walls. *What's this style called? Oh, yes. Tabby.* Angel had seen one or two houses like this in Florida because of the Spanish influence, but out here on Toch Island? As she walked to the door she ran her fingers along the rough texture of the shells. The house looked out of place among the fir and spruce trees in Dr. Kate's yard and the wooden cottages that made up the rest of the neighborhood.

A small painted sign shaped like an arrow indicated the direction of the office entrance, which was on the side, almost to the very back of the house. A high, Tabby fence encircled the back yard. Angel pushed the door open and entered the room.

A young woman with long blond hair and pale freckles sat behind a wooden desk covered with file folders. When she looked up, her smile filled her entire face. She rose from her seat and stood at the end of the desk. She wore a long-sleeve shirt, jeans, and work boots, with leather gloves tucked into her belt.

"Can I help you?" she asked.

"Um…my name's Angel. I was hoping I could speak with Dr. Kate." Angel heard the tenseness in her own voice and tried to relax, but she was doubting her decision.

"She's busy with a patient right now, but she'll be done in just a bit. Do you have a dragon that needs care?" The girl's tone, and kind, welcoming eyes, reassured Angel, but the information was for Dr. Kate's ears only.

"No, it's more of a personal matter."

"Well, then, make yourself comfortable. My name's Gwen. I'm Dr. Solberg's assistant. Let me know if there's anything you need."

"Thank you."

Gwen smiled and went back to her work at the desk.

Angel walked around the waiting room. Dragons of every shape and size peered at her from paintings and drawings, sat as statues on top of tables and shelves, and even hovered in the air just below the ceiling. The room was furnished with heavy wooden chairs and chunky wooden side tables. One larger table was pushed into the corner of the room with three high-backed chairs askew around it. As Angel approached the table she saw what lay on top—an incomplete puzzle for the dragon owners to work on while they waited. She wondered if Dr. Kate got the idea from Sir Benjamin or vice versa.

Scratches and gouges marred the stone floors. From dragon claws? As she stood pondering the claws that were required to make such marks in solid rock, the door opened.

"Hello, Mrs. Anderson. How's little Maggie today?" Gwen's smile traveled across her face again and she walked around the desk to peek into the carrier.

"Much better. She's eating normally again and her scales look like polished gold."

Mrs. Anderson sat and placed the carrier in her lap. Angel's curiosity took over and she sidled into the seat next to Mrs. Anderson.

"What kind of dragon do you have?"

"Oh, Maggie's a miniature…well, I'm not really sure. She's a mutt, I guess you could say."

Mrs. Anderson reminded Angel of Mrs. Mason's aunt—petite, curly gray hair, glasses that sat ever so slightly crooked on her tiny nose. She unzipped the flap on the carrier and let Angel peek in.

"May I pet her?"

Mrs. Anderson nodded.

Maggie felt smooth and snakelike just like Spike, but her scales were much smaller and shone a lovely golden yellow marbled with deep brown. She was like a scaled Chihuahua, without the fiery temperament. She held her little head up so Angel could scratch under her chin, dreamily closing her walnut-colored eyes. Zack had always wanted a Chihuahua—if only he could have one of these.

"Angel, Dr. Kate can see you now."

As Angel traveled the hallway to Dr. Kate's office, a man walked toward the waiting room. A midnight blue dragon the size of a Great Dane lumbered ahead of him, tugging at the leash and harness. He tugged even harder when he spied Angel.

"He's friendly," the man said as they neared her. "The worst he'd do is lick ya ta death." The dragon lunged forward, dragging the man about three feet. Then he abruptly plopped down on his haunches, and furiously licked Angel's outstretched hand with a prickly cat-like tongue.

"C'mon, Luke. Let's get goin', boy." The man yanked the leash and Luke jumped to his feet and lunged toward the door. Angel looked behind her as they passed. Gwen stood in the doorway dangling some kind of biscuit. Angel continued on to the door at the end of the hall.

"Welcome," Dr. Kate said as Angel entered the office. She sat behind a mahogany desk much like Sir Benjamin's, but the feet were dragon talons and the desktop was covered with glass. The cozy office was decorated in gem tones and deep-stained woods. More dragon statues were housed on the built-in shelves and a large Chinese dragon guarded the plant stand in the corner of the room.

"To what do I owe this pleasure? I'm afraid I don't have time to give you a tour today."

Angel stood inside the doorway, fidgeting with the strap on her bag. She'd rehearsed this conversation a dozen times in her head, but she still didn't know how to ask Dr. Kate about the liquid in the syringe without lying to her. Guilt threatened to stop her altogether, but she had to find out for sure who was involved in Siophra's death and help clear Gregor's name with Mr. Halvard.

"Dr. Kate, I've got a favor to ask. I hope this won't be much trouble and I can pay you for it..."

"What is it, sweetie? Go ahead, I don't bite. At least not unless I'm bitten first." Dr. Kate smiled slyly, but her eyes twinkled.

"Okay, I found this liquid in a broken bottle in the pasture. I think one of the sheep may have drank some and I wanted to see if you could analyze it."

Dr. Kate's eyebrow arched over her glasses.

"Did it make the sheep sick?" She motioned Angel to the chair in front of the desk. Angel sat stiffly and pulled the vial out of her bag.

"Well, she's not acting right at all. She won't let me close enough to tell if she's really sick. I'm not even sure she actually drank any, but I just want to be safe."

"You brought it with you?" Dr. Kate nodded toward Angel's hand, which was wrapped tightly around the vial.

"Yes, here." She handed it to Dr. Kate and held her breath as the dragon doctor examined its contents through the glass.

"A few simple tests should give me an idea what it is."

Angel let out her breath. "Really?"

"Absolutely. Give me a couple days, though. And don't worry about paying me. Gwen needs some training on this kind of thing anyway." Dr. Kate increased the volume of her voice as she spoke the last sentence and gave Angel a conspiring look.

"I heard that!" Gwen called from the hallway.

Dr. Kate let out a hearty laugh. "I never get enough of teasing her. She's a great sport."

Angel smiled. "Thank you, Dr. Kate. I really appreciate this."

"Not a problem. Ben told me you're Gregor Halvard's cousin, and he seems very fond of you. I'd do anything to help him out."

Angel shifted nervously in her seat. She'd forgotten that Dr. Kate might mention her visit to Sir Benjamin. *I hope she doesn't find out I never asked him for directions.*

Dr. Kate eyed the vial one more time. "You said the sheep's acting strangely, but not showing signs of illness?"

"Pretty much. But I can't help but worry."

"How long has she been acting this way?"

"A couple of days, but I didn't find this until last night."

Dr. Kate's face brightened. "Try not to worry. It sounds like she's agitated about something, rather than having a reaction to a toxin, but we'll get to the bottom of it. Could be she's just on edge because of the Lunicor that's around—you did say she's female?"

Angel nodded.

"Women's intuition," Dr. Kate added with a wink.

Angel shuddered involuntarily. *It was my intuition I was listening to that told me Dr. Damian was a good guy. And look where that's gotten me.*

Angel stood and held her hand out. But Dr. Kate rose from her chair and walked around the desk. She put her arm around Angel's shoulders like a mother hen.

"It's great seeing you again, Angel. Are you enjoying your stay here?"

"Very much. Gregor's wonderful, and this place is just beautiful."

"Well, I'm glad. I have to agree that this is a pretty great town. And please, come back so I can give you that tour. I wish I could have today, but I've had to schedule a surgery for this afternoon."

"I understand. And thanks again."

Dr. Kate gave Angel's shoulder another quick squeeze and she returned to her seat behind the desk.

"Would you tell Gwen to send in Mrs. Anderson for me?" she asked.

Gwen called from the hallway, "She's already on her way in!"

Dr. Kate chortled again as Angel left the room.

Chapter Twenty-Six
The Visit

"How's Spike doing?" Angel asked as she sat down at the puzzle table across from Sir Benjamin. Spike snoozed on his pillow as usual. His metallic scales glistened in the light of the lantern on Sir Benjamin's desk, flickers of dark and pale green dancing across his side. His snout was tucked under his wing, which muffled his snoring.

"Much better. Kate has such a gift. I don't know what I'd do without her. He had me worried for a while there, but he's back to his old self again and he's even gained some weight." He beamed at her and glanced over at Spike.

"Awesome." She turned her attention to the box in his hand. "New puzzle?"

"Yes, yes." He scrutinized the picture on the box top. "Dr. Damian got this for me. It's one of the spiders I've been studying for my book. This one's going to be quite difficult. Look here, how the web looks the same all the way around and the foliage behind it is monochromatic. And the bark on that tree…"

"You saw Dr. Damian?" Angel tried to sound casual, but her heart thumped hard against her ribs.

"He came by just last night with this. He was so excited that he'd found it he couldn't wait another day to give it to me. He must've flown Lightning here full-speed. You okay, Angel?"

Sir Benjamin was staring at her, and she tried unsuccessfully to remove the blank look on her face.

"Lightning?" she asked.

"His winged horse. Surely he told you about Lightning. That horse is his pride and joy."

Angel felt Sir Benjamin's eyes bearing down on her.

"Of course, he did. But he never mentioned the horse's name. Um…you said he came last night on Lightning?" *That's why I couldn't Find him properly! He was flying too fast for me to pinpoint.*

"He barely made it before I had the shop locked up. Impatient, that one." Sir Benjamin continued peering at her curiously.

Angel fidgeted with her hair as she processed Sir Benjamin's words. *Impatient, nothing. He needed an alibi! That was almost the same time as Siophra's death.* But even on Lightning it would have been a push to get to the bookstore by closing time. It was such a close call. Whatever the truth, Sir Benjamin obviously had no idea about Siophra.

"Sir Benjamin…" Angel bit her lip and forced the words out. "I've got bad news for you. Siophra was killed yesterday. We found her in the forest with a poison dart of some kind stuck in her chest. Gregor and Kalek took her body back home. Gregor's…well…"

Sir Benjamin sat back in his chair and stared, mouth agape. He shook his head and uttered a quiet, "No, not Siophra. Not her. How can this be? Where's Gregor now?"

"Out in the forest as far as I can tell. He left before I woke up this morning and he was still gone when I left the house. This has got to be the worst thing he's gone through beside his parents' deaths. I think he just wants to be alone."

"Sounds like you've learned a lot about your cousin. That's exactly how he grieved over his parents. He went camping by himself all the time. You may find he takes off quite a bit again. I'm so sorry this had to happen while you're staying with him. Please let me know if there's anything I can do to help. I know Gregor will never ask. If anything, he'll get more independent and push away. So you make sure you come to me if you need anything at all." Sir Benjamin leaned forward, his eyes full of fatherly concern.

"I promise I will. But for now I think I'll be okay. I just want to make sure I'm there for Gregor."

Sir Benjamin's gaze warmed her heart. Gregor had truly begun to feel like family, and Sir Benjamin was beginning to as well. With him gazing at her, she lost hold against the emotion she'd been fighting. Tears broke loose, and she let them flow freely down her cheeks.

Sir Benjamin grabbed her hand and squeezed.

"Sorry," she said when the tears began to slow. "I'm just…afraid this is going to push Gregor over the edge. He said Mr. Halvard is actually blaming him for Siophra's death."

Sir Benjamin's face contorted. "He's got some nerve. As if Gregor could ever be to blame for anyone's death. He loved that girl, and the old man would have done good to realize it." He seemed to want to say more, but held his tongue.

"Kalek told me about the whole situation with the Halvards, but I just don't understand how someone can be so mean and selfish and still get people to do what he wants."

"Did Gregor ever tell you about Dawric?"

Angel's tears stopped instantly. She'd never talked to anyone except Gregor about Dawric. "He's—he's the one who tried to kill that, um, little girl…and started the fire that killed Gregor's parents." A chill traveled down Angel's spine. Speaking of herself as if she were a different person didn't make it any less real.

"Did he also tell you that the whole town believes it's Mr. Halvard who has kept Dawric away?"

Angel shook her head. That's why he'd never elaborate when he said the island was protected. He didn't want to admit that Old Aldrik could be responsible for anything good.

"Um, do *you* believe he's kept Dawric away?"

"The truth? I'd love to say no way. But I can't deny that there's been neither hide nor hair of the man in seven years. Aldrik Halvard has no qualms about wielding his power and money. He may be a tyrannical maniac, but if something needs to be done, you can be sure he's got the means and the will."

"What if Dawric did come back? Do you think that's possible? Do you think…I mean, could he be the one who killed Siophra?" Angel couldn't believe she was voicing this.

"Oh, my dear Angel. Don't get yourself worked up about that. This doesn't look like Dawric's style at all. It's more likely someone trying to dart the Lunicor and Siophra got in the way."

Angel had never thought of that. But it only made her feel torn. On one hand, it was reassuring to think that everything really could fall back on the presence of a Lunicor. On the other hand, it would mean that she was wrong about the prophecy, and she didn't want to let that go.

"But, what if he's changed his ways, to throw everyone off? If Aldrik Halvard really did keep him away for years, Dawric might come for revenge. And what better way than with Mr. Halvard's daughter?"

Sir Benjamin squeezed her hand again. "The man got himself in too deep and he knows it. All it took was one fire to teach him that. He won't show his face around here again. He tread on dangerous ground, trying to steal magic, and he'll face the punishment for that. Mark my words. It's out of our hands, even Aldrik Halvard's. You've got to have faith."

"But it's been seven years."

"I know, Angel. But things don't always happen on our timetable." His expression deepened for a moment and then his eyes refocused on Angel. "If you're truly concerned, stay out of the forest except when you're with Gregor. You're in good hands with him—as he is with you."

"Thank you, Sir Benjamin. That means a lot to me."

A loud chiming broke Angel's concentration and she set down the puzzle piece she'd been trying to place for the past ten minutes. The clock still vibrated when Angel looked up and read the hands.

"I've got to head back! Poor Zoe's gonna burst if I don't get home to let her out. She's probably already chewing up something to let me know she's mad at me for leaving her." Angel scooted her chair back and jumped up, dashed over and gave Sir Benjamin a quick peck on the cheek, then high-tailed it to Old Man Brady's.

Not bothering to unsaddle Juliet, she called as she ran into the house, "I'll be right back to take care of you, girl."

Zoe sat, ears pulled down against the side of her head, big eyes drooping, and torn bits of leather and paper scattered around her. Shakespeare stood staring at his food bowl as if someone had made his food disappear and he couldn't believe Angel hadn't refilled it hours ago.

"I'm so sorry, guys." Angel filled Shakespeare's bowl with milk and he wound around her ankles, purring his forgiveness. She scooped up Zoe and got her into the back yard just in time.

Gregor barely made it home before dinner, and despite Angel's first successful attempt at making lasagna, he refused to eat a bite. He went straight to the closet, pulled out a broom, and began sweeping the wood floors.

"I can do that later, Gregor. Come eat." Angel tried to take the broom from Gregor's hands. He gripped the handle even harder and swept as though he were trying to beat the dirt out of the floor.

"I've been thinking all day about what we can do about Dr. Damian," he said, "but I haven't been able to come up with a single answer that doesn't involve exposing you."

"Well, you may have to face me being exposed. Those verses are coming true, Gregor. I was thinking about it, and the verses said *the guardian shall leave his post*. That could be Siophra if you think of guardian in the sense of a protector."

Gregor stopped sweeping and glared at her. "You've got to give up on those verses. I admit I blew you off before. I was angry with Kalek and didn't want to deal with two dramas at once. But *now* you could be in real danger. And I can't lose you, too. Whatever *work* The Finder is supposed to do will have to be done from the safety of home. I should never have left you alone today. It won't happen again."

Angel tried to sound calm. "If it's fated for me to be a part of this there's nothing we can do to stop it. And if the verses are true, then I'll be successful at whatever it is I'm supposed to do."

"No place in those verses does it say that you won't get hurt. And if it's fated to happen, then it'll happen with you right here. Besides, there is no 'treasure' in this world worth losing you over. The lock can stay shut!" Gregor began beating at the floor again.

"I don't understand you. You jump into everything—searching for me, taking your anger out on Kalek, thinking the worst of Dr. Damian. But when you've got something right in front of your nose"—Angel pulled the key out of her shirt—"like an ancient book that mentions *me* and a magic key, you act like it's all got to be coincidence. You have no problem going out on a limb over something you're not even sure about, but…oh…urgh, you're just so frustrating! I thought men were supposed to be logical."

The swishing of Gregor's broom stopped.

"That's the point. I didn't use logic in any of those decisions you mentioned. And they were all about me. I wanted to make up for my mistake by finding you, so I could feel like my parents hadn't died in vain. I wanted Siophra for myself and I was willing to blame Kalek because I felt like a failure for not being the one who could have her. And as for Dr. Damian—"

"Gregor, are you sure you saw what you thought you saw? I mean, how do you know *for sure* he's the one who killed that sheep?"

"I know what I saw!" Gregor slammed the broom on the floor.

"And it has nothing to do with Siophra going to him for help with the unicorn?"

"Angel, I didn't even know about that until you told me, remember? And that was *after* I saw him in the forest."

"Oh, yeah." Angel's mind was about to explode. She believed Gregor about the sheep, but if Dr. Damian were Siophra's killer it would mean she was on the wrong track about the verses. *I feel like I'm fighting myself as much as I am Gregor.*

"Listen," Gregor said, "as far as you're concerned it doesn't matter if I'm right or wrong about Dr. Damian. The fact is there's someone out there killing. If it's Dr. Damian, you need to stay away from him. If those verses are true, and somehow Dawric is back, then you still need to stay here and keep safe. No matter what, I don't want you in danger. It won't be for long." He sighed. "I hate to admit this, but Ole Aldrik has every resource out there and he'll find Siophra's killer. He may have no problem letting the supposed killer of someone else's little girl run loose, but trust me, not *his* little girl." His voice resonated like steel against steel.

"Ouch."

"Angel, you know what I mean. That's nothing against you. It's just how heartless and determined he is." Gregor leaned down and picked up the broom again.

"I know, but the key, and the lock, and all that. It's still happening and I feel like I wasted time in the beginning. What if I'd Found the lock or whatever right away. Maybe Siophra wouldn't have been killed."

Gregor flinched, and gripped the broom tightly, and then he pointed over the end of it at Angel.

"Do *not* start blaming yourself for this. I should know how that turns out. I've done it long enough. Maybe the key is just a symbol, and Ole Aldrik is the true heir. Maybe this is just what had to happen to reveal who Dawric really is." Gregor cocked an eyebrow and met her gaze directly. "Maybe Dawric was Dr. Damian all along."

Dr. Damian...

"But wasn't that before he moved here? And you said yourself you saw Dawric leave in a helicopter. Gregor, you're just not making sense. You saw Dr. Damian with the sheep, okay, but would he really kill Siophra? That would strip his powers."

"The man is a geneticist. He could have figured out a way to make himself immune to the physical effects of murder. Maybe he genetically altered himself or something. See, it has nothing to do with you. He tried one way—using you—and it didn't work, so now he's done this."

"Oh, and then he moved to the island disguised as an Empowered, perfectly satisfied with his power as an animal-Tamer, and decided to live a quiet life as a University professor and give up killing."

Gregor cocked his head to the side, but his voice remained cool. "Not give up killing. Just switch his target. From humans to animals with more pure magic. And now the Elven."

"So what if you're right about Dr. Damian? What if he really is Dawric and he's genetically altered himself? Do you think Mr. Halvard is prepared for that? And it doesn't change the fact that this key exists and I'm mentioned in that book. All it does is change the person we have to stop."

Gregor's knuckles turned white as he squeezed the broom handle. "And how do you propose we stop Dr. Damian if he really is Dawric? We can't overpower him on our own, and without the support of someone else we've got no chance against Ole Aldrik. If anything, he'd probably go enlisting Dr. Damian's help just to prove me wrong. And who's going to believe anything bad about the ever-trusted Tamer? Even Sir Benjamin thinks the world of him."

"But Dr. Randall doesn't. We could tell him."

Angel couldn't believe she'd just heard those words coming out of her own mouth. But it was true. She'd taken the vial to Dr. Kate, but Dr. Randall could have tested the liquid from the syringe just as easily. And he'd probably believe them about Dr. Damian. It gave Angel shivers to think about turning to him, but they may have no other choice.

Gregor's eyebrow lifted. "Really? I wouldn't have thought you'd want to go to Dr. Randall. But, we could I suppose. Only..."

"What?"

"I didn't want to tell you this before. I know you said he gave you the creeps and all, and I was still mad at you for going to see Kalek that day we had the fight."

"Gregor, get to the point."

Gregor huffed at her. "I defended him because he's not very well-liked by Ole Aldrik. Kalek told me a long time ago that Dr. Randall really ticked his father off one day by showing up at their door demanding money for his research. He said it would benefit the Elven and Ole Aldrik had an obligation to help him with it. That's one thing you don't tell the old man— that he has an obligation to anything. Randall's never been able to get a serious grant since."

"What kind of research was he doing?"

"I have no idea," he said. "It was years ago. But, I can guarantee you Ole Aldrik has not forgotten that day and I doubt he'd take Dr. Randall seriously even if he believed us. I want Siophra's killer caught, especially if it's Dr. Damian and he's been slashing those animals. But right now I think the best thing is to lie low and let him get exposed on his own." He leaned against the broom, finally calmed down. The muscles in his arms still strained, but his expression and voice were no longer filled with irritation.

"So you at least think something is going to happen? Maybe not something involving me directly, but *something*?"

"I don't know. I'll have to think about it. But for now, please promise me you'll stay here and not go wandering."

"Fine, but only if you spend some time with that book. It's got the answer in it somewhere. Maybe something your dad told you about sank in and you'll be able to piece it together. I'm not giving up until you give this a real chance." Angel stepped closer to Gregor and crossed her arms.

Gregor nodded and sent the broom back into the cupboard. Angel knew he'd be true to his word, but she also knew he'd be spending plenty of that reading time mourning Siophra. She couldn't fault him for that, of course, but it did make her feel a little less guilty about the plan she was forming.

~Transferring Power~

He took the dagger from the scientist's trembling hand. "I never should have trusted you. Far too much time has been wasted."

"It has not been a waste. We have what we need. I can get the girl now."

"You mean *I* can get her now. This is my privilege."

The scientist gazed down at the crimson gash on his forearm with somber eyes. "I can't promise both will be transferred. But at least the other one is out of the way, and can no longer Protect the girl."

"You don't look happy, doctor."

The scientist's head snapped up. "I should have been affected. I don't understand why killing her did not harm me...my soul."

He smiled, the skin on his cheek protesting. "Maybe one can't harm what one doesn't have."

The scientist's eyes narrowed. "Go ahead. Finish it. Get it over with. I have things to do—the research is nearly ready. One last specimen is needed and we will both have what we want."

He raised the dagger and brought it down against his own, scarred arm. Blood oozed from the cut and ran toward his gloved palm.

Chapter Twenty-Seven
The Dagger

Angel had expected Kalek to be at the Temple and didn't even think to Find him before setting out the following morning. When she arrived she realized what a mistake that was. So she concentrated, Found him seated on the ground in a clearing, then took off in that direction.

She trudged through the unfamiliar forest, eyes cast down. Gregor would freak if he knew what she was doing.

A tree branch snagged her sleeve, and when she looked up to pull her shirt free it felt as if the tree were trying to stop her. As if…a part of Gregor was watching her. She untangled her sleeve from the branch and moved on.

Sorry, Gregor, but I've got to talk to Kalek and find out what the Elves know about Dawric, and who Aldrik's looking for. And if he knows anything about the prophecy. I just know that book is Elven.

As she drew close to the clearing a strange sense of familiarity set in.

It was too quiet.

No birds, no rustling branches, no distant dragon calls…nothing came from the surrounding trees to compete with the crunch of dry leaves beneath her feet.

Angel had experienced quiet like this in the forest only once before—the day of her first Finding lessons. A cold breeze swirled up from out of nowhere, sending chills up Angel's spine. Icy fingers ran across her shoulders and she spun around as if expecting to see a ghost behind her. But there was no one. Everything stood as statues despite the breeze.

And then, something moved amid the trees.

A tall, slender plant swayed in the shadow of a great tree, its iridescent green stalks moving like seaweed on the bottom of the ocean floor. Angel took a few cautious steps closer and the plant's shimmering light brightened. It bore into Angel's eyes, as the forest around her closed in under a blanket of darkness. Soon, all she could see was the undulating glow.

The midsection of the stalks gathered together to form a single mass that pinched inward, shaping itself into the curvy hips and torso of a woman. Tendrils emerged from the sides of the figure and began to twist and sway like the arms of a belly dancer. The lower portion split into two legs that remained seated in the earth. The top thrust up and bent double, creating a mane of hair that cascaded down the figure's back, her curves enhanced by the dance-like movement.

The figure's arms beckoned Angel toward it, and when Angel hesitated the plant-woman's feet pulled free from the ground. She waltzed toward Angel, her light pulsing as if in time to unheard music.

Angel stood transfixed as the figure moved closer and began to circle around her. She resisted the pull of the dance, but her hips moved to one side and her feet followed even as she fought to keep them in place. A sickening thrill coursed through her, pushing her to join the figure in the eurhythmic ring. Her pounding pulse and the rushing blood followed the cadence of the soundless music.

The plant-woman continued to shimmer and gleam, but the light reminded Angel of plastic that glowed after being left in the light, a pale copy of light that eerily contrasted with the dark shadow of forest behind her.

The urge to touch the figure was overwhelming. Angel copied her movements, drawing closer and closer only to have her move farther away, always beckoning for Angel to follow.

As they approached the deep shadow that darkened the tree trunks of the cursed area, Angel's heart pounded even harder. Her head spun and she tried to take a deep breath to ease the dizziness, but her ribs would not expand to allow her lungs to fill.

She tried to scream but had no air to exhale.

Blackness closed more tightly around her as she crumpled to the forest floor. The glowing figure moved toward Angel, a ghostly form hovering in the blackness. Faceless and eyeless, the iridescent mass opened a dark hole in its center, forming a ghoulish mouth that mocked Angel with its hysterical laughter, and then the dark overtook completely.

Angel awoke to hard ground pressed against her lower back and strong hands supporting her shoulders. Her eyelids fluttered, and the brightness of the daylight scorched her eyes.

The hands moved from her shoulders to the back of her head, gently guiding it to the ground. Her ribs nearly broke with her inhale of the crisp, cool air. She gagged and coughed until her breathing stabilized, and then pulled herself up so she was leaning back on her hands. Kalek's face was inches from her own when her eyes finally focused.

"You okay, Angel?"

She nodded and looked around. They were in the clearing where Siophra had been killed.

"What on earth were you doing over there? Didn't Gregor explain to you about the Cursed Region?"

Angel scooted herself back so she was sitting upright.

"I was looking for you and didn't realize I was so close to it. Then this thing came out and it looked like a glowing woman, and before I knew it I was following her."

Kalek nodded knowingly. "A Fire Nymph. The ones in the Cursed Region no longer live to light the way for the lost…now they lure people into the dark."

"The curse did that to them?"

"Only after they found themselves trapped within it."

Kalek held out his hand to help Angel to her feet. Her legs felt flimsy beneath her, but after standing for a moment her strength returned.

She pulled Kalek's dagger out of her bag.

"I thought you'd like this back."

"Oh…yes…" Kalek looked at the dagger with disgust then placed it in the sheath strapped to his thigh. "I suppose I do need it back, not that it does me any good. You might as well have left it stuck in the tree."

"Why do you say that?" The dagger was beautiful, with its pearl grip and ruby-set pommel.

"This was only supposed to be a temporary blade. It's nothing compared to the one I usually carry. *Used to* carry, I should say. I made the mistake of loaning my dagger to the University. It was made by my great-great-grandfather and has magic powers like no other blade on the island. If I'd had it with me on the day Siophra was killed I would have never missed my target!"

Kalek's anger flared through the tears that welled in his eyes. He breathed in heavily and pulled back his shoulders. "I should never have handed that blade over. My father warned me not to, but I didn't listen. It's the one time in my life I should have."

"So that was the object that was stolen? Mrs. Crick wouldn't tell us what it was."

Angel and Kalek began walking toward the main path of the forest.

"My father hit the roof when he found out. He's been holding it over my head ever since. But he doesn't want anyone to know about it. Another reason to be ashamed of his son, I guess. I never even told Gregor. Of course, I wasn't exactly on his best side back then."

"Do you know if that blade can cut through dragon hide?"

"Absolutely." Kalek stopped in his tracks and looked hard at Angel. "Wait a minute. You think Dr. Damian killed more than that sheep and unicorn, don't you? You think he's the one killing all those animals, not the Lunicor. And if he has my blade…"

"Well…" Angel squirmed under Kalek's piercing gaze. "Gregor's been thinking it was him ever since he saw Dr. Damian with the sheep. But we didn't know about your dagger, and you know how Gregor jumps to conclusions when he's angry. He even believes Dr. Damian killed Siophra. I can see that he was right about the animals, especially if Dr. Damian really does have your dagger. But—"

"But not about Siophra," Kalek cut in.

"No. He can't be. That'd mean I was wrong about—" Angel snapped her mouth shut.

"What, Angel?" Kalek said sternly. "Do you know something you're not telling me?"

"Not exactly. I just…well, I was actually beginning to think Dawric is back. Before Gregor saw the sheep, I thought he was the one killing the animals too, looking for one with magical powers that will stay with him."

Kalek shook his head. "There's no way he's back. He's unempowered, so he has no way to get here except by air or boat, and those areas are constantly patrolled. My father made sure of that. It may be the safety of his belongings and position that he's trying to protect rather than the citizens of Toch, but at least we reap that benefit."

"But he couldn't even stop your dagger from being stolen."

"That is altogether different. He didn't even know I had loaned it out. And no unempowered could have ever broken into the museum. Trust me, with my father's men guarding the island, powerful magic would be necessary to get here."

"But what about Siophra? You agree with Gregor?" Angel felt her eyes watering, but held back the tears with all her might. She would not let her frustration sway her. *I don't care what they all think. Gregor, Sir Benjamin, Kalek. Dawric's back, I can feel it.*

Kalek tucked a tangle of curls behind a pointed ear. "I'm not sure. It could have been someone out hunting the Lunicor. And even if it was Dr. Damian, he'll be exposed. His powers will be stripped from him, and Siophra will regain hers in the Realm Beyond. He will get his punishment, far worse than anything a mere mortal could impose. That is, unless my father gets to him first."

His expression turned more serious. "In the meantime, stay away from Dr. Damian. And don't enter the forest alone again."

"But what if his powers aren't taken? What if there's more to it—a plan we know nothing about? What if the killer figured out a way to keep the powers of his victims? Killing never affected Dawric like it does Empowereds. If he's back, or he never really left…"

"Gregor witnessed Dawric leaving. If he'd kept his powers when he left don't you think there would be news of that? Somewhere he'd be killing again, yet nowhere has there been word of anything. That's why the Kleidons are searching the unempowered regions for him."

Angel flinched at the mention of her parents' names and hoped Kalek didn't notice. That was yet another reason Angel wanted Siophra's killer to be Dawric. If he was caught, the search would be over and her parents could return and stay for good.

"And if there was evidence that the killer was not from here…"

Kalek's onyx eyes flared. "Angel, what do you know? You've only been on this island for a matter of weeks and you think you've solved a mystery that's baffled everyone seven years. What makes you think you have anything to do with this?"

Angel faced Kalek and reached for the strength she knew was in her somewhere.

"Do you know anything about a book, an ancient history book that belonged to Gregor's father? A book with a prophecy about The Finder. Wasn't that what the little girl was?"

"So that's it? It figures Gregor's father would have a copy of that." Kalek scowled and crossed his tattooed arms. "Yes, it's an Elven history book and much more, but the Prophecies have been misread more often than not. The Prophecy of The Finder will have its day, but it won't happen until an Elven Finder is born. Read more closely and you'll see that. It has nothing to do with Dawric."

Angel's resolve began to crumble. She had to admit Kalek had an understanding of the book she and Gregor didn't have. A single tear escaped and she wiped it away.

Kalek placed his hand on her shoulder. "Trust me, Angel. My father has studied the prophecies, and so have I. We disagree on many of the recent passages surrounding the Temple, but he's not wrong about the prophecy you're speaking of."

"You still haven't told me about the Temple."

"I will, I promise. Very soon. But right now I have to get back home to help with the...funeral preparations." He inhaled. "I'm already late. And I don't have the desire to argue with my father today." His eyes dulled as his hand dropped back to his side, and Angel's heart broke for him.

"I'm so sorry, Kalek. I know how much you miss her."

"Thank you. But we will be united again someday." The shine returned to his eyes before he turned to leave.

As he stepped away, Angel made one last plea. "Kalek…"

He stopped walking and looked over his shoulder at her.

"Please tell your father to search for Dawric on the island anyway. Even you said the Prophecies are misread."

"You are too much like your cousin, you know." Kalek smiled, but his eyes warned her not to take things too far. "Are you sure you're not from the Halvard side of the family?"

Chapter Twenty-Eight
The Substance of Man

When Angel came in through the back of the farmhouse, she found Gregor standing in the open front door with his back to her.

"Are you sure it was Angel Mason who brought that in?" he said as Angel approached and peeked over his shoulder. "She didn't say anything to me about it."

Gwen stood at the top of the steps of the front porch. A horse-sized, turquoise dragon sat on the grass at the bottom of the steps, poised like a sentry.

"It was definitely Angel. The doctor remembered her from Sir Benjamin's—oh, Angel, there you are…"

Angel nudged Gregor over and walked out onto the porch to greet Gwen. The dragon flared its nostrils and kept its eyes pinned on her, but didn't move.

Gwen wagged her finger at the dragon. "Lighten up, Wyatt."

The dragon huffed at her, a thin plume of smoke blowing from his nostrils. He stepped away and sniffed at Shakespeare, who was seated by the bushes, and then at Zoe, who frolicked around the front yard.

"What's going on?" Angel asked.

"That sample you left for Kate—where did you say it came from?"

Angel shot a quick glance at Gregor, who stood in the doorway with a bemused expression.

"Angel, what's going on here? What sample? What is she talking about?" He moved toward them, his arms crossing his chest and his forearm twitching.

"Gregor, we'll talk about this later. Please." Angel took hold of his arm and urged him back toward the house. "I'll explain everything, I promise. Just let me and Gwen talk for a few minutes."

Gregor reached up and ran his fingers through his hair, then turned and walked back into the house, Shakespeare on his heels. He let the door slam behind him.

"I'm sorry, Angel. I didn't mean to get you in trouble. But Kate wanted me to talk to you right away."

"It's okay, but what's so important? Did you figure out what that liquid is?" Angel peeked through the window and saw that Gregor was sitting in the leather chair by the fireplace. Shakespeare curled up on the arm of the chair while Gregor absentmindedly stroked the cat's back from shoulder to tail.

"Well sort of. It's mostly a common extract, something you can buy locally. Or at least you could until recently."

Gwen's eyes told Angel that she was suspicious about something.

"What do you mean?"

"Well...last time we needed some, just a few days ago, Roger said he was all out. He said his last bit was stolen and he's been missing vials here and there for a few months now."

The sound of Roger screaming about stolen inventory echoed in the back of Angel's mind.

"But what is it exactly? And what do you mean it's mostly a common extract?" Angel found herself running her fingers through her bangs again, and jerked her hand away.

"The extract is generally used as a dragon sedative. But that's not the strange part. It has components that we've never seen before. Something has been added to the extract, a substance that's not found anywhere on this island or anywhere else Kate has ever been. And she's been to every Empowered community on this side of the globe."

"What does that mean?" Angel already thought she knew.

"When we placed a drop on a tissue sample, we noticed definite, and immediate, cellular changes. Changes that would inhibit the animal's magical qualities if the substance were fed directly to it." Gwen's voice matched the concerned expression on her face.

"Or injected..." Angel said under her breath. Gwen didn't seem to hear.

"Um, the point is, you don't need to worry about the sheep. There's no way she drank any of that because...well, with the strength of the sedative..."

"She'd be dead?" Angel didn't tell Gwen that the sheep was already dead from something else much worse than a sedative overdose.

"Right. And now that you got it out of the pasture, none of the other animals can get into it either. So that's good." Gwen's eyes brightened and she gave Angel an assuring smile. "Chances are someone put this out to catch or kill that Lunicor and the container rolled into your pasture since it's so close to the forest. It's a shame." Gwen shook her head. "Last time one of those things was around here, animals were attacked all over. Kate was busier than ever with injured dragons. But once Dr. Damian caught it, we thought the trouble was over."

"Dr. Damian?"

"Yes, he's—"

"Oh, I know him. I just didn't realize he'd caught a Lunicor here before."

"Yeah, he's the best. I don't know what we ever did before he came to the island. Anyway, keep an eye on that pasture and please let us know if you find any more strange liquids. We've got to find out what's contaminated it. If it hadn't been stolen, we'd have record of who has the rest and could test the whole batch. But since that's not an option, we'll just keep running tests on what little you brought in."

"Does Dr. Kate have any ideas about where the contaminant came from?" Angel asked.

"Her present theory is that it's from a mutated plant in the Cursed Region. The glitch in that is, of course, that there's no one who could go in there with all the crazy wildlife that's taken over."

Gwen hadn't even seen the irony of what she'd just said. *Who could go in there? Dr. Damian of course.* Another point for Gregor.

"And if it were man-made?"

"Well, I suppose that's a possibility to consider. Man-made substances are never used here, though, as far as I know. I'll bring it up to Kate, but I'm sure she's right about it being from a mutated plant."

"I'd appreciate that."

Gwen looked past Angel and smiled sweetly. "Looks like someone's ready for you to come inside."

Angel glanced over her shoulder and saw Gregor staring at her through the window. "Yeah, I better get in there and talk to him." She glanced again, and he hadn't moved. "Thanks for coming all the way over here, Gwen. Thank Dr. Kate for me, too. I feel much better about the sheep now. And I promise I'll let you know if I find anything else."

Angel watched Gwen fly off on Wyatt's back. Zoe pounced at his spiked tail as it scraped across the lawn, leaving a stripe of upturned grass behind. Angel waved her hand and the grass flipped over and filled in the trench.

"Explain," ordered Gregor.

Angel sat down on the couch opposite him. Zoe hopped into the seat next to her and curled up with her head in Angel's lap. Angel played with Zoe's ear, examining the downy fur to keep her eyes averted from Gregor's gaze while she spoke.

"I went to see Dr. Kate yesterday. I wanted her to test the poison that killed Siophra."

"And what purpose would that serve? Anyone around here could have gotten their hands on something strong enough to kill her and make a poison dart."

"Not if the poison was man-made. And not if it wasn't a dart." Angel lifted her eyes tentatively. Gregor looked livid.

"Angel, I pulled the dart from her chest myself. What are you talking about?"

"It wasn't a dart, Gregor. It was a plastic hypodermic needle. You just didn't notice because you were so upset at the time."

"So where is it? We could've used that for evidence. I could've shown that to Kalek's father!" Gregor edged forward as if he were about to bound out of his seat.

"It disintegrated in the forest." Angel described all that had happened, and Gregor's anger seemed to subside.

"I wish you'd told me about this."

"You had enough on your mind. I figured I could find out what was in it, and if it were a man-made poison Dr. Kate would tell the right people and word would get out. Mr. Halvard would have to take it seriously."

"That wouldn't mean he'd go after Dr. Damian, though," Gregor said, and then his eyes lit with understanding. "You think if it's a man-made substance than he'd assume Dawric is back just like you think. Okay, I see …but—"

"I went to see Kalek today, too." She fiddled with Zoe's ear and the puppy licked her hand.

Gregor scooted back in his seat and sighed. "I figured as much…when I found you gone and saw that his dagger was gone, too. I thought about heading out to find you. You promised not to leave the house."

"I just wanted to take his dagger back to him. And find out what Mr. Halvard was doing so far. To let him know to look for Dawric."

"Angel, really—"

"The substance in the syringe is man-made."

"Dr. Kate said that?"

"No, but Gwen said they couldn't identify a compound in it. Most of it was a dragon sedative that was stolen from Roger's. But the compound makes it deadly by disarming magical powers. That's what killed Siophra. She was murdered, not from a distance and not by an Empowered. She was murdered by Dawric."

Gregor just stared at her. He seemed dumbfounded.

"It's coming true." Angel lifted her face and looked at him. "It's the next-to-last line of the verses. *And the truth is exposed by the substance of man.* You see it, don't you?"

Later, Angel and Gregor sat at the kitchen table devouring a plate of turkey sandwiches and fruit. It was nearly four-thirty and neither of them had eaten since early morning.

"Why didn't you tell me Dr. Damian had captured a Lunicor before?" she asked.

"It happened a long time ago, right after he moved here. I was gone a lot, searching for you. I guess it just didn't stick out in my mind as important." Gregor sat back in his chair to take a deep breath. "I ate too much."

"So, did Dr. Damian move here right after I got lost?"

"Pretty soon after. It was Sir Benjamin's last year teaching and the year he and I became friends. He was setting up his bookshop so he could open it right away when he retired. Haven't I told you all this before?"

"Not all of it," she said as the information clicked into place. "I never put the time line together with Dr. Damian. It could be what you said, that Dr. Damian was here killing as an unempowered, and then came back pretending to be a real Empowered. The timing does all line up. But, there's just something missing..." Angel couldn't keep her mind going in the direction she wanted it.

Gregor ignored her meandering monologue about Dr. Damian and Dawric. He'd situated himself facing away from the kitchen window, so his gaze couldn't wander to the forest. He'd also taken half an hour to cut every piece of fruit into perfect squares and made their sandwiches by hand without any magic at all. The tension was worse than anything they'd experienced during the three-day rainstorm, and their conversation felt fake. It made Angel nauseous despite how ravenous she was.

"Speaking of missing," Gregor said as though he were at some sort of business meeting, "I seem to have lost track of one of the steak knives. Do you think you could do your thing and—"

"A missing knife! Oh, I can't believe I forgot to tell you this!" Angel dropped her sandwich onto her plate and perched forward in her chair. "Kalek said the thing that was stolen from the museum was his dagger. The one his great-great-grandfather made. That's the artifact Mr. Halvard didn't want everyone knowing about. The reason he had the museum closed."

Gregor snapped out of his robotic mode. "Kalek never told me. That knife is priceless. I bet Ole Aldrik had a fit!"

He gave the first genuine smile Angel had seen on him in days.

"That's what he said. He said it's magical too and can cut through dragon hide. It could be what Dawric is using to kill those animals. Maybe it's what gives the powers over permanently."

Gregor's face morphed into the strangest expression Angel had ever seen. Then he scrunched his eyes and pinched the bridge of his nose, and laughed. He lifted his head, stood up and started pacing.

"We were goofing around in the forest one day. I was twelve and Kalek was fourteen. Kalek's father had just given him the dagger and we couldn't help testing it out. We chopped plant after plant, the thickest vines we could find. We sliced everything we could think of and then gathered a bunch of wood and took turns chopping it with the dagger.

"At one point Kalek slapped a thick branch onto the rock we were using as a chopping block and I realized he'd grabbed a piece of Diamond Wood. I knew even his blade would be destroyed by that, so I put my hand out to stop him. The dagger sliced me right here." Gregor stopped pacing and pointed to a long, pale scar that ran along his forearm.

"Oh, he must have felt awful."

"He did. He felt so bad he held his arm out and cut himself in the same spot. He said, 'My brother, everything that pains you, pains me.' I thought he was crazy. I can't believe I ever doubted him. I forgot all about that day until now…" Gregor's hand found its way into his bangs and stayed there for a minute.

"What happened? You didn't just stand there bleeding, I hope. You could heal it with magic, right?"

"Oh, yeah, but we didn't right away. Kalek grabbed my hand and held our arms up like one of us had just won a fight or something." Gregor clasped his hands together and held them over his head like a prizefighter.

"And then the strangest thing happened." Gregor's hands dropped down, his eyes widened, and he returned to his seat. "When we went to leave, Kalek was imitating me, the way I hold my hand when I Gate, and when he touched the tree his hand went through."

"You mean he made a Gate?"

"I think so. I couldn't be sure. We didn't try going through or anything. The next time we got together, though, we tried to make it happen again, but couldn't figure out what did it. We held the Diamond Wood, and even cut ourselves in the same spots again, but nothing ever happened. We figured it was some kind of fluke."

He sat back and gazed at Angel with an expression she couldn't read. She realized she was staring.

"When you cut yourselves the second time, did you hold your hands up like before?" she asked.

"I don't think so. Why?"

"When you did it the first time, were the cuts touching?"

"I don't know. Maybe. Why? What are you getting at?"

"Blood brothers."

"What?" Gregor stared at her as if she'd suddenly started speaking a different language.

"That's what it's called—you're talking about a ritual. I think it's a really old ceremony and I don't know where it comes from, but I remember seeing it in a movie where two boys who were best friends swore to be like brothers. No one does it anymore because of diseases." Angel crinkled her nose. "But that's what it's called when you both cut yourselves like that and press the cuts together. It's supposed to bind you to each other."

"Blood brothers…"

Angel could see the gears turning in Gregor's head again as he said the words.

"So, that wouldn't happen with any old blade, right?" she asked. "It's just the one Kalek's great-great-grandfather made. Right, Gregor? Gregor?"

Gregor stared at the tabletop as if trying to will the answer to appear before him. Angel snapped her fingers in front of his eyes.

"I-I don't know. The dagger is just supposed to be super-strong. The grip is inlaid with Iron Oak, and the blade is a type of magical steel, made from the iron found in the tree. It's different from ordinary iron…it has magical powers that strengthen physical and chemical bonds. And Kalek's great-great-grandfather was an Enhancer. He enhanced the magic in the iron from the tree, and made the blade able to cut anything."

His frozen expression brightened. The silver flecks in his eyes caught the sunlight from the kitchen window and sparkled.

"Wow…that's it!" Gregor slammed his hand on the table. "I guess he enhanced more than he expected. It strengthens the bonds between people."

He jumped to his feet. "Dawric and Dr. Damian used that blade in a ritual like blood brothers. And they can share powers. Or, I guess, Dawric gets Dr. Damian's, but…what does Dr. Damian get?"

Angel's heartbeat quickened. She hadn't been wrong. And neither had Gregor.

"I don't know. Maybe Dawric is supplying him something, like the syringes, or the substance Dr. Kate found in the liquid I gave her. Maybe he's doing something to suppress the powers of the magical animals. Whatever it is, he's getting something he can't get from another Empowered."

Gregor lifted his eyebrow before running into the other room.

He returned seconds later with the book Angel had gotten from Mrs. Crick.

"Didn't you tell me Mrs. Crick said some of Ole Aldrik's personal collection was in here?" He thumbed through the book.

"Careful, you're gonna rip the pages like that."

Gregor glanced up at her and continued flipping.

"I'll buy you a new one if I do."

Many crumpled pages and discouraged grunts later, Gregor finally stopped and turned the book around for Angel to see.

"That's it right there." He pointed to a picture of a very mundane looking dagger. It had none of the style of the dagger Kalek carried in its place. No iridescent pearl handle or sparkling ruby inset in the pommel. Nothing engraved on the blade, except a crudely drawn letter J. The wood in the grip didn't gleam with polish or lacquer. It looked like something that would be sold for a few dollars at a flea market and given to a child to use for whittling a block of soft pinewood.

"Can you Find it?"

Chapter Twenty-Nine
The Arrest

"It's at the University," Angel said. "In Dr. Damian's lab. I can see the seedlings he was watering that day…it's just lying there on the table! You've got to report this, Gregor. No more worrying about exposing who I am."

Gregor nodded, then opened the back door and dashed through toward the forest. Angel followed, waving the door shut behind her.

Gregor stood on the edge of the forest, his hand already held up, holding the Gate open. As soon as Angel caught up to him he went through and she followed.

They stepped out in the middle of a line of trees outside of what looked like a courthouse. Square windows were set symmetrically to either side of a huge pair of double doors, and broad columns spread wide on the marble portico. Angel scanned her surroundings in search of something familiar to gain an idea of where they were, but found nothing.

Gregor was halfway up the steps of the portico when Angel realized he was no longer beside her, and she ran to catch up. The doors swung open when she and Gregor reached the rectangular mat in front of them.

Inside, their footsteps echoed in the deserted lobby. Uncomfortable-looking wrought iron chairs and small tables lined the walls. There were several hallways leading off from the lobby, but no signs indicating which one, if any, Angel and Gregor should follow.

Angel glanced at Gregor as if to say, *well, what do we do now?* He only shrugged and headed toward a window set in the far wall. A mass of blond curls peeked over the edge of a file cabinet in the corner of the room behind the window. Angel heard a *slam*, and the middle-aged woman to whom the curls belonged clicked across the floor towards them.

"Can I help you, um, children?" she asked as though Angel and Gregor were four years old and had lost their mommy.

Angel wanted to pinch the woman for her tone, but stood back and let Gregor handle things.

"Yes, ma'am," said Gregor. "We think we have information regarding the missing artifact from the University museum, as well as possibly the animal slayings that have occurred around the island. We'd like to report what we know. Can you tell us who we should speak to?"

"May I ask what ya've found out?" The woman grabbed a pencil and licked the lead before placing it on the paper.

"We believe it's one of the professors at the University. Um—"

"Oh, that's been taken care of, *Mr*—?"

There was that condescending attitude again. Angel ground her teeth.

"Halvard."

"Are you...I mean...you don't look anything—"

A glimmer of fear shot across the woman's face.

"Aldrik Halvard is a second cousin of sorts. I'm Gregor."

Angel frowned. *Too bad Gregor can't use that name to pull some weight for himself.*

"Hmm, if you say so. No matter. Like I said, that's been taken care of. Unless you've got something new." The woman tossed the pencil back into a pile of other perfectly sharpened pencils and turned to walk away.

"What do you mean it's *taken care of?*" Gregor shouted after her.

The woman paused, then slowly turned back around. Her head no longer in a haughty tilt, she looked at Gregor and nodded.

"Well, hon, we got a call just a little while ago from a woman at the University. She said one of the professors had evidence against his colleague. We've already sent officers there to arrest him. They should be out there as we speak. And, no, I can't tell you *who* they're arresting. I've already told you more than I should have. Now if you two would kindly head out. This is no place for kids." The woman clicked toward the back of the office and out of sight.

Angel beamed at Gregor and nearly jumped for joy. With Dr. Damian arrested, Dawric wouldn't have access to powers again and would be trapped on the island. He'd be found for sure now and probably have the truth of who killed Siophra tortured out of him by Ole Aldrik. That left Angel and Gregor free to find the lock and fulfill the prophecy.

Gregor grabbed Angel and pulled her toward the door. "I want to witness this *myself*."

Gregor Gated them to edge of the forest in front of the main entrance of the University. A carriage sat off to the side of the steps with two pewter-gray dragons harnessed to it. The oranges and reds of the nearly-set sun reflected on their metallic scales, setting them ablaze. There was no sign of anyone else outside the building, and Gregor motioned Angel to follow him.

Before either of them took a step toward the building, a commotion arose in the main entrance. Angel and Gregor craned their necks around the tree in front of them. A group of men fought to drag something through the doorway.

Silhouettes shuffled in the lobby. The men pulled their burden into the fading daylight. They were wearing uniforms.

"Come quietly, now!" a gruff voice said. "You're only making this worse for yourself."

"He's lying! He's lying!" a frantic voice cried. "He's the one! It was in his desk!" The uniformed men pulled the struggling prisoner farther out onto the front portico. Angel blinked, not trusting what she perceived. It looked like there was no one there, and the officers were fighting to control air.

Then a man appeared instantaneously, yanking hard against the officer's arms. He squirmed until his back was toward Angel revealing arms bound by shackles. One of the officers stepped to the side, tugging the prisoner around so that he faced the spot where Angel and Gregor hid.

Dr. Randall.

An expression of sheer panic contorted his face, and he repeated over and over, "It was him! Not me! It was in *his desk*!"

He had to be talking about the dagger. But why was *he* being arrested and not Dr. Damian? Angel grabbed Gregor's arm. *They've got the wrong man!*

Dr. Randall disappeared again, and the gruff-sounding officer said, "I told you to stop doing that. Royce, take him down." Another officer, the one that had pulled Dr. Randall over to the side, reached out a hand and held it in mid air. At least it looked like he was holding it in mid air, but a second later, Dr. Randall appeared again with the officer's hand set firmly on the top of his head. Dr. Randall slumped to the ground.

"His Talent is Invisibility," said Gregor. "That's how he knew what Dr. Damian was up to. He was able to spy on him and he must have been the one who told Mrs. Crick. But why do they have *him* instead of Dr. Damian?"

Angel didn't answer.

The officers dragged Dr. Randall's limp body to the carriage and hoisted him onto the back. Bars emerged from all sides of the carriage's open top, extending upward and arcing toward the center. The ends joined with a loud *clank*, enclosing Dr. Randall in what looked like a birdcage. Two of the officers climbed into the open front seat of the carriage, one of them grabbing the reins of the harnessed dragons.

One of the dragons reared up when the reins tugged at his neck, and Dr. Randall bolted upright in the back of the carriage.

"I'll get you, Damian! You won't get away with this!" He clawed at the bars and flashed in and out of visibility.

The dragons spread their wings and took off into the air. Dr. Randall's screams became fainter and fainter until the carriage was too high and far away to hear them at all. The other officers mounted horses and headed toward the main road. The people that had been milling around the doorway disappeared back into the lobby.

Angel and Gregor stayed hidden behind the trees until the portico was empty.

"You stay here, Angel," said Gregor, still staring at the doorway. His eyes were narrow slits. If his jaw had been any tenser, the bone would have shattered under the strain. "I'm going to find a way to bust him. There's got to be something in that lab, some piece of evidence that will give him away. But it's too dangerous for you now."

He stalked toward the steps and Angel followed.

He spun on his heel. "I said stay here!"

She stared at him defiantly. "He's working with the man who tried to kill me. Who may have kidnapped or killed my parents by now. I'm going with you. Maybe I can Find something in there. He might have moved the dagger. I'm not letting you do this alone." She set off toward the steps again.

They entered the empty lobby and turned down the hallway that led to the science wing. It was deserted as well. Angel tried to swallow the lump in her throat.

Gregor reached the spiral staircase that led to the science labs and climbed up. Angel followed as closely as she could. They paused at the top of the stairs.

Mrs. Crick was leaning over a box, rifling around inside. Dr. Damian walked toward her holding a dagger that looked covered in dried blood. Gregor jumped out from the staircase doorway and spread his body in front of Mrs. Crick like a shield.

"Stay back! I know what you've done, and you're not going to get away with it!"

Mrs. Crick spun around, looking terrified and confused. Angel ran over and stood next to Gregor. She shook with both rage and fear.

Mrs. Crick dropped to the floor behind Angel and Gregor. She spoke in a quivering voice. "What are you two doing? What are you talking about?"

"He's the one who's been killing animals, not Dr. Randall. And he's helping Dawric search for a way to steal powers." Gregor stared Dr. Damian in the eye.

Dr. Damian fumbled with his collar with one hand and held the dagger down at his side with the other. Both hands trembled.

"Get out of here, Mrs. Crick," ordered Gregor. "Go downstairs. Summon the officers who just left and tell them they have the wrong man."

"But Dr. Damian said...he said Dr. Randall was the one," cracked Mrs. Crick's voice from behind them. "I thought Dr. Randall was the one killing the animals."

"He couldn't be," Gregor said. "One of the animals was a unicorn, and Dr. Damian is the only human capable of getting near one."

Mrs. Crick crawled to the stairway and descended. Dr. Damian looked defeated. He raised the dagger in the air, gripped in his fist as he extended his finger and pointed at them.

"I would never have harmed a unicorn. Dr. Randall was the one killing them. And I don't know what you mean by helping Dawric." Dr. Damian's eyes darted back and forth between Gregor and Angel, and the dagger twitched in his hand.

"You're lying," said Gregor. "I've never trusted you, and now I know you—or that madman you're helping—killed Siophra. And you framed Dr. Randall. If you try to escape before the officers get here, I will kill you." His eyes blazed.

Angel's stomach churned with fear. Gregor may have been much bigger than Dr. Damian, but Dr. Damian still had the dagger.

Chapter Thirty
The Lab

"I never killed *anyone*."

Dr Damian's voice sounded distant and melodic, like the tinkling of bells carried on the wind. It caressed Angel like fingers down the nape of her neck. He moved slowly and smoothly toward them, the dagger still gripped in his fist. He no longer fumbled with his collar, and looked Angel squarely in the eye.

"You believe me don't you?" His gaze shifted to Gregor. "I'm not a murderer. I'm not a murderer and I didn't hurt anyone."

Angel believed him. How could she not? He was so sincere. Calmness enveloped her like a warm blanket. *He'll never hurt me. He's here to help me.*

She wanted to look at Gregor and tell him that they'd made a mistake, but her gaze held to Dr. Damian like a magnet, drawn to the intense ice-blue of his eyes. He shifted his gaze back and forth between her and Gregor, never unlocking his eyes from either of theirs for more than a second.

Angel reached out automatically and took Gregor's hand. He grasped hers tightly in return and they moved closer together.

Dr. Damian continued looking at them both, his eyes darting back and forth between hers and Gregor's, unblinking.

So kind. I can't believe I ever suspected him of anything.

"Come with me." His voice soothed her like the sound of waves breaking on the ocean shore. Relaxation seeped into her the way it always did when she lay on the sand at the beach, wishing she could float along the current forever.

She and Gregor moved simultaneously toward Dr. Damian, who walked backward with his eyes fixed on them both. Angel felt drawn to follow him…to go anywhere with him, to do anything he asked.

Down this hallway…to safety…through this door…yes.

The light dimmed, but not enough to block out the face and mesmerizing eyes of her rescuer.

Stop here. Okay, anything.

His voice traveled through her mind like music. "I'm going to lock the door now."

Yes, lock us in here where it's safe, where you can protect us.

Dr. Damian eased his way around her and Gregor. The lock clicked. He eased his way back past them again to where he was standing before.

"I need to show you something." He began walking backward again. Angel followed, gaze locked on Dr. Damian, pulling away from Gregor. Gregor's grip on her hand increased, his arm stiff and resistant, but his footsteps followed along with her. She squeezed his hand and felt a surge of strength.

Why are we following Dr. Damian?

The thought sent a shock of pain through her head and she released it, refocusing on Dr. Damian. Gregor squeezed her hand even tighter and she felt a desire to pull her eyes from the ice-blue intensity.

No, I can't. He doesn't want me to. He needs me.

She relaxed her hand again. Gregor tightened his grip even more. Angel could suddenly focus beyond the man in front of her, and saw out of the corner of her eye that Gregor's head was moving back and forth.

"Just a little farther," Dr. Damian cooed. "You have to see this and you'll believe me. You have to believe me."

Angel's calmness slipped. Her heart skipped and she sensed danger.

Gregor's hand squeezed harder than ever, and his head moved back and forth more forcefully. He whipped his upper body away from Dr. Damian and yanked on Angel's arm. Everything in the room jumped into focus.

"We're not going any farther!" shouted Gregor, and he pulled Angel to him.

She pressed against Gregor, his strong arm a shield. Dr. Damian made no attempt to recapture her eyes. He looked horrified and guilty, but it wasn't the guilt of being caught in the act of wrongdoing.

It was the guilt of remorse.

"You have to see what's in here," he said in his normal voice. A door stood slightly open behind him. "It's the only way you'll believe me." He fidgeted with his collar again.

"Put down the dagger and we'll come with you." Angel pushed away from Gregor but still within his grasp.

Gregor glared at her.

"No way, Angel. We're getting out of here and locking the door behind us, and this sick-o is going to jail. Or I'm going to kill him." Gregor grabbed Angel's arm.

Dr. Damian looked down at the dagger in his hand as though he had just realized he was holding it. He set it on the desk next to him.

"Please, you have to believe me," he said. "I never killed anyone. This is Dr. Randall's office. And through this door is his lab." He pointed over his shoulder to the door behind him. "And through that lab is another lab. A secret lab, where Dr. Randall was conducting his real research. Research I found out about. I turned him in. He planted the dagger in my desk. He's the murderer, not me."

"He's telling the truth," said Angel.

Gregor loosened his grip on Angel's arm but didn't let go. Dr. Damian moved toward the door behind him.

"You can take the dagger if you don't believe me, Gregor. I'm only trying to show you that I'm innocent."

Gregor walked over to the desk, pulling Angel with him, and picked up the dagger. He looked at the blood-covered blade with disgust and pointed it at Dr. Damian. "All right, show us the lab. But you try anything and this goes in your neck."

Dr. Damian pushed the door all the way open and stepped through to the lab. Angel and Gregor followed, Gregor's hand still holding Angel's arm. They walked through the lab. It looked spotless, unused.

"I always thought it was odd that he'd lock the door to go in here," said Dr. Damian, "but it looked like he never did anything. He spoke about his research like it was something top secret but would take us by storm when he revealed it. He was always bringing in new vials and materials, but when I came in here, everything was the same."

They continued through the room, Gregor pointing the dagger at Dr. Damian and holding Angel's arm, until they reached the back wall. They faced a set of cabinets with doors that ran from floor to ceiling, like a huge closet. There were windows on either side of the cabinet that looked out over dense trees just outside the wall.

"This room backs up to the forest right at the base of the mountain. The other lab is underground." Dr. Damian reached down and grabbed the handle on the cabinet door. The lock on the door was broken. "He had this sealed with an enchantment, but I broke that. The lock is ordinary. I just forced it with a screwdriver." Dr. Damian opened the cabinet and moved to the side.

The cabinet was empty, but in the bottom was a hole about three feet in diameter, dug directly into the rocky ground. The top of a ladder poked out of the gaping blackness, mounted to the side of the hole. Angel did not want to climb down that ladder, but she had to see what Dr. Damian wanted to show them.

"I'll go first," said Dr. Damian. "Maybe that will show you that I don't want to hurt you." He sat down on the floor and dangled his feet into the hole. He turned over and slid the rest of himself down, grabbing the ladder as he went. Gregor let go of Angel, and followed, holding the ladder with one hand and clutching the dagger with the other. He paused with his head sticking out of the hole.

"Are you sure you want to come?"

"Absolutely." She stepped closer to the cabinet.

Gregor's head disappeared down the hole.

Angel sat on the floor and dangled her feet over the top of the ladder. Her heart pounded, and she felt like the walls were closing in on her.

What if Dr. Damian was trying to trick them? He had helped Dr. Randall and Dr. Stieber with research according to the conversation she and Gregor overheard. Could he have framed Dr. Randall to get him out of the picture and take credit for their research?

She had to see for herself. She'd heard nothing except the *thunks* of Dr. Damian and Gregor's feet hitting the floor. No scuffling or fighting, and no screams.

She flipped onto her stomach and pushed herself farther into the hole until her feet caught a rung on the ladder. She closed her eyes and felt with her foot down to the next one, and moved one rung at a time as quickly as she could, eyelids clamped until she felt the floor beneath her foot.

The floor was smooth stone, not dirt like she had expected. But the walls were even more surprising. They were transparent—through them Angel saw dirt, rocks and tree roots. It was like being inside an aquarium embedded in the ground.

The walls to her left and right curved upward, creating a solid arc that ran the full length of the room. An arc, of course, because it was the strongest structure and the glass needed to support the ground above. The flat walls at either end enclosed them in a hollow, semicircular prism.

She recalled the day Gregor had turned the dirt into a mirror. Dr. Randall must have done the same thing to the entire room, but instead of pushing the dark particles to the back to make a mirror, he'd pulled the pure sand particles forward and made clear sheets of glass. They reflected the light from the torches mounted on the corners of the long laboratory table in the middle of the room.

Cabinets lined the length of the room in either side, set away from the curved walls. Bizarre pieces of equipment of shiny steel and hard wood and rusty metal sat atop the counters of the waist-high cabinets.

Gregor leaned over the lab table, which was covered with lumps of something. Dr. Damian stood next to him. His eyes were kind, she realized, of their own accord, no longer a result of his Taming. He'd been telling the truth. Gregor knew, as evidenced by the way he loosely held the dagger. Angel moved closer.

"I must warn you, Angel, before you look at these," said Dr. Damian. "They're not going to be easy to take."

She slowed her pace. She'd seen some pretty gruesome things before, but what met her eyes when she reached the table still made her stomach turn.

Animal fetuses lay on the tabletop, in various states of dissection. Some were simply sliced open, while others had their insides partially or completely removed. Dismembered bits and pieces lay on a trays. Some of the fetuses had been cut up so much they were unidentifiable, or made into thin slices of tissue mounted on glass slides next to a microscope.

The animals she'd seen in school were preserved in formaldehyde and came from a science supply store. *These* were babies that belonged to animals she'd seen in the forest. They had been taken from the mothers by force, unmercifully. The mothers had been sliced open and left to die, and their unborn babies used as a sick experiment.

The fetuses weren't ordinary animals. They were hybrids made of vastly differing species: a pig's body with the head of a snake and a rattle at the end of its tail, the body covered with black scales; a colt encased in the slimy skin of a frog, with bulging eyes and undeveloped stumps for legs; and what looked like a fawn whose body tapered down and twisted to the shape of a lizard with a long scaly tail.

Angel thought of the doe they'd seen at the stream, and the strange rippling caused by something unseen. She shivered. *Dr. Randall...he was there.* The doe had escaped that day, but Angel wondered as she stared at the half-reptilian fetus if later the mother had not been so lucky.

Not all of the hybrids were recognizable, though. Some had odd numbers of legs, or body parts protruding from the wrong locations. Skin and fur mingled in matted clumps along bloated torsos, eyes were absent from their sockets having never developed, and faces were a smear of flesh instead of distinct features.

Angel remembered the wobbling fence that Shakespeare had noticed, with the pregnant ewe lying beside it. Dr. Randall had literally been experimenting in Gregor's back yard. Her anger swelled as she moved to the end of the table.

A lone lump of flesh set apart from the others lay on a tray, not dissected at all like the rest. Most of the body was covered in patchy fur, the hind feet were hoofed, and the torso was hunched forward unnaturally for any animal. The fur grew more thickly around the fetus' neck and shoulders, goat-like ears protruded from the sides of its head, and small, nubby horns had just begun to form on its forehead.

Angel stooped over to get a look at the face, and then stepped back, smacking into the cabinet behind her. Gregor reached out and wrapped his arm protectively around her. She peeked at the fetus one more time. Its contorted face was pasty flesh, wrinkled and pursed, its snout elongated, but most definitely human behind the patchy pelage.

She dug her fingers into Gregor's sides, and tears of anger stung her eyes. *What's the point of this? Why would anyone hybridize these animals? And how did he get human DNA to use for it?*

As if reading her thoughts, Dr. Damian spoke.

"I believe Dr. Randall was trying to create new species out of existing ones. He must have snuck up on the females while invisible and injected them with a sedative. I found these in one of the drawers."

He opened a drawer and pulled out a bag of hypodermic needles just like the one they had found in Siophra. Gregor flinched and turned away, letting go of Angel's shoulder. Angel took a deep breath and turned her back to the horrid display on the table, shaking the images from her mind.

"We thought you had done it because you could Tame the animals," Angel said. "We didn't know Dr. Randall's Talent was Invisibility."

"Neither did I," he replied. "A lot of people keep their Talents secret. But *he* was keeping his secret so he could use it for this, I guess. He must've been harvesting eggs and fertilizing them in vitro. Under normal circumstances, all he would need is a DNA sample from a male animal. A skin cell would work. As long as he separated the two chromosomal sets and only used one, he could combine it with the single set of chromosomes inside the egg. Very simple magic is all that's needed for the process as long as both parents are the same species."

He sighed and shook his head. "But I have no idea how he broke the species barrier and created viable, or even nearly viable, hybrid embryos. It should be impossible. Animals can only breed after their own kind." A pained look moved across his face. "Nothing in the realm of true magic would have enabled him to accomplish something like this."

Gregor turned back and faced Dr. Damian. "You say true magic, but you study those ridiculous books filled with crazy theories written by that Dr.Watkins. I don't get where you're coming from."

"I analyze them, that's it." Dr. Damian's eyes flashed, and then his face softened. "I take what makes sense and drop the rest. His are *theories,* as you said after all."

"How did you figure out what Dr. Randall was doing?" asked Angel.

Dr. Damian turned to her, his words pouring out in a torrent.

"I was in the forest gathering saplings for my research, and found a dead sheep. Her gut was split wide open. I used my dagger to push open the wound and saw that there was a fetus in the ewe's womb. Then I heard a dog growl. A stray puppy was peeking around a tree. I thought it was growling at me, but I couldn't make eye contact with it to Tame it and quiet it down. It was looking over my shoulder.

"I heard the leaves rustling behind me. I remembered how Dr. Randall had mentioned something I'd said in a private conversation, and I realized he must be able to hide somehow, spying on me. I knew someone else was there in the forest, and I knew it had to be him. I reached into the ewe and grabbed the fetus and took it back to my lab.

"It wasn't entirely a sheep. It was so genetically mangled, though, that it was impossible to tell what he'd try to hybridize it with. But then I knew where the Cagon had come from. And that there was no Lunicor." Dr. Damian sat on one of the stools.

"I broke into his lab and searched it. I found the cabinet leading down here was locked and sealed with enchantments and it took me a while to figure out how to break them. That's when I decided what I needed to do."

"Why hasn't this room been searched by anyone but you?" asked Angel. "Why isn't it *being* searched?"

His shoulders drooped, and he met Angel's gaze with deep and sober eyes. The ice-blue irises clouded over and he merely shook his head. "I had to catch him killing a mother animal in the wild to have him arrested. I took a camera into the forest, knowing there was a pregnant unicorn in trouble, and I figured Dr. Randall would follow me when I went out to find it. I'd been searching for the unicorn for days, but she was nowhere to be found, and Siophra never showed up to help like she was supposed to. I had no idea what had happened to her. I'm sorry, Gregor."

Gregor nodded but remained silent.

"I never found the unicorn, but the next day I did happen upon a dragon giving birth. It was obvious she was dying, and nothing would save her, so I hid nearby and waited. The dragon was lying down, nearly unconscious when Dr. Randall got there, but the baby hadn't been born.

"Dr. Randall just slashed her stomach wide open, and I jumped out and took a picture of him. Of course, he came after me. But I'd discovered one day when I had a student get hysterical about a failing grade that my Taming worked on people. I'd never tried it before, but I couldn't get the girl to calm down. I just wanted her to stop crying."

Dr. Damian's face flushed, but he went on, "So I Tamed Dr. Randall and brought him and the baby dragon back to the University, then reported him. The picture was all the evidence they needed. The dragon's head had risen when he cut her, so she was obviously alive, and her mouth was open in a howl of pain. That alone was enough to have him arrested. Only the dagger from the museum could have cut through its scales."

"But the dagger, why was it in your lab?" asked Gregor.

"My Taming doesn't work perfectly on humans, as you both can attest to. He still had enough control to conjure it away before I could get it out of his hands, even though he couldn't get away himself. But he had it in his hand in the picture. Of course he kept telling the officers I had framed him, that I had put the dagger in his hand while I had him Tamed and made him do it.

"Anyway, that's not all. I tested the blood on the dagger. There was other blood mixed with the dragon blood. Human blood. I was going to give the dagger back to Mrs. Crick when you arrived, and turn in the test results."

But Angel and Gregor had botched that. And now the officers would be back any time to arrest Dr. Damian.

"The human blood wasn't just Dr. Randall's, was it?" asked Gregor.

"No, it wasn't. How did you know?"

"I can explain that," said a voice from behind them.

Chapter Thirty-One
The Madman

A cloaked man stood at the base of the ladder.

Dr. Stieber.

He stepped toward them.

"See what you have caused, Dr. Damian? Another worthy scientist is being persecuted for his research, *real* research, while you make pretty flowers in your lab." His heavy accent had disappeared.

As he moved closer, his hooded face came under the light of the torches, his eye still covered by a patch. Only now Angel noticed that the skin between it and his beard was rough and shiny, like skin healed over after a burn.

"You call this research, Dr. Stieber?" said Dr. Damian. "This is sickening. And if you have been working on this too, I'll have you arrested as well."

Dr. Stieber threw back his head and laughed. His hood fell behind his shoulders, but he turned away before Angel could clearly see his face. He walked partially along the perimeter of the room, running one gloved hand along the glass.

"I'm not helping him, no. Not directly, anyway. I only let him access my knowledge in exchange for his. What he does with my knowledge is his business. But what I do with his will be everyone's business before long. With your help, that is, Miss Angel." He paused and stepped away from the wall.

"Or should I say...Anna."

Angel felt as though someone had run long fingernails across a chalkboard.

"Did you hear me, *Anna*? Why don't you answer? "

Ringing screamed in her ears, just as it had the day Gregor had shoved her through the Gate to save her from the speeding truck. She gripped her ears and dug her fingers into her hair. Her hands trembled against her skull as the ringing ground her bones.

But she would not let herself give in to it.

She struggled against the nausea, and it didn't take hold. The ringing eased, and her muscles stilled their trembling. Her determination was stronger than the memory this time. *She* was stronger.

She banished the ringing with a scream that came from the very depths of her soul.

"You cannot use me! I'm not a little girl anymore! I have strength you'll never have access to!" Her hands balled into fists at her sides.

Dr. Stieber turned to face them and the torchlight caught his uncovered eye. An eye that looked exactly like the eyes of her friend, Melinda. Except there was none of Melinda's sadness in this eye, only arrogance.

Dr. Watkins.

His face had vastly changed since the taking of the picture in his book. His brow was lined with age. Gray invaded his dark hair and had already taken over his beard. The burn-scarred skin on the side of his patched eye ran under his beard and down his neck.

He laughed.

"You like the marks I've taken? If it is what it costs me to gain magic, then it is worth it, I assure you. I only keep it hidden to conceal my identity for now, not because I am ashamed." And with that he tugged on each finger until his gloves loosened, and then pulled them off completely. He tucked the gloves into his cloak, and displayed his hands before them. Deep burn scars grooved the skin from the gnarled fingers down to his wrists.

"When I have found what I'm looking for...or should I say, when you have *Found* it for me...I will be able to gain enough magic to heal my scars, and to accomplish anything I choose."

"You can't gain magic by force." Steel in Gregor's voice sharpened his words and tingled the air. "It destroys your soul." He wrapped his arm protectively around Angel, and he and Dr. Damian moved closer to her, blocking her from Dr. Watkins.

"Destroys your *soul?*" Dr. Watkins said. "You honestly believe that? You have no soul, you fool! Magic is a trait, just a trait like any other, controlled by your genes. And genes can be moved from one organism to another. Scientists do it all the time. Dr. Randall was kind enough to loan me his from time to time in exchange for my knowledge about species hybridization. He was most gracious when I solved his little problem."

"That's ridiculous!" shouted Dr. Damian. "Magic isn't something you attain by splicing genes."

Dr. Watkins turned on Dr. Damian. "Thank you so much for sharing your review of my lecture with him. He could see the possibilities my hypothesis presented, even if you couldn't. Not that I would have chosen to work with someone like you." He sneered. "Your little magic display in the back of the lecture hall was intriguing, but I could see once I found you in Germany that you had nothing to offer." He inhaled through his teeth and smiled wickedly. "Well, except the conversation you had with your roommate about the isolated little magical island you'd be moving to when you graduated. Your description of its location was all I needed."

"That *was* you at the table next to us. I can't believe I was too in awe of you to even approach you." Dr. Damian's face dropped.

"Don't look so glum. I fell in love with this place, just as you did. Well, maybe for different reasons. I learned so much here, about magic and your culture, and about *little girls* with very important *Talents.*"

"But what were you going to use me to Find?" Angel asked over Dr. Damian's shoulder. "Do you even know?"

"A single amino acid, actually. One that is produced only by a certain magical plant that grows in the deepest parts of your forest. The problem is that it is very rare and difficult to locate, as it likes to grow hidden below the underbrush."

"I wouldn't have done it then, and I won't do it now. Not ever."

"You won't have to," said Dr. Damian. "I know the plant he's talking about. It all makes sense now. Dr. Randall said he was looking for it for his research, but of course I couldn't figure out why. That must be why he sought you out. You could synthesize the amino acid for him. Create a man-made version of it. He would have figured that out once I told him about your lecture. Oh, how stupid I am!"

"On the contrary, Dr. Damian. I think it's quite brilliant of you to have figured it out, but Dr. Randall is much more brilliant. He knew from the beginning a synthesized version would never work, but he soon derived a plan for us to combine our skills, to create a…symbiotic relationship with me. Of course, as is the way of nature, symbiosis often evolves into parasitism. Survival of the fittest, you know." He smiled as if becoming a parasite were some glorious evolutionary crest.

"Survival of the fittest?" Dr. Damian glowered at Dr. Watkins. "Parasitism is the equivalent of dependency. That's not survival of the fittest. Going from symbiosis to parasitism would be the breakdown of a balanced system, not an improvement."

"Oh, but you're wrong!" Dr. Watkins raised a hand in the air. "It's the first step to independence. When organisms rely on each other, it's total dependence. But if one can figure out how to take advantage of the other, using it as its resource and eliminating it at the same time, then it becomes the sole survivor. No more competition. Total independence and control!"

His eye gleamed as he paced the end of the room. "But there is a catalyst I need to complete the process. The genes degrade too quickly once spliced into my genome. I need the magic catalyst that will fuse it into the DNA of all of my cells. And for that I need the amino acid."

"You're mad!" Dr. Damian trembled, face red and jaw straining. "You can't take someone else's power permanently. It's part of their soul, not their genome. That's not competition, or parasitism. It's murder."

"How is it murder?" Dr. Watkins said. "The genes survive. That's what survival truly is. The body is just a vehicle. I'm merely moving the desirable genes from a less fit host into a more fit one." He spoke as though he were talking about rearranging the furniture, rather than DNA. But the frenzy in his eyes betrayed the calmness of his voice.

Dr. Damian lunged forward. Angel and Gregor grabbed him and held him back. He struggled in their arms. "You're talking in circles. You say it's eliminating the competition, then talk as if you're saving the very thing you're trying to eliminate. It doesn't make sense."

Dr. Damian stopped struggling, but Angel and Gregor didn't let go.

"Why so emotional?" Dr. Watkins said, leering. "I'm merely following the course of nature. Improving my chances of survival, and ensuring that my offspring take the next evolutionary step."

But despite his outward composure, Angel saw as much anger in Dr. Watkins as she did in Dr. Damian.

"I told you, magic isn't genetic." Dr. Damian was still tense but no longer pulled against Angel and Gregor's grasp.

"And even if it was," Angel added, "you're not doing it for your offspring. Melinda's already been born. This is for you, for your own selfish gain."

"All progress is selfish, my dear."

"That's not true," said Dr. Damian. "At least it doesn't have to be. You don't have to lie, steal, and murder to progress."

Dr. Watkins began to shout, lashing at the air with his gnarled fingers. "You're just jealous! You don't want to admit the truth, because it might shatter your little world. You cling to your antiquated beliefs, on this technologically backward island. You all deserve to be taken out of the gene pool! You all deserve to die!"

Angel stood shoulder to shoulder between Gregor and Dr. Damian in the middle of the room as Dr. Watkins paced in front of the ladder. They needed to overcome him to escape the room. If they all performed the same magic together, they could stop him, kill him. They could constrict his throat, or stop his heart from beating.

But if they killed him, they would suffer the consequence—lost powers. And their souls could be damaged beyond repair. Or would they not be affected because it was really self-defense? Angel had no desire to find out for sure.

Dr. Watkins slowed his pace and then stopped altogether, blocking the ladder. He stood arrogantly before them, considering his prey. Angel, Gregor, and Dr. Damian began to inch their way to the other end of the room at Gregor's lead. Dr. Watkins watched their progress, but made no move in their direction.

Their feet slid noiselessly across the smooth stone floor and Angel focused her attention on Dr. Watkins until she felt Gregor halt his steps. They had made it to the far wall.

Dr. Watkins moved slowly toward them, eyeing them with a sneer. He reached his gnarled hand into his cloak.

Angel felt Gregor's arm moving back and forth behind them and she glanced down. Sand fell from the wall where his arm waved, and the glass was disappearing in front of a large tree root. *That's right! That's all he needs to*

Gate us out of here!

Angel tried not to let her excitement show. She wanted to show Dr. Damian what Gregor was doing, but was equally afraid that that would also draw Dr. Watkins' attention to Gregor's actions.

She glanced at Dr. Damian and noticed he was trying to make eye contact with Dr. Watkins. *He's going to try and Tame him!*

"It's fine, Dr. Watkins," Dr. Damian said in that dulcimer voice. "We see your point now. We can help you." He stepped toward Dr. Watkins.

Angel tried to pull him back but she wasn't strong enough. Gregor had nearly made the hole large enough to Gate the three of them through. He couldn't raise his hand to stop Dr. Damian.

Dr. Watkins lifted his head and let out a roar of laughter.

"You think you can Tame me like a little beast!" he said. "I know better than to allow the gaze of a Tamer to attract my attention. *But I can tame you.*"

Dr. Watkins pulled his hand out of his cloak—he held a bullwhip. He cracked the whip in front of them, and the end wrapped around Dr. Damian's neck before Angel or Gregor could do anything to stop it. He yanked on the whip and Dr. Damian hit the floor.

"*Nooo...*" The scream gurgled out of Angel's throat. She cringed at the sight of Dr. Damian's body lying limp, blood pooling around his splayed ponytail, crimson staining the strawberry blond.

Dr. Damian's head jerked and then lolled to the side as Dr. Watkins snapped the whip free. Angel gasped, tears flooding her eyes.

She lunged forward, but Dr. Watkins stepped over Dr. Damian's motionless body and reached for her.

Sand shot from Gregor's hand, the particles whizzing through the air like millions of miniscule bullets, pelting Dr. Watkins' scarred face and single bared eye like a sandblaster. He screamed as the skin scoured from his face while Gregor grabbed Angel's arm and pulled her, stumbling, through the Gate he'd made in the tree root.

Chapter Thirty-Two
The Reunions

They stepped out on the edge of the clearing that surrounded the Elven Temple, and Angel turned to Gregor with tears streaming down her cheeks. His eyes reflected the moonlight.

"He killed Dr. Damian." Her heart pounded. "Dr. Watkins has the power to Tame us now! He can't come through the Gate, can he?"

"I closed it behind us. But that doesn't mean he can't make it here. Didn't Dr. Damian say he owns a winged horse?"

"Yes!" Panic gripped her, squeezing, shortening her breath.

"Angel." Gregor grabbed her shoulders. "Calm down. It will take time for him to get here, but right now I need you to do something."

"Me?" She looked around the clearing and glanced toward the sky. Dr. Watkins could arrive any minute and take control of her and her Talent, or kill her for refusing to Find the plant.

"Yes, you. I've been thinking about those verses. *As the bearer stands on the threshold.* I don't know why, but my instinct told me to bring us here. To a *door.* A door made from the most magical wood ever known. Angel, you've got to walk up those steps right now and stand in front of the door."

It made no sense at all. But she trusted him.

She walked toward the Temple and up the stone steps, constantly peering into the night sky for the image of Dr. Watkins on Lightning. She saw only the moon and its light reflecting off the clouds.

As she ascended the steps, she felt drawn to the door, as though an electric current ran between them. She continued walking, her eyes fixed on the magical wood planks. She stopped only when she stood inches from its rough, metallic grain.

A strange tingling prickled her skin and the air began to rustle around her. She looked beyond the roofless portico, but everywhere else was still. The movement increased and the tingling intensified, especially around her head. The air lifted tendrils of her hair. Several dark-brown tresses danced in front of her face.

The brown faded before her eyes, lightening to an auburn that shifted hue until her former flame-red color took its place. Her hair waved around as though it had a life of its own, the redness brightening until Angel was sure she saw flames amid the strands.

She turned to Gregor, who didn't appear nearly as amazed by what was happening as she felt. *He figured it out—I am the flame from the prophecy, the flame that burns with no fuel.*

"Do you have the key?" Gregor didn't move from where he stood on the grass.

Was this something she had to do alone?

She lifted the key out of the neckline of her shirt, and then showed it to him, dangling on the end of the ribbon. Then she tried to pull the ribbon over her head, but her hair waved around too wildly. She fumbled with the knot in the ribbon instead. Again and again she dug at the knot until an edge pulled loose.

The key slid off the ribbon and clinked on the stone floor below. Angel picked it up and stood with it held tightly between her trembling fingers. *It's too small for the lock.* Tears burned her eyes. She and Gregor must have missed some crucial part of the puzzle.

Then the key began to glow.

Slowly, it turned from polished silver to bright white, and a faint heat radiated from the metal. Angel ignored her hair whipping around as she stared at the key in her palm, which grew and stretched to fill her hand. The white glow turned to pale yellow, then deep gold, and finally subsided altogether, leaving the key the dull color of tarnished brass. She turned the key around and held it between her thumb and forefinger, but her hand shook too hard to get the key into the lock.

The air around her slowed until her hair ended its dance and settled around her shoulders.

She took a deep breath, her heart threatening to pound out of her chest. *I've got to do this. It's what I've been brought here for.* She willed her hand to be still. This time, she steadily placed the key in the lock. There was a quiet click as she turned the key, and then…nothing. She pulled the key back out of the lock, searching for an indication of what she'd done wrong.

"Gregor! Gregor, it didn't work! The lock won't open! Gregor—"

She spun around, but Gregor was standing still as a statue, staring into the forest on the other side of the clearing, eyes wide like a deer caught in headlights.

Angel ran to his side and shook his shoulder. "Gregor! What's wrong? Gregor!"

He didn't respond, still staring, eyes glazed over. Angel shook his shoulder more frantically, but his face remained stone and his eyes unblinking. After several moments he collapsed. Angel dropped to her knees and knelt over him, silent tears spilling over her lids and running down her cheeks to drip on his chest.

"Gregor, wake up," she said weakly. "You've got to. Dr. Watkins is on his way."

Gregor's eyelids fluttered open. His eyes shifted left to right, and then he jumped to his feet. He reached down and pulled Angel up.

"Angel, give me the key."

"But, it doesn't work, Gregor. I tried to tell you." She sobbed.

"Not for you, it doesn't. But it will for me. Give it to me *now*." He pushed his open hand toward her, his eyes demanding her to obey.

She put the key in his palm, and he wrapped his fingers around it.

"Angel, it's me. I have to open it. This is the way we can stop him, for good. It's a Gate I have to make in the door…and go through. And you can't go with me."

"But where does the Gate go? Why can't I go with you?" She grabbed his forearm, and when she saw the look in his eyes her heart skipped. "Are you coming back?"

He shook his head. "It's a Gate to the Realm Beyond. I have to go through and take the key with me. It's the only way." He stood, determination planted on his face. He suddenly seemed much older, decades beyond his seventeen years.

Angel lowered her head. *He doesn't just have to do this, he wants to do it.* She felt his hand pressing on her chin, and let him pull her face up to meet his eyes again.

"They'll be there waiting for me." His eyes pleaded for her to understand. "My mom and dad…"

"And Siophra."

"Yes, Siophra. I can't…" He looked deeper into her eyes, his silver flecks like sparks of energy emanating from his soul. "I can't live without her. I'm ready, Angel. I can do this."

His gaze broke from her as he spun around and looked skyward. Angel followed the direction of his gaze and spotted what had gotten his attention. Cast across the moon was the silhouette of a winged horse bearing a cloaked rider. It traveled fast, moving toward the clearing in a great arc.

"You've got to hide, Angel. Quickly! He needs to think you've gone through already. It's the only way he'll follow me in."

"Follow you? But—" The words caught in her throat, and she dug her fingers into his arm. *No, that's not what you said!*

"*Now*, Angel. He's nearly here."

She threw her arms around Gregor's neck and clung to him. He'd become like a brother to her, the kind of older brother Josh and Jacob had never been, the kind of brother Zack couldn't quite be because he was too young. She'd already lost her family—twice—and now he was asking her to give him up too.

She squeezed tighter, and his arms wrapped around her shoulders in return. He shuddered in her embrace. He was making the same decision she had made when she left the Masons', and she was only making it harder for him.

She forced herself to let go and stepped back. Tears glistened in his eyes, made brighter by the silver flecks. Sadness lurked in the darkness of his eyes, but so did hope.

Angel reached out one last time and touched his cheek, following the trail of tears with her fingertip. Her hand dropped to her side. She couldn't deny that he was right, no matter how empty she felt. *He'll be with Siophra forever now, and Dawric will be banished for good.*

She inhaled, shoving the pain deep inside, then turned and ran into the forest. She ducked behind a thick oak, not caring that the bark scraped against her as she sank to her knees.

She peeked around the trunk as Gregor walked resolutely up the Temple steps, her heart squeezing tighter with each of his steps. He placed his hand on the door, and put the key in the lock. When he turned the key, the click echoed through the clearing. The lock fell open and the chains snaked to the stone floor, leaving Gregor still holding the key in place in the lock. The door shimmered, then disappeared, replaced by a thick haze.

Gregor didn't move.

There was a sudden crunch as the winged horse and rider landed on the clearing in front of the Temple. Dr. Watkins dived off the horse and ran to the base of the Temple, his cloak billowing behind him. The winged horse reared up on his hind legs and then ran several steps before taking flight. He nearly grazed the top of a tree on the edge of the clearing and vanished into the night sky.

Gregor shouted, "She's gone! And you'll never get her!" and disappeared through the Gate.

Gone…he was gone.

Angel's fingernails dug into the tree bark. She strained against the hollow ache, and pulled herself to her feet. With Gregor no longer there, she needed to be ready to run if Dr. Watkins caught sight of her.

Dr. Watkins roared, bounded up the steps, and skidded to a halt in front of the open gateway. He carefully put one hand through and pulled it back out. Angel fought the urge to run up the steps and push him through.

His own cruel determination sent him through without her help. The tail of his cloak trailed behind him, before it, too, disappeared.

Angel stood frozen behind the tree, barely able to breathe. She clung to the tree trunk, unable to pull her eyes away from the Temple door, which still glimmered with haze in the moonlight.

Something occurred to her, making her heart race again. Gregor had just lured Dr. Watkins through the Gate to the Realm Beyond. *That means Dr. Watkins is there too, and will be for eternity.* Had Gregor misunderstood and released a murderer into Heaven? She wondered if she should go through. *Maybe I'm still needed. Maybe the Finder's work is not complete after all.*

She tried to run through the verses in her head to see if they had all come true, but the words tangled together in her brain. Powers given, taken …in birth, in death…the bearer and the threshold. The place of beginning and ending…the circle…could that mean the Temple?

She was the flame, and she'd found the key, and the *truth* about Dawric had been *exposed by the substance of man*. Gregor had found the lock…*and he's finding his treasure*, Siophra and his parents. *Happily gained when all else is lost.* But the rest was still unfinished as far as she could tell.

My work's not done but I don't know what else to do. Do I go after him? What if I'm trapped in the Realm Beyond and it's not my time? There's got to be something else.

A huge crash of thunder bellowed through the trees and shook the crumbled walls of the Temple. A brilliant light blazed up through the roofless ceiling and blared through the open gateway as though lightning flashed inside the building. Angel put her hands over her eyes to protect them. The wind began to blow, first gently, and then with more and more force as each second sped by, and the light still broke through the gaps between Angel's fingers.

A howling added to the din, but it wasn't wind. It came from the direction of the Temple. Angel wanted to go see if it was Gregor, but she couldn't get near the Gate without being blinded.

The light slowly dimmed, until it was merely a faint glow around the open Temple ceiling and amid the haze of the open Gate.

Angel took her hands from her eyes. And pushed her hair back against the still-powerful wind.

A shadow appeared in the middle of the glimmering haze of the Gate. A figure lunged through, and Angel nearly ran toward him thinking it was Gregor. But the man was wearing a cloak. He continued down the steps, and onto the clearing, stumbling as he stared around as if blind.

The wind picked up even more, thrashing Dr. Watkins' cloak, and whisking Angel's hair so it stung her face. She fought to keep her hair out of her eyes as she looked closely at Dr. Watkins. His eye patch was gone and both eyes were cloudy white and glazed with panic.

His scarred face contorted in pain. The burn scars stretched into an inhuman mask, a twisted, hideous monster. His gnarled hands balled into fists and he beat at his head as if insects swarmed him. Then he grabbed his hair and yanked. He remained standing, but convulsed, pulling his head back and turned so he was facing Angel. His mouth was open wide, twisted in a silent scream.

A ring of blood-red fire sprouted up around him, and the ground beneath his boots loosened and swirled like molten steel. His feet began to sink into the earth as he fought savagely to free them, releasing the grip on his hair. He reached down to his legs, pulling on them one at a time. His legs disappeared into the ground inch by inch, while he clawed the air around him. Soon he was buried to his waist, and his cloak was ablaze from the licking flames that encircled him.

Angel shifted against the tree and her heart pounded even harder. She wanted to turn away from the horrific scene playing before her, but her gaze held fast.

Dr. Watkins sank farther into the swirling ground and the flames grabbed at his arms and face. His scream broke through, and an explosion of glass shattered inside Angel's chest, the shards impaling her ribs. Dr. Watkins was buried up to his neck. No chance of escape.

Angel could still barely breathe, but her panic began to subside, easing her heartbeat, and she released her grip on the tree.

She felt pressure around her shoulders, and looked up into Kalek's onyx eyes. Sobbing, she buried her face against his chest as his arms enclosed her. She held tightly to him and let his strength flow into her. Then she lifted her head from his chest and turned to face the Temple.

Dr. Watkins was gone, the place where he'd been devoured marked only by a still-smoldering patch of scorched grass. She raised her eyes to the Temple door, but solid wall filled its place.

A movement above the door caught Angel's eye. It was the stone gargoyle. Kalek's arms tightened around her and she knew he'd seen it too. The gargoyle had risen to its hind legs and spread its bat-like wings, claws extended. It released a lion-sized roar that joined the howling of the wind in an eerie chorus. Angel watched transfixed as the creature launched from its perch and soared into the darkness.

The guardian shall leave his post.

The wind died down to a gentle breeze, and Angel leaned into Kalek for support. He guided her to the Temple and helped her sit, resting her against a pillar in the shadows that cloaked the steps.

"Are you okay?" Kalek asked, and she nodded.

"What happened here? I was walking through the forest, when the trees along the path disappeared. It was like a trail just opened up. Then I saw a bright light and the wind started blowing. Who was that?" He pointed at the smoldering patch of grass.

"It was Dawric. We found out what he was looking for. But even he was wrong. There was no object, or plant, or anything like that. It was a Gate—a Gate to the Realm Beyond. Gregor took the key and went through. He had to make the Gate, and he insisted he had to be the one to go through. We thought it was supposed to be me at first, but then..."

Angel knew she wasn't making sense, but the words streamed out of her. "Wait, what path opened up? It's the prophecy! *When the hidden path is unmasked.* All of it...it all came true, and we were all part of it, not just me, like we thought..."

Kalek seemed to be trying to follow her words. "What do you mean you thought it had to be you?"

"This." She raised her arm out of the shadows to reveal the charm bracelet, which now had only three charms to reflect the moonlight. "It was a key, and Gregor used it to open a Gate to the Realm Beyond. He's with Siophra now..."

Kalek's eyes widened at the sight of the bracelet. "But that's—"

"ANNA!" a voice called, followed by two voices together, *"ANNA!"*

Angel and Kalek looked in the direction of the voices. Two people were running toward them. Even in the dark one was obviously a woman, with long hair trailing behind her. The other was a man, much taller than his companion—well over six feet, Angel guessed—his legs pounding the ground. Leading their way was a fluttering black shadow, which the moonlight suddenly hit, revealing its sparkling silver flecks.

"Horatio!" cried Angel. *Then they must be—*

Angel's parents bounded up the steps and dropped to their knees in front of her.

"Anna, is that you?" Her mother burst into tears.

Angel smiled broadly and sat up. Her father threw his arms around her, followed quickly by his wife, and the three of them clung to each other for minutes that could have gone on forever. When their embrace ended, they stared into each other's eyes, tears flowing despite their smiles.

Angel searched their features for signs of her own. She found them in her mother easily. The same red hair and dark brown eyes. But her mom's face was rounder, with deep dimples in her cheeks that Angel didn't have.

Angel reached out and touched her mother's cheek. *Finally, I can see her face!*

The features of her father's face brought forth a vision of a painting. Every detail was the same except the eyes. Where the eyes in the painting had shadows of sadness, her father's real eyes sparkled with joy.

She stared at them, soaking in every curve, every wrinkle, every strand of hair. *My Mom and Dad...*

Kalek stood to the side, mouth open wide. "Then...you're Anna Kleidon. Your hair..."

Her red hair blazed in the moonlight now that she was no longer in the shadows.

"He's gone..." Angel said to the loving faces staring at her. "Dawric, that is. Gregor made him go through a Gate to the Realm Beyond and he was thrown out and sucked into the ground." She pointed to the spot where it had happened. "Did you know that the charm bracelet had the key to the Gate?"

"We knew it was a key to something important, but, no, we didn't know it was that," her father said. "There was a paper handed down along with the bracelet, but we never understood what it meant. Only that we were to keep it safe."

"Gregor's gone?" Kalek looked stunned now that her words had sunk in.

Angel nodded.

"Gregor Halvard?" asked her mother, and Angel nodded again.

"He went through the Gate." She tried to work up the strength to tell them the whole story. "We found verses in the book his father had and then we found the paper in your painting." She and her mother gripped each other's hands. "We thought Dawric was after a magic object that would empower him permanently, but it turned out to be a Gate. I just had to help Gregor find it, but he insisted he was the one that had to go through.

"He *wanted* to go," she said when she saw Kalek's expression. "He wanted to be with his parents and Siophra."

"Siophra?" said Angel's father.

Before Angel could say anything to him, her mother cut in.

"We need to get her out of here. She has to be exhausted—she needs to lie down. Anna, you can tell us later. Right now, let's get you home."

Angel's heart soared. She looked at her parents kneeling next to her.

Everything she'd been waiting for was finally happening. She was going home. They were going to be a family now. Tears filled her eyes all over again, her joy pushing the corners of her mouth into a wide smile. She let her parents help her up, and they all walked down the main forest path that led from the clearing to Gregor's farm.

Chapter Thirty-Three
The Confession

The gilded box that contained the Elven girl, Siophra, glinted in the sunlight as it rested in the bed of leaves that layered the forest floor. The Halvards had chosen the most beautiful spot in all the forest for their daughter's funeral, a clearing surrounded by towering trees with pure gold graining their rich, coppery bark and sinewy branches bejeweled with golden leaves that stretched into the crystal-clear azure sky. It seemed the sun had painted everything with brightness and glitter to wash the sorrow from the ceremony honoring the life of the beautiful girl who had been loved too much.

The Elven sang songs and told stories, rejoicing in the knowledge that Siophra had moved on to a place of perfection and pure magic. The few funerals Angel had attended before had been filled with tears and mournful faces, sobs punctuated with "Why?" and "It's not fair." They were funerals for people who had not known true magic.

As the singing abated, Kalek stepped out of the milling group and up onto a tree-stump a few feet from Siophra's casket. There was no podium, nor chairs or shelters, only Elven standing under the shade of the outstretched branches that reached into the open circle of the clearing. Those Elven guests who were too feeble to stand sat on tree-stumps or giant toadstools. A few of the younger Elven sat perched in tree branches.

Angel's father and mother stood on either side of her, holding her hands tightly in theirs. After one night's sleep at Gregor's farmhouse, they'd only had a single day together before the funeral. Angel's memories had flooded back to her, exactly as she'd wished for. They'd spent hours talking, laughing—all the while Angel's mother insisting she get some rest.

But Angel couldn't hold back the stories she had to tell of her time with Gregor and their defeat of Dawric, discovering the Prophecy, and her newfound friendship with Sir Benjamin. She also told them about the Masons, bittersweet emotions bringing fresh tears to her eyes as she thought about no longer being part of their family. In her heart, though, Zack remained her little brother.

In return, she'd made her father tell her about the places her parents had searched. After breakfast they'd gone back to their own house, Shakespeare, Zoe and Horatio in tow, and begun the process of restoring it to accommodate them all…as a family.

"Friends," began Kalek, bringing Angel out of her reverie, "we are gathered here to say farewell to Siophra. Farewell for the present, that is, for we shall all be reunited in the Realm Beyond. Siophra has received the greatest gift bestowed upon the Elven, and because of the fulfillment of the Temple Prophecy, the non-Elven as well."

Several of the older Elven muttered under their breaths, but the remainder of the group held their hands high and shouted, "It is so! It is so!"

Kalek held his head proudly above the crowd, sunlight bouncing off the tangled mass of curls that hung to his shoulders. He looked like royalty in his silk tunic and polished leather boots. A gold cord draped across his chest from shoulder to waist, and his great-great-grandfather's dagger was strapped to his leg.

"'Tis only your body that we bury today, dear Sister, for your soul has moved Beyond, but as physical life is taken away, so that body must be returned to the dust from which it came."

The crowd moved into a circle around Siophra's casket and Kalek stepped down from the tree-stump platform. Three Elven men stepped forward to join him, one taking his place at the foot of the casket, and the other two standing one on each side. The four men held their hands over the gilded box, and without a word began to lower it into the earth.

No soil was displaced, nor so much as a leaf disturbed, on the solid earth under the casket. The glimmering box silently fused into the ground,

267

inch by inch, until it disappeared completely.

Horatio shifted on her shoulder, his melodic chirping deep and mournful. Angel sensed meaning in his song, if not the words.

She released her father's hand to wipe a tear from her cheek and felt her mother squeeze her other hand. Her father wrapped his arm around her waist.

Kalek remained standing in place as the other three men rejoined the crowd. Angel tried to read the mixed expression on his face. He missed Siophra dearly, but his joy for her new life with Gregor overtook the sadness. There was more to it as well, and Kalek promised to tell her everything soon, the story of the Temple—*Mori Zede*—and how it had changed his life. His onyx eyes glistened as he stared at the grave and spoke again.

"As life is taken, so life is also given. In remembrance of Siophra, I cast this seed."

Kalek held out his arm, opening his hand. A tiny seed fell to the ground over Siophra's grave. The leaves on the ground began to rustle without the aid of wind, skidding across the dirt as if vibrations from below the ground were resonating along the surface. As a small patch of dirt cleared, a crack in the soil appeared through which burst a pale green seedling. It was as if time sped forward in only that spot as the seedling stretched higher and higher, sprouting leaves and thickening its stalk until a sapling stood before the crowd.

The sapling continued to grow, albeit at a slower pace, until a full-grown fir towered majestically over Siophra's grave. The dense needles sparkled with gold and silver woven throughout the deep green. Angel stared, awestruck by its beauty. *It looks like a Christmas tree.* The most glorious Christmas tree Angel had ever seen, one that did not need the added decoration of dangling ornaments, tinsel, or electric lights, because its beauty came from the magic with which it was infused.

The funeral crowd dispersed over the next several minutes, some heading off in different directions between the trees, and others forming groups around the clearing, leaving only a few Elven clustered at the base of the great fir. Kalek was among them, but Angel didn't approach him.

He was deep in conversation with his mother, whose tear-streaked face was an older version of Siophra's. She looked every bit the wife of an Elven patriarch in her flowing black velvet gown that set off the magnificence of the Halvard teardrop emerald suspended around her graceful neck. The sunlight burnished her dark, cascading hair with amber highlights. Kalek reached out to embrace his mother.

Angel turned away, not wanting to invade their private moment.

Her parents had joined a group of Elven some distance away where her mother was hugging what appeared to be a close friend. Angel caught a few of their words carried along the gentle breeze, exclamations of "It's been so long," and "You haven't changed a bit." Her mother glanced at her and beckoned with an outstretched hand. But Angel's father looked at her with understanding and nodded.

Angel smiled a *thank you* and walked on. She couldn't face introductions and the reactions of those who would soon be discovering that the Finder was still alive.

Horatio chirped and fluttered off toward Angel's father. Again, Angel sensed meaning in the sound—Horatio knew his presence would draw attention to her.

She didn't know where to settle herself until she found the right moment to approach Kalek. Her gaze jumped from guest to guest as she wandered along the edge of the clearing, until it fell on a frail, aged man sitting next to an unoccupied toadstool. His clothes were far more elegant than anyone else's, and gold banded each of his fingers. His hand gripped a walking stick made of richly-stained wood with bright gold grain.

Aldrik Halvard. It had to be.

He caught Angel staring at him and she blushed, but she couldn't turn her head away. Mr. Halvard's eyes shone brilliantly with emotion, but Angel couldn't tell what kind of emotion from where she stood.

A slight smile crept onto Mr. Halvard's face and he gave an almost imperceptible wave of his long, bony hand, beckoning Angel to come to him. She steeled herself for a confrontation in case she had misread his gesture, but when she stood before him he looked at her with brokenness and remorse.

"Anna." He spoke with a voice that was worn down as though his tears had eroded it like sand at the beach. "I have something to tell you, and something to ask of you as well. Please sit," he said with a remnant of authority.

Angel obeyed, but it was out of curiosity rather than the fear it would have been only weeks before.

"First, I must say that I have been a fool. An old stubborn fool at that! I have come to realize the error of my ways—the pride and greed that has clouded my judgment all these years. I could not accept the truth about many things, but I now know that I was wrong. You are the Finder of the ancient Prophecy, and what I must tell you is that I knew that from the beginning."

The words slammed into Angel's brain, and she sat dazed.

"How...how did you know?" Her curiosity held down her anger. She would give him a chance to explain himself before condemning him.

Mr. Halvard's eyelids closed for a moment, and when they opened, he breathed deeply. "Kalek told me that he's apprised you of the Halvard legacy, but even he did not know what I am about to tell you. You see, the emerald necklace was not the only Halvard heirloom. The parents of the twins, Rastus and Rurik, had *two* heirlooms to pass down. Most often a second heirloom is given to the second-born, but in this case the twins' parents decided to hold out and give their second heirloom to their first-born daughter. As you know from the story, that daughter was never born."

Mr. Halvard's breath came shallow and raspy. "They decided to give both heirlooms to Rastus, because of his maturity and responsibility, which they considered far above that of his brother, Rurik. They had no understanding of Rurik's shrewd business sense... oh, but, I am not here to defend him. He is my ancestor, and deserves my respect. However, I know *now* that there are much more important things than wealth and power." Mr. Halvard's gaze shifted over to rest on Kalek, who stood nobly next to the tree over Siophra's grave.

Why did it have to take the death of someone so close to him to make him realize how important his family was?

"What does this have to do with me being the Finder, Mr. Halvard?"

"Haven't you guessed?" he said as his eyes trailed back to hers. "Your bracelet was the other heirloom. Rastus had a daughter and he passed it on to her. She in turn, passed it on to her daughter, and then to each first-born son or daughter for generations, until it reached your hands. The story of its origin was lost after some time because your ancestors leading back to Rastus chose to depart from Elven ways. But Elven blood runs in your veins, Anna."

The implication of his words struck as she sat, transfixed. She was a descendant of Rastus...the same Rastus whom Gregor had descended from. *We were cousins. Really and truly cousins!*

Angel shook her head to clear her thoughts and asked the question she could no longer wait to hear answered.

"Why did you want me dead, then? If you knew I was part of the Prophecy? Didn't you know what it meant?"

"What I knew was that the key to the Gate to the Realm Beyond would be handed over to the wrong heir. I was convinced that the key should belong to someone from my side of the family and I wanted one of my children to take the honor. But I did not want you dead, Anna. Please know that. I am not a killer."

Not a killer? But selfish enough to let someone die if she was in the way. Angel swallowed, jaw clenching as she forced the thoughts down.

Mr. Halvard cleared his throat. "However, when you appeared to be dead by the hand of another, I cannot deny that I was secretly glad to be rid of you. I thought that maybe the Prophecy was to be fulfilled by my family after all, because I was the rightful heir of the bracelet. I had no idea that the bracelet was the key itself, though. Nor did I know that the Key-bearer must cross over to the Realm Beyond. I only wanted what I felt was rightfully mine."

"Why wasn't Kalek aware of all this? He didn't know that I have Elven blood. He was convinced I couldn't have been the Finder because of that."

"Why would I have told him? It would have given him more reason to rebel! He wanted nothing but to be free of the life into which he was born. I've known that all along, but I could never understand it. He prizes music over wealth, harmony over power. He would have left years ago if it were not for Siophra and his desire to keep her well cared for. He loved her enough to give up his friendship with Gregor. And it is my fault he had to choose. My selfishness and greed…"

Mr. Halvard threw his face into his hands and sobbed. Angel suddenly felt only pity for him. She placed her hand on his quivering shoulder and his sobs slowly subsided. He straightened up in his seat, wiping away tears with a quivering hand.

"Anna, I'm a wretched old man and I know I have no right to ask this, but I must. For my sanity, I must. I need to know if there is any chance that I could find your forgiveness."

"My forgiveness?"

His eyes pleaded with her, vacant of everything except remorse.

"It is too late to gain my daughter's forgiveness, and Gregor's as well, at least in this Realm. But I have petitioned Kalek for his forgiveness. I shall have it some day, but it will be a long and difficult road. I can freely seek it, however, if I can attain yours. Were it not for me, you would have had seven years of happiness with your family. I could have put my resources to work searching for you, and Dawric as well, and you would have been free to fulfill your destiny without loss."

Angel reached out and touched his withered hand. "Mr. Halvard, that may not be true. If you hadn't stopped the search for me, I may have never fulfilled my destiny at all. There's no way of knowing for sure. It was all part of a plan beyond our comprehension."

"You sound like my son." A smile lifted the corners of his mouth. "He has such faith in the unknown. I suppose he has told you the story of the Temple, and you believe him?"

"He hasn't told me yet, but I already believe what he's going to tell me is true. He said you don't believe. Why not?"

"I could not before. It meant letting go of my pride and possessions. But that is not an obstacle anymore." He looked at the ground, shaking his head slightly.

"And I don't want to give you any other obstacles." Angel wrapped her fingers around his hand. "I forgive you. And Kalek will, too. I'll talk to him." She glanced over at Kalek and saw him staring at her and Mr. Halvard with confusion.

"He will listen to you. He has only spoken of you with admiration. 'An Angel who appeared out of nowhere,' he said. And now, I need you to be an Angel to watch over him."

"Me? Watch over Kalek?"

Kalek was at least five years older than Angel, and one of the strongest people she'd ever met. His faith permeated his every action, his every word. She began to wonder if Mr. Halvard's mind was disintegrating in the same manner as his body.

"Oh, yes. Siophra and Gregor were the only ones who had a firm place in Kalek's heart. And now they are both gone. His faith will bring him through his sorrow, but once he has moved past it, he will need someone who can keep his head out of the clouds, without breaking his spirit. I think you will be more than capable.

"And to ensure that you do, I am relinquishing any claim I have on

272

Gregor's land. It is to be passed to you and Kalek together. And it must remain your joint land until you reach eighteen. That will be long enough, I believe." He gave Angel a tender smile. He was still shrewd, that was sure, but his motives seemed genuine.

"And as for the emerald," he added, apparently aware of where Angel's eyes had just wandered, "that will become yours when you've reached your eighteenth birthday as well."

Angel's head swam with all the information.

Gregor was her relative, distant as it were, and Angel was now co-owner of his farm. And she was the rightful heir of the Halvard family emerald. She felt as though she'd been transported yet again into another life, and she'd barely had time to get used to the one she'd experienced the past couple of months.

Angel's mother approached. Mr. Halvard smiled warmly and excused himself. Angel wasn't sure if his gesture was politeness, or avoidance. He had apologized to her, but there were many more owed.

"Anna." Her mother's voice was still music to Angel's ears. "Sir Benjamin stopped by to pay his respects a few moments ago. He apologized for not speaking with you, but he said you seemed busy." There was a hint of irritation in her voice as her eyes darted to where Mr. Halvard stood next to his wife. "Anyway, he said he wants you to stop by the shop after the funeral. He's got a surprise for you."

Angel looked around. Most of the funeral guests had left. "Can I go now?" She jumped to her feet before her mother had a chance to answer.

"Sure. Your dad and I will meet you back at the house. We have a special surprise of our own."

She gave Angel no chance to reply, winking and walking away to join Angel's dad and the group of Elves he was entertaining. Angel caught a snippet of one of the stories he'd told her about their search for Dawric.

Angel noticed before she left that Kalek had moved away from his parents, and she approached him. His face, although still shadowed, widened with a welcoming smile.

"My Angel, I know you weren't going to leave without speaking to me."

"Of course not."

Angel was swept by emotion and tears began to flow down her cheeks. "Kalek, I'm going to miss Gregor so much. And I didn't even get to know

Siophra. I'm happy they're together, in a place where they can never be kept apart again. But I wish that place could be here, with us."

Kalek put his arm around her and stroked her bangs out of her face with his other hand. His touch was comforting and gentle. *Musician's hands.*

"Tomorrow, can you meet me at the Temple, Angel?"

Angel choked back a sob and nodded. "Are you going to tell me the story?"

"Yes, it's time. Long overdue, actually. And while we're there, you can tell me what you and my father were talking about so secretly." He didn't look angry, but Angel hoped that Mr. Halvard would explain at least some of it to Kalek before the next day.

"Okay, tomorrow, then. Sir Benjamin wants to see me, so I'm heading into town right now. Take care, Kalek." Angel leaned in to kiss him on the cheek before she left on Juliet.

Chapter Thirty-Four
The Gifts

Angel stopped at home to change before going on to Sir Benjamin's. *Home.*

For the first time that word rang true.

She entered Sir Benjamin's lost in thought, and nearly crashed into a big, stuffed chair next to the couch. She stopped and crinkled her eyebrows at it. *Wasn't that always in the back, behind Sir B's desk?* She took a closer look. Yes, it was the one. *Why'd he move it out here?*

"Angel, is that you?" Sir Benjamin's familiar voice called from across the room. The tip of his salt-and-pepper head showed above the desk. She walked to where he was crouched and gasped when she saw what he held in his arms—the baby Cagon.

"How did you get that?" She crouched next to Sir Benjamin. Spike lay sleeping as usual on his purple pillow, which now sat adjacent to a green one that took the place of the chair Angel had nearly tripped over. "The authorities found him when they investigated Dr. Damian's death. Sweet little thing, isn't he? Apparently, they searched his notes, which confirmed that he had nothing to do with Dr. Randall's research, for lack of a better word. I still can't get over that. I knew he was a putz, but really..."

"Sir B!"

"Sorry, I digress," he said with his best Santa smile. "The point is, they discovered Dr. Damian found this little guy in the forest, abandoned by his mother, and he intended to give the kit to me as a gift. He just wanted to make sure its temperament was stable enough first. I've decided to name him Niles. What do you think?"

"I like it. He's so cute." Angel's hand instinctively found its way to Niles' back, and she stroked the soft fur. It did feel exactly like cat fur; although, when she scratched underneath, the hide felt rough and thick.

Niles had grown substantially since Angel had seen him only weeks ago in the cage in Dr. Damian's office. His body was more in proportion with his paws and head, but his emerald-green eyes were still larger and rounder than a typical dragon's. The tabby stripes that covered his body had become more distinctive, so that his coat varied from the darkest black to the palest gray, with bits of tan and gold bursting though here and there.

"Spike's okay with him?"

"He's doing just fine. I know he's a bit jealous, but it's not as if he demands much attention these days anyway. Worthless lump of scales…"

The last words dripped with love. Angel scratched behind Niles's ear and gave Sir Benjamin a look that said, *you haven't got me fooled.*

Sir Benjamin cleared his throat. "Wasn't the funeral beautiful? Her parents made a very good choice for her burial tree. Lovely and full of light, just like Siophra."

"It was amazing. Nothing like what I expected. But speaking of funerals, will there be one for Dr. Damian?"

With all that had happened over the last two days, Angel had nearly forgotten that it was not only Siophra and Gregor who'd been lost. Gregor had no family left, and there was no body to bury, so there had been no service. He wouldn't have wanted one anyway.

"I'm sure there will be, but not here. Dr. Damian's family is back in Germany, and that's where he'd requested to be buried."

Nothing more was spoken of death or funerals. Angel and Sir Benjamin discussed the progress of his book and played with Niles. The Cagon ran out of energy and fell asleep on the green pillow. "Brings out his eyes," Sir Benjamin said.

Angel found her mother in the kitchen, dressed in a paint-smeared smock and stirring a pot of stew. Zoe dashed over to her and pounced on her legs, then scrambled to the door and whimpered.

Such a normal scene. Strangely normal. Had it really only been two days since she was reunited with her parents? The seven years between her disappearance from the island and her return seemed more a dream than the distant memories from her childhood before the disappearance. It didn't make sense. Shouldn't she feel like a stranger with them?

"Hi, Mom. That smells awesome." Angel opened the door to let Zoe out and then sidled up to the stew pot and reached to grab a spoon.

Her mom swatted her hand playfully. "It's not finished. It's needs to simmer some more."

A chittering sound came from the direction of the kitchen window. Angel turned toward it and saw Horatio sitting on the sill. She scrunched her face into a fake glower.

"No laughing!"

Horatio chittered again, then zoomed past, narrowly missing her, and zipped into the hallway.

Angel scooted around to the bar stool and sat down. Her mom sat next to her, then reached out and brushed Angel's hair behind her ear the way Mrs. Mason used to do. It opened another ache in Angel's heart, but she wouldn't change things. Sometimes choices are not between good and bad. Sometimes they are between good and better, and those can be the hardest.

"Go into the living room, sweetie, and I'll get your father. I think it's time for that surprise we promised you." Her mother winked and walked out of the room. Angel went into the living room and sat in the chair next to the fireplace. It wasn't as comfortable as the one at Gregor's, but its proportions were just right for her and she adored the new rich, caramel color. With Angel's help, her father had convinced her mother to get rid of the red.

Her parents walked in together, hand in hand. Her father sat on the couch opposite Angel, and her mother plopped onto the floor in front of him, leaning against his legs. Her father placed his hands on his wife's shoulders and spoke to Angel.

"Your mom told you that we have a surprise for you." He hesitated for a moment.

Angel assumed for dramatic effect. It worked. She fidgeted in her seat, trying to be patient. But after counting thirty-seven seconds, she nearly burst.

"What? Come on, tell me. What is it?"

"First, let us explain." He sounded serious despite the hint of a smirk. "We may have not known about the Prophecy and your charm bracelet's role in it, but we've always known there was something very special about the bracelet."

"Open the charm," her mother said.

"But I already know what's inside. It's just a wood chip. What's so special about that?"

"It's no ordinary wood chip," said her father. "It's from a very magical tree."

"Magical door, is more like it." Her mother reached up to squeeze her husband's hand.

Magical door?

"You mean the door at the Temple, don't you?" Angel opened the locket and peered inside. Now she noticed the bit of silver in the wood chip. She looked back up when her parents didn't answer. They didn't need to—it was written in their smiles.

Excitement started like a spark and built quickly. "So, what does that mean? Will it enhance my Talent like magical trees did for Gregor?"

"No, I doubt it will do that," her father said, "but it has powers of its own, linked to the heritage of the bracelet."

"What does that mean?" She let her fingertip slide across the tiny, rough chip.

"It means the powers are only accessible to the owner of the bracelet," her mother answered, "and in this case, that's you."

"What kind of power?" Angel's finger stopped stroking the wood.

"A wish. A *single* wish. You will be able to make one wish that is guaranteed to come true."

Angel's heart beat faster. *I can wish for anything in the world and it will happen?* Her brain began spinning with ideas: the dress she'd seen on her first day in town with Gregor, a real stone castle to live in…with a library full of books, to be bilingual without having to *learn* another language. Smaller feet.

"But be careful," he added. "That wish may come with consequences.

You've heard the saying before, I'm sure. But it's very true. You need to think this through very carefully. Promise?" There was no hint of a smirk on his face now.

Angel promised she'd think long and hard before making her wish.

She lay in bed that night, stroking Shakespeare's back as he slept by her side. Horatio hummed quietly from his perch on her dresser top and Zoe snuffled in her sleep on the floor. The words of her promise lay hard on her heart. *Yes, I'll be careful. Very, very careful.* But not about the wish itself. She knew that what she *really* had to think long and hard about was the *wording* of her wish...her wish to have Zack back at her side.

Little Book of Magic

A short story
by Kat Heckenbach

*When you finally find the person who believes in you enough to take
a chance, you simply have to thank her with a story about her.
This is for my Space Kiwi publisher, Grace Bridges.*

"It is my little book of magic," the girl said to the man who sat on the other side of the wide, wooden desk. "I have put my heart and soul in it. I want to share it."

The man pulled his glasses off and rubbed his nose. "No one wants a little book of magic, dear girl. Heart and soul or not, it won't make money."

She swallowed as her stomach twisted. "But it is magic. It's meant to be shared."

"I'm sorry. It's not for us." He returned to his work, and she noticed the deep stress lines in his forehead, the rumpled slouch of his suit jacket. His hands were a blur as he ran pen over paper, ignoring her.

She stood and left, her little book of magic tucked tightly inside her backpack.

The next door held a similar office, with a similar man behind a similar desk. He gave the same answer as the other, and she moved on.

The hallway grew as she walked, doors adding to doors, stretching far behind her. Each door locked with a forever click as she exited, and her heart and head sank lower with each step.

And the little book of magic weighed heavy on her back.

"Maybe I should just go home," the girl muttered to herself. She stopped and turned around, looking down the narrow hallway. A door at the end swayed open. But darkness pulsed on the other side—a tempting darkness that promised both relief and despair.

The girl slid the backpack off her shoulder and opened it. She pulled out the little book of magic, then clutched it to her chest. The door slammed shut, and even from a distance the girl could read the words scrolled across the wood: *The Land of What-If.*

She sighed, and reached again for her backpack.

"Oy, little girl, what have you there?"

The lilted voice startled her and she spun, nearly dropping the book. A space suit stood before her, although she could not see who—or what— filled it.

"It—it's a book. My book. My little book of magic," she said, her heart sputtering back to a normal rhythm.

One arm of the space suit rose then, and the gloved hand pushed a button on the side of the helmet. The dark shield clicked and slid upward, revealing the face beneath.

The little girl gasped. The creature's face was covered in downy feathers, with bright, round eyes. A pair of metal-framed spectacles perched on its narrow beak.

"You're a bird!"

"A kiwi, to be precise," the creature said, and a smile ruffled the feathered face.

Comfort flooded the little girl as she gazed at the kiwi's warm expression. "Would you like to see it?"

The kiwi's eyes lit up. "Oh, may I?"

She handed the little book of magic over, and it was grasped lovingly by the gloved hand. The kiwi sat against the wall then, and opened the book. The girl held her breath in anticipation as those bright eyes scanned page after page.

Finally, the kiwi looked up and closed the book. The bright eyes blinked. "Why have you not shared this little book of magic, dear girl?"

"I have no means to share it myself, and those who do will not help me." She turned toward the hallway behind her and stared at the forever-locked doors, refusing to let loose the tears that burned the edges of her eyelids.

She heard scuffling, and then the kiwi's voice again. "Would you come with me if I offered to help you share your little book of magic?"

The girl eased around to face the now-standing kiwi once more. "Yes," she said, and followed the kiwi far, far from the dreary hallway.

Acknowledgements

Jeff, without you I wouldn't be here.

Nickie and Anna, thank you for putting up with Mommy's moods and writing time, and for being my biggest cheerleaders.

To my parents—Mom, Dad, thank you for believing in me always. And to the rest of the family…this is why I'm so nuts.

To my best friend, Barbi—without you I wouldn't have made it past my first day of writing.

To my red-penned critters—Kathryn ("kill your darlings"), Shawna (so many hours and emails…), Lexi and Kaylee (teen readers rock), and Diane (the only one who gets to call me Chicky)—and Amy Deardon who lent her editing skills—this diamond lost its roughness because of you.

To my dear Word Weavers, especially Janet, Jan, Sheryl, Tina, and Sharron…to the wonderful members of Brandon Christian Writers…to my friends who read my various early drafts (Susan, Barb S., Scott, Kecia, Tina, Robin, Robynn) and to those who were spared that punishment—thank you all for standing by me.

To the New Authors' Fellowship—I can't wait until we are ALL in the granny flat together.

To the Lost Genre Guild—continue your mission to reach out to those of us who write in the void.

And last, but surely not least, thank you to Grace Bridges and Splashdown Books. Grace, you believed in me and taught me more than I can possibly thank you for. I am honored to be a part of your team.

about kat heckenbach

Kat Heckenbach grew up in the small town of Riverview, Florida, where she spent most of her time either drawing or sitting in her "reading tree" with her nose buried in a fantasy novel...except for the hours pretending her back yard was an enchanted forest that could only be reached through the secret passage in her closet...

She never could give up on the idea that maybe she really was magic, mistakenly placed in a world not her own...but as the years passed, and no elves or fairies carted her away...she realized she was just going to have to create the life of her fantasies. She shares that life with her husband and two homeschooling kids.

Kat is a graduate of the University of Tampa, Magna Cum Laude, B.S. in Biology. She spent several years teaching, but never in a traditional classroom–everything from Art to Algebra II. Her writing spans the gamut from inspirational personal essays to dark and disturbing fantasy and horror, with over forty short fiction and nonfiction credits to her name.

www.katheckenbach.com

Made in the USA
Columbia, SC
12 June 2018